BERKLEY UK

DEATHWISH

Rob Thurman lives in Indiana, land of rolling hills and cows. Lots and lots of cows. *Nightlife* and *Moonshine*, the previous novels in the Cal Leandros series, are also published by Penguin. Visit Rob at www.robthurman.net.

Deathwish

ROB THURMAN

BERKLEY UK
PENGUIN

BERKLEY UK

Published by the Penguin Group

Penguin Books Ltd, 80 Strand, London WC2R ORL, England

Penguin Group (USA) Inc., 375 Hudson Street, New York, New York 10014, USA

Penguin Group (Canada), 90 Eglinton Avenue East, Suite 700, Toronto, Ontario, Canada M4P 2Y3
(a division of Pearson Penguin Canada Inc.)

Penguin Ireland, 25 St Stephen's Green, Dublin 2, Ireland
(a division of Penguin Books Ltd)

Penguin Group (Australia), 250 Camberwell Road,
Camberwell, Victoria 3124, Australia (a division of Pearson Australia Group Pty Ltd)

Penguin Books India Pvt Ltd, 11 Community Centre, Panchsheel Park, New Delhi – 110 017, India

Penguin Group (NZ), 67 Apollo Drive, Rosedale, Auckland 0632, New Zealand
(a division of Pearson New Zealand Ltd)

Penguin Books (South Africa) (Pty) Ltd, Block D, Rosebank Office Park, 181 Jan Smuts Avenue, Parktown North,
Gauteng 2193, South Africa

Penguin Books Ltd, Registered Offices: 80 Strand, London WC2R ORL, England

www.penguin.com

First published in the USA by Roc, an imprint of New American Library,
a division of Penguin Group (USA) Inc. 2009
First published in Great Britain by Berkley UK 2012

001

ISBN: 978-0-718-19279-2

To Shannon, who saved my ass, but didn't physically touch it, I swear—my best friend, my twin, my sherpa/pack mule. I love you, man.

ACKNOWLEDGMENTS

I would like to thank, first and foremost, my mom, without whose incesssant nagging I would never have written my first book at all. I would also like to thank my editor, Anne Sowards; Jessica Wade, who can keep a secret; Cam Dufty, who didn't once get annoyed when I called her asking, "What's this copy editor's squiggly line mean again?"; magnificent author Charlaine Harris, who has been most kind to me and my work even though she didn't actually personally know me—an anonymous fairy godmother, and when I finally did meet her, grace herself; Brian McKay—a helluva copywriter and one who genuinely gets the feel of Cal and Niko's world (he doesn't even *know* the word "perky," and say "Hallelujah" for that); Agent Jeff Thurman of the FBI, for advising me on something that may or may not exist; my eleventh grade English teacher, Earl Perry, who actually let us write what we *wanted* to write in the creative writing section of class—he inspired students when my college English teachers instead sedated them; the incomparable art and design team of Chris McGrath (an art *god*) and Ray Lundgren; my agent, Jennifer Jackson; doctors Linda and Richard, for being convention pals extraordinaire; Shawn Van for keeping my Web site up and running; Jordana for all the cookies; Mara for finally being recognized for her amazing talent; to Michael and Sara—congratulations on a wonderful marriage; and last but never least—my fans. Devoted, faithful, and somewhat frighteningly obsessed with the cover models. Without you . . . hell, I wouldn't be writing these acknowledgments at all.

1

Cal

Once, when I was seven, I was chased by a dog.

We lived in a trailer park then, my brother, our mother, and me. There were lots of dogs around, most of them running loose. I didn't mind. I like dogs. But dogs . . . dogs don't much like me in return. Puppies do. Puppies like everyone. They'd crawl in my lap, chew happily on a finger or the tattered edge of my sneaker. Dogs are different—one sniff of me was enough. The upper lip would peel back, ears would flatten, and the warm brown eyes would go glassy and slide sideways as they hunched away with tail tucked beneath their legs. Dogs don't just not like me; they're afraid of me.

Except for Hammer. Hammer wasn't right; not right being flat-out crazy. One hundred pounds of shepherd mixed with Rottweiler mixed with God knew what else, Hammer wasn't afraid to look at me as the other dogs were. No, Hammer liked to look at me. He liked to think about me. If anyone thought animals didn't think, didn't plot, didn't plan, then they'd never met Hammer. Two trailers down and one of the few dogs in the park kept on a chain, he watched me every day as my brother and I walked to school. He never barked. He never growled. He never even moved. He just watched.

Because of his lack of apparent aggression, any other kid might have been tempted to pet him. Not me. Even at seven, I knew a monster when I saw one. It didn't matter whether his owner had made him into one or he'd been born one like me. Hammer was Hammer. You didn't pet him any more than you petted a rabid grizzly bear. You just walked by and kept your eyes on the ground. You never looked. . . . Just as Hammer never moved.

Until he did.

Hammer was bad inside, *wrong*, and as I recognized him, he recognized me. And when drunk old Mr. McGee let the chain finally rust through, Hammer came for me. I had my dollar-store sneakers and a bagged lunch my brother had made for me, but I didn't have my brother. He'd gone ahead, although he was still in sight. He never failed to make sure I was in sight. I'd forgotten my backpack like kids do. I'd catch up. No big deal, until Hammer made it one.

He'd been lying in the same position he lay in every day. Bowl of dirty water, gnawed club of wood. That day, like every day, I wondered why he didn't like me. We were both twisted. Both wrong. So why? I didn't get a chance to wonder any further than that. There was a blur of fur, jaws clamped into my backpack, and my body was thrown sideways. He dragged me several feet before he tore the pack completely off me.

I didn't think. As I said, I'd seen monsters. You didn't hang around and ponder the situation. I got up and ran. While I'd seen monsters before, been followed, watched, I hadn't ever been chased by one. It was my first taste of death at my heels, my first taste of running for my life.

It wasn't my last.

In fact, I ended up spending a vast amount of my life running. Not just living my life on the run, which I had as well, but actually *running*. I wasn't seven anymore, but I was still flat-out hauling ass. Like the wind—like the ░░░░░░░░ Running from this, running from that—usually from something with teeth, claws, and the attitude of a great white on steroids. Things that made Hammer look like a toy poodle.

I hated it, the running. Hated it like poison. Which may be why I had finally decided I'd had enough and committed to staying in one place more than a year ago, and that place was New York City. A veritable Mecca for monsters like me, as well as monsters like Hammer—those that had me literally running for my life or the life of one of the few people I gave a shit about. There weren't many of those. Part-time bartender, private investigator/bodyguard/jack-of-all-trades to the nonhuman world, and one suspicious son of a bitch, that was me. Not precisely Mr. Social. It paid to be wary in a dark world thought to be nothing more than fairy tales and ghost stories by most people—most people being the blindly oblivious, the cheerfully clueless, the ever-so-lucky assholes.

The handful of people, humans and non-, that I did give a crap about had all ended up in New York, too—in the City That Never Sleeps, a good place for us creatures of the night. Everyone I cared about, and one in particular: my brother. He had been with me since the beginning, *my* beginning, and now had me running through the streets to make sure my beginning didn't bring him to an end.

The running—it always came back to that. A pity, because I was an inherently lazy son of a bitch. Burning lungs, knotting muscles, stuttering heart—I could do without any of that, thanks. But now I was running toward something, although there was plenty to run from. Death behind me; the unimaginable before me—an unholy situation, and it only made me run faster. The bus that nearly clipped me as I ran across the street? That wasn't even a blip on the radar. I had bigger, badder, and far more destructive things on my mind.

"Traitorous cousin."

The side of that bus brushed my jacket as I looked up at the sound of the icy hiss. For a second I saw it crouched on top, proving that mass transport wasn't just for hygienically challenged humans. I saw metal teeth, red eyes, and hair the color and drift of jellyfish stingers. I saw a killer. I saw a monster.

I saw family.

Then I saw something more immediately relevant—the front of a cab barreling at me. I dodged to one side as it braked. I rolled across the hood, taking down a bike messenger. Vaulting the cursing man, I ran on. I didn't look behind me. I didn't have to. I knew what was there. I knew what was coming, and I knew it wasn't alone. But that was the least of my concerns. What was important to me now was getting to the park, because I had other family. Real family.

My brother was at Washington Square Park, waiting for me. We were supposed to spar. "Spar" was a word Niko used when he meant he was going to beat the shit out of me for my own good. He kept me sharp and quick. He kept me evading monsters and taxis with equal alacrity. He was the reason I'd lived this long. The ones that followed me, the Auphe, knew that too. They hated him nearly as much as they hated me. And hate was like air to an Auphe. When something was as easy as breathing, you got pretty damned good at it. But the Auphe weren't good. No . . .

They were the best.

That's why I ran. Not because they were behind me, but because I suspected they were also in front of me. They'd been waiting for me at the apartment building at St. Marks's, where Niko and I lived. I'd come home to see them lining the roof, and I'd felt the internal wrench as they ripped holes in reality and slithered through. The dread was instant. If they knew for sure where I lived, they knew where I went. If they knew that, they knew the same about Niko. Months ago they had said they'd kill everyone in my life before they killed me. I believed them. Reapers and rippers and older than time—living murder wrapped in cold flesh. They didn't lie. Why would they when blood-soaked destruction was so much more entertaining?

Yeah, it had been months, but they said it, I believed it, and now was apparently the time. Long months of waiting, but, hell, I'd have been happy to wait a little longer.

No such goddamn luck.

I came off East Eighth Street, crossed Astor, then hit Broadway and kept running. This time I was hit, a big, ancient black Lincoln, but it only grazed my hip. There was the screech of brakes as I was knocked to the asphalt. As I scrambled back to my feet and kept moving, the skies opened up and dropped a waterfall of icy rain. I was soaked instantly, but the cold I felt on the outside couldn't touch what swirled inside me. Once on Fourth, I was running through the people. The human and the non-. The blissfully ignorant and the voraciously aware. The dinner and the diner.

Among the walking, talking snacks that were now cursing the rain, I could see the occasional pale amber eye, the gleam of a bared tooth. Upright Hammers. And they knew me as Hammer had. Smelled me. Were-wolves were good at that. Leg humping and sniffing out a half-Auphe—it was all a piece of cake.

There were other monsters among the unwitting, but I didn't bother to pick them out. I didn't have time. I didn't have time for anything except getting to Nik. It was a fifteen-minute run, going as fast as I could. Fifteen minutes was a long time. I didn't let myself think it might be pointless, that Nik had been at the park for more than an hour now. I just gulped wet air, tried not to think how much easier it would be if I shot the people milling in front of me, blocking my way, and kept running.

There were people in the park, but they were all

leaving—running themselves, although not as desperately as me, for shelter from the unexpected downpour. When it was cold enough to shrink your balls and wet enough to prune up everything else, it tended to put an end to casual walks and Frisbee playing. Niko would be on the far side of the green. There were bunches of trees gathered around the perimeter of the park. We worked out by a particular group of them in the northwest corner. As I ran toward it, I smelled the grass crushed under my feet, the mud, the dead leaves, the acid-free oil Nik used to clean his swords. . . .

And Auphe. I smelled Auphe.

Elf and Auphe, one and the same. Proof that mythology never failed to get it wrong. How it had gotten blond, prissy, silk-wearing elves from the world's very first monsters, I would never know. After pointed ears and pale skin, the resemblance stopped, and the steel teeth, razor claws, and lava eyes of a demon started.

I ignored the few people who gave me quick stares as they ran in the opposite direction, and tried to get more speed. I couldn't—I was giving it all I had and more. But then I was there. I was in the trees. The leaves had all fallen and the dark branches should've been bare as they split from the trunk to spread against the sky. They weren't. They were filled with Auphe, as pallid as the winter sky behind them. They were hidden enough by the rain that I could barely see them, but they were there. There had been no one behind me because they had beaten me here, the same twenty from the apartment building. From the roof to the trees—it was only a step for them. Open a door in reality, pass through, and there you were.

The one on the bus hadn't been following me. It had been playing with me. Homicide and humor—it was one and the same to the Auphe.

And Niko faced them all.

Revealing himself, he stepped from behind a glistening black tree trunk. Jesus. Alive. Fucking *alive*. And he was ready, with dark blond hair pulled back and katana held high in the pounding rain. The Auphe didn't blink, didn't move. "Gun," Nik said calmly.

I was already reaching under my jacket for the Glock .40 in my shoulder holster. My grip should've been tight and cramped with adrenaline, but I'd pointed one weapon or another so many times over the past four years that my touch was light and confident. The rest of me could've taken a lesson. Normally I was good at this—I saw monsters all the time and faced them head-on. Kicked ass, tail, flipper . . . whatever they had. But this . . . this was the Auphe. Half of my gene pool. They'd been not only the bogeymen of my childhood, but of my whole damn life. Outside windows at night, around darkened corners, trailing behind me from the time I was born until I was fourteen. Bad, right?

Wrong.

There was worse. They took me. For two years. I didn't remember those years and I probably never would, but inside, at a level I couldn't access, I somehow knew what they had done. Could feel it. Seeing just one was enough to have the taste of screams and blood in my mouth and a chunk of ice in my gut.

Seeing twenty of them was like seeing the end of the world.

Pointing a gun at the end of the world seems fairly goddamn futile. I did it anyway. "It's broad daylight, assholes. Seems bold even for you," I said tightly. I didn't freeze, not this time. I swallowed the bile, grew a pair, and kept the Glock steady. Two-headed werewolves, mass murderers, dead bodies hanging like fruit in a tree, I'd faced all of that—I'd face this. "Or did you get the weather report I missed out on?"

"Faithless cousin." Hundreds of titanium needle teeth bared at me as the closest one spoke. "The blind do not see us."

"And when your eyes are ripped from their sockets," hissed another, "neither will you."

Jesus, family. It was a bitch.

But maybe they were right. Even if the water falling from the sky hadn't been the next best thing to the biblical flood, it still might not have mattered. Because if you saw them, you'd have to be insane, wouldn't you? So instead, maybe you'd just turn your head and keep moving as your brain glossed over what simply couldn't be. Maybe your average human was smarter than I gave him credit for.

"We nearly wiped your race from the face of the earth." We'd also gotten our asses spanked and handed to us on a silver platter in the process, but Niko didn't feel the need to mention that. Show the enemy no weakness. A throwing knife appeared in his free hand as he continued without hesitation, "We finish what we start."

That's when they fell from the trees. Predators who had no equal. The hundred others we had killed had been a suicide run we'd unexpectedly survived. A big-ass explosion, a collapsing building, and the good fortune of several lifetimes; I didn't think we'd get that lucky again.

They were like lightning as they fell—that quick, that deadly, and that inescapable. I heard steel hit flesh as Niko swung his blade, and I also heard the thud of my back hitting a tree as clawed hands lifted and threw me before I could get a shot off. God, they were so damn *quick*. Another one snatched at my shirt, scoring the skin of my chest, and tossed me to the wet ground and then landed on me to pin me there. I could see my skewed reflection in the mirror of its teeth as I jammed the muzzle of the gun under an unnaturally pointed chin and pulled the trigger. The bullet hit nothing but the rain. The gate, one of twenty opening, gobbled up the Auphe just as it gobbled up the others.

They were just *playing* with us.

Blocking the rain, the gray light of the gate shimmered above me, hypnotic in the twists and turns of it. It slowed me for less than a second—I'd seen my share—but that was long enough. The hand came through to wrap around my throat, black nails snagging in my shirt and my flesh. I didn't wait for the muscular jerk that would yank me into the light. I emptied my clip into it instead. As the bullets vanished, the hand against my skin spasmed tight enough to cut off my air, then went limp. When it did, the gate closed, leaving a pale arm severed at the elbow lying across my chest. Dark blood pooled on my stomach as the arm suddenly twitched, fingers opening and closing before slowly stilling, this time for good. Dr. Frankenstein couldn't have done any better. "Shit." I pried it off of my neck and with a lifetime of revulsion threw it to one side. "Shit. Shit. Shit."

"So"—there was no whisper of drenched grass, no ghost of the faintest of footsteps, but suddenly Niko was looking down at me anyway—"other than that, how was your day?"

Actually the day had sucked ass before the park, during the park, and it didn't look to be getting any better.

We'd called Promise and Georgina to warn them about the Auphe. Niko spoke to both of them; my call wouldn't have been precisely welcome on George's part. She had cut me out of her life as of that morning. I'd worked toward that for a year now and I'd finally gotten what I'd wanted, although I'd never really wanted it. But I had bad genes, and not wimpy little alcoholic or schizophrenic tendencies either. I had the DNA of Dahmer and Godzilla combined, and I wasn't passing that on.

Promise was a vampire and George a psychic, when she wanted to be, and they weren't helpless against

the Auphe. Not completely. It didn't make me feel
any better. The Auphe were the Auphe.

Now we were here to warn the third person in our
lives. He was a cocky, annoying, conceited, lazy son
of a bitch. He was also a friend, one who'd had a few
bad days of his own this week. He was currently holed
up in his apartment and had been for three days. No
one went out; no one went in. For a chronically social,
not to mention horny, puck, that was alarming behavior.

I pounded on the door of his Chelsea apartment. I
was slowly drying off; the rain had stopped not long
after we'd left the park. "Goodfellow, open the hell
up!"

There was silence, then a muffled but cutting reply.
"How did *you* get in the building? You can't afford
to piss on the topiary out front much less walk through
the door. Go away." I heard something hit the door
with a shattering of glass. "When I want to see belligerent, fashion-impaired monkeys, I'll go to the zoo
and watch the feces fly."

That would be Rob Fellows, car salesman of the
month, year, decade. Better known to us as Robin
Goodfellow . . . Pan . . . Puck, whatever name he'd
been passing off at the time. Immortal, stubborn, and
could talk shit with the best of them. He'd also saved
our lives more than once. That made his nonstop
mouth a little more bearable.

"This lost its entertainment value as of yesterday."
Niko folded his arms and leaned against the wall.
"Kick in the door."

Unlike most siblings, I listen to my big brother. I
kicked in the door. It was a good door—solid, thick.
It took a few tries to get it open. There was quite a
bit of damage—splintered wood, locks ripped free of
the frame—none of which I planned on paying for.
Goodfellow was right. I couldn't afford to piss on his
bushes, and he had money to burn. Besides, tough

love was tough love. And right now that's what the infamous Robin Goodfellow needed.

"Oh, good." Wavy brown hair disheveled, green eyes bloodshot, the puck was sprawled on his couch in pajama bottoms and an open, wrinkled silk robe. "The Hardy Boys are here to show me the light."

I walked into the apartment, which was an unholy mess. Considering his housekeeper, Seraglio, had been killed just days ago, that wasn't much of a surprise. As she had been trying to kill us all at the time, I wasn't crying a river over that. On the other hand, I still remembered how she'd made me peach pancakes. It was a concept that was hard to fathom. Pancakes and assassination. What a mix.

There were empty wine bottles everywhere I looked, littering the floor, the granite counters, and there was even one embedded in the screen of the plasma TV. Damn, I'd loved that TV.

I nudged a bottle out of my path, moved closer, and winced at the sheer volume of alcohol fumes seeping through Goodfellow's pores. I had a good nose, as good as your average dog, thanks to my Auphe sperm donor. But even a normal human nose could've picked this up easily. "Jesus." My eyes watered as I squinted at him. "How are you not dead?"

"I was there when the first grape was fermented," he grunted. "It makes for a tolerance a fetus like you couldn't begin to comprehend."

"So you were the one who taught Bacchus to drink?" Niko asked with a gleam of skepticism in his gray eyes that came from a year's familiarity with Goodfellow and his . . . er . . . exaggerations. He didn't wait for the answer, instead making his way to the kitchen.

"Actually, I did. Of course, I think he's in AA now." Mournfully, he lifted a bottle into the air, then drank. "It is to weep."

"Yeah, I'm sure." I sat on the massive rock crystal

coffee table in front of him. "Okay, Robin, you deserved a little holing-up time, but now you've got to shake this off. The Auphe are back playing their games. They messed with Nik and me in the park. They could come here next. They were toying with us. They might be more serious with you. As in rip you open and get drunk on that alcohol you call blood. You have to be ready. Sober your ass up."

"*Gamo* the Auphe." Goodfellow had known the Auphe when people were still living in caves, gnawing on mammoth bones and picking fleas off one another. He had a healthy fear of and respect for them. Very healthy. At least up until now, apparently. "Bring them on." He took another drink. "Lead their pasty asses hither. I'll give them something to chew on."

I wasn't sure whether he meant his sword or himself, and that worried the hell out of me. He'd been through it, I knew, but I wasn't sure how to deal with a depressed and ashamed puck. I'd never seen him less than confident—brazen as hell. Cocky and way too willing to show you why that word was appropriate in more ways than one. Anything different from that, I wouldn't have been able to picture as of last week. Now . . . now I'd seen it and it wasn't right. It wasn't puck—it wasn't Robin. I didn't like it. Goodfellow had lived a long, long time. Now wasn't the time to give up.

I reached over and snatched the bottle out of his hand. "Okay, fine, you fooled some people into worshipping you as a god. And, yeah, their descendants chased you for thousands of years, wanting to kill you for deserting them. So what? They failed. Get over it already."

The glassy eyes blinked several times before he gave a slurred drawl. "You know, say it that way and it doesn't sound so bad." Of course it had been more than that. Two people had died—died very bloody, terrible deaths because of his massive puck ego, when he had been their "god." He hadn't meant for it to happen, but it had and that's what had him in the bottle, not being worshipped and nearly killed by the last of his followers' tribe. Speaking of bottles, he grabbed at it and missed. I'd seen Robin drink, but I'd only ever seen him drunk twice before. The first time had been when he'd met us, and the last time had been days ago. Both had been for only a few hours. This time, I would bet he'd spent every minute of these past three days like this.

"Look," I said sharply, "we don't care what you did back then. We only care what you do now. You're a friend, and you were a friend to us when any person with the sense God gave a mentally challenged rock would've run the other way."

He let his head flop against the back of the couch. Looking up at the ceiling, he exhaled, then reminded me with a faint note of nostalgia, "Don't forget that you threatened to slit my throat when we first met."

"And even that didn't dissuade you from talking endlessly." Niko appeared and deposited a plate on Robin's lap. There was a sandwich on it and what looked like homemade potato salad. I tried not to think how Seraglio had no doubt made it herself. "Now eat, sober up, and face up to the fact that what you did was wrong, but not wrong enough to justify your murder as penance."

Goodfellow remained motionless, either thinking about it or ignoring us entirely. Niko leaned in, planted a hand on each side of Robin's head, looked down at him, and asked silkily, "Did I or did I not say 'now'?"

Yeah, the tough love. Niko was all about it.

There was more silence, a grunt; then the puck straightened marginally and reached for the sandwich. "I hate you both." He took a bite, chewed, swallowed, and added grudgingly, "But I'm glad the Auphe didn't kill you. The massive hero worship you have for me brightens my day."

"Yeah, I can imagine." I pushed a few bottles off the coffee table and spread out a little while Niko distanced himself to stand at the other end of the couch from Robin. I doubted it helped with the alcohol reek, but I gave him credit for trying.

Making his way methodically through the sandwich, Robin looked us both up and down, and then asked between bites, "The Auphe came at you and neither of you have a scratch? How did you manage that? Are you carrying nuclear armament now, Caliban? Did you give up on the pop guns?"

"Like I said, they were just playing with us. Talking shit." I did have a few claw marks, but in our work if you could still walk and talk, that didn't count. "They were on the roof of our apartment building when I came home, and then they traveled to the park where Nik was practicing."

I often thought of going through the gates as traveling now. I'd been called "traveler" repeatedly by a homicidal asshole in the past two weeks. Sawney, mass murderer and one seriously crazy son of a bitch, was dead and less than ash now, but the term had stuck with me. It was as good a description as any for what the Auphe did . . . for what I could do. And as it also covered my other half—Rom—it fit.

"And you"—he grimaced—"*traveled* after them?" He'd gone through a gate with me on one occasion. It wasn't a pleasant sensation for non-Auphe; not unless you were into puking your guts out.

"No. I ran my ass off." Traveling, once difficult, had suddenly become easy. Too easy. It put me in touch with my homicidal Auphe roots more than was good for me . . . or for anyone around me. I'd told my brother I wouldn't do it again if I could avoid it, but if I hadn't been in the midst of a sidewalk full of people I would've done it in a hot second. He was a helluva lot more important than wrestling with the wrong half of my Jekyll-and-Hyde issue. He was worth losing a piece of my soul. . . . If I had one, it was only because of him anyway.

Still, it wasn't anything I wanted to talk about. How I felt the mental stirrings of a bloodthirsty heritage when I passed through the gray light wasn't my favorite topic right now. The Auphe nature wasn't mine. I wouldn't let it be. And if I said that to myself over and over and sprinkled enough frigging fairy dust around, maybe it would be true.

Clap your hands. Clap them goddamn hard and wish like a mother.

"But why—" He stopped when he saw Niko's eyes narrow fractionally, effectively ending the subject. When your overprotective big brother carries a sword, people tend to pay attention. "Moving on." Robin tossed the plate onto the table's surface, knocking over yet another bottle, and rubbed his eyes. "I need a new housekeeper."

I didn't say anything. He'd liked her; he'd lusted after her; he'd even respected her—a rarity for Goodfellow—and she'd tried to kill him. What was there to say in the face of that?

Actually, I did have something to say, although it was not about Seraglio. It was about what had happened in the park. I hadn't been completely sure then. . . . No, that was a lie. I had been sure, but I didn't know how I was sure and I didn't want to talk about that—that the only way I could know was because of my two stolen years. The Auphe were a subject I avoided, but discussing those two years—that I avoided at all costs. I was afraid—hell, terrified—that talking about it might one day peel back the darkness that swallowed those years, which would then swallow me. And I'd lose my mind. For good this time.

"Yeah, or you could pick up after yourself," I said

distractedly, then went on before his outraged laziness hit me in the face. "Nik, Robin, in the park . . ." I ran a thumb over the smooth stone of the table's surface and grimaced before going on. "They were all female. The Auphe." I tended to think of the Auphe as "he" or "it," because physically there was no difference between male and female to the eye and because I didn't want to give them the label of actual biological organisms. They were too goddamn horrific for that. Too alien.

Niko frowned, both at the knowledge and the fact I hadn't told him sooner, I knew. "What are they usually?" I could see he was annoyed with himself for never asking that question before. He was dedicated to knowing every fact about the Auphe that he could gather, because one day one of those facts might save me.

"I don't know." I gave a defensive shift of my shoulders. "I usually pay more attention to not pissing my pants and staying alive, so I guess they've just been a mix."

"How do you know they were all female?" Robin asked curiously, his reddened eyes slightly more alert. "It's not like the male Auphe keep them swinging in the breeze, and I assume they have something to swing or one couldn't have impregnated your mother." He considered the matter as he popped in the last bite of sandwich. "Perhaps they recede up inside the body. There are some animals—"

"Robin," Niko said matter-of-factly, "be quiet."

Goodfellow caught a look at my face, which, considering how much I wanted to hurl right now, probably wasn't the best it had ever looked. "Ah yes. Well. Sorry," he apologized sincerely before making a washing movement of his hands to scatter any remaining crumbs. "The male and female no doubt have a difference in scent."

He was probably right, but what the hell did it

mean? It didn't do jack shit for us if we didn't know what it meant. I said as much and changed the subject abruptly. "Where do we go from here? A rehab center for Goodfellow here?"

Niko was silent just long enough that I knew he would bring this up later when we were alone—whether I wanted to or not—but then he said smoothly, "Promise wants to talk to us. She may have some work for us." Most of our work wended its way through our favorite vampire. "That includes you, Robin."

The brown head dropped into waiting hands. You could virtually see the hangover forming. "Why? I'm highly looking forward to the alcoholic coma due me, thanks so much."

"Because with the Auphe reappearing, we all need to stay alert. And you"—Niko flicked the side of Goodfellow's head with enough force that I heard the *thwack* that was usually reserved for me—"you are not alert. Shower and dress. You have fifteen minutes."

"And we charge fifty an hour for babysitting," I added, "so grab your wallet." As green as Robin was when he swayed upright, I'd be happy just not to have a gallon of vomit hurled onto my shoes.

There was no vomit, but the fifteen-minute timetable went right out the window. Considering the shape and smell of him, I didn't mind waiting longer for a clean and slightly more sober Goodfellow to walk back into the room. He was as pasty as the Auphe ass he'd been referring to earlier, but he was moving under his own power. That had to be a good thing. When we reached the street he hadn't recovered any color and he had a faint wobble to his step, but that didn't stop him from leering at a passing woman. "Well, hello."

When she didn't respond, he switched his gaze to the man behind her. "Well, hello."

"Three days without sex," I snorted. "I'm surprised your dick hasn't deserted you for greener pastures."

Goodfellow glared at me as he swayed. Niko reached out to steady him and said reprovingly, "I wish, especially now, that you had not done this to yourself."

"Yes, yes. I'm sure you take your Metamucil shaken, not stirred," he griped. "But some of us like the grape." He walked . . . weaved, whatever. "We need a cab before I fall on my face."

By the time we reached Promise's building on the Upper East Side—60th and Park, another place too expensive for my bladder—Robin had sobered up more. Pucks—they have one helluva metabolism. It didn't stop Promise from taking a second look at him when we walked into her place. "You are well?" she asked dubiously.

"I'm alive," he said tersely. "I think that counts, but ask me again later." Trudging to Promise's ivory couch, he collapsed. "Perhaps I could get a little hair of the canine?"

"No," Niko replied firmly. Leaning in, he kissed Promise lightly. "If you have a key to your liquor cabinet," he said to her, "this may be the time to employ it."

She touched her fingertips to his jaw, and then turned to look at Goodfellow. She didn't say anything further, but I could see the sympathy in her eyes. She knew. She'd been there with us when Seraglio and her clan had nearly killed Robin. She was often exasperated with him, more often pissed as hell, but she was still fond of him—although somewhat less fond after he'd once turned her apartment into the scene of an orgy.

Robin looked away from her gaze. It was bad enough, I knew, that Niko and I had seen him so vulnerable. One more was too much. "I'm not here for an intervention or the entertainment, and I do have my own business to run. Can we move this alcohol-free ordeal along?" Yes, Robin Goodfellow, Puck, Pan, the Goat in the Green, did have his own business that he ran with a ruthless hand. He was worse than any monster. Worse than any beast from a mythical hell.

Like I'd said, he was a car salesman.

Worse still, a *used*-car salesman, the type of man that bragged that he could sell a condom to a eunuch or life insurance to the undead.

"I'll come to the point, then, so that you may return to fleecing the sheep." With a parting kiss to Niko's cheek, Promise walked to the darkly tinted window and pulled the curtains. In a gray silk skirt slit just above the knee and a scoop-neck sweater that was a soft shimmer of violet, she looked at us with equally violet eyes. Her hair, striped moon pale and earth brown, was pulled back in three braids, tumbling in loose waves at the crown and falling to the small of her back. "I have an old acquaintance. He wants to hire us."

She was generous with the "us." Promise, like the vast majority of vampires, didn't drink blood anymore, but she had gone through five very wealthy, very elderly husbands in the past ten years. However, I was sure every one of them had died with smiles on their wrinkled faces and gratitude in their shriveled hearts. Consequently, she didn't need the money we brought in; she did it for the love of the game . . . or the love of something else. Someone else.

"An old acquaintance?" Robin waggled his eyebrows. "The naked kind?"

Promise sighed, then ignored him. "Seamus. A vampire like me. He seems to have a bit of an interesting problem."

"Huh. A vampire. What's he want?" A vampire acquaintance, eh? Robin might not be so far off. Niko wouldn't be annoyed. He wasn't that possessive, and insecurity was only a word in the dictionary to him. But I was more than ready and willing to be annoyed for him. That's what brothers are for.

"Yes, a vampire." A finely arched eyebrow lifted. "As for his situation, this is something unusual, Seamus says. This is nothing completely . . . apparent. It's a subtle thing, and perhaps nothing at all. But to determine that I think we'll need a team approach."

"There's no *I* in 'team,' " Robin pointed out, starting to get up, "There's an *I* in 'intercourse,' 'iniquity,' 'illegal,' 'intoxication,' and did I mention 'intercourse'? But there is no *I* in 'team.' And I'm all about the *I*, which means that *I* will see you later."

"There's also an *I* in 'I'll kick your ass,' so sit down," I ordered darkly. "Maybe if you're lucky and finish sobering up, we'll tag your ass and turn you loose in the wild."

He gave a silent snarl, but by the time we got out of a cab at Seamus's place, an artistically clichéd loft in the artistically clichéd SoHo, he was sober. Despite that, he made no move to go back home. He might have had only a reluctant interest, but reluctant or not, it kept him there. "Art." He looked up at the walls of the loft, where the artist's work was liberally displayed. Not seeing any paintings of himself, he gave a disgruntled snort. "Theoretically."

Seamus slid his eyes toward Promise. "Humans and a puck. *Mo chroi*, I fear for your social standing."

Promise had said Seamus's problem was interesting, which was funny, because Seamus himself turned out to be just as interesting. Stick him in a kilt, paint his face blue, and he could've stepped into a Mel Gibson movie without missing a beat. Maybe because he'd actually lived through similar battles—the nighttime ones anyway. He wasn't tall, although hundreds of years ago he would've been. About five-nine, he was built with broad strokes. Wide shoulders and chest, muscular arms and legs; he wasn't your typical lithe and languid, ruffle-wearing vampire of pulp fiction. Except for one small braid that hung from temple to stubbled jaw, the wavy, deep red hair was pulled back into a short club at the base of his neck. That with the tawny eyes made him into a lion of a man, a giant cat walking on two legs. Which would make me a scruffy alley cat, an ill-tempered one who already had a headache from the Auphe situation. . . . It damn sure wasn't improved by the surroundings.

Seamus was an artist. His massive warehouse loft was wall-to-wall with his work. He liked bright, vibrant colors. Very bright, and vibrating right through my goddamn skull. After the day I'd had, this was like an ice pick between the eyes. I groaned and dug into my pocket for Tylenol, as Promise discarded her ivory hooded cloak onto a battered old chair to embrace Seamus lightly.

"Seamus, it's been a long time." Her expression was one of fondness, pleasure to see an old friend, and . . . something else. It was so brief I would've thought I'd imagined it, if I hadn't watched Sophia size up a mark thousands of times. Neither Niko nor I could hope to read people like our thieving mother had, but we held our own.

An old acquaintance, my ass.

I glanced sideways at Niko to see a perfectly blank face. No reason for him to feel threatened by Promise's past relationships, although this was the first one he'd come across where the participant wasn't dead and who hadn't been profoundly geriatric before he slipped into that state. I shook out two painkillers into my hand and then offered him the bottle. He bared his teeth for a fraction of a second, and I took that as a no. Putting the bottle back into my pocket, I popped the pills dry as Seamus welcomed us. Hands on Promise's shoulders after she pulled back, he leaned forward to brush a kiss across her cheek. "Paris was a cold and lifeless city without you, *leannan*. I'm glad our paths have crossed again."

"You're dusting off the Gaelic, Seamus," she said reprovingly. "Are the women not falling for 'lassie' any longer?"

He grinned, his strong white teeth gleaming a bright contrast to the copper shadow on his jaw. "You've caught me, then. The last pretty maid I tried it on branded me a cheesy pervert, I believe. Back in London. A feisty one, that, but I won her over in the end." Dropping his hands to his sides, he said, "But let us then get down to business, *mo chroi*."

"She's not your heart anymore, no matter what your nostalgia tells you," Nik said very mildly. There was no edge to the words, but there was one in Niko's sheath if Seamus wanted to make an issue of it. No jealousy, but a definite line drawn in the sand. And didn't it figure my brother would pick up Gaelic in his spare time?

"My nostalgia lasts longer than your lifetime, human," Seamus replied as mildly. "I shall be waiting at a finish line you will never see."

Promise didn't look amused by the exchange, and Goodfellow didn't help things any. "Men fighting over you," Robin said as he started opening cabinets and rifling through them, looking for that hair of the dog he'd mentioned earlier. Since he was sober now, I let it go. One or two wouldn't hurt him, and it might help us. "It's like old times for you, eh? Or it would be if both of them were dueling with their walkers."

She was even less amused now. Seamus repeated with a snort of disdain, "A puck, Promise? Sincerely, lass, what would possess you?"

"My company is my business, Seamus. Don't make assumptions on an old acquaintance," she warned. "You make it difficult to want to give you our assistance."

He gave her an abashed look from mellow whiskey-colored eyes. Curling his lips, he put a hand to his chest and bowed slightly. "I'm a poor client and a poor host. Forgive me."

Robin finally stumbled on a bottle of wine and toasted us. "You're forgiven. *Sla inte chugat*. Now where's your corkscrew?"

"As I have no brothel to offer you, Puck, a meager good health to you as well. And in the drawer by the stove," Seamus answered, suddenly good-natured . . . even toward an odious puck. He waved a hand at the couch and chairs, simple wood and natural fabrics that contrasted against the bold colors of the paintings. The Tylenol was beginning to let me see them as bold rather than eye-melting. "My apologies. Please."

I didn't believe the apology or accept it, but I did accept the invitation to sit. Sprawling in a chair, I looked over at Robin pouring a glass of ruby red. I held up one finger, cutting him off with the single glass. He rolled his eyes and ignored me. I may as well have been at work at the bar.

Promise sat on the couch, and Niko stood. Niko usually stood. You never knew when the couch might come alive and eat you. You had to stay alert. Constantly vigilant. Although after the Auphe attack, I didn't blame him. I dealt with it a little differently. Every cell inside me vibrated with the need to runrunrun. Sitting, slouching, watching Robin, looking at art I didn't get . . . it kept a small part of my mind occupied. Kept me from grabbing Niko's arm and tearing down the street. Getting out of town like the old days. Going anywhere. Anywhere but here. Anywhere the Auphe weren't. Just like a dozen times before.

Good times. Jesus.

It was also a helluva ride waiting . . . balancing on the knife's edge as I just waited. Waited to feel that heads-up, that gut twist of an Auphe gate opening. The sensation of theirs ripping open were a distant echo of mine, but I could still feel them. It was a nice alarm system, good to have. But it was no fun, the nerve-shredding anticipation. No goddamn fun at all.

"Have one, kid. It will do you good."

I looked up to see a wineglass in front of me. Robin was right. At the moment, one wouldn't kill me. The Auphe would, but wine wouldn't. "Thanks." I took it and had a swallow. I made a face. It was the good stuff. I didn't drink much—with an alcoholic mother, I didn't like to take chances—but I did know the better the wine, the worse it tasted. I liked the cheap stuff. The more it tasted like Kool-Aid, the happier I was. You could take the boy out of the trailer park . . .

Robin clicked his glass against mine and toasted. "As they say, it never rains; it pours. Pours liquid fire from the sky, sets us aflame, and scorches the earth to barren bedrock." Goodfellow's glass was now half-empty, but he stuck to the one-glass rule. "Cheers."

Niko shook his head when the bottle was held in his direction, as did Promise and Seamus, who said, bemused, "You are, without a doubt, the most grim and gloomy puck it's been my pleasure to come across."

No one commented. Aware he'd breached a touchy subject, he continued briskly, "On to my difficulty, annoyance that it is. It started nearly a week ago." He frowned. "I'm being followed. At least it seems that way. Ordinarily, I would know, but this . . . this is different. I do not see anyone tailing me, as they say, yet wherever I go, someone is there, already waiting. Someone who has far too much interest in me. Always in a public place where I cannot *discuss* the situation with them." White teeth, fangs and all, were shown in a humorless and savage grin. "And before I am to leave, they disappear. I turn away for a moment, and they are gone. It seems they know my intention before I do."

"Same guy?" I asked.

"No, which makes it more perplexing." He shook his head. "They're smart, whoever these sons of bitches be, but after four hundred years, I know when I'm being watched. I know when someone's a little too curious about my affairs."

"So you see the need for the team dynamic," Promise said, her hands clasped loosely over her knee. The oval pearlescent nails gleamed. "We can surround whatever curious gentleman shows up. He can't evade us all."

Well, if nothing else, it seemed easier than our last few jobs. No flesh-eating kidnappers. No fire-spewing serpents. No dead little girls. And with the Auphe back, something easy was all we could probably handle. If we even wanted to. Yeah, we needed the money, but trying to stay alive trumped that. I had doubts, serious doubts we could do both. I had doubts we could do even the most important one. I looked over at Nik and voted no with two words: "The Auphe."

Seamus's face slid into an expression of pure disgust. "Those *diabhail* creatures. What of them? I'd heard they were no more."

Promise hadn't told him I was half Auphe, and vampires don't have the sense of smell werewolves do. The wolves always knew. Seamus, however, didn't seem to have any idea about me, which was fine. I'd seen enough of those same looks of disgust shot my way. Disgust and fear. I was beginning to take a perverse pleasure in the last one. Not such a great thing to admit, but being hated for who you were right down to the genetic level leads to some defense mechanisms. Unhealthy ones, probably, but what the hell?

"Yeah, well, you heard wrong." I pulled the tie from my hair to let the dark strands fall free against my neck. I stretched the black elastic until it dug into my fingers with a painful bite. "They have a problem with us. And an Auphe problem is one fucking big problem. We don't need the distraction right now."

Niko disagreed with me. "Job or not, Cal, we still have a problem," he pointed out with inarguable logic. I hated logic. It was never on my side. "They'll come when they come; we can't change that. Whether we're working a case or not. Putting our lives on hold won't make us any safer."

Or any more likely to survive, I added silently. But he was right, and it wasn't about the money. It was about what I'd said earlier, keeping at least some of your thoughts somewhere else. Not enough to be truly distracted, but enough to keep from drowning in dread and apprehension. I shifted my shoulders to loosen the tension in my neck, and exhaled. "Okay, okay. I'm in." Moving from kidnapping to extermination to babysitting—our cases weren't quite heading in the right direction. Thoughts for another time . . . like when our asses weren't in such a sling. Or when we were dead.

Plenty of time then.

So we took the job. Robin, unable to help himself, jumped in to haggle Seamus up to an outrageous fee. It was a wonder he left the poor bastard with the tartan boxers on his ass. On that slightly disturbing thought, I turned toward the door with the others, leaving behind echoing spaces, powerfully raw art, and Seamus . . . Seamus, who was staring at Niko's back as I looked over my shoulder. Not at Promise as I'd expected. But at Nik. Staring and staring hard.

This could be a problem.

2

Niko

The seven deadly sins.

Wrath, lust, gluttony, greed, sloth, envy, pride.

The puck pillowing his head on the bar counter of the Ninth Circle, sleeping the sleep of the exhausted and overindulged, had the latter six covered. But Cal, my brother, had the first all to himself. He tried to hide it, and from anyone but me, I believe he most likely succeeded. He'd come a long way in a year. Then it would've rolled off him in waves, choppy and fierce. Some emotions still did show: annoyance and impatience being the primary ones, and annoyance was threatening enough when others knew you were half Auphe.

Discipline would come. He was only twenty. Twenty and missing two years of his life. Eighteen mentally, the cynicism of a forty-year-old, and one of the bravest men I knew. He would deny it, but it was true. Kidnapped by the Auphe, possessed by a creature that had all but eaten his soul, and he went on. He clawed his way from the pit and went on—balanced on a knife's edge. The Auphe were determined to snatch his sanity before they took his life. He'd already seen things, experienced horrors that I hadn't been able to save him from. But I wouldn't let what had happened before happen again. I would kill anything.

Anyone.

He was my brother.

I'd been handed a newborn at the age of four. Our mother must've fed me and changed me. She must have given me the bare necessities to survive, but she didn't do the same for Cal. From the moment he came into this world, she had never wasted one moment of affection or attention on him. After handing him to me, I don't think she ever touched him again, not on purpose, in his entire life. Sophia took the Auphe's gold to bear a half-human, half-Auphe child, but I don't think she saw him as a child, just as a *thing*. She'd even named him Caliban—the offspring of witch and demon from Shakespeare, a deformed monster, and she made sure he knew what it meant.

Bitch. It wasn't a word I said often, but it was the only description that suited her.

Sophia had died a horrible death, and I couldn't say I once felt an ounce of sympathy for her. She'd have made a good Auphe: sociopathic and utterly without compassion. She might have not physically touched Cal. In fact, she barely acknowledged his existence, but when she did, she said things to him—gloating, evil words, and I couldn't protect him from them all. Call a child a monster often enough and he'll believe you, maybe all of his life.

After the home birth—no hospitals if they could avoid it for the Rom, living below the government's radar—pale and sweating, she had cut the umbilical cord, tied it off with a strip of yarn, and handed the bloody, writhing bundle to me. "You've been wanting a pet," she had said, voice hoarse from grunts and restrained screams. "Here you are."

Four years old. What do you do with a baby when you're four years old? You learn responsibility. You go next door to the next run-down row house and ask the woman there, the one with five children of her own. She tells you how often and how to feed, because

Sophia can't be bothered, gives you a few cans of formula, a half box of diapers, and an old bottle. Then she sends you away with a look in her eyes that says she's done all she's going to do. You're not her problem, so don't darken her door again. There are worthless monsters and worthless human beings, and sometimes it's hard to tell the difference between the two.

I'd been lucky Cal had rarely been sick. Never a cold, never colic, only once with something like the stomach flu; the healthiest baby in the world, thanks in part, I was sure, to Auphe genes. If he hadn't been, he might not have survived. Best intentions, especially at the age of four, don't always count.

Bad memories and dark bars—the two seemed to go hand in hand.

We'd come to Cal's work, his day job, so to speak, after agreeing to take Seamus's case. It was early afternoon, but the bar was half full. I'd taken a table in the corner by the bar. I flipped my dagger as I opened my book, Thucydides's *History of the Peloponnesian War*, and ruthlessly vanquished the desire to slam the blade into the polished wood of the tabletop.

I moved on to practicing grips before my control wavered and I did bury the dagger in the table. Memories—you can't escape them, but you can't let them rule you either. Or you won't be any good to yourself or your brother. I should concentrate on this new development on the Auphe front. All female— what could it mean?

"You're late."

I didn't look up at Ishiah's annoyance. Cal's employer was both bark and bite. Either way, Cal could handle it.

"It's funny. You say that every time." I heard Cal toss his jacket behind the bar. "Like you expect something different."

Ishiah owned the bar the Ninth Circle. He hired Cal as a favor to Goodfellow. The two of them, peri and puck, had issues with one another, Cal had told me. Actually, he'd said they bitched about each other until they made his ears bleed. Always with the turn of phrase, my brother. Apparently, the behavior ranged from cool exchanges to out-and-out threats of violence. While it was entertaining as hell, Cal had yawned one night after work, he never had figured out what their history was. For all their sharp words, they had a certain respect for one another, it seemed. If it hadn't been for Ishiah swooping in, literally, at the last minute earlier in the week, Robin would be dead. That said something. And I knew Cal was grateful.

But that didn't mean he was going to be on time.

It was an understanding the two had. Ishiah had given Cal a job when he didn't particularly want to. And as Cal tended to alarm a good deal of the clientele, it was no doubt best to get some liquor in them most days before he showed up. Sedate them somewhat. But with an understanding or not, Ishiah still called Cal out on it. He was the boss; that was his job. It wouldn't do to let the other employees see Cal get any special treatment . . . especially as he was the only one without wings. Peris, like every other creature on the planet, weren't without their prejudices.

The Circle was a peri bar. That meant quite a lot of plants and birds. Peris had a fondness for birds. It also meant Ishiah, Danyel, Samyel, Cambriel, and another peri whose name Cal had never mentioned beyond "it has a lot of z's in it," were all peris. The average peri might look like the customary depiction of angels, through a very dark lens, but they weren't. No one was sure what they were or how long they'd been around.

Myth said they were half angel, half demon, but I had serious doubts that that was the truth—I'd yet to see mythology get anything completely correct. The big picture was close, if you blurred your eyes, but every one of the details was twisted or flat-out wrong.

It's annoying when information doesn't live up to your standards. Someday your life might depend on it, and when you're bleeding to death on the ground, you may wish you'd taken it with a grain of salt.

As for peris: Peris had wings, peris had tempers, and peris kicked ass. I gave a quirk of my lips. Cal had told me that in exactly those words after working there for a time. That was my brother: the succinctness of the truly lazy.

I looked up from the book for a moment, the flat of the dagger balanced on the back of my hand. There were ten or so werewolves in the evening crowd. I'd focused on them the moment we'd entered. As one their heads had come up and their eyes had all been aimed at Cal. Gold, orange, reddish brown, pale blue, some wolf, some human—they all widened and then turned to slits at the sight and scent of him. There were some growling, snarls, and bared teeth, but no one marked their territory by urinating on a table leg. It was a nice change of pace.

"Why the hell do they keep coming back?" Cal muttered as he reached for a gray apron and wrapped it twice around his waist.

"Pride," Ishiah responded, folding his arms.

"Pride?" Cal took a bottle of tequila and poured a large shot as a chupracabra approached the bar. "Yeah, I guess I can see that." Facing your fear and spitting in its eye. I knew that was something he could relate to. Depositing the tequila in front of the goat sucker, he said, "Five bucks. Or you want to run a tab?"

The chupa, who looked remarkably like a shaved dog in a hooded jacket, looked at him with the dull blankness of the barely sentient before putting a dirty five on the counter and moving off with his drink. I wasn't surprised. Cal complained often that monsters weren't big tippers.

A rustle of feathers shifted my attention from the departing chupa to Ishiah. Aside from the gold-barred wings, which flickered in and out of existence, he didn't look like anything that belonged on the roof of your typical manger scene. He was not quite the same as other peris. He was bigger, had more presence. Tall and broad-shouldered with light blond hair, fierce blue-gray eyes, a pronounced scar along his jaw, and one extremely large sword under the bar, not many of the patrons started anything when Ishiah was around.

"So you managed to pry Robin out of his well of self-pity?" he asked, looking down at a lightly snoring Goodfellow.

That was somewhat harsh. True perhaps, but harsh nonetheless.

"Wouldn't let you in either, huh?" Cal said knowingly. "Yeah, we got him out and sobered him up. He's doing better."

Ishiah seemed relieved. He was hard to read, but our mother had spent Cal's and my childhood sizing up many a mark. You couldn't be Sophia's get without picking up a few things. Looking back down at my book, I continued the dagger practice as I read. Relieved or not, Ishiah didn't say anything further about Robin as I multitasked, reading about the fall of Potidaea, flipping the blade, and thinking of the Auphe in the park. Instead he asked, "Why is your brother here? He's hardly a drinker."

True, and it was rare that I came to the Ninth Circle. Drunken werecats spewing hairballs far and wide wasn't my idea of an enjoyable evening, but I did make exceptions and this was one. I kept my eyes on my book as I tossed the dagger up into the air yet again and caught it blind. One: because it was good practice. You always know where your weapon is, whether you can see it or not. Always. Second: It annoyed Cal, as he couldn't do it. I smiled to myself. Being an older brother wasn't always about protection.

"We have business after work," Cal said, although that wasn't the real reason. We did have business, Seamus's business, but that wasn't why I was here. Ordinarily I would've met Cal after work, here or at the stakeout location, but with the Auphe in the here and now, things were different. Now none of us were to go out alone after dark in the more deserted areas of the city if we could avoid it.

Not that the Auphe wouldn't appear in broad daylight—we'd seen that and their no doubt justified faith in the human desire to not see what it didn't want to see—but it was rare. Georgina had promised me she wouldn't go out at all once the sun set, although I was hoping that the Auphe had forgotten about her or decided that Cal himself had. As monsters went, they weren't precisely plugged into the community gossip, and Cal had seen next to nothing of her in the past months. Even if the Auphe had been following him for some time, they could take it that she didn't mean a thing to him. With their twisted brains, I doubted they could even imagine she meant anything at all to him if he didn't spend nearly every day with her.

It wasn't true, or it hadn't been. Cal had cared enough that he'd done everything he could to push her out of his life. To keep her safe. And he had. Hopefully, the Auphe would believe what he'd so desperately attempted to make true, or had missed those incredibly rare visits altogether.

"Auphe business?" Ishiah's voice darkened a fraction.

"Is that a good guess or do you know something?" And at that moment, Ishiah wasn't Cal's employer.

The peri wasn't Robin's sometime friend, sometime enemy right then. He was someone who might have information that could save us.

The only thing Cal and I had in common physically were gray eyes, and I raised mine to see his turn empty and cool. Ishiah wasn't easily intimidated, but when it came to the Auphe, he had the same reaction as everyone else. He certainly wasn't going to do anything in their favor, but seeing is believing, and I wanted to see this very clearly. I closed my book and stared at the peri with a gaze as empty as my brother's. And if my dagger did embed itself in the table this time, it wasn't anger, it wasn't a loss of control. . . .

It was incentive.

"No. I haven't heard anything . . . yet." He looked at the table, the dagger, and then at me. I wasn't here often enough for Ishiah to have much insight into me, not firsthand, but I thought he caught a glimpse now.

He went on, his eyes still taking my measure. "But we peris suspected the Auphe weren't all destroyed. Millions of years of survival have served them well." Shaking his head grimly, he added, "And when there's one Auphe left, people are going to die." He turned back to Cal and nodded toward his throat. "As for how I know . . . the Auphe have a distinctive saw-toothed edge on their claws. Makes for an interesting pattern."

"That's astounding, Sherlock. Take a bow." Cal poured a beer with a whiskey back for a wolf that slunk up to the bar. "Let me know if you do hear anything. Things are going to get nasty. You might have to find a new employee of the month."

"One who doesn't terrorize, impale, and melt the clientele?" he said, brows lowering in an annoyed scowl. "Pity me. I'll have to scour the city."

"You just can't let that go," he grumbled as he cleaned the bar top, the tension passing. "And, come on, only one of those was intentional. Accidents happen." Now, those were work stories he hadn't shared with me. He caught my narrowed glance from the corner of his eye, dropped his head, and groaned.

"Yes, I'm rather particular about the mutilation of my patrons. My apologies." Ishiah turned and went about the business of running the bar, and Cal kept serving up the drinks, avoiding my gaze when he could, and muttering, "Ah, shit," when he couldn't. I saw a discussion in our future. A very long, detailed, unfortunate discussion . . . unfortunate for my brother, at any rate.

When eleven came, the peri Samyel came in to work the rest of Cal's shift for him. For a peri, he was considered mellow. From the one thing Cal *had* bothered to tell me, Sammy hadn't heaved anyone through the wooden door of the bar for almost several days now. They must've gone through quite a few doors. A temper can be an expensive habit.

Cal took off the apron, passed it over, and turned to me. I was standing at the bar with book in hand. "Ready?" I asked.

"Yeah," he answered, retrieving his leather jacket and shoulder holster from beneath the bar. Lifting the hinged countertop, he walked through. "Although I think this sounds like a waste of time. Probably a crock cooked up by Seamus to get some Promise time. I don't trust that haggis-eating son of a bitch one damned bit."

"Cal," I said with amusement as I shrugged into the long gray duster that covered the sword strapped to my back, "you don't trust anyone. It's your religion, your mantra, and I believe you have it on a T-shirt." Not that I trusted Seamus either; I didn't, but I did trust Promise.

"Hey, not true," he scowled defensively. "I trust you. I trust Robin."

"And?" I prodded patiently.

"I trust Promise to do what's best for you," he

evaded. He did trust her for that, but just as I came first with my brother, so did I come first with Promise. That could lead to situations. It *had* led to a situation in the past that hadn't ended well for Cal. She'd pushed him to access his lost memories even though I'd told her before of the one previous attempt, which had had a catastrophic effect on my brother. She knew the danger, but because of me—*for* me—she'd pushed him regardless. And because Cal wanted to keep me safe as much if not more than she did, he let her. It hadn't ended quite as badly as the first time, but badly enough that Cal nearly lost himself in a black pit of memories that could have destroyed him. He'd also unconsciously built a gate that led straight to Auphe hell, Tumulus, and had had absolutely no control of it or himself. I'd had to knock him unconscious.

To say that had strained things between Promise and me would be an understatement, but we'd moved past it, thanks in part to more pushing, this time on my brother's part. But there couldn't be a repeat of what she'd done. Promise had given her word she wouldn't put Cal at risk again. I knew she was telling the truth. If I hadn't known that, well . . . Cal and I had more in common than our eyes. If there is no trust, there is nothing. Trust is all.

But Promise had never lied to me. She hadn't told me much about her past. I didn't blame her. A vampire's bloody pretreatment history could only be painful. I understood wanting to forget the predator that biology had once forced her to be. So I didn't mind that I heard only bits and pieces—the places she'd lived and the historical events that she'd seen. All I cared was that she had never lied. She was honest in a world just the opposite, and a cool oasis in my life. She was who she said she was, and everything Sophia, my mother, the pathologically manipulative liar, had never been.

She was also an accomplished fighter, practiced, efficient, and deceptively deadly. I'd seen her snap a revenant's neck in an instant and put a crossbow bolt dead center in the eye of a *vodynoi*.

Common interests—they really do enhance a relationship.

"As for George," he went on, "I trust her to do what's best for the universe, life, existence . . . whatever." Unfortunately, Cal was usually at odds with all those things. He didn't see the big picture that she did. And he didn't want to. His life, whatever he made of it, was enough for him. Georgina loved Cal or had loved him—I wasn't certain which it was now—but she also had a calling. I wasn't sure that one could trust a calling . . . not on a personal level. Georgina had enormous compassion, but she also had, in her eyes, an even larger responsibility. Fall leaves are brilliant with gold and red. You can cup them in your hand and wonder at them, be amazed at their uniqueness and glory. But eventually they are gone, brown, crumbling, and scattered on the wind. But the tree remains. The tree is what is important. The tree lives on. That was a difficult knowledge to bear, and an even more difficult life to live.

Of course, being the leaf wasn't exactly desirable either.

"Being wise is a burden." There was sympathy in my voice that I didn't bother to hide.

"Being a smart-ass moron is no cakewalk either," Cal retorted.

"So true," I offered dryly. "Yet you struggle on." I was about to step forward to shake Robin's shoulder when I noticed the snoring had a subtly different quality, and his hand was moving inch by slow inch across the bar. When it made it to the plastic container, I threw the dagger. It slid between his index and middle fingers to punch a hole in the plastic. "That is a tip jar," I observed mildly, "not an ATM."

He sat up and glowered. "I'm simply trying to stay in practice. I would've put the paltry pilfer back."

"Yes, I'm sure." Robin was at the very least as good at lying as our mother, but with his trickster race it was genetic. I couldn't hold his DNA against him, and his lies were never meant to actually deceive us. Annoy us, entertain us, convince us to change our sexual orientation, but never to actually deceive us. He certainly didn't use his powers for good per se, but with us he didn't use them for otherwise either. I retrieved my blade, then took his shoulder to heave him upright. "Time to work, not to steal."

"Stealing is teaching a valuable lesson to the naive. It's a community service. I should be honored for my heritage, not condemned." He shrugged off my hand to carefully smooth the material of his shirt, which would no doubt take the contents of a hundred tip jars to pay for.

We all moved outside onto Eldridge Street, Good-fellow and Cal behind me as I stopped and scanned the street. "Do you feel anything?" I asked.

"Gates? No." Cal put his hand inside his jacket, and I knew he was feeling the reassuring textured grip of his Glock. "Of course, they could've taken a cab, right? Who wouldn't stop for a clawed, fanged killer freak of nature?"

I gripped his shoulder at the bravado. He always tried to pull it off and he most often did. Not this time. "We've handled them all our life, little brother. We've survived. That's not going to change now."

"Yeah, sure." He looked away . . . up at the roof of the building. Up where the Auphe would roost.

I exhaled and dropped my hand. It was hard to reassure him when I had doubts myself. I wouldn't let them take Cal again, but I couldn't guarantee we wouldn't die in the process. I couldn't guarantee I would be quick enough, strong enough, no matter how many hours I practiced, how many miles I ran, how many books I read on the art of war. So I practiced more, ran more, read more, and one day maybe I would feel like it would be enough. One day.

The street in front of the Ninth Circle was packed bumper-to-bumper. Promise had called on my cell and said her car was parked illegally in front of the Tenement Museum three blocks down. Three pathetic blocks, but that didn't stop my indolent brother from grumbling. Any excuse to share his laziness with the world. He was slightly ahead of us when the revenant sprang out of a deeply recessed doorway. Dressed like a homeless man in ragged layers of clothing to conceal what it really was, it came boiling out of the gloom with claws like ten knives. Cal wouldn't have caught his scent. The entire block the Ninth Circle was situated on was saturated in so much supernatural scent, he couldn't separate one from the other. It didn't stop him from grabbing the clammy wrist, twisting the hand away, and avoiding the slashing claws of the other one. Then he proceeded to seize the hissing creature by its filthy jacket and pound its head against the brick wall.

"I am so"—*bang*—"*not*"—*bang*—"in the mood," Cal snarled.

The revenant's companion came out of the same doorway. As with cockroaches, if there's one revenant, there's bound to be more. Unfortunately, Raid had yet to come up with a solution to the next best thing to the undead. They might look deceased and mildly decomposing, with moist, clammy gray-green skin and milky white eyes, but revenants were alive and had never been human. They simply had good camouflage. Is that a corpse? Should we investigate? By the time the second question was out, the revenant had already eaten your leg—unfortunately for you.

This second one also had no weapons but what nature had given it and that . . . that was far from being enough. Cal, however, believed in using what nature and the local gun trafficker had gifted him with. He dropped the first creature, whose head had lost its original shape for something even less attractive. He then pulled his gun, a Glock .40, with lightning speed, shooting the other revenant in the face before it had a chance to take another step. I gave an inner nod of approval. Cal practiced. Frequently. I had to force him to run and spar, but he had never needed pushing to keep up his gun skills. Little boys and their toys—the bigger and louder, the better.

The revenant fell with a half-strangled scream. It wasn't done yet, though. It tried to crawl toward Cal, claws scoring the concrete beneath it. It had perhaps a spoonful of brains left in its shattered skull, but revenants were like cockroaches in that respect as well. "You got balls," Cal said with a grunt. "I gotta give you that." And then he shot him again, this time at the base of the skull. That time it did the trick. Nothing quite takes the fight out of a revenant like a severed spinal column.

Cal turned to see Robin and me leaning against the wall, observing the show. I didn't wear a watch, but I took Goodfellow's arm and tapped the face of his Rolex meaningfully. "We are on a schedule," I said mildly.

"Gee, Nik, I hate to slow you down. By the way, thanks for the help," he said caustically.

"If you had needed it, then I've taught you nothing. You barely broke stride." I pulled out my cell phone and called Ishiah to tell him he had a pile of garbage half a block from his door and he might want to clean it up. Muggers had once been New York's bane years ago. The police, and the boggles in Central Park, might have cleaned up that problem, but the revenants had taken their place. It wasn't quite a trade for the better. At least the muggers wouldn't have eaten you. As for witnesses, the bar and this block belonged to the supernatural. The majority of humans avoided it.

They might not know why, but a prehistoric instinct that had kept their ancestors alive knew that here there be monsters.

We reached Promise's limo minutes later. She'd brought the larger car this time to accommodate the extra passengers. I opened the door. Robin promptly climbed in out of the cold. I waited and Cal gave a mock-aggrieved sigh. "Cut the cord already, Cyrano. I just kicked ass."

"Revenants," I said with disdain. "That hardly counts. The day you spar a full three hours with me is the day I let you watch your own back," I retorted, looking down a nose that I had no problem admitting was Romanesque, if not Cyranoesque.

He gave a grin. It was a faint one, but considering the day he'd had, I'd take it. "Never gonna happen." He followed Goodfellow, and I followed him, closing the door behind us. Robin was sitting opposite us, beside two wolves. He brushed at his shirt as if ridding it of fur, but that was just Robin being the ass he was so often very good at being. These wolves were high breeds or fine-breds. They were of completely human shape and features when they wanted to be, not like the wolves in the bar. That didn't stop them from baring their suddenly elongating teeth at Cal, who sat on one side of Promise, as I sat on the other.

"These are your bodyguards?" I asked with eyebrows raised.

She gave an elegant nod. "Courtesy of Delilah. They are Kin, but loyal to her." Which was good. The Kin, the equivalent of a werewolf Mafia, had strong suspicions we'd been involved in the death of one of their Alphas. They were right.

Delilah was the sister of the wolf who had helped us. She, unlike her brother, was still in good standing with the Kin . . . for now. She was playing a dangerous game to advance her rank, making allies on any side she could. She was also sleeping with Cal. Whether that was a good thing was debatable, but it wasn't my business. Having sex simply to have it was what being twenty was all about—as long as I didn't have to hear any of the more furry details.

There was a soft kiss to my jaw. I turned to Promise and smiled. "I see you dressed for the occasion."

She'd hidden her glorious and definitely noticeable hair under a black cap that matched her sweater, snug pants, and boots. She would blend into the typical art crowd, which is where we would be. Seamus was attending an art show opening and we would be there to spot anyone who might be following him. Although, like Cal, I had my doubts.

With her warm weight against my shoulder, we arrived soon enough at yet one more converted loft in the Lower East Side. We left the wolves in the car and paired up to move into the crowd. As Cal moved off and Robin started to follow, I took his arm. "Watch him," I said quietly. "Watch him every moment. Are we clear?"

"It's too crowded here for the Auphe, but I will. I swear it," he returned as quietly, before heading off in Cal's wake.

Slim fingers looped around my wrist. "He's right. The Auphe won't come here."

"Never take anything for granted." I reached over with my other hand to tuck a willful strand of blond hair behind her ear. "Georgina?"

"Delilah was kind enough to send two wolves to her as well." She ran the soft pad of her thumb, like silk, along the inner part of my wrist, then let her hand fall. "There's Seamus, the center of attention as always." There was part exasperation and part affection in her voice.

"Nostalgic?" I asked. She'd made it clear to Seamus where her loyalties lay, but that didn't mean she couldn't have fond memories.

She thought about it for a moment, eyes distant.

"He was a friend when I needed one," she said finally, "but never more than that, although I thought differently. It simply took me several years to realize that. And the jealousy was the last straw."

"He's still jealous," I pointed out as I focused on him, surrounded by enough women to give Goodfellow a run for his money.

"Oh no. He hasn't attempted to behead a single person." She smiled, eyes now bright, bold, and entertained. "He changed for the better over a century ago, I'm glad to say. I wouldn't have let him near you otherwise." And of the group, I was thought to be the protective one. "Now"—she bent to check the dagger in her boot—"I'll go ask if one of his mysterious followers is here."

I looked over the crowd as she vanished into it. It wasn't an extraordinarily large amount of people, but it was crammed into a small space with art that even several university classes in the subject couldn't help me appreciate. There didn't seem to be anyone especially interested in Seamus besides the women. . . .

Wait.

On the edge of the crowd, studying a hunk of metal vomiting forth several jagged pieces of glass, there was a man. Completely inconspicuous, he was of average height, average weight, with short brown hair and a brown jacket. In the midst of this crowd wearing either the ridiculously bright or all in black, he didn't quite fit. He was *too* average. His body language said "Don't look at me" so strongly that I was surprised he didn't blend into the wall like a chameleon. I didn't need to wait for Promise to return to know this was the one.

I looked across the room for Cal and Robin. Taller than Promise, I spotted them instantly and caught their eye. Then I moved toward our chameleon of the ordinary. He didn't see me at first. Most don't. By the time he did, I had his collar fisted in my hand and was moving him briskly toward the door. He gurgled as the collar of his shirt cut into his airway. He turned red but not blue, so I wasn't too concerned about his health. I took him into the empty stairwell and gave him a shake, not hard, but not precisely gentle either. "Who are you?" I demanded.

He *was* turning slightly blue now—annoying—and I eased my grip a fraction as I repeated, "Who are you? Why are you following him?" No need to name Seamus. He knew whom I was talking about. I could see it in his brown eyes—completely average as well. I could also see he wasn't going to say a word, not without some encouragement. I let the dagger slide out from my sleeve. I didn't plan on using it—yet. I didn't know whether he meant Seamus any harm, not so far, but a blade to the throat is one of the better bluffs.

That's when I heard it. Below. The click of metal against metal.

I released the man as I threw myself to one side, feeling a tug that pulled at my duster and pinned it to a stair. Freed, he clattered, wheezing, down the stairs, as I yanked my coat free. Another long bolt of metal shot by, close enough to tell a story, but not close enough to kill. I listened to the story and stayed still as the footsteps faded away. When they disappeared, I looked down at the long rod of metal embedded in the stair a bare two inches from my leg. Well . . .

That was interesting.

3

Cal

"A speargun? A goddamn speargun?"

"You've said that five times now, little brother. I don't think it's going to change with repetition." Niko had laid the two metal spears on our kitchen table to examine them. "It's rather an ingenious weapon for fighting nonhumans . . . if it weren't for the ammunition difficulties."

"Yeah, they're a little larger than crossbow quarrels. Hard to haul around. Good for a couple of bad guys; not so much for more," I said. I was examining something myself—the hole in Niko's coat. "You're sure they weren't trying to kill you?" Trying to kill him while Robin and I had been making our way through the crowd. Fast, but not fast enough. Goddamnit.

Promise's driver had dropped Robin, then us off after our less-than-successful job. Promise went home with her wolves. Robin went home alone. Promise was one helluva fighter, but while she'd been around centuries, Goodfellow had been around almost as long as the Auphe. If push came to shove, he had enough millennia of weapons practice to take either Niko or me, maybe both at once . . . if he were sober. If any of us could handle the Auphe, it would be him . . . especially in his home territory. Although he damn sure would sooner avoid it if he could.

And while it was now two thirty in the morning in our own home territory, I was too wired to sleep. "You're sure?" I repeated, sticking my finger through the hole in the gray cloth. If it wasn't bad enough the Auphe were back, now someone had tried to spear Nik like a goddamn sea bass. Jesus.

"Yes. They had the opportunity and they didn't take it." He was sitting on a kitchen chair with hands folded across his stomach. "Which is quite curious. I think . . ." He frowned. "I think we're going to have to do something neither one of us is going to like."

"Oh, Christ, what?" I asked apprehensively. If Nik didn't think we were going to like it, I really wasn't going to like it. It'd be up there with a Drano enema.

He stood. "Think about it. I'm sure it will come to you. Do you want first watch?"

When we thought we'd lost the Auphe while running or when we thought the Auphe were gone for good, we hadn't kept watch. Now here we were, the bad old times again. "Yeah, no way I'll sleep yet." I continued to fiddle with his duster until he pulled it from my hands.

"We have enough to occupy our minds." He pinched the nerve right above my elbow. There was that tough love again. "No what-ifs, understand?"

"Fine. Jeez." I rubbed my arm. "I'll let your dry cleaner worry about it."

"Good," he nodded. "If you get bored, try reading a book instead of making paper airplanes out of the pages."

"What? You're not going to grill me about the park? About how they were all female? We're not going to go over that for hours and hours until I try to skin you with a butter knife?" I asked, surprised. I'd been waiting for the discussion all day. I'd seen that unrelenting look in his eye. What had changed since then?

"No," he paused, then shook his head. "I want to

think about it first. And I'm familiar with your record of noticing details in any given situation."

"Pathetic?" I freely admitted.

"Nonexistent," he corrected. "Read a comic book or color if you can't handle that. There are crayons in the desk drawer." He disappeared down the hall to his bedroom. Crayons. Smart-ass bastard.

Naturally, I skipped any of his suggestions and went straight to why he didn't want me thinking about the Auphe. What was that about? What happened to two heads are better than one? And you couldn't say anyone knew more about the Auphe than I did, personally anyway. I might not be detail oriented, but those details were part of my genetic code. I couldn't avoid them if I wanted. What was Nik up to? After contemplating that long enough to make me bat-shit crazy and getting nowhere, I distracted myself by thinking about what Niko had said before that.

With Seamus's case—spearguns and all—what were we going to have to do that neither of us would like? It took me nearly half an hour to figure it out. And he was right.

I didn't like it one damn bit.

I surprised myself by sleeping for a few hours after Nik took over. I'd learned to do that on the run, no matter how scared or emotionally screwed, you had to sleep or you couldn't function. You couldn't run from the Auphe if you can't run at all. When I woke up and staggered down the hall in a T-shirt and pair of sweatpants to the living area, the first thing I said was, "No fucking way."

Niko was already dressed and doing his morning katas with his sword in the living room. "Figured it out, did you?"

Yeah, I had, and there was no way. "Wahanket tried to kill us last time." Wahanket, an informant also known as Hank when he wasn't trying to kill us, lived in the basement of the Metropolitan Museum. It was a good place for a walking, talking mummy with a fondness for cowboy hats.

"No, he tried to kill *you*, although I'm sure he would've gotten around to the rest of us if you hadn't taken his hand off." He gave a quick movement of his blade, a flick to rid it of imaginary blood. "Besides, Goodfellow's informants always try to kill us. It's tradition." He whirled, and I dodged the swipe of the katana. "Unfortunately," he continued, nodding in approval at my footwork, "only the more homicidal of snitches have anything worthwhile to say."

"Great." I went over to the fridge and stuck my head in. There was Nik's carrot juice, wheat-free bagels, cottage cheese, some sort of soy thing, and my week-old Chinese. I took the Chinese. "You know he makes mummy rats? Undead bony things running around." I made a face as I stuck a fork in the cardboard container. "Can you imagine what else is down there? Gah." I took a bite and chewed. "Then again, I could get to blow another piece off of him. There's a plus."

"No explosive rounds this time." He sheathed his sword with the proper respect. "I don't think Sangrida would appreciate that, considering all the artifacts down there. Best to stick with your Glock. No Desert Eagle." Sangrida was a Valkyrie and the museum director. It probably wouldn't do to piss her off. If the myths were true, she'd dragged many a warrior kicking and screaming off to Valhalla. And if the myths weren't true, she was strong enough to take a cab from the museum curb and beat us to death with it. She was definitely tall and muscular enough to.

"If we go, and I don't think we should." I took another bite, considered the odd taste of the chicken, shrugged, and went on. Food poisoning was the least of my concerns. Assuming I could even get it. I never had, and I'd eaten things five seconds away from growing penicillin. "The hell with Seamus and his money.

He's not worth that kind of grief. And I don't want to be a mummy. I definitely don't want a certain part of me mummified. It's just now getting some action."

"Yes, yes, your sexual exploits aside . . . there were the whole two of them, yes?" he asked with mock curiosity. He didn't wait for an answer and ignored my glare. "Those aside, we can't assume this is only about Seamus. It seems odd someone would follow a vampire only to watch him. If they don't want to kill him or me, what do they want? I don't think this is just about him."

"And you're doing it for Promise." I finished the carton and dumped it in the garbage.

"Yes. If this is about all vampires, I'd like to know as soon as possible." He didn't say he could go see Wahanket without me. He knew better than that.

"Okay. We'll go." I sighed and scratched my ass absently. "Should we take Robin?"

"I don't know. What does the Magic 8 Ball that is your ass say?" he asked dryly.

We took Robin without any input from my ass, thanks for asking.

"We should've brought an offering. Hank doesn't like it when you don't bring an offering," Robin said glumly. We'd managed to get him through the museum with a minimum of the I-slept-with-her, I-slept-with-him patented Goodfellow tour. When he started in on taking Cleopatra's virginity and how the legend of the asp was simply Octavian's Freudian longing for a penis . . . or for a bigger penis, as his was virtually nonexistent, we'd yanked him along.

"I don't think a present and some Get Well Soon balloons are going to do the trick." I snorted. "He's going to be pissed. I cut off his damn *hand*. Only Darth Vader gets away with shit like that."

The basement was the same as it was during my last visit, a virtual city of crates and forgotten exhibits.

Robin led us through it as easily as he had before, only this time I heard several cries from different directions. The croak of dried vocal cords. There was also the sound of claws tearing at the wood of crates. Those weren't rats. Great. Hank had gone from homicidal maniac to crazy cat lady. I wasn't sure which was worse. At least mummified cats didn't piss. All I smelled was the dust of years and years.

When we finally came across Wahanket's lair, Robin had gotten bored and was now telling us Brutus hadn't even been at the forum when Julius Caesar was killed. "A vicious rumor. And he had it all over Octavian, let me tell you. Hung like Pegasus, he was." It was enough to make you wish for an attack of mummified cats after all.

"You."

It was a death rattle from beneath the sand. It was Wahanket, and he sounded every bit as pissed as I expected.

"*You.* Mutilator. Maimer. Auphe."

Robin's informants really did know their shit. He knew I was Auphe. And if he knew that . . . "Then you know I came by the maiming hobby honestly," I said coldly and without remorse. I might hate the Auphe, but I wasn't above using their reputation if I had to, and why not? Most believed it anyway. "And it's not like you didn't deserve it, you withered son of a bitch." I had my gun, but it was holstered. If I couldn't use explosive rounds, I had something that would be more effective than the Glock. I held a sword, short and thicker than Niko's katana, and perfectly capable of taking more than a hand off.

"Why not come out, Wahanket? And we can discuss things without any mutilation." Niko said. "Perhaps," he added matter-of-factly.

There was a moment of stillness, then Wahanket stepped into the dim light. The first thing I noticed was he had a new hand. Sort of. It was scaled with wickedly curved black claws. I had a feeling a stuffed Komodo dragon down here somewhere was missing a piece. The rest of him was the same. Blackened flesh, resin-soaked bandages, a pit of a nose, and empty eye sockets that held a faint yellow glow. He wasn't slow like the mummies in the old black-and-white movies. He was quick when he wanted to be, with the scuttle of a cockroach. A very fast, murderous cockroach—something you definitely didn't want living under your sink.

Robin raised eyebrows at the "hand," but said smoothly, "See? That's not bad at all. Caliban did you a favor. It's very . . . ah . . . fashionable. Useful as well. A can opener has nothing on you, I'm sure."

Dark brown teeth clicked as he moved closer. I could see a rib bone sticking through cracked flesh, and something on the claws of the dragon hand . . . brown, crusted—I had no problem figuring out what it was. Maybe we should ask Sangrida if any of her security guards had gone missing.

"What do you seek here?" he hissed with a curled scrap of leathery tongue. "What do you think I would possibly give unto you?"

Like that was fair. Yeah, sure, I had blown off his hand; there was that. But *he* had started it. Had tried to kill me with a malicious glee, and if you think a mummy is bad, a mummy with a gun is much worse. Luckily, he had lost that along with the hand and it seemed he hadn't gotten a replacement yet.

"Information per usual," Robin replied, rocking back on his heels and smothering a yawn. It could've been a hangover remnant or his deal-making bullshit extraordinaire. "Remember the good old days, Hank, before you tried to kill us? VCRs, DVD players—who showed you how to connect to the Internet? To the really good porn? At the very least, you owe me, if not them. You are a scholar—when not on a killing rampage. I made life down here bearable for you. And

I doubt you can find a replacement for me." He cocked his head toward a gaunt, furless cat that had clawed its way, slithering like a snake, up to the top of a nearby crate. The same yellow light that dwelled in Wahanket's eye hollows were in its as well. "Mummifying piss pots for entertainment is going to get old after a while."

"Or if you don't want to play ball, asshole, we can start chopping off other parts until you have to stitch yourself together like a goddamn quilt." I patted the sword against my knee suggestively.

Niko sighed, "Your lack of diplomatic skills are appalling." He then said to Wahanket, "The sooner you tell us what we want, the sooner we'll leave you in peace." He drew his own blade, only more diplomatically, naturally. "And I won't dismember you and toss the pieces in the river for trying to kill my brother. A reasonable option, don't you think?"

I really didn't see how that was any different than what I said, minus my trademark colorful language, but apparently the "in peace" worked. That or the fact that if he hadn't been a match for me, he wasn't going to be one for all three of us. Plus, Wahanket seemed to be as tired of looking at us as we were of him. Taking his hand might've taken some of the spirit out of him, but I doubted it. The son of a bitch was probably just biding his time. "Very well. Ask and begone."

Niko described Seamus's problem, our failure to do much about that problem, and the man he'd tangled with. "He was utterly average. Purposely so, I believe, except for the scar behind his ear. An inch in size, half-moon shape, it was so regular and even that I believe it was self-inflicted."

"Or inflicted by someone else," the mummy grunted, curling his one set of claws in demonstration. "I believe I know of what you seek."

Considering we'd had next to nothing to go on, I

was surprised he knew so quickly of what it might be. . . . A remote possibility, he said, the rumor of two-thousand-plus years, but it could be what we'd come across. "I've heard of men with this scar before. There is an order called the Vigil. Human. They have existed since several hundred years B.C. Barely." He dismissed the age with the superiority of a creature that had walked the earth when the first pyramid was built. "I have heard they follow the inhuman, unhuman, the monsters among the world. They seem to have no other desire than to watch on occasion, or so it seems. As to why they do this thing . . ." The hardened upper lip cracked as it revealed the blackened maw in a sneer. "Bring one to me and I shall make him speak the truth." The claws swiped the air in a decisive, eviscerating curl. "I could do with a companion. One would be amazed at how removing internal organs leads to the most interesting of conversations. Information does flow." The flesh-encased skull turned toward me, as what passed for his eyes flared with a harsh light. "Perhaps you will be on my table one day. My knife in you, cutting you away. Your liver, stomach, intestines. I will save your heart for last to see how long I can coax it to beat. Perhaps minutes, perhaps an hour. Bound to an agony so total and savage that it will strip you of sanity itself."

Oh, sure.

Now, who wouldn't love that?

"Right," I drawled. "I'll call and make an appointment for that. Be sure to wait by the phone."

That was all we got out of Wahanket, and a little more than I wanted to know, because I didn't have any doubt one day he'd try to make good on his threat.

Get in line.

As we made our way out at about the halfway point, I heard a skittering behind. I didn't smell anything, but I heard it. And if I heard it, then Niko and Robin had probably heard it before me. "What now?" I asked, starting to turn.

Niko shook his head and gave a dismissive shrug. "Just one of the cats."

Oh, sure. Just one of the undead mummified cats. No big deal. I grimaced as I heard the croaking cry. That Wahanket was one sick bastard. As we walked on, the croaking got closer until finally Robin jerked and cursed in the gloom between the dim bulbs, "Bast's bountiful breasts," and shook his leg. That skinny, zombie-gray, wrinkly fleshed cat from Wahanket's lair had leapt, hooked its claws into Goodfellow's pants, and it wasn't letting go. Flickering jack-o'-lantern eyes looked upward and it croaked again.

"Do something," Robin demanded, shaking his leg again.

"What would you have us do?" Niko asked blandly. "It's already dead."

"And it's just a cat," I observed, hiding the grimace this time. Just a cat. Just an undead, walking, croaking, creepy-as-hell cat.

"Monster killers, my immortal ass. Fine. I'll take care of it myself," he muttered as he tried to yank it off. It didn't budge; it had to be strong as hell. Robin then drew out a blade as long as my forearm from within his long brown leather coat. He tried, without luck, to slide the blade between his leg and its body. It was clamped on too tightly. "All right, then," he said with determination. "If that's the way it has to be." He angled the blade under its chin, and that's when we heard it. Loud and clear.

The purr from beyond the grave.

It was like the rattle of bones, but that's what it was, all right. Rough and coarse and rapturous.

"No." Robin shook his head. "Absolutely not." The blade fell away. "Absolutely *not*."

As Niko had said last night: Repetition didn't change a thing.

By the time we reached the stairs it had climbed Robin's leg, slithered under the coat, and wedged itself under his arm. And Goodfellow, who always had an answer for anything—whether you asked for it or not—had an expression of disgust and despair on his face. "I don't like cats. Even live ones. They're demanding and annoying, they imagine themselves to be so very superior, and they shed."

"That one won't shed," I grinned. "As for the rest . . . sounds familiar, doesn't it?" I ignored his snarl and turned to Nik to say, "Think we should tell Sangrida? Before there's a mummified security guard walking around here too?"

"I already passed that message along through Promise once Wahanket went rogue." Niko had had his sword in hand, wary of any traps the mummy might have set. Bad things happened down here. We'd seen that on a previous visit. Now he sheathed it as we reached the top. "No one comes down here now without Sangrida, and she is capable of handling Wahanket."

Maybe. She could break him like a twig if she could catch him, but he was cunning as hell. Still, her museum, her problem. Hell, we had more than enough of our own to worry about at the moment.

We parted ways with Robin and his new best friend at the front entrance as Niko dragged me to the main branch of the New York Public Library. I wasn't a fan. Not that I didn't read. I read—and not comic books, as Niko claimed. And not porno mags—well, yeah, okay, I did look at porno mags on occasion. What twenty-year-old didn't? But I read mysteries and sci-fi once in a while too, which I picked up in used bookstores. I liked older books. These days, the space suits on the front of books aren't made to showcase the proud Double D astronaut. And you couldn't tell me Spandex couldn't keep out the vacuum of space. NASA had no idea what they were doing.

Despite my perfectly valid literary choices, Nik had made sure I knew my way around the library the first week we'd moved to New York. The mythology section was home base for months. I had to give credit where it was due: My brother had done all he could to shove the knowledge in my head, and some stuck. But mostly? Mostly, I read a sentence and forgot it the second I hit the period. Having the knowledge of the Auphe in my head was monster news plenty. I didn't want to study the other kinds hanging around. Enough . . . hell, enough was just enough. I picked up the info I needed on the streets and during fights— Nik was the only person who'd give you a lecture on the monster you were fighting *during* the fight itself.

". . . and is well-known for the barbed poisonous tail." Duck and slice said tail from body. "It also builds a nest of mud and clay, and lays eggs in the chest cavity of its dead victim as a means of procreation." A thrust of steel and a jet of dark blue blood comes spurting from its heart. "Are you paying attention, Cal?"

Honestly, wasn't that enough studying?

This time as I trudged through the main lobby, about to call Internet shotgun while Nik dealt with the books, is when I saw it. "Hey, look." I nudged Niko in the ribs and nodded my head toward a guy sprawled in one of the chairs reading the *Post*. On the front page in the bottom corner read the headline: NAKED ALBINO MENTAL PATIENT GOES BUS SURFING.

Had that naked albino mental patient not been a creature bent on the torture and murder of my family, friends, and me, it might've been funny. As it was, the lack of humor I was feeling had me snarling at the man, who started to protest when I moved over and yanked the paper out of his hand. He then took one look at my face and backed away slowly.

"I apologize for the rudeness," Niko said. "He's off his medications and consequently more himself than usual." He handed the man a couple of dollars for the paper. I ignored the guy as he slid carefully past me with the money and worked at putting a lot of space between himself and me.

"If I hear voices, it's because of whatever freaky-ass vitamin you put in my morning coffee when I'm not looking," I muttered as I scanned the short article.

"If you hear voices, it's because you only eat irradi-ated nitrates and have grown a microwave-spawned tumor in your frontal lobe." He took the paper from me. "Assuming you have a frontal lobe or a lobe of any kind. My latest theory is your skull hosts a ham-ster running in a wheel that keeps you upright and less coherent."

"Don't you mean 'more or less coherent'?" I snorted and continued reading over his shoulder.

"No."

I thought about a light punch to his kidney, thought about the elbow I'd get jammed in my diaphragm be-fore I got halfway through the punch, and decided to finish the article instead. It wasn't much. A few people had spotted something on top of a bus that had looked pretty abnormal, and somebody in the police depart-ment had filled them in on the melanin- and clothing-challenged mental patient, but he'd been captured and returned to the hospital. All was well. These aren't the 'droids you're looking for and all that. No, of course, the name of the hospital or patient couldn't be revealed. Confidentiality rules. Blah, blah.

"Somebody actually covered it up," I said, sur-prised. This wasn't a random reporter spotting a bog-gle in Central Park and doing a Bigfoot-hits-the-big-city story on it. This was a genuine cover-up with an authority figure involved and everything.

"That they did. But who are they and why did they do it?" He folded the paper. "How is a good question as well."

They were all good questions, but . . . "We don't

really have time for any more mysteries right now. Hell, we don't have time for Seamus's," I pointed out. I thought it was too bad the spear had gone through Niko's coat instead of Seamus's heart. It would've solved at least one of our problems, because, truthfully, I didn't give a damn if the guys shadowing Seamus were a threat to him or not. "Screw the mysteries and let's go have a hot dog."

Niko looked at me and shook his head. "Where did I go wrong?"

I flopped in the chair the guy with the paper had just vacated. "Okay, Cyrano. Spoon-feed it to me. Bruce Willis was a ghost. Darth is Luke's father. The *Crying Game* chick is packing sausage and it's not for a picnic." I raised my eyebrows and made a come-on gesture with my hand. "And?"

"If an organization that follows and watches supernatural creatures has existed for thousands of years and we have proof that someone is covering up the existence of these creatures, doesn't it seem logical that they might be connected? Or even the same entity?"

He was so smug. "Not necessarily," I said, just to be contrary.

Sighing, he swatted me with the paper. "Bad dog. Go and research. And if I find you playing Minesweeper or looking at pornographic sites—"

"Yeah, yeah. You'll kick my ass."

"See? You can be logical when you want," he said as I heaved out of the chair and headed for the computer section.

I didn't find anything, and I looked, but other than a thousand sites for candlelight vigils, and one paramilitary skinhead group out in Wyoming, I was out of luck. No super secret organizations mentioned, and they definitely didn't have their own Web site. What a crock, considering this was the Internet age. How'd they recruit? Hang around haunted houses on Halloween and say, "Hey, wanna see something *really* cool?"

Niko didn't have any luck either, which made me feel somewhat better, until he took over my computer. Then he found something. A year ago, most of the Auphe had died in a collapsing warehouse. Thanks to the wild energy of an impossible gate I'd created, it went down so quickly that apparently only a few had a chance to gate their own way out. Lucky us.

The archived newspaper article called it a gas explosion. When Nik and George had been kidnapped months ago, we'd left a church littered with dead *vodyanoi*, man-shaped, oversized leech creatures that were big and heavy enough to be damn hard to dispose of. The church had burned to the ground. Arson, the police said. Someone had cleaned up two very big messes of ours. Maybe there was a Vigil; maybe not, but there was something going on out there. And weeks ago when Sawney Beane, our least favorite mass-murdering monster, had left a tree full of dead bodies in Central Park . . . those bodies had disappeared. They hadn't made the news at all.

Mysteries on top of mysteries. I didn't like mysteries. Mysteries only meant trouble.

Like I'd thought earlier at the museum about Sangrida and Wahanket, we had trouble enough without looking for more.

Or so I'd hoped anyway . . . until Nik's cell phone rang.

Enough was never enough, was it? Seamus wasn't enough, and now this. One thing we'd learned over the past few months: Work doesn't stop when things turn bad. Our lives were, in a word, complicated as shit. Okay, three words, but "complicated" didn't really get the point across. Family, serial killers, allies who were anything but . . . day to day, it seemed like a miracle if I lived long enough to eat my lunchtime chili cheese dog. So, when you got the karmic swat, as Nik would probably call it, we kept going. We kept living. We kept working, because if we didn't, Christ, we would *never* work. And Nik's teacher's assistant salary from the university combined with my bartender pay was about enough to pay our utilities. It was our other work, our real job, that paid the bills. And while it was more interesting than serving drinks to the frequently inebriated and the occasionally incontinent, it was also a damn sight more gory.

We did it all. Ransom deliveries, de-bodaching carnivals, exterminations. Whatever someone was willing to pay us for that didn't involve compromising too much of our souls. Which is how we ended up freezing our asses off under the pier at Coney Island later that evening. Promise had found us another client, because a Scottish vampire wasn't enough of a pain. I sat cross-legged in the sand, waves colored the purple-gray of the twilight sky nearly reaching my shoes, and sifted absently for a rock. Over the three hours we'd been sitting there, I heard one set of footsteps above us over the sound of the waves, and the occasional shout and laughter from the boardwalk, but that was it. The wind off the water had a vicious bite, and if I didn't have to be there, my ass would've been someplace warm like everyone else's.

But it wasn't the frigid air that I was thinking of. Or whatever client we had, what they wanted. I wasn't thinking of the Vigil either. Did they exist? Did they not exist? Did I care? Nope.

Right now I was thinking the same thing that had come to me yesterday morning as I'd lain on my back in Washington Square Park, surprised that the world hadn't ended then and there. It was something more important than cold, clients, and mystery organizations combined. Something that had to do with our problem. Our lives . . . or deaths. I was thinking of something that actually mattered. I couldn't picture doing it, not really, and that didn't say too much about me. Not at all. Because it might be the best thing to do—if I had the guts. In fact, it might be the only thing that would work, and it didn't have to be permanent. If I survived.

"You know," I started diffidently, flinging the pebble I'd found into the water, "I was thinking . . . if I—"

"I'd find you," Niko said, watching the water. He had his hair pulled back in a short ponytail, and was in a long black coat, gray shirt, and black pants, and had his sword lying across his lap. He looked every bit as deadly as he was and every bit as confident. I missed his long braid. It had hung to his waist and been good for annoying him with a tug. It had also been a sign of simpler days. Days when we'd been totally in the dark about why the Auphe had wanted me, days when they'd wanted only me. Ignorance/bliss, all that. I wished I really were as ignorant as Niko had accused me of being when he'd homeschooled me when I was sixteen. Ignorance can get you killed, but at least you'd be happy up until the hammer fell and shattered your clueless skull to bone fragments.

Nik turned his view from the water to look at me and emphasized, "Wherever you went. I'd find you, little brother."

"Yeah," I admitted, not surprised he knew what I was thinking. A lifetime of familiarity will do that. "You would."

No, running wasn't the answer. Even if there were a chance the Auphe would follow me if I left the others—after all, where was the fun in mentally torturing your prey if he wasn't around to see it? Yeah, even if . . . Niko wouldn't let me. I could run and disappear as well as any fox, or any Rom, for that matter, but Niko was the one who had taught me. Anywhere I could think of, he could do the same. Probably beat me there.

"We've made our stand, Cal. All of us. You can't take that choice from us. Now . . ." He gave a stinging swat with the flat of his sword to my knees. "Watch the water or you'll be dinner. Of course, the creature would promptly vomit you back up. All the bitching and moaning." He curled his lips. "No one could suffer that on their stomach."

I snorted and tossed another rock. "If anything comes out of there, their balls will be icicles. Kind of cuts down on the agility. I think we'll be okay." But when it came out of the water, it didn't have balls . . . at least none that I could see. Not that I was looking for them or anything.

Swear to God.

It was like nothing I'd seen before, and I'd seen quite a bit in the past few years. The flesh was a mottled light gray on dark and was covered with a thick layer of slime. Its head was featureless except for round black eyes and a backward slash of mouth filled with a double row of triangular teeth. It had no neck; its wide chest was smooth and without nipples; the arms were short, with webbed hands; and the rest of it was a muscular fish tail. It looked like a shark with human arms. Like it was evolving slowly toward the land, and if that was the case, I was never coming to the beach again.

It threw itself up on the wet sand, tail thrashing, and its mouth opened wide enough that I could've stuck my entire head in it. "Holy shit!" I sprang to my feet and yanked my gun free.

"Wait." Niko grabbed my wrist. "That's our client."

"You're shitting me, right? Tell me you're kidding." I looked at the polished black eyes and the gnashing mouth. "What the hell is it?"

"A mermaid." He frowned. "Merman? I think Mer

is correct. Either way, this is the client Promise passed our way. Now, help me pull him farther up. I imagine whatever is chasing him will be right behind him."

"A mermaid? Jesus, Disney was way off the mark there, weren't they?" I holstered the gun, seized one slippery, thick arm and helped Nik drag the heavy body farther up into the sand. "What the hell is after it?" . . . that could possibly be worse than this, I silently finished.

Most of the time I went into a job with at least a sketchy knowledge of what we were after, and sometimes sketchy is all we had. But this time I hadn't asked, my mind still on the Auphe, and Niko, always the teacher, had let me get away with it . . . for a reason. Learn your lesson the hard way and you'll always remember it. And this was the result of that lesson—being more than mildly freaked out by our own client, and wishing like hell I'd worn some gloves. I wiped the slime on my jeans as I waited for Nik's answer.

"Promise wasn't sure. It seems no one speaks their language very well." The immediate whistling shriek from the Little Mermaid proved that, as Niko continued, "It was all the go-between could do to figure out it wanted help, that something was attacking the local school of Mers."

As swimmers rarely disappeared here, I guessed the Mer weren't eating people, though they certainly looked capable of it. I supposed that made them if not the good guys at least not the bad ones. But, damn, what the hell was it they couldn't handle? And a whole school of them to boot. I wasn't shy about asking that either as I pulled my gun again.

"They're a peaceful people, apparently." He actually said that with a straight face, like he hadn't seen those teeth. "And my best guess is this one was working as bait to lead their attacker or attackers to us, so be ready."

I was. When one third of it slid out of the water onto the sand under the pier, I was as ready as I was going to be—which turned out to be not very.

It was the length of three SUVs, I was guessing, end to end and as big around as a Volkswagen. Part of it was hidden in the crashing waves. Dead black, it had scarlet eyes with pupils as big as my fist. It also had a spray of teeth exploding at an outward angle from barracuda jaws that looked perfectly capable of snapping a boat in half while Spielberg pissed his pants.

"We're going to need a bigger beach," Niko murmured.

"Funny. Real funny." I hadn't brought the explosive rounds. I rarely needed them and they made a lot of noise. Attracted a lot of unwanted attention out in the open like this. Not as unwanted as the kind that was trained on us now, though.

I backed up as the jaws opened and slammed shut. "What the *hell* is that thing?"

"I think it's a Jinshin-uwo. In Japanese mythology, it's an eel that . . ." Niko's usual pre-battle lecture was cut short when the massive head heaved up and forward before coming down on the ground with a force that would've crushed anything beneath it to jelly.

Like our client.

"Oh, *shit*." It wasn't much of a eulogy for the poor guy, but at that moment I was more concerned that the same wasn't going to happen to me. Although seeing those two-feet-long teeth designed to do nothing but tear flesh, crushed might be the better way to go.

As the head turned, the jaws clamped around the dead Mer, ripped it in half, and ate both pieces. Two bites, snap, snap—gone. I, along with Nik, backed farther under the pier. "The eyes?" I said.

"The eyes," he confirmed.

Confronted with something this big, short of crawling into its stomach and stabbing it before you were digested, the eyes were pretty much the only way to go. And while it was fast, it didn't seem to be as quick as many of the things we'd faced. The eyes were doable. I aimed my Glock at one grapefruit-sized eye and that . . . well, that was pretty much all I remembered until I woke up facedown in the sand.

It was hard to breathe. Why? Why was it so damn hard? Where was the air?

I sucked in a breath and something soft and powdery spilled into my mouth. Coughing and choking, I got an arm under me and struggled to turn over. I wavered on my side for a second and then dropped onto my back. Still coughing, I could see the sky above me. Purple. Good color, purple. I was a fan of purple. Grape soda and twilight skies . . . good stuff.

Good . . . wait. Wasn't there something I should be doing?

Christ. Nik.

I got my elbows under me as I finally pulled some air into my lungs and blinked at what I saw. I was at least forty feet from the darkness under the pier and if the pain slowly blooming across my back was any indication, I was lucky my spine wasn't broken. I also saw the reason I'd ended up facedown. The giant eel had moved farther under the pier, its midsection still in the water, but its tail was out and whipping with violent fury. It was safe to say it had gotten me but good. I must've hurtled through the air like a crashing plane. Down in flames.

"Cal!"

I couldn't see Niko, but I could hear him, and that was enough to snap me back to full alertness. I staggered halfway up, fell back down, then got back up again . . . all the way this time. My gun was still clenched tightly in my hand and as I lurched across the sand I fired. There were five muffled pops from the silencer and, just as I'd thought, not a single reaction from the eel. The rubbery flesh was too thick. The bullets probably felt like a fly bite to it, if it felt anything at all. I could've left the gun at home and brought a goddamn sushi chef for all the luck I was having with this giant unagi roll. I stumbled on through the shifting sand, gaining momentum and steadiness with every step.

Closer, I could see Niko's sword flashing, reflecting the stray beams of the streetlamps from the board-walk. The eel's head was moving back and forth just as fast. A lot faster than I'd anticipated. Apparently, it had figured out its eyes were its weak point, the same as we had. Or maybe that's a knowledge that big bad-ass eels are born with. I didn't know and I didn't care. What I cared about was that Nik was taking on that thing alone. I ran faster, then dove to the ground as the tail headed my way. It passed over my head with only inches to spare. I smelled the dank salt water that sprayed over me. I turned my head to one side and flattened myself as much as possible as the tail swung back. This time I felt the skim of flesh against my ear. It was ice cold and unnaturally smooth, like a leech. I gritted my teeth, refused to shudder at the sensation, got up, and moved. And I mean *moved*. I kicked off my shoes and tore ass up the length of the monster, and when it turned its head away from Nik's sword, I put eleven silenced rounds right in its bloodred eye.

That it noticed.

It didn't die. It didn't thrash about in agony. It just noticed.

But that was enough to put its attention squarely on me. Its right eye turned to jelly, it opened its mouth—the teeth cutting through the air like the maiming snap of a bear trap. I could smell the Mer on its breath. The blood, the flesh. I could smell other flesh, too, caught in its teeth. Decaying. Rotting for days, weeks. I gagged at the reek of it as I desperately dived to one side. Out of the corner of my eye, I saw Niko go for the other eye. But the thing wasn't surprised from behind this time. It knew where Nik was, knew that danger well. It snapped its head back. Niko was hit by the snout and flung across the beach, narrowly missing one of the pier columns. That would've broken him . . . shattered every bone to pieces no one could put back together again.

I slammed another clip home as he landed on his back. He wasn't moving, but he would. I'd survived it, and he was stronger than I was. More conditioned. Tougher. He'd get back up, and that's the way it was going to be. So help me God.

But since I didn't believe in God, I was going to have to help myself. I rolled, got back to my feet, to be faced with an open mouth as tall as I was. The head turned slightly to get me into the sight of its one good eye as its flesh bunched muscularly, ready to surge forward. I jerked backward as I fired into the maw. Nothing. *Nothing*. Not a damn thing fazed it.

Until the gate opened.

And out they came. A swarm of the deadly, the fatal, the world's first murderers. They'd hunted dinosaurs once, Goodfellow had said. For fun. There'd been easier things to catch and eat. But for a helluva good time, for a real party, they killed dinosaurs. The eel wasn't much different.

Thirty-eight sets of claws were buried in the black meat. As one, they dragged it foot by foot across the sand. With jaws snapping and long body twisting, it tried to escape. It didn't. Section by section, it was wrenched backward into the largest gate I'd seen since . . . hell, since I'd tried to destroy the world. Black blood spilled on the pale sand as half of it disappeared into the whirl of gray light. Metal teeth buried in rubbery flesh and wrenched massive pieces free to toss away onto the sand, a pack of hyenas savaging their crippled prey. Those same teeth, now stained black, all grinned in my direction as they called me, voices as one—the crooning of a chlorine gas–tainted wind.

"Cal-i-ban."

Death in the air, death in my name.

Then they went back to the business—the *fun*—at hand, taking the eel to a hell that put anything in the Bible in the shade. The last attacker visible clawed its way up onto the eel's back. Hand over hand it ripped into the now slowly thrashing body—they were eating the eel, I thought numbly. On the other side. They were eating it while it was still alive. The last Auphe kept up its bloody passage until it was behind the now-sluggish head.

"You," it hissed, bloodred eyes fixed on mine, teeth bared in the same happy, insanely twisted grin, but not murderous—it was possessive. *Coveting.* And that was worse. God, that was so much worse. "You are ours. For no other. *Ours.*" The hot-lava gaze slid to Niko. "And you, sheep, you are no more. Blood to soak the ground, screams to tear the air. Meat. Meat to feed us." The grin shimmered black and silver. "Meat to feed your brother."

Then they were gone. Eel and Auphe. The gate closed. There were only sand, dark waves, a rising sliver of moon, and . . .

And . . .

And we were going to die. All of us. They were going to kill every last one of us, and I didn't see any way around it. But . . .

The way it—*she*—had looked at me. It meant something. I didn't want to know. I didn't. If she coveted anything, it was my death. That's all. That's all it could be. Fuck, I almost laughed, wasn't that enough?

My legs wanted to give out and dump me hard in the sand, but I refused to let them. Dinosaurs had never ruled the earth—the Auphe had. And if it weren't for humans breeding like rabbits, they still would. Now billions of humans might live on, but we were soon to be as extinct as those dinosaurs. Buried and gone. All of us, me included.

But not now, I thought as I caught grip of the last gossamer strip of sanity as it went sailing by. I held on tight, held on for all I was worth. Not now, I reaffirmed savagely. Not yet.

I turned to see Nik sitting up and staring back at me. For once he looked as stunned as I felt. As if he didn't have the answer. Even though he always had the answer. Even though he always came through. Never failed. Which wasn't fair. It was a weight no one should have to carry, but he did it day after day. Battle after battle. Catastrophe after fucking catastrophe. He never hesitated and he never gave up. On anything. On me. He should have. There were times that if he had we wouldn't be here right now. In this place, this position. Niko, Promise, and Robin . . . they'd be living their lives. I'd be gone, but it would've been worth it. To save the only family, the only friends I'd ever had.

But that chance was gone. That ship had fucking sailed.

But I had another chance. A chance to do something good. Something I should've done a while ago.

I walked over to put my hand down and help Niko up. Not that he needed it, but he took it all the same. He stood, one arm cradling his ribs. Hopefully, they were only bruised, not cracked or broken. His jaw was set against the pain, and broken ribs or not, I knew he'd make the climb back up to the boardwalk stoically. That was Nik.

"It's okay," I said. I couldn't feel his hand against mine or the sand beneath my bare feet, but that didn't matter. I had one focus now. One.

"Okay," he echoed dubiously, head turned down toward me. He said it as if he couldn't believe that I had, as if he wondered how I could imagine that *any* of this could possibly be okay. Doubt; Niko hadn't ever shown it, not on the outside. Not when we were kids—not last year when he had to kill me to save me. But I saw the faint shadow of it now. It was time for me to take the burden for a while. Time that I was the one to never give in, never give up. To believe, against all odds and logic, that we would make it. Force myself to believe, because that's what was needed. To do what Niko had done for me his whole life.

Even if it was a lie.

"It's more than okay," I said, trying to sound optimistic. I'd never actually *felt* optimistic, so pulling off a completely unknown emotion was a stretch, but I gave it my best shot. I put my hand on his arm to support him if the ribs were broken and he needed it. He wouldn't, but I did it anyway. "I'll think of something. We'll kick so much pasty nightmare ass, we'll be limping for a week. Blisters on our soles the size of lemons." Bullshit, utter and complete, but then again . . . maybe not. Maybe it wasn't bullshit or a lie. I'd always claimed to be a monster. Now was the time to step up to the plate and live it. "I'll think like them. I'll anticipate them. I'll be ready."

And why not?

Who better to think like the Auphe than their own family?

4

Niko

Pearls were everywhere.

In shades of white, old ivory, and cream, hundreds of them spilled across Promise's violet and gray rug. It was an amazing sight, the contrast between the soft pale shimmer and the dark colors of the rug. Beautiful. I recognized that, but I didn't feel it. I felt many other things not nearly as pleasant, but not that.

But I did feel the fingers combing their way through my hair. Slow and sure. Patient. When I remained silent for nearly an hour, sitting on the floor with my back against the couch, the fingers remained patient. Scooping up a handful of pearls didn't change the pattern. Faithful, soothing—the only thing I felt. At the moment, the only thing I wanted to.

The Mer had come out of the water when the Jinshin-uwo and the Auphe had vanished. The rip in reality sealed itself, and only Cal and I were left in the icy December evening. Slowly, one by one, they came to the edge of the waves to balance upright on curled muscular tails. Each hand was filled with pearls. We hadn't completed the job. The Auphe had done that, but we were paid nonetheless. Then, with the pockets of both our coats filled to the top with gems, we came home. Not ours, but Promise's home. Cal had suggested it and I hadn't disagreed. He thought I needed it, and he wasn't wrong.

"He grew up on me." One last pearl fell and I smiled slightly. "I didn't see it coming. Isn't that odd? I always see everything about Cal, but I didn't see that."

Promise finished smoothing my hair. With her legs tucked under her on the sofa cushion, her knees touched the back of my neck. They were warm, as warm as the hand that came over my shoulder to rest on my chest over my heart. Legend told you vampires were cold. Legend, as usual, lied.

"I imagine he'll still be a cranky little boy now and again." There was a smile in her voice as she bent to press her cheek against mine. "But you did teach him well. No one else could've brought him through it all as you have. Sane, intact, his soul clean."

"Clean soul and the filthiest mouth around," I mused. "Where'd I go wrong?"

"Not a single place." She straightened and patted her lap. "Lie with me. Tell me everything. The more I know, the more Auphe blood I can spill." A cloud of black drifted across her eyes for an instant and then they were violet again. "And I will so enjoy spilling it."

So I moved up to the couch, rested my head in her lap, and gave her every detail of the night. She'd been given a quick sketch by Cal, who was on the phone with Robin as we'd walked in. "Sharks with arms. Big-ass eel. Goddamn Auphe. Watch your ass." No one could say my brother wasn't succinct when he wanted to be, or that he couldn't paint a picture with his words. Granted, it was a picture made up of red and black crayon slashes, but it got the point across.

The painter was now asleep in one of Promise's spare bedrooms. Robin was hosting something large and loud, from the shouting Cal had to do to be heard over the phone, so he was most likely safe. At least in the respect that by the time the Auphe killed all the partygoers he'd be long gone. Georgina had her wolves and her anonymity, thanks to Cal's refusal to see her. It was all we had and all we could do.

We gave Promise's wolves the night off, and as they left, I had thought that we couldn't live this way. Not for long. Trying to encase every second of our daily lives in safety glass. You could see through it, see everyone else walking, breathing, living, but you couldn't live yourself. You were caught like a fly in amber. It wasn't a life; it was an existence. And that wasn't much of a substitute. Even when Cal and I had been on the run for three years, it hadn't been like this. We knew the Auphe were after us, but we didn't know why they were, other than Cal having their blood. We knew it would be a bad thing if they caught us, but we didn't know how bad . . . not until they finally did.

We'd thought that they didn't know where we were most of the time. Thought we'd lost them time and time again. I didn't know if that was true. I did know no matter where we went they eventually found us, but they were only biding their time. All along they had been waiting for Cal to mature physically, to be able to build the giant gate they needed and travel, as he called it. And so they had trailed us from place to place, and when they finally actually did want Cal they simply reached out and took him. That easily.

I couldn't imagine underestimating the Auphe, but I had. And because I had, we had lives, Cal and I. That delusion had let us breathe. We had watched over our shoulders, given fake names, practiced the martial art of staying alive daily, stayed ghosts to everyone we came into contact with, but we had still lived. We hadn't hunched under the knowledge that every second could have been the killing one.

Faith; it could support a life if you had it. It was the undoing of one if you didn't.

I always had faith that things would end up as they should. We would escape the Auphe. When that didn't happen, I had faith I'd get Cal back, because I literally couldn't accept anything else. He was my responsibility. My brother. They hadn't taken him, I had *lost* him. Twice in my life I had lost him.

I'd forced myself to believe I would get him back. There could be no doubt. I would get him back.

Faith again.

And I had gotten him back. But in the process, I had learned something. I had my eyes opened. I'd seen the Auphe up close. I'd seen what had happened to the people around them, people the Auphe cared nothing about one way or the other. They died. They died very easily—killed by something that barely knew they were alive to begin with.

And the Auphe knew we were alive. Like the eye of God, their sight was on us. Inescapable.

They hated Cal with all the passion of a betrayed race. They knew Robin and I had taken Cal away from them. Promise was simply swept up in the murderous wake. No matter how we'd gotten there, we were all under the eye.

And now I thought there might be something far worse. I suspected, but . . . no, I was wrong. I had to be. Even an uncaring universe wouldn't allow that. Death, yes, but not that.

"Niko?"

I'd closed my eyes as I told Promise what had happened on the beach. And when I'd stopped talking I left them shut, just for a moment. A denial of the tightening noose. Something I rarely allowed myself. I opened them now and looked up at her. Large eyes, skin a little too pale, a mouth a little too wide, and eyebrows that winged upward like a bird in flight. It was an imperfect beauty and all the more beautiful for it. She put the multitude of pearls to shame.

"Niko?" she said again, cupping my face with her hands.

I took one of her hands, kissed the palm, and gave her the truth.

"We are fucked."

She laughed, showing the small pointed incisors of a predator in her own right. "It seems you weren't the only teacher over the years. Cal taught you something as well."

He had. He'd taught me many things, but first and foremost, he'd taught me that faith. Sophia never would have. Cal had given me a reason to have faith. How would I honor my teacher if I deserted that faith now?

"But Cal says we'll get through it." I kissed her hand again, this time lightly nipping the skin at the base of her thumb. Without Cal I wouldn't have faith. I wouldn't be the man I was today.

I wouldn't have this.

The night haze swam across her eyes again, this time for a different reason. "And what do you say?" she asked as her finger lazily traced the line of my jaw.

"I have faith," I said simply.

And in Cal, I did.

Of course, the next day the cause of all that faith was trying to kill me before the Auphe had their chance. The morning sun drifted through the tinted windows as, after my shower, I padded into the kitchen, dressed in one of the pair of sweatpants I kept at Promise's. Leaning over Cal's shoulder as he stirred, I frowned at the bumpy kaleidoscope of red, yellow, and pale brown in the bowl. "What could you possibly be concocting there, Dr. Frankenstein?"

"Chocolate, cherry, banana pancakes. Want some?" He pulled the spoon out and licked it.

"Very hygienic." I nodded at the sink. "I can explain the use of the tap again for you if you like."

"Like the doctor takes advice from Igor," he snorted. He yawned and licked the spoon again. "You want some or not?"

"I think one bite might lodge in an artery and stop my heart," I said truthfully.

"Worse ways to go," he pointed out with a dark grin as he poured the batter on the griddle. "We were nearly eaten by vengeful sushi last night. Live a little." He boosted himself up and sat on the counter. "How are the ribs? They don't look too bad."

I pulled on the black shirt that I'd been carrying in my hand and replied, "Bruising. Nothing more." He was moving with only a little stiffness, and I knew his back was no worse. He'd showered not long before I had. I could tell by the still-wet black hair and the water spots on the T-shirt that I'd lent him last night. The sopping washcloth half covering the drain, the toppled shampoo bottles, and the towels on the floor had been a clue as well.

He gave another grin, this one not as dark. "I was going to ask if she was gentle with you, but I think I'll sit here and smirk instead."

"You're a gentleman without compare." I went to the refrigerator, saying over my shoulder, "Your pancakes are burning."

There was a curse, a thud of feet on the floor, and the smell of singed batter. By the time I sat at the table with my juice and yogurt-granola mix, he had a plate of half-runny, half-burnt pancakes and was squirting syrup over them. The typical feeding habits of the Cal Leandros in his natural habitat. I was long used to them.

"No Promise?" He took a sticky, dripping bite. "I made enough for her."

"So you plan to poison her and leave me a celibate and lost soul. Cunning." I dipped a spoon in the bowl. "She's sleeping in. Centuries of habit are hard to break." I studied the yogurt before me, then made a decision. Cal was right. I should live a little. "I'll take some after all."

"You're shitting me. Really?" He slid the plate closer. "Help yourself."

I reached over with the spoon, carved off a piece, and took a bite. I chewed, swallowed, and made the best decision of my life. I went back to my yogurt. We ate in companionable silence. Cal was not a morning person. I was surprised he was as coherent as he was this one. When I finished, I pushed the bowl away and looked at him. This time I wasn't looking at wet hair and shirt or the casual slouch as he chased the last bite of pancake around the plate with his fork. I was looking past that—past the still-sleepy gray eyes to where Cal could be his own worst enemy. The place where he stuffed all his fears, his misplaced guilt, his anger . . . his rage. Hid them away. Tried his very best to forget about them. I looked there for the beach we had stood on last night.

I didn't find it.

"So, then." I tapped my spoon on his plate to get his attention. "We're going to be all right, are we?"

"Yep," he said agreeably, giving up on that remaining bit of pancake.

"And if we're not?" I wouldn't give up my faith, but it had to be factored in with reality. Believe, but be ready.

"Then we take those bitches with us." The eyes weren't sleepy anymore. They'd gone from drowsy to dark, savage, and ruthless.

"There's my brother." My lips twitched. "I was afraid you'd taken all my Zen."

"Like I'd want it," he retorted. "Jesus. I'd need a pack mule for all the granola."

"I am stunned with your witty riposte. Give me a moment to recover." I took another spoonful of yogurt that I didn't particularly want, but my body required. I needed to ask Cal something, and it was a memory that wasn't going to do much for either of our appetites, which is why I'd waited until he was finished with his pancakes. Pushing the almost-empty bowl and spoon away, I asked, "The Auphe you killed last year, the one that attacked us on the way back from Florida"—when George had been kidnapped and we'd needed help from a Rom clan to obtain her ransom—"was it a male or female?"

For a second, his eyes went blank. Completely. For a moment Cal was gone. I reached over and squeezed his wrist hard and said his name as forcefully as if we were in the midst of a battle—which, for all intents and purposes, we were. I was about to repeat his name when he blinked. "Sorry." I let his wrist go and he used both hands to scrub at his face. "Yeah . . . Florida. I was a little . . . distracted." "Distracted" was Cal's way of saying "walking a very fine line between sanity and the alternative." "Shit." He shook his head. "I don't remember. Male, I think." His pupils dilated and I could see the past sucking him down. The Auphe trying to drag me through a gate to Tumulus. Cal all but disintegrating its head with the entire clip of his gun while the door to hell stood hungry and open only feet away.

Enough. I'd needed to know, but I wouldn't make him see anymore. He'd seen too much already. I took his plate and promptly pushed it into his stomach. "Enough ancient history. Cleanup time."

He was slower to come back this time, but he did come, grumbled, glared, and cleared the table. What he didn't do was ask me why I'd wanted to know. He may not have remembered my even asking, or he may not have wanted to know the reason. Either way . . . I was grateful. Because I still could be wrong.

Let me be wrong.

Forty minutes later, the wolves were at the door, literally. I left Promise with a kiss to her bare shoulder, and we were gone. Outside, the sky was blue for the first time in days. With the sun the day felt warmer than it really was. Cal didn't seem to notice. He kept sliding a glance at me from the corner of his eye as we went down the stairs. It was a look both alternately worried and confused. Finally, I said with mild exasperation, "Enough. I feel like the last movie I forced you to watch that had subtitles. What is it?"

He didn't snipe back in our usual give-and-take of his cultural, scholastic, or martial arts lack. We had just passed through the front entrance to Promise's building and taken a few steps when he shook his head, growled, grabbed two handfuls of my coat and shoved me up against the stone facade of the building. Then he pressed his nose to my neck and jaw and smelled me. I ignored the looks of the people jostling by. I knew my brother. He did some odd things, but he always had a reason . . . maybe not a safe reason or a particularly good reason, but he always had a purpose of some sort.

"I think you may be spending too much time with either Delilah or Robin," I said equably.

He didn't react to the humor. Letting go of me, he backed up. "Jesus, Cyrano." He seemed both disgusted and angry. "You smell like him. You smell like that goddamn Seamus."

Seamus, who, although I had spent time with him in his loft and later at the art show, I would've showered away his scent at least three times by now. The last shower was this morning before we left, but it hadn't been the last thing I'd done before leaving the apartment. I'd kissed Promise's bare skin in good-bye. I hadn't asked where she'd been when Cal and I had been fighting a giant eel. We hardly kept track of each other's every movement. She very well could've met Seamus to further discuss his case. It would've been a professional courtesy.

But she hadn't mentioned it.

Considering that we'd decided last night that everything was to be put on hold until the Auphe were dealt with, it skirted along the border of suspicious. If it had been anyone but Promise, it would've been far beyond the border and seeking, no doubt Cal would say, a fake green card. But this was Promise. She and Seamus were old friends, old companions. I had no reason to think "old" had changed to "current" or that she was keeping anything from me. I had never seen anything like that in her. And being suspicious of her now would only taint everything we had. I wouldn't do that—no matter what Sophia had taught me all her life: that everyone lies. Everyone deceives. Cal didn't—not unless it was to save my life; then he would lie like the proverbial dog. But otherwise, Cal wouldn't deceive me.

Neither would Promise. If I believed she would, then I let Sophia win.

"I didn't catch it last night. I just went flying past her to the guest room while telling Robin to watch his ass. I wasn't paying attention. What the hell is wrong with me? You should kick my ass for it. I actually deserve it this time." He moved back away from the sidewalk, toward me, and leaned against the wall next to me. "I'm sorry," he said, his mouth twisted.

In all his life I think I was the only one Cal had said that word to, and he said it more often than our acquaintances might think. He didn't need to now, although I don't think he himself knew why he said it: for not noticing last night or for noticing this morning.

"It's Promise, little brother. He's a part of her past. I wouldn't tell her who she could or couldn't see, no more than she would tell me."

He straightened as the wind carried a candy bar wrapper across his boot, snagged it there, and then took it on down the street. "She told you, then?" he asked, relieved. "Told you they met?"

"No."

The relief in his eyes transmuted to suspicion so

quickly that there wasn't a split second between of thought. He didn't say anything, but then again he didn't have to. I knew that expression, borne of our mother years ago, and I knew my brother. He didn't trust Promise to tell the truth about Seamus, and he didn't want to hurt me by saying so.

I took his shoulder and pulled him away from the building and into motion. "This is Promise, Cal. In the past year there were several occasions she could've died because of us or we could've died if she hadn't helped us. Don't be this way."

"What way?" he demanded.

"Yourself." I gave him my customary affectionate tug on his ponytail. "And whatever you do, please don't sniff her like a wayward dog when we get back. She might not be as understanding as I am."

"Okay, okay. You're right. It is Promise." It sounded much more dubious when he said it, but it was an effort, a considerable one for him, and I appreciated it as such. "Although you didn't see the look Seamus gave you when we left his loft."

"I saw it." He'd been sizing me up. Let him. "But we don't have to trust him, only Promise. And she's not given us reason not to."

He frowned, but let it go for now. Checking his watch, he said, "You know, we have enough time before your first class to go to Central Park."

"And why would you want to do that?" I asked dryly. "I would want to run or practice, but why would *you* want to go?"

"More revenants."

"Revenants?" Not that there were as many as you'd think in Central Park. Boggle and her brood ate most of them. But the revenants couldn't help themselves. The draw of all those people running, walking, Rollerblading, all those people just begging to be dragged into the trees and devoured—it was too much temptation for them. They kept going, and occasionally they

did get a runner here and there, but mainly they were
the equivalent of Meals on Wheels for Boggle and her
children, who were faster and more predatory than a
hundred revenants.

"Yeah. Spearguns, giant eels, the Auphe. I think we
need to kick some ass just to prove we're badder than
somebody in this city. In the past two days even an old
lady with a walker could've taken our asses down," he
grumbled in disgust.

"Exaggeration served up with a fine whine. Entertaining as always. And we don't have a time issue. I
called the university yesterday and told them I was
taking leave. Family emergency."

"And if this doesn't count as an emergency . . ."
He shook his head and shoved his hands in his jacket
pockets. I'd never been able to break him of that, to
always have your hands free, just in case. As often as
I'd swatted the back of his head or pinched a nerve
cluster, he just couldn't remember. You have to pick
your battles, and I'd realized years ago Cal was most
certainly his own person. He wasn't me, couldn't be
me.

I have a bigger sword.

We took the subway to the Ninth Circle, where Cal
was going to tell Ishiah he needed a little time off as
well. Right now we needed to focus on our situation
and nothing but that. Seamus would get the same
speech from Promise. This one I knew about, at least.
It was a petty thought and I pushed it away. Yes,
Seamus would have to deal with his mystery stalker
himself. Normally, we kept working, regardless of the
situation. The world didn't stop because this or that
was trying to kill you. That happened too frequently
in our lives. You had to work or you would be on the
streets and starving in no time. This . . . this was an
exception. I knew it the minute that gate had opened
on the beach and those nightmare monsters had come

boiling out to kill what Cal and I couldn't. And they had done it in less than thirty seconds.

Luckily, with last night's payment we could actually afford the time off. No teaching, no bartending, none of our jobs. We were in the best financial situation of our lives. Assuming, of course, that we could hold on to those lives.

Delilah was at the bar when we arrived. Since she worked at another bar, a strip club, as a bouncer during the day and did her work for the Kin at night, I assumed she was waiting for Cal and not simply hanging out for the feathery ambience. She sat at the bar, very much the fox in the henhouse. Confident, clever, and more than a little carnivorous. She was dressed in brown leather pants, a discarded matching jacket, and a long-sleeve amber-colored sweater that stopped a few inches above her navel. No matter the temperature, Delilah was a wolf and she was proud. She had survived and she would show you the proof—scars white and jagged across her stomach. They were bright against skin that was only a few shades lighter than her sweater. She wore them as boldly as she did the wolf eyes and Celtic swirl design she had tattooed choker style around her neck. Those scars were the reason Cal could be with her. She couldn't have children. Cal was adamant . . . there would be no more Auphe-human hybrids. Not if he could help it. It was smart of my brother, smart, mature, self-sacrificing, and up there with genuinely phobic status.

Georgina . . . she could have children, and had been willing to let the future unfold however it would. Cal was not as trusting of the universe, and I didn't blame him for it.

Delilah's hair was almost as pale as her brother's. His was albino white; hers was silver blond, long enough to fall to the middle of her back when pulled up, as it was now, in a tail at the crown of her head.

She looked fully human, if exotic, like the high breeds did, but she wasn't. High breeds were considered original werewolf stock. Purely human at one moment and completely wolf at the next. But some wolves didn't want that. They sought what they felt was the more desirable form—a wolf at all times. Pure and wild, untouched by civilization and "monkey" genes. So they bred for what high breeds considered faults and mutations; some even inbred as well to further the cause. And it was an ongoing cause, since as of now they only had some wolves who at best were half-and-half. Human with wolf teeth, fur in odd places, lupine eyes and claws. Sometimes they were beautiful and sometimes hideous. Sometimes they could pass on the street without effort and sometimes they couldn't.

They were still a minority in the werewolf community, Kin and non-Kin, and considered by their brothers in fur to be a little less worthy. And because of that prejudice, Delilah could never be an Alpha in the Kin. Females could be Alphas, unlike in genuine wolf packs. The Kin were practical: they realized the females could be deadlier than the males. Male or female, if you killed on all takers, then you were Alpha, but a non–high breed Alpha was out of the question. Then again, Delilah might change that custom. She had a presence that let you know she was no ordinary wolf, no ordinary Kin, no ordinary killer.

And quite definitely no ordinary woman.

"I'm not sure if I'm impressed or afraid she'll eat you as a midday snack," I murmured as the door closed behind us.

Almond eyes of pale copper that showed the Asian blood in her were already on us. I probably didn't smell much different than your average human, but the wolves could smell the Auphe in Cal from the metaphorical mile away. They hated it, except for Delilah. She hadn't minded when we had once hired her to heal Cal with the benefits of wolf saliva, and she obviously didn't mind now. It was that presence again. Delilah had a quality about her—she was completely fearless. Unfortunately, a little fear was often what kept you alive.

"Promise could go off the wagon anytime," he snorted as he moved off. "Then it's just you, her, and a giant twisty straw."

The vast majority of vampires had been off blood for sixty years now, thanks to a few hematology advances on their part, but he had a point. One way or the other, we were all food for something else. Every creature on the planet.

As he sat next to her, Delilah tapped a disapproving finger on his knee. "Playing with Auphe. Not smart. Come with me." She tilted her head, lips curving. "Play better games."

And that was the only sign Delilah wasn't a high breed. Her vocal cords were somewhere between human and wolf. Her brother had it as well, although his was much worse. Delilah sounded as if she had a strong accent, was just learning the language. It was as exotic as the rest of her, something the patrons of her bar would've enjoyed thoroughly . . . if it hadn't been a gay male strip club. And I doubted when she tossed the drunks and troublemakers out onto the concrete that she wasted many words on them.

I went over to the far end of the bar, giving Cal some privacy to tell Delilah that the sex games were over temporarily. He'd only met her just over a week ago. She wouldn't be an Auphe target yet. Fearless or not, it was best she stayed that way.

Ishiah came up as I sat. "I heard what happened last night. Going on a trip?"

"No. We've learned the hard way that there is nowhere we can go that the Auphe can't follow." I didn't ask how he knew. Peris were the grapevine of the supernatural world, but that quickly? He could only have gotten it from Goodfellow. I suppose that tipped the Ishiah scales more toward friend than enemy . . . at least for today. I accepted a bottle of water he offered and rolled the blue glass between my palms. "But Cal won't be back here until this is taken care of."

"Business will boom." Beneath the gruffness, I heard a reluctant sympathy. "He blames himself. He snaps and snarls as much as I do, but I've been around a long time. I see."

My face didn't move, but whatever he saw behind it was the end of the conversation. Without further word, he put a glass before me on the bar and left.

Cal blamed himself . . . as if I didn't know.

The Auphe had given Cal every reason to blame himself. It was part of their game. It wasn't enough to kill us or him. There had to be suffering, agony . . . torment. Months ago, before Cal had killed the Auphe in Florida, they had told my brother they would save him for last as we were torn to pieces before him. They wanted him to blame himself for every one of our deaths. They would be happy to know he already did. Cal had already lived that moment hundreds of times in his head, I knew. Would live it hundreds more before this was all over. And no matter what I said or did, that wouldn't change.

My grip tightened on the bottle and I put it down with exquisite care before I shattered it. I couldn't change it, but I could make sure he only lived the nightmare of it, not the reality.

The first step would be to stay together as much as possible. Robin would take some persuading, but I was rather in the mood for some persuasion. I'd missed my workout this morning. Dragging him kicking and screaming from his den of debauchery could be a substitute.

I stood as Delilah gave Cal something to remember her by. As she turned her back on him, I waited for him to walk over before I commented on the bright red handprint on his cheek. "Things went well, then."

He gave me an irritable glance and rubbed his face gingerly. "Funny, it doesn't feel like it did."

Delilah slapped her hand on the bar, snapping, "Pigeon! Whiskey. Now."

Amusing though it might be, I didn't have time to see the fun and games that were going to start with Ishiah. Herding Cal toward the door, I said, "She could've broken your neck with one blow if she'd wanted. That's the tap a mother gives her cub."

"Being smacked by a she wolf," he muttered, "it gives new meaning to 'bitch slap.' "

"Don't complain." I opened the door and shoved him out just as I saw Ishiah pull his sword from beneath the bar. "You could've stopped her."

"Maybe." He scowled, then let it go. "Relationships. I never claimed I was good at them."

"When you actually have one," I advised, "we'll return to the subject."

Coincidentally, as we arrived at Robin's, he was in the process of not having relationships as well. Standing on black-and-white marble in tastefully subdued lighting, I wondered not for the first time how Goodfellow had managed to weasel his way past the co-op board of this place. They couldn't have any idea what went on behind that door. I'd only seen glimpses, and as much as I appreciated education, that was one no one needed.

After several minutes of Cal's pounding, we were finally let in by a shirtless Robin. His pants were still on, though, and that was something. Not much, but something.

Tapping a bare foot impatiently on the floor, he asked, "What? What do you want? It's never-ending with you two. I would think a giant eel attack would have you taking at least one day off."

"We're . . . oh, hell. What are you doing now?" Cal asked as we both caught sight of the rumpled clothes on the living room floor—a Salvation Army uniform, a sweatshirt that read ABSTINENCE MAKES THE HEART GROW FONDER, and, if I wasn't mistaken, a Shriner's fez.

That was the type of day it was going to be, then. I pinched the bridge of my nose at the oncoming headache.

Robin folded his arms and raised his eyebrows as if it were obvious. "I'm trying to change my ways. I'm helping the poor, the deluded, and the medically needy. Who could find fault in that?" he said with a self-satisfied smirk.

Trying to change. More like trying very hard not to change. His brush with death as a result of similar behavior had him trying to prove to the world that he was fine the way that he was—and trying even harder to prove it to himself.

"You . . ." Cal started, then gave up immediately. I didn't blame him. This was Robin as he was and as he would no doubt always be. Which was fine. I liked him . . . well, I was *used* to him the way he was. Semantics.

"Just don't tell us the cat is involved as well," I said. "There's a line to be drawn, and necrophiliac bestiality would be it."

"The cat." He gritted his teeth. "Do you have an idea what my life is like now? No, you do not, and why? Let me tell you. Yesterday she got out and . . ."

"She?" Cal interrupted before inhaling. I could smell the cat in the apartment as well, and my sense of smell had nothing on his. The mummifying spices of cinnamon and ginger floated on the air, winding about us. "Hey, that's nice," Cal grinned. "You can't beat a walking undead deodorizer for that domestic touch, can you, Nik?"

"She?" I prompted, returning to the subject at hand

and giving his ribs the reprovingly sharp point of my elbow. The sooner Robin vented, the sooner we could get on with it.

"Yes, *she*," Goodfellow snarled, "and a complete and utterly psycho bitch she is. Like many of my past liaisons, as a matter of fact. Yesterday she somehow opened the locks, got out the door, and ran into Mrs. Federstein's Great Dane. The woman"—he made a seesawing gesture as if he wasn't quite sure she qualified for the gender—"wholly unattractive and not especially bright, lets the dog roam up and down the hall for exercise. The poor, wretched creature is a hundred years old, completely deaf, mostly blind, and no brighter than his owner. Up and down the hall he weaves, bouncing off the walls, probably praying for death from whatever god dogs worship." He sighed and ran an agitated hand into his wavy hair and clenched it there. "Well, he got his wish. I come home from the dealership last evening to find a 'present' on my pillow—one very big, very dead dog. Do you have any idea how hard it is to get a Great Dane into the incinerator? Do you?"

"Aw, she loves you." Cal's grin stretched a little wider. It was a rare one for him, neither dark nor sarcastic. For one brief second he wasn't thinking of the Auphe, and that made Robin's rant more than worth listening to.

"What are you naming her?" I asked, as genuinely curious as I was genuinely amazed that he had kept her after all.

"Salome. She was a bitch too," he replied, disgruntled. "All she could talk about was John the Baptist. Bring me his head on a platter. I want his head on a platter. Now, where's that platter? Blah, blah. I was willing to serve up my dick on a platter, still attached, of course, but was that good enough for her? Nooo."

"Robin, we're starting without you."

I could say if it was a female or male voice coming

from the bedroom, but what was the point? Robin lived a restriction-free life in that area. All areas, actually. It was too bad for him that was about to come to an abrupt, if hopefully temporary, end.

He turned and walked away, waving us off with a "Thanks for visiting. Drop by anytime. My best to the family. Pick a platitude and leave with it."

"I don't think so." I tapped his shoulder with the blade of my katana, stopping him in his tracks. "Pack. You're coming with us. We're all staying at Promise's until the Auphe situation is resolved."

He looked in the direction of the bedroom and then back at me. "I most certainly am not."

I gave a smile sharp as my sword. "Yes, you most certainly are."

Twenty minutes later Goodfellow, still not at peak performance after his drunken three days, was in a cab on his way to Promise's penthouse apartment. His playmates had left fifteen minutes prior to that. Apparently, a sword fight in the living room wasn't the aphrodisiac one might imagine.

"You enjoyed that way too much," Cal observed as he watched the cab pull into traffic.

"Did I?" Salome, the Great Dane–loving feline, was staying behind. She didn't need to eat, drink, or eliminate. She would be fine on her own. All in all, other than the killing of domesticated animals twenty times her size, she was the perfect pet. Robin would be selling them via infomercial within the month. Goodfellow's Mummy Cats—Gummy Cats no doubt.

"You're getting cranky in your old age, Cyrano," he snorted at the satisfaction in my voice.

"Children need boundaries." I had enjoyed it; there was no denying it. And if he hadn't been up all night doing things Caligula had only dreamed of, he would've been able to hold his own. As it was, work-outwise . . .

I shifted a speculative gaze to Cal, and he groaned.

"Nik, damn. My back hurts. I'm still tired from last night. Come on."

It was several hours and dark before we made it home to do packing of our own. We stayed away from the park this time and used a dojo where I'd once taught. One student had offered to spar with Cal during one of our breaks. Cal, sweaty and tired, had given him the highly pissed-off reply of, "Niko can keep me from killing him. You can't. Go away." Not precisely tactful, but true. His form was virtually nonexistent, the results undeniably deadly. He wasn't as good as I was—there was only so much inherent laziness one could overcome, but he was good.

Good enough that he noticed it the same moment I did. We'd finished sparring and went home to pick up clothes and gear to take to Promise's penthouse. Reaching our apartment door, we entered, and it came that quickly before I had a chance to turn the light on. The sensation of something slicing through the air—headed in our direction. I gave Cal one hard push to the side and dove to the floor. It passed over my head and hit the wall with a distinctive chopping sound. A sword. Not Auphe, then. An Auphe didn't need a sword.

"Vampire," Cal said, his voice coming from near the floor by the couch. "I smell you, Seamus. You ambushing piece of shit."

Seamus, whose jealousy phase had passed a century ago. I'd trusted Promise's normally excellent judgment. I should've trusted Cal's; I should've trusted my own. I heard the sound of metal ripped free of plaster, and then I could see him as he moved back. Silhouetted against the city lights streaming through the cracked window blinds, the bulk of him paused for a moment, then slid with a fluid speed to the right.

"I never knew I wanted her back, all these years. But then I saw her again. Smelled her. Touched her. And I do want her back. She should be with me," he spat. "She belongs with me. Her mate. Her *true* mate."

I'd moved to my feet, silent and smooth. I caught the next swing of his blade on my own before I spoke. "Her choice, not yours."

Vampires could see better than humans in the dark, but my eyes had adjusted now. I could see him, albeit in shades of dark gray and black. "Then I shall narrow her options," he said coldly.

There were no further words, only the sound of blade against blade. Cal would have his Glock in hand, but Seamus and I were moving too fast for him to get a shot lined up. The vampire was quick and he was good—the type of good that was learned from time on a battlefield. Years. But I'd been in battles myself, faced creatures I doubt even Seamus had ever seen. Yes, vampires were quick and lethal.

But so was I.

I twisted and swung the katana. Inches from having his head severed, Seamus jerked to one side and sliced toward me again. From the shadowy length and breadth of it, he was carrying a broadsword. He swung it like it was one. Two-handed and with the weight of a mountain behind it. In the dim light, I could see his eyes were all black—the eyes of a vampire in the midst of strong emotion. Fury, I was guessing. I used it. His next strike, full of rage, took him slightly off balance. Barely detectable, but I caught it. I slammed a boot in his gut. He staggered, but less than he should have. His breed was stronger than humans, and Seamus, big and broad, was no exception. I slid around his next blow, but it was close. The point of the sword cut through my skin, tracing a superficial slice. He gave an incoherent growl at the miss and with one furious kick sent the couch flying up on end to then promptly topple over. I heard Cal curse as he leapt out of the way. Then I heard him say one more thing.

"Lights."

Vampires could see well in the dark, yes, but humans saw well in the light. As our lights flared on, Seamus closed his eyes against it for a fraction of a second. That was about half as long as I needed. He swiveled, but not before I carved off a slice of flesh over his ribs. He didn't let that slow him. He kept coming . . . right into Cal's crosshairs. Three bullets hit his upper back before he shifted direction and made it to the door, split it in half with his weight, and was gone. Cal, by the light switch, instantly vaulted over the shattered wood to follow him.

It was too late. If he'd thought it through, he'd know that. Short of chasing Seamus down to the lobby and killing him in front of anyone who happened to be strolling through, this fight was over. I reached through the doorway and caught Cal by the back of his jacket as the door to the stairwell slammed shut at the end of the hall. I saw it on the wall down there and on the doorknob, swipes and smears of dark red. Blood. Some would say quite a bit.

I would say not nearly enough.

5

Cal

"He's good."

That's what Niko said in the aftermath of the fight while mopping the small amount of blood from his chest with a washcloth. "He's good." Like he'd say, "It's hot today," or "Darn, I'm out of tofu."

He'd tagged Nik during a sword fight. He was more than good. And those three shots I'd put in him weren't going to slow him down. Vampires healed fast and had an incredible tolerance for pain. All of that made Seamus a problem. Because, hey, the Auphe weren't enough. Let's add another goddamned monster gunning for my brother.

The couch had already been tossed over. What was one more kick? I slammed my foot against it. It didn't make me feel any better, but it didn't make me feel any worse either. "I told you I didn't trust him," I said grimly, as he pulled a new shirt on. "Being followed, my ass. He planned that."

"No, that was real. Or whoever shot that spear would've killed me then. But there's no denying Seamus used being followed as an opportunity to get closer to Promise." The meeting she'd had yesterday with him that she hadn't told Niko about. "And if he killed us both . . ." Niko's eyes glittered with an anger he normally would've kept hidden. Niko didn't have many buttons, but Seamus was pushing the ones he had—Promise and me. "Who's to say it couldn't be blamed on those following him?"

"And how hard could killing us be? Two humans." I wasn't really human, though, and Niko was by no means your average one, but Seamus hadn't known that. He knew now . . . at least when it came to Nik. No matter how long the bastard had been around, Niko was his match—even in an ambush.

So what would he try next time? How much further would he go to get what he wanted?

Far.

"We don't have time for this. Not now," Niko said firmly, the anger already squelched under his customary control. "We'll deal with it later."

He was right. We didn't have time for it, but Seamus had plenty of time. All the time in the world. The son of a bitch. "Promise isn't going to be too happy." I wasn't too happy about it myself. Then again, I hadn't had a secret meeting with the Scottish bastard. Maybe Promise wouldn't be happy in an entirely different way. Niko said he trusted her, and that should've been good enough for me. And for him, I was trying damn hard to make it be. I hefted the duffel bag I'd stuffed with clothes, weapons, and ammunition, my grip tight enough to whiten my knuckles.

"Naivete in you, little brother. I'm surprised." He lifted his own bag and stepped over the wreckage of our door. The landlord was not going to be pleased, but for a hundred bucks we could get him to nail it shut with plywood before the place was emptied out.

I guess I was naive, because it looked like Niko had been right about her after all. When we made it to her place and told our story, Promise wasn't unhappy. She was *pissed*.

"He is dead. *Dead*."

Eyes ebony, whiteless, and frozen with rage, Promise was saying all the right things, in my book. Seamus dead. Yep. Totally on board with that. As icy as Niko himself, I hadn't seen her like this often. It made me wonder what she'd been like back in the blood-drinking days. She might be an omnivore now, but she'd been a carnivore once. Niko said she didn't talk much about her past, and there was probably good reason for that. To see her sweeping out of the dark-ness at you—you'd think angel, you'd think demon. And you'd be right on both counts.

"Dead," she repeated. This time I saw her fangs and I saw them lengthen before my eyes. I'd seen her climb walls, seen her snap necks, but that was a new one for me.

Nik didn't seem surprised, but when you have a kid brother who's half monster, not much can shake you. "We'll take care of it," he said, catching her wrist lightly as she paced past him. Her hair loose and a mass of motion around her, she was like a wind—the gale-force kind that takes down everything in its path. "After the Auphe, we will deal with Seamus. To-gether."

"If Seamus is cooperative enough to not attack you again before then," Robin added.

"Not helping," I muttered as I continued to unpack my guns onto Promise's dining room table—even if I was thinking the same thing.

He drained his wineglass and raised his eyebrows. "Who said I was trying to?" He sighed, green eyes somber. "Helpful or not, it's the truth. But, really, what's the difference? We're already watching for the Auphe. We'll watch for him as well. When you're neck-deep in it, what's one more dollop of manure?"

Maybe the death of Niko, that's what. Seamus was determined. Then again, I thought as I stared down at my guns, he wasn't the only one.

Robin's hand moved past mine into the long bag and pulled out a sword. "Something for every occa-sion. Except clothes. I hope you don't expect to wear mine. Your skin would probably melt at the touch of true fashion."

"I have clothes, jackass." I pushed his hand away, and looked back at Promise and Niko.

"I brought this on us." She stood still now, and I could see glints of purple behind the black clouding her eyes. "If I hadn't suggested we take his case. If I hadn't let him fool me for an entire *century* that he had changed his ways." Her face was stone. "I'll have his heart, scarlet and still in my hand, and none of you will interfere. He is mine."

"The challenge was to me," Niko countered. "We will finish him face-to-face." Face-to-face. Face-to-goddamn-face, because although he had drilled in me over and over that there was no honor in battle, only survival, Nik did have honor. Maybe the only person in the world who did.

"The challenge may be to you," Promise argued back, "but the insult is to me, that my affection could be transferred so easily."

I didn't know if Niko would've gone further with it, or asked about that meeting she hadn't mentioned yet. Considering Promise's mood, it probably wouldn't have done any good. But it didn't come to that. One phone call ended the topic.

That same one phone call had us sitting at a diner across the street from a church in Brooklyn. There George's father was having a memorial service on the first anniversary of his death. He'd been sick a long time, George had said, before he died. He'd kicked the drugs, but he hadn't been able to survive the deadly present a few dirty needles had left behind. We hadn't been able to go to the funeral, as we were recuperating from some serious wounds at the time, but we could pay our respects now—for George— from a safe distance away. If the Auphe were watching, we were having lunch. Nothing more. I doubted

they understood the concept of mourning death anyway. It was a ceremony that escaped or bored them,
and they most likely ignored it entirely. Why bury
what you can eat? Why mourn a long-gone snack?

As for George, I thought she'd know we were there.
She might refuse to look far into the future, but the
little things were just there to her. We'd arrived too
late to watch her go into the church. I hadn't seen her
dark red cap of hair or deep gold skin. She wouldn't
have worn black. That wasn't her. Whatever she believed about death—I'd never asked—she wouldn't
honor her father by looking different than she always
was. He wouldn't have wanted that.

Hell, I'd never met the man. How did I know what
he would've wanted?

I clicked the salt and pepper shakers against each
other and looked away from the church. If she'd been
there, why would I want to see her anyway? Seeing
was just the next best thing to not having. They both
sucked, but it was my choice. I would live with it.

"I'm not eating here." Robin looked at the lami-
nated menu with unadulterated horror. "They think
grease is a marinade and that a Band-Aid in your food
is à la carte."

"We're not here to eat. So just order something and
sneer at it like you normally do," I ordered.

Promise, in one of her hooded cloaks, was sitting
across from me and farthest from the window. Niko
sat next to her, eyes moving from the people in the
place to the street outside. He was always on watch.
He'd taught me, and I was good enough. But there
was good enough and there was Nik.

He tensed minutely and that was something I *was*
good at picking up on. I turned back toward the window, blinked, then narrowed my eyes. "Holy shit."
When a dead guy shows up at a memorial service and
he's not the one being eulogized, you take notice.

"Samuel," Niko said. "Unexpected."

"Unexpected" was the word for it. Samuel had once worked for the Auphe, keeping close to me while in a band that played at the hole-in-the-wall bar I'd worked at—keeping an eye on me from feet away. Even the Auphe couldn't do that. But then he had changed his mind, had died to save us from them. He'd worked for them in the beginning for the promise of saving his brother. I couldn't say I might not have done the same. And I hope I would've died to make up for the mistake like I thought he had when I found out how horrific a mistake it was. But now he was standing in front of the church. Alive. It was his brother that they were holding the service for, and I wondered why George had never felt the need to bring up the fact her uncle was still alive. I knew the answer to that the instant I asked it. She thought it was his decision to tell us.

And that's what he was there to do.

He looked away from the church over to the diner. He saw us immediately through the glass. He saw us, because he'd been looking for us. One of the little things George was willing to share—that we would be there. Where'd she draw the line? Between what was little and what was big? How did she know? How did she know she couldn't look at our future, hers and mine, but she could look at this? And why did both of us have to be so damn stubborn?

Either way, it was over. No point in thinking about it now . . . or ever again.

I watched as Samuel crossed the street toward us. He was a tall black guy with a close-shaven goatee, big and tough . . . now moving with a limp. He hadn't had that before. His head was shaved too, new as well. It showed a half-moon scar behind his ear, clear as day—the same kind that Niko had described on the guy following Seamus. Samuel hadn't seen me since the days before Niko and Robin had managed to get the Auphe-hired hitchhiker out of my head. So when he hesitated after coming through the door before moving over to us, I understood it. Darkling had been every bit the son of a bitch the Auphe were, and when it had squatted inside me, I hadn't been the safest person—safest *thing*—to be around.

I took off my sunglasses to show my eyes were gray, not possessed silver, and he nodded and pulled up a chair. "Sorry. Georgie told me they got that thing out of you, but . . ." He shook his head at the memories. "Seeing is believing."

"You've got that right." I planted the muzzle of the Glock, hidden under the red plastic tablecloth, in his abdomen. "You know, I felt pretty forgiving when you died to save our lives. I'm feeling a little less than that now that you're still walking around."

He rested his hands carefully on the table. "I can see that. I think I'd probably feel the same way."

I half expected Niko to reel me in. For him to say that Samuel hadn't known what the Auphe were capable of. That we barely had ourselves. But Niko had spent a week looking for me then, not knowing where I was . . . if I was still even alive. An entire week of that. I'd been possessed, but in my mind Nik had had the worst end of it by far. Now he sat, his eyes impenetrable. "Samuel," he said, voice empty. "I thought you died with honor. I see I was wrong about one. Now I have to wonder at the other."

Promise, who had never known Samuel, remained silent. Robin, who had, drawled, "Order him the tuna casserole. That will kill him faster than any bullet."

"In this place? I'd say you're right." Other than speaking, Samuel didn't move. He was mostly as I remembered him: calm, easygoing. A trustworthy sort of guy, if you were into that sort of thing. I hadn't been then, and he damn sure hadn't earned it now.

"What are you doing here?" I asked flatly. "I get what you're doing over there." I jerked my head at the church. "But what are you doing *here*?"

"Because I do owe you, and I know it." He added seriously, "Then there's the Auphe. They're back and that's trouble for more than just you. It's trouble for the Vigil too. You do know about us, right? Our psychics were able to pick up that you were poking around. Investigating. Something about a mummy. They weren't able to get a clearer picture."

"Psychics." Niko gave a quick glance back toward the church.

"No, not like Georgie. If only," Samuel said ruefully. "Ours are much weaker. They have no future sight, but they can pinpoint when something has happened as it happens. They know when we need to get moving."

"To do what?" I demanded. The Vigil did exist. Wahanket hadn't lied. He was a killer, but he wasn't a liar. Good to know. Gotta have your priorities straight.

"Clean up. We don't always get there in time, but mostly we do. And if it's a mess someone else, like the Kin, will clean up, we let it alone. Those mutts are damn good about cleaning up after themselves. I have to give them that." It made sense. The Kin didn't want attention any more than their human Mafia counterparts did.

Samuel tapped his fingers on the table, but kept the rest of his hands still—respecting the gun. "Basically, we're supernatural janitors." He gave a self-deprecating smile. "At least that's what I consider us. The Vigil found me when they were cleaning up that Auphe mess we were all caught up in. The collapsed warehouse was explained as a gas-main explosion. That's why I'm alive today. The Vigil."

"Yeah, we read about the so-called gas-main explosion. So you escaped? It didn't look that way from our point of view," I challenged.

"I didn't escape, not entirely." He moved his hand, very carefully, to knock on his leg just below his knee.

There was a hollow sound. "My leg was crushed. They did their best to save it, but I lost it below the knee." He flashed a slow grin. "But half is better than nothing, not to mention the fact that I'm alive and that's damn amazing in my book. A miracle, one I know I didn't deserve." He placed his hand back on the table. "I knew about the Auphe, so it was recruit me or commit me. The Vigil's been around a long time and they have their philosophy. I don't totally agree with it, but I'll take it over a mental institute any day."

"And what is this no doubt fascinating philosophy?" Robin dropped the offending menu and pushed it away.

"We protect the human world from the knowledge of the supernatural one. People couldn't handle it. If they found out, there'd be war, and no matter who won, the results wouldn't be pretty." He focused in on Niko. "You wouldn't want the entire world knowing about your brother, would you? I doubt he'd last long. It might take the military, but they'd get him sooner or later."

"So you just clean up?" I said skeptically, basking in the whole right to exist. Whoopee for me. "Wipe up after some monster's snack. You don't interfere?"

"We make exceptions, but they're rare. Only when a nonhuman is so overt, so out there in what he's doing, that he'll give away the secrecy we've kept so long. There might not be as many nonhumans as humans, not that we know for sure, but there's no guarantee humans would be on the winning side. Keeping the secret is everything, you understand? Everything. If we have to kill a werewolf or boggle who can't bother to hold their buffets in private, we will."

"Watching us for thousands of years. The pucks must have given you quite the show." Promise clasped her gloved hands on the table.

"I'll bet we did." Robin curled his lips smugly, not ashamed at all. "We should've charged admission."

"So, what of the Auphe?" Promise continued, ignoring Goodfellow. "They grow more bold all the time. What are you doing about that?" she demanded.

"Not a damn thing," Samuel admitted. "By the time our psychics know where they are, they're already gone. We're hoping you can succeed where we've failed. The Auphe were mad—don't think I don't remember—but they're worse now. They have to go before it's too late and the world wakes up and sees them. There's only so many fake escaped-mental-patient stories you can put out. But if we can't find them, we can't stop them. . . . Making the assumption we're even capable of stopping them." He exhaled with the confession. "They're the Auphe."

And that said it all.

I pulled my gun back slowly and slid it back under my jacket. "Nik?"

"It's an interesting story." Niko didn't look particularly interested. "What I don't know is why you're bothering to tell it to us, and why now."

"It took me this long to get up and mobile again. To be trained. And like I said, I owe you." With the threat of being shot gone for the moment, he slipped a hand in his pocket. Placing a card with a phone number on the table, he said, "Call me if you need me. Any time. I have a lot of making up for what I did to you guys. Not to mention the entire Vigil owes you for taking care of Sawney Beane. He was the damn definition of overt and psychotic as the cherry on top. He had to be taken down, and I don't think we could've done it."

And that's how all the bodies had gotten cleaned up a week ago when we were fighting the supernatural mass murderer, why none of his victims' pieces had turned up in the park, the college, or were discovered by subway workers. The Vigil had tidied up but good. Niko had been right. Our mystery janitors and the Vigil were one and the same.

He rapped a fist on the table and gave me an amused smile. "I tried to talk them into recruiting you and Niko, you know, but they say you're our biggest annoyance. You cause us quite a bit of work." Pushing halfway up with one hand on the back of his chair, he asked curiously, "Am I leaving?"

It was a good question. Niko considered him for several seconds, then gave impassive permission. "You're leaving."

"You'll call if you need my help?"

"You're leaving," Nik repeated, his voice cooling even further.

Samuel nodded in acceptance. "If you change your mind." He pulled a few bills out of his wallet and let them fall by Niko's plate. It was only when he was at the door that he called back over his shoulder, "Sorry about the coat. Hope that covers it." The door shut behind him and he headed back toward the church.

Niko's coat? What . . . ? Oh, hell. The speargun. The Vigil guy with the scar. Samuel had just confirmed they were behind that . . . were watching Seamus. Why? Did they think he was going to be overt? Noticed? Whatever. I only hoped they killed the bastard. It would be one less thing on our plate to worry about. Less worry, I could use more of that. I didn't need the distraction, not with what I was trying to do.

What I was still trying to do hours later.

You didn't notice the tinting at night on the windows. Promise's guest room, one of four, looked over Central Park—it was a blot of darkness surrounded by thousands of lights. Fairy lights, if you lived in some fantasy world. I'd never seen that world, not even in my dreams.

Not that all my dreams were bad; they weren't. I had nightmares, more now that the Auphe were back, but I had good dreams too. I usually didn't remember them, but I'd wake up with the sensation of warmth on my face, of floating. No details, but I'd take it.

Then there were the XXX-variety dreams. Now, they were all about the details. Testosterone, gotta love it.

But dreams would have to wait. I had things to do. Things to think.

Think like an Auphe.

I told Nik that I would. Told myself that I could. Whether I wanted to or not.

Auphe blood—was that the same as an Auphe brain? An Auphe soul? Stupid question—they didn't have souls. No damn way. But the blood . . .

Last week to fight a killer, I'd opened a gate and traveled through it. It was one of a handful I'd opened and one of the few times I'd felt it. Slippery, cold, savage. Carnivorous and content with that. Very content. It had only lasted a few seconds, but that was long enough for me to decide traveling wasn't a good idea. Opening a door in reality could open a door in me. It let the Auphe part of me out. Let it take a peek around. It had disappeared with the gate, and hadn't shown up again. If I guarded myself, it might never. Yet here I was, inviting it in. Sit down, have a beer. Let's talk.

How 'bout those Yankees?

I sat on the bed and stared out the window, watching as the lights slowly began to swim. And I thought. Ugly, bile-black, murder-red thoughts. They crept in and I let them. I liked to think they weren't mine . . . that they were the result of two years of being held by the Auphe. Two years of a prisoner's intimacy with his captors, knowing what roamed in their twisted brains. I didn't remember that lost time, but it was there. I wanted to think that's where the thoughts came from. I wanted to deny they were mine. Deny they were me. Then I said, Fuck it, and just thought them.

For a long, long time.

"Cal, stop it."

I heard the words, but I didn't understand them.

They were just sounds. They came and went, but they didn't mean anything.

"Stop it. Now." A hand fastened tightly on my forearm and gave it a hard shake, bringing me back to myself. Words were words again. "What are you doing?"

My hand, it was haloed in gray light. A gate . . . very small, contained. I blinked and let the light bleed into nothingness. I raised eyes from my now-normal hand to Niko. "Thinking."

Bad things. Such bad, bad things.

He didn't let go of my arm. "Don't. I know you said you would, but we'll get out of this without that. It's not worth it."

To save Nik and my friends? It was worth it. It could eat my soul if I had one, and I thought it just might. It could turn me inside out; I didn't give a damn. If it saved my brother, it was worth it. "I think they'll come tomorrow or the next day," I evaded. "Not all of them. Three or four. Probe our defenses. A suicide run, if they have the chance." Because vengeance is all. Sacrifices have to be made. "It's what I would—" My lips twisted and I corrected, "It's what an Auphe would do."

Niko hesitated, not like he doubted me, but more as if I didn't have all the facts. But if there was something I didn't know, he didn't fill me in. Instead, he just said, "All right. That's good intelligence to have." He moved his hand from my forearm down to my wrist, squeezing tightly. "But don't do it again. Don't go to that place. I mean it, Cal. No more." To that place in my head where things were dark and memories were black holes, sucking up everything around them until you forgot there had ever been anything to remember at all. Or to forget.

"Cyrano, shit," I dropped my head and rubbed at weary eyes with the heel of my free hand. "It's all we have. How goddamn selfish would I be if I didn't use it?" The lights had gone still again outside the window. Fairy land. I pulled loose of Niko's grip— because he let me—and in turn I yanked at his arm until he sat on the edge of the bed. "You've put it on the line for me all your life. It's my turn to step up. You can't stop me. You can kick my ass, yeah, on a daily basis if you want. But you can't stop me. Not until this is over."

He studied me, frowning. "You are so damn stubborn."

"Learned from the best," I said truthfully.

He exhaled. "Be careful, then. Can you at least do that?"

I was saved from answering by the car crash from the living room. For a second I forgot we were several stories up. The sound was exactly the same. A waterfall smash of shattering glass and the scream of twisted metal. Niko lunged into motion and I was on his heels.

In the living room, Promise's largest window was gone. With curtains billowing, the cold air whipped through to carry with it tiny pieces of glass—a razor-edged wind. On the floor was a thick carpet of shining stuff. Misshapen pieces of the metal framework were embedded in two walls, the ceiling, and glittered in the light as much as the glass did. Diamonds and silver.

In the middle of it all, she stood.

Not Auphe. I eased my finger fractionally off the trigger of my Glock. Not Auphe. Don't pull the trigger. Not Auphe.

Straight black hair whipped around her shoulders, blood covered her hands and sword, and her eyes . . . I saw those eyes almost every day. Wildflowers in spring.

"They're right behind me."

Although Niko and I had moved into the room, it wasn't said to us. Violet eyes found violet eyes as Promise appeared in the hall. She had a crossbow in

her hand and an expression of wary affection and resignation on her face.

"Cherish, what trouble have you brought now?"

A dimple flashed by a very familiar mouth. "It's
only a little trouble, *Madre*."

Robin had been the one to pull the first watch and
was in the living room when the window had ex-
ploded. He now stood, back pressed to the wall, next
to the absent window, with his own sword high. He
took off the head of Cherish's trouble as it flowed
over the bottom edge of the window. The first of her
troubles, rather. They weren't as little as she claimed.
More and more came, pouring into the apartment in
an undulating wave.

That's when the big picture hit me, jerked from
Auphe dread to an almost equally crappy reality. She
had crawled . . . no. With that much force, she must
have *raced* up the side of the building to throw herself
through Promise's window. And the trouble she was
talking about had come right behind her.

"Black cadejos," Robin said as he took another
head. "Whatever they bite will rot off in a matter of
days. Nothing can heal it." He swung his sword again.
"And, worse yet, they smell like dog piss."

"Don't feel bad," I murmured to Niko, the icy
clamp at the base of my spine easing. Cadejos. Big,
ugly, and flesh rotting, but not Auphe. "I'm sure you
knew that."

He growled and stepped into the fray, beheading
two cadejos with one blow. Several across the room
had leapt up to the wall and were running along it. I
nailed them in their low-slung foreheads. They did
smell like dog piss. Not surprising—they looked like
dogs as well . . . if you crossed one with a weasel.
Black skin, sleek black hair, short legs, long length,
and a whiplike tail. They were like a living puddle of
oil, but with baleful yellow eyes and a mouthful of

teeth that could've come from the dinosaur that made
that oil.

I fired again at one that vaulted toward me. The
silencer chuffed as I hit it midchest. I ducked as it
tumbled over my head. Another one, the size of a
German shepherd, was hurtling toward me. I jerked
my gun over, but before I had the shot lined up the
thing was down, chopped into three separate pieces.
Niko stood on one side of the body and Cherish stood
on the other, both with bloody blades buried in the
cadejo's flesh. "Little boys," she smiled at him, her
dimple appearing again. A vampire with a dimple . . .
what the hell was up with that? "They need protecting."

Crossbow bolts went through the eyes of three cadejos sweeping up behind Cherish. As she looked over
her shoulder, eyes widening slightly, I drawled, "When
your mommy's done watching your ass, we'll let the
adults set up a playdate for us."

She wasn't offended. Instead she laughed. If you
didn't know she was a vampire, you would've guessed
her to be only ten years younger than her mother—
she looked about nineteen or twenty. And her mouth
and eyes were the same as Promise's. Her chin,
though, was more pointed, her face a little wider at
the cheekbones, her nose thinner. But it was the perfectly black, perfectly straight hair parted precisely in
the middle to fall just past her shoulders that was the
first definitive sign. The light brown skin was the second: Cherish's father had left his biological stamp on
his daughter too. The third, and obvious even to me,
was the *madre*. Spanish for "mother." Cherish's father
was either a Spanish or Latin American vampire.

Still laughing, she whirled and took out another cadejo. Robin handled the last two that eeled through
the window. That left five. Niko took two, Promise
and Cherish one each, and I shot the last in the head.

And then I aimed at what had wriggled in behind the couch. It wasn't a cadejo. It was wearing clothes. I could see a slice of jeans and a bit of red sweatshirt.

"No." Cherish stepped between us. "He is with me." She turned. "Come out, Xolo. Come out, *perrito*."

Pale fingers edged around the couch and *perrito* slowly edged into view. My Spanish was pretty rusty, despite Niko's best educational efforts, but that I recognized. Puppy. And I could see why she called him that. It was a chupacabra, like the one from the bar. Puppy was a good name for something that looked like a cross between a bald dog and a lizard. It was the size of a small human—about five-three; no hair; round, mellow brown eyes; and with a bony spinal ridge that started midskull. As it moved out into the open, it pulled the hood of the sweatshirt up to cover the ridge and ducked its head shyly. I didn't know much about chupas aside from what I'd seen in the bar. They didn't talk as far as I could tell, they drank tequila, kept to themselves, and they didn't tip.

"Oh, hey, another big spender. So glad I could save your life at no charge," I snorted and let the muzzle of the gun fall toward the floor.

Cherish let her arm drape around the goat sucker's red-clad shoulders. "Xolo. Xolo. He is a good *perrito*. Safe and good. I promise."

He leaned into her side like a child and watched us with those unblinking soft brown eyes. He was a pet, not that bright, or was one introverted son of a bitch. She patted him on the shoulder and pointed to the couch. "Rest. Nap. There will be food soon."

Unless Promise kept a goat in her freezer, "soon" seemed a little optimistic, but Xolo took her at her word. He went to the couch, like a good *perrito*, curled up, and was out like a light. With a bifurcated upper lip, eyes closed, and sneakers that could've been mine, he wasn't much to look at. There were bloodsuckers and then there were bloodsuckers, and a goat sucker didn't stand up too high next to the vampires, trolls, bodachs, wolves . . . the usual. Unless you were a goat, they weren't much to worry about—as far as I knew. Trouble was, that wasn't very far.

"Nik?"

He moved next to me, the blood staining his boots with each step. Promise's beautiful rug was ruined, a sopping mess of cadejo blood. The entire room was a battlefield of the fallen, and the dog piss smell was not improving matters. "Chupacabras suck blood from animals. They have a mild telepathic ability said to be used to freeze their prey. Most references say they are harmless to humans."

"Just lousy tippers." I looked over to the piano where Promise had several photographs in polished silver frames. One I'd noticed before. It was old, a black image on tarnished metal. Promise and a little girl, dressed in clothes I'd only seen in movies. Promise sat in a chair, the little girl at her feet. The pose was stiff, but the small hand held in the larger one . . . that was warm. I'd wondered about that photo before. Vampirism isn't a contagious disease. You're born a vampire. Vampires have children, and I guessed now that that little dark-haired girl was Promise's daughter.

Had Nik wondered like me, or had Promise told him? I don't think she had, and while I was doing this whole thinking fest, I went on to the next thought, which was: That was a mistake. She had really screwed up. Seamus, now this. The past was the past, but family was family—it could fuck up things in a heartbeat. I was living proof.

"I'm not looking for a step-niece, in case you were wondering," I told him lightly as I dug a hand into my jeans pocket. With cell phone in one hand and card in the other, I muttered as I punched buttons, "Payback time, Samuel." When he answered, I said brusquely, "Promise's place. Bring a van." I took another look around. "Forget that. Bring a truck." I was sure their psychics would know where her place was. Flipping the phone shut, I crossed my arms and took my first good, detailed look at Cherish. She was dressed in a long-sleeved, high-necked, sleek black dress. It was slit to her thighs, the skirt separated into four pieces for easy movement. Beneath it she wore black leggings and black boots. Vampires . . . they could never wear jeans like a normal person.

"Cherish, what have you done now?" Promise demanded with a weary tone to the words. The bottom of her silk robe fluttered in the rush of air circling the apartment.

Not done . . . but done *now*.

She had Promise's eyes, but while the color was the same, what was in them was far different. There was a swirl, wild and wicked. It reminded me of what I saw in Goodfellow. I'd seen a street performer doing origami once—folding brightly colored squares of paper into cranes, tigers, horses, dragons, you name it. That was the quality I saw in Cherish and Robin. They treated life the same way. They twisted and folded it until they got the result they wanted. Life, like the paper, didn't have much to say about it. But the two of them enjoyed themselves, so normally I would've said what the hell? Live it up.

If not for the Auphe, Seamus, and a horde of flesh rotters. If that wasn't a hat trick of shittiness, I didn't know what was. Cherish's trouble was one trouble too many.

"You're always so quick to think badly of me, *Madre*." Scarlet-stained sword still in hand, she kissed Promise's cheek. Blood and daughterly affection; it was a weird mix. Goodfellow was probably getting turned on. I made sure not to look and see. "And it was so very bright and sparkly," she smiled, "not even you could've resisted taking it."

"Strangely enough, I think I could have." Promise returned the kiss but it seemed strained. "But you have made your bed, Cherish, as you have so many times in the past. You must handle this alone. We're in dire straits ourselves."

"She's right. Next to our shit," I nudged a dead cadejo with my foot, "this is playtime at doggie day care."

"The Auphe are coming for us," Niko said impassively. "If you stay here, they'll be after you as well. I don't believe you or your mother would want that."

She definitely hadn't told him. Promise had messed up indeed. Knowing Niko, knowing how he felt about Promise—how he trusted her, he might have thought that long-ago-photographed little girl was dead. Not a matter of honesty—a matter of too much pain for her to talk about.

Cherish would've been a lot less trouble dead, and that was my honesty—because from the set of her chin and the desperate spark in her eyes, she wasn't going anywhere. "The Auphe." The olive skin grayed. "How did you get involved . . . never mind." She shook her head, the sweep of hair coming to rest on her shoulders in a fall of black silk. "I can't leave. I can't do this alone. And *Tío* Seamus told me to come to you if I needed help. That you had friends, strong ones. I'll need all the friends and all the assistance I can get. Oshossi wants me, and he won't stop. He will never stop. This is what he does."

"Hunts," Robin cleared up our confusion. He'd turned over a glass-sprinkled cushion and dropped onto the couch. "Never met him, but he's some sort of immortal creature. Likes to hunt. Likes to fight. Usually sticks to South America. He's a forest type. Nature and whatnot. Likes dogs too. Obviously. If he's come all this way to this place of concrete and steel, he is wholly pissed." He propped his feet on a dead cadejo-canine. "So you stole from him, eh? Thievery. Tsk." He raised eyebrows at Nik and me with his next words, "Uncle Seamus, eh?"

Cherish gave a deceptively delicate shrug, recognizing a kindred spirit. "It's a hobby. Everyone should have one." It was said breezily, but the pallor remained. Between the Auphe and this Oshossi guy apparently wasn't the best place to be, but it didn't have her offering to leave. "And, yes, if it is any concern of yours, Uncle Seamus. Step-papa Seamus, whatever you wish to call him. Family takes care of family. But when I told him that what I took I had already sold and couldn't retrieve it, he sent me here. He knew he and I couldn't handle Oshossi alone." Damn Seamus, jumping at the chance to make things harder for Niko. The more distractions, the easier he'd be to kill. Then again, he wanted Promise. He wouldn't want to risk her. He might have genuinely thought the group of us had a better chance than just he and Cherish. And when Promise told him the case was off, I doubted she'd brought up that the reason was the Auphe . . . for my sake.

Cherish sighed, a self-deprecating downward curve to her lips. "No matter how much they glitter, the things I 'borrow' tend to bore me quickly. I did try to make up for it. I gave Oshossi the name of who I sold it to, but either he can't find them or he'd rather have his revenge instead."

"Or maybe," I said, "you really pissed him off at, I don't know, the worst possible time for everyone in this whole goddamn room. You think maybe that's it?" I didn't care if I sounded bitter—I was. Uncle Seamus. Step-daddy Seamus. A full-grown daughter out of nowhere. An entire *family*. What the hell had Promise done to my brother?

That had some color returning to her face as she said frostily, "And what did *you* do to piss off the Auphe, *hijo de puta*?"

"I missed the family reunion." I bared my teeth in a humorless grin. "And, yeah, Mom was a whore. Thanks for the reminder."

It was true. I existed solely because Sophia had taken gold to screw an Auphe. I existed because not only had Sophia whored herself out to anyone, but also to anything. Like Cherish herself had said, everyone needed a hobby. And despite what Niko had thought . . .

It looked like Promise's hobby was lying.

6

Niko

"She didn't know about your mother. She didn't mean it, not that way. She's one hundred and sixty-five, but in human terms that makes her barely eighteen."

I didn't care about Cherish's age, and I barely heard Promise's words.

Samuel and his colleagues had come and gone. They'd taken the cadejos with them as well as the rug that was ruined beyond repair. They hadn't said a word other than a murmured "careful of the teeth" amongst themselves as they rolled the bodies in tarps. They were knowledgeable; Samuel hadn't been wrong about that. He didn't ask any questions when he arrived or when he left. He simply did the work, paying his debt.

If he thought he was done, he was mistaken. He may have helped to save Cal, but he had helped to betray him first. Seeing him made me remember things I'd sooner not. The sensation of my sword's blade sliding into Cal's abdomen. The absolute certainty that I was going to have to kill my brother to save his soul. That I had failed him. Knowing I chose to die with him hadn't changed what had twisted my gut, had frozen my brain . . . the feeling of . . .

There were no words.

I, who had read so many of them in my life, had

no words for it. The blade slipping through the resistance of his flesh. The blood. On me, Cal's blood, warm and flowing. Dripping from my hands to the floor. Red with a quick patter like rain. Images and sensations; I had those. So many. But no words. Words were for defining, capturing. I didn't want that moment defined. I only wanted it gone. Over a year later and I still just wanted it gone.

Samuel could clean up every dead body in the city if he desired. I didn't know that it would ever be enough.

I leaned my forehead against the glass and watched the lights below, the nearly empty street. Promise's bedroom was large, her apartment spacious, but now it felt tight and small. I wanted to be down there running. Running was like meditating. It stilled your mind, sank your thoughts in a pool of calm until there were no thoughts at all. There were only light and peace and the ground thudding beneath your feet. Clarity.

Sometimes.

It should've put Promise's deception in perspective, the dark memory of my brother dying in my hands . . . by my hand. Yet somehow it didn't.

"She didn't know." Hands rested on my shoulders and a warm weight leaned into me from behind. "I promise you, Niko. She didn't."

"I know." But Cal didn't. He thought it was written on his forehead. Son of a whore. Gypsy trash. Monster. All the lies Sophia had told him for fourteen years were always waiting for the opportunity to whisper: They know. They look at you and they know. *Everyone* knows. No one was quicker to think the worst of my brother than he himself.

But he dealt with it. He always had; he always would. He was strong. Promise knew that and she knew this wasn't the conversation I was going to have. Not now.

"But Cal doesn't know." The breath at my ear was touched with regret. "I'll have her apologize."

"Promise," I said coolly as I straightened. "Stop."

When she'd asked in the past—most often among tangled sheets, I'd told her about my life, childhood, and time on the run. I told her about Sophia, amorality made flesh, a woman who'd tarnished our lives as equally as the Auphe. The reason I required absolute trust, the reason Cal thought everyone but me lied. I talked more about Cal, the things he wouldn't have minded her knowing. She'd already inadvertently learned the worst. I told her all. From the beginning of our relationship, I had given her only the truth. And when I asked her about her past . . . I received quick snapshots. The Great Plague of London in the 1600s. How blood was hard to come by then. It was the only time she'd ever mentioned feeding. How you drank to survive and tried not to kill. "Dead cows don't give milk, do they?" she'd said with a sadly bleak smile. Yes, you tried not to kill, but trying wasn't always succeeding.

Ugly truth, but truth.

She told me how she had come to America following the Civil War, how vampires blended into the larger cities. Her parents were long dead, or so she'd heard. Vampires didn't stay together long in large groups. They didn't crave the contact of their own kind the way humans do. Nature's way of keeping the predators from outbreeding their food source. She didn't talk much of her lovers. The hundreds of years she'd lived, I didn't expect to hear of every one. She hadn't mentioned Seamus.

She did tell stories of her five human husbands. Elderly and wealthy, but she'd been fond of each one. She'd lived through the Great Plague. I didn't blame her for wanting to be surrounded by beauty and life after that. I could understand her wanting to feel safe no matter what might arise. And if it took millions for her to feel that way, I didn't judge. I understood and I trusted—me, who, like Cal so very rarely trusted anyone.

Cherish might have shattered more than a window tonight. I didn't know. Not yet.

We all had our needs. Promise needed safety. I needed trust. Complete trust. No daughters swept under the rug. No lovers so close that she'd considered them uncle or father to that daughter. She had an entire family and hadn't told me. Had us work for the vampire who'd once been her *mate* and hadn't felt the need to mention it. I had always been honest with her, and it seemed now she had been anything but.

I moved from beneath her and took my sword from the bed. "It's my watch."

"Wait." Regret was still there, stronger than ever, but so was temper. The ivory sheath of a nightgown rippled as she turned over to face me. Waves of hair were twisted into a loose braid for sleep, and a rainbow-chased black pearl choker was fastened around her neck. She slept in pearls. She always slept in pearls . . . even when she slept in nothing else. A slim nude form and pearls—proof that poetry could live and breathe. And keep secrets.

Like Sophia.

She took a handful of my shirt to hold me still. She was strong enough that she might succeed if I put it to the test. "You should've told me," I said without compromise. Because wasn't that who I was? Niko Leandros, who had his brother and his honor. You fell between the two or you fell outside. It sounded inflexible and it was, but Cal and I had shared that same lying, manipulative mother. We both had survived her in different ways. I doubted I could change my ways now.

"I should have but . . ." She took a deep breath. "You, Niko. You raised a good man. Despite all that he had against him, you did that with Cal. I raised a thief, one who has little care for anyone but herself. I raised a predator who was reluctant to give up drinking when the rest of us did. I raised a liar, who would say anything to get what she wanted." Her hand released the cloth and flattened on my chest as she went on somberly, "She's also charming and bright and loves me . . . I hope." Her eyes clouded. "I didn't do well. It shames me. I keep hoping she'll mature. She was loved, and yet right and wrong are only words to her. My failure, and it's hard to live with, much less tell."

Cherish wasn't so different from Goodfellow, then. But that wasn't true. Robin did have a care. They were few and far between, but he did care for us and stood with us when we needed him. And if we needed him to stand away, he would do that as well. Cherish didn't seem inclined to go anywhere. She feared the Auphe, but they were legend to her. She'd not ever seen one, and consequently, in her mind, this Oshossi was as much of a threat. Survival—it was pass or fail. She'd thrown herself decisively on what might be the failing side—and was dragging our chances ever further down.

I waited as she looked away and then back, eyes blacker than the night outside. "And Seamus . . . Seamus, Cherish, and me, we lived in the time of blood. We were a family of predators. We took blood wherever we found it. Sometimes we didn't kill, but sometimes we did. Three take so much more blood to nourish than just one. I endured it. Cherish wasn't old enough to know it was wrong, and Seamus . . . Seamus enjoyed it. I didn't see it in him at first, but more and more he showed it. He had a passion for killing, far more than he had for his art or for me. And because of that, I left him, but not as soon as I should have. I was fond of him. Cherish and I were safer with him than alone, so I closed my eyes when I should've been running."

"But you did leave," I said, "finally." There was judgment in that last word. There was no denying it.

"Finally." Her voice hardened slightly. "And I heard he changed. I saw him again, and he seemed to have genuinely altered his ways. I wouldn't have involved us with him otherwise, never, but tell you about him and my past?" Her lips tightened. "You don't know the time we lived in. What we had to do to survive. What the humans would've done to the three of us if we'd been caught. You have no idea."

"No, I don't, because you didn't tell me." Not once as we lay there with sheets twisted around our bodies.

"No, I didn't, did I?" Her temper spiked. "Maybe I didn't want to see how you would look at me when I told you in detail the killer that I used to be. That my family was no more than a trio of monsters, living no matter the cost to the innocent." The temper, the regret—it faded, to be replaced with puzzlement. "You're difficult to live up to, Niko. You are not quite twenty-three years old. You're a *child* in comparison to me, but you live this life, this black-and-white life. You have this unbreakable core." Her hand rose to my cheek, then fell away. "Honor. It's a wonder. It's a curse." The hand went back to my chest and she pushed me away. "You have your watch. Go."

I didn't. I needed trust, but I needed Promise as well. She hadn't lied. I held on to that. She hadn't actually lied. But neither had she told the truth—and it was a great deal of truth not to tell.

And that was something I couldn't pretend hadn't happened. I couldn't close my eyes and pretend she hadn't held back a major part of her life, that she had hidden the knowledge of her family from me. And more.

"You met him while Cal and I were fighting on the beach. He smelled him on you." I stared, unblinking, at her. "A business meeting or reminiscing about that past you don't want to talk about?"

"Business, although it is honestly none of yours." The heat was back, but she reined it in and tried again when I didn't move, saying, "Except for Seamus and Cherish, I've been honest with you since we've been together, Niko."

Except for my family, my mate, my life. Except for all that.

"Except" . . . a small word to do so much damage. This time I did go. Silently. Leaving her behind.

And I felt . . . nothing. I walked to the living room, hollowed out—an empty shell called honor. I didn't believe in ghosts, not even in our world, yet at that moment I was one.

So be it.

If I was a cold ideal, with every bit of compromise stripped away, then that was survival. If I were an abstract, that's how it had to be. Never mind the things it made me wonder. As in, Had Sophia won? As in, Outside honor, did I truly exist at all?

Then Cal punched me in the nose and, as a starburst of pain flared behind my eyes and I tasted blood, I decided that I did. I wasn't precisely happy about it at the moment, but I did exist. "Better?" he asked, shaking out the ache in his hand.

I wiped at the trickle of blood on my upper lip and replied honestly, "Actually, yes."

"I didn't break it. Hell, I'd need a baseball bat to take out something that big." He went to the kitchen and returned with a hand towel full of ice. "Here." He was the one I was relieving. During his watch, he'd finished taping up the window with black plastic. The Vigil, ever efficient, had removed all the blood and glass with the bodies. If not for the missing window and rug, you wouldn't have known what had taken place. "And since you let me hit you," he added, "I figured you needed it."

I had let him and I had needed it. An odd thing to need, pain. A smaller one to set a much larger one free. If it's not free, you can't acknowledge it, you can't see it. And if you can't see it, you can't fight it.

I hadn't known, but Cal had. Cal wasn't black-and-white like me. Cal was all shades of gray. He knew right from wrong, unlike Cherish, but that didn't mean the end result was any different. He never let that knowing stop him from making the necessary choice. He had a care for some, and such a ferocious carelessness for others that the contrast was . . . stark. Cal wasn't the good man Promise labeled him, but he was a man. He struggled every day to be one—to be that and not the monster he suspected was ready to crawl out at any second. Endlessly stubborn, utterly loyal, and could throw a fairly decent punch when needed. Compared to that, good was highly overrated.

With black hair shoved behind his ears, he wiped a blood smear from his knuckles onto his jeans and offered, "You know, I've never had a problem with hitting a girl."

Promise was correct: I really had raised him right.

I pulled the ice pack away from my nose and felt the bridge—straight and unmarred. As he'd said, unbroken. "A girl might be one thing," I said, the taste of salt still on my tongue. "You'd be hitting a woman who would then paddle your ass like the Whiffle-ball-bat wielding child that you are."

"Ye of little faith." There was a dark tone under the flippant words that had me shaking my head.

I cuffed his head lightly. I did have one person to depend on always. It was well worth remembering. I filled him in on what Promise had told me. Seamus's agenda had more history behind it than we suspected. It made his brutal jealousy easier to understand.

"In all honesty, I'm not sure who's to blame, Promise or me." Everyone else—Robin, Cherish, and her companion—had gone to bed. Cal and I stood alone in the living room. The lights were low but I could still see my breath form in the cold air leaking around the plastic. "Sophia made sure you and I both have our issues."

"Issues?" he echoed incredulously. "Jesus, Nik. People on Dr. Phil have issues. We have atomic-powered, demonic-flavored, fresh-from-the-pits-of-hell, full-blown fucking neuroses. Freud would've been in a corner sucking his thumb after one session with us. And don't ever think our bitch of a mother did worse by me than you. She stole your childhood, she was the reason you had to stand between me and her again and again, she made you the one that *had* to tell the truth, because all she could do was lie. Thanks to her, we both have walls around us like steel. If she ever taught us anything, it was that the only one we can trust is each other."

He looked at me and winced. "Black eyes. Sorry." Pushing my hand with the ice pack back toward my nose, he continued, "We learned differently with Robin. He lies for fun. He doesn't mean it. He's so full of shit with us we wouldn't believe him for a second." Which was true, and a puck's way of being honest. "But Promise . . ." Cal shrugged.

I waited for him to say "I told you so." He was the one who had smelled Seamus's scent transferred from her to me. I expected him to tell me to cut her loose immediately. But he didn't. Not quite.

"She didn't tell you the truth," he went on. "Maybe she didn't lie outright, but she didn't tell you she has a kid, about Seamus, that they were a family. That's a big deal. Huge. If she's not telling you that, what else isn't she telling you?"

"You think I should give her up, then?" That freed pain wasn't going anywhere. It simmered and swelled like the ache of a broken bone. It wasn't alone. There was anger there as well—anger and betrayal.

His lips turned downward at the corners. "What do I think? Let's see. I have a woman who loved me but

I couldn't be with because—forget truth—she wouldn't tell me any damn thing at all. And I'm sleeping with a wolf who if she wants an after-sex snack might decide that's me, but I still like her anyway."

I hadn't known that . . . that there might be the potential for more than sex between Delilah and him. I should have. Delilah wasn't afraid of Cal. That was rare among the supernatural community, and I knew how incredible that must've felt to him—to be accepted. How could he not want more of that?

"What do I think?" He mused as he bent to pick up his gun from the coffee table. "I think you deserve the best," he murmured, studiously not looking at me as he turned away to absently eject the clip from his Glock and slam it home again. "But there's no such thing as the best. There's good enough, though. Sometimes. Can you trust her for good enough?" He started for the hall, pausing only to say, "She made you happy, Nik. A happy brother's not such a bad thing. And, Nik? I don't have a problem being suspicious enough for both of us."

When he was gone, I thought of how Promise hoped her daughter cared for her. I never had to hope my family cared for me. I knew.

Family—it can be the making of you or the breaking of you. If it had been only me as a child with Sophia, with no one to protect, to stand with, to share that cold, empty life . . . Sophia could've been the breaking of me. Cal . . . Cal had been the making of me.

I settled in to watch for the Auphe, Seamus, and any more of Cherish's problems. I turned the lights all the way down and did silent katas in the dark. You could lose yourself in the smooth movements, in the structure and the balance. If you let yourself. I didn't. I moved and listened and watched. I shifted the inner tangle of emotions aside and pushed away the image of pale blond and earth-brown hair spread over a silver-gray pillowcase. I ignored the phantom sensation of skin against mine, intermingled breath, and a giving warmth under my hands.

Conflict and confusion could get you killed. Focus and a calm mind kept you alive.

I doubted Seamus felt conflicted or confused—he knew exactly what he wanted—but that next morning he was dead nonetheless.

The sun was barely coming up when Cal's cell phone rang. It was lying on the couch where he'd discarded it after calling Samuel hours before. I wasn't surprised it was Samuel again. Cal wasn't the most social of creatures. Very few people had his number, especially since he'd convinced Robin to stop writing it on bathroom walls.

"Yes?" I answered.

"Niko?" Samuel said.

"Yes," I repeated evenly. Despite his help with the cadejos, I was still on the fence regarding Samuel. I couldn't imagine that would change anytime soon.

From his reserved tone, he picked up on that. "We have a cleanup at your friend Seamus's place. You might want to take a look first, since he was your client."

"He's hardly our friend and no longer our client," I said shortly. "If we do go there and he's alive, I'll kill him. And as I'm human, I can be as overt as I care to be. And right now I'm in the mood to be extremely overt."

"Trust me, the alive thing, you don't have to worry about that."

He was right. An hour later we were looking at Seamus's body and head, neither of which shared a relationship anymore. When that person was trying to kill you, you like to see that sort of thing with your own eyes. To be certain—and I was certain: Seamus wouldn't be a problem for me anymore.

"Well, this has to be the best news you've had all week," Robin observed, nudging the decapitated head with a foot covered in one highly expensive shoe. There was very little mess. Once the heart stops beating, which would've been nearly instantaneously, there's nothing to pump the blood out. Despite what most literature said, vampires did have hearts that beat as human ones did, and they stopped just the same.

"He's been drinking blood," Cal reappeared from a quick recon of the loft.

Promise, who'd been looking at Seamus without a hint of emotion in her eyes, lifted her gaze. "Drinking? How do you know?"

"The dead girl in the bathtub was pretty much a dead giveaway," he answered grimly. "Her neck's torn out. I guess Seamus wasn't taking those Flintstone vitamins you guys swear by. Bastard." He delivered a perfunctory kick to Seamus's body, which rocked under the blow.

Although she had said she would kill him herself, Promise now winced and said with dark melancholy, "Seamus, *cara mo anam*, how far you fell."

I almost reached out and ran my hand in one sweep from her shoulder down to her wrist, but I didn't. Although, current differences aside, I understood how she could feel that way about him considering their history—bloody and violent though it may have been. She wasn't feeling for him, but for what she thought he had managed to become. Another lie—his this time.

"Cal."

"What?" He folded his arms stubbornly and glared at me. "He tried to kill you, and it looks like he killed enough girls to have the Vigil on his ass. He deserves exactly what he got."

Robin, for once defusing the pressure rather than

adding to it, said lightly while scanning the walls, "His art will most likely triple in value. Anyone for a souvenir?"

Only Cherish seemed shocked and upset. She knelt by his torso and rested her head on the still chest. *"Tío. Papa."* There were no tears, but grief hung gray beneath the pale brown of her skin. Xolo, in what was turning out to be typical behavior, lurked in her shadow. Cherish raised her eyes to Promise. "This is your Seamus, *Madre*. Our Seamus. Why do you just stand there?"

"Yes, this is Seamus, and he was a killer long past our killing days. He killed innocents and he tried to kill Niko. He's my Seamus no more." Promise's melancholy disappeared under an iron determination. "Obviously, he won't be needing his place any longer, and Oshossi's cadejos don't know of it. They do know of my penthouse. You will be safer from them here as well as from the Auphe, *hija*." She reached down and smoothed the black hair.

"But Oshossi . . ." Cherish began instantly, her mood shifting just as quickly to demanding and desperate as she rose from Seamus's body.

"No matter what you think, Cherish, Oshossi isn't nearly the threat the Auphe are. This is the best way to protect you, and I do want you protected. Call us if he manages to find you again and we'll do what we can to help you." Pausing, she corrected, "I'll do what I can to help you." She felt she couldn't speak for me, and I certainly wasn't sure I could speak for Cal in this case. He watched out for me the same as I did for him, and while he had suggested last night that I would be happier with Promise than without, there was no guarantee he would want to lend our support to Cherish when we could least afford to give it. I'd say Robin would be even less inclined. But as for me . . . I couldn't not say it.

"I'll come as well."

Cal's jaw tightened, Cherish's son-of-a-whore remark still with him, I knew, but he gave in. "Shit.
Fine. *We'll* help." The "but I don't have to like it"
hung unspoken in the air.

"Lemmings," Robin sighed, "all of us. Still, it
should be entertaining if we don't end up dead and
buried." He walked to one wall and took a painting
of blues, purples, and an acid green. "I wonder who
did our artist friend in. The Vigil is good, but good
enough to take Seamus's head without a struggle?
They would definitely be a force to be reckoned with."
He considered another painting and took it as well.
"Ah, now, this one I like." It was a nude, of course,
in a startling primary red.

"A force indeed." I gave Seamus one last look and
then dismissed him as ancient and decomposing history. If I nursed a feral satisfaction, no one need know
about it. "Are we done here?" I addressed everyone,
but Cal in particular, whose face had gone from annoyed to bored in a heartbeat as Robin had rambled
on about the power needed to kill Seamus.

"Yeah, I'm more than done." He headed for the
door.

Cherish's eyes followed us as we left, and they
weren't saddened anymore. They were brilliant with
anger and fear. She really was in a trap of her own
making, but from what I'd seen, she could hold her
own in a fight. Young or not. It might be enough. It
might not. The same could be said of us.

"You would go with them?" she demanded incredulously. "You would choose them over me?"

Promise stopped in the doorway at that, softening
further. "If you had seen the Auphe but even once,
you would know the escape I'm giving you. Now,
there are those outside who will be in to clean this all
up. Get the keys from them. And please be as careful
as you can. Know I'm never far."

"But I am never close, am I?" she said softly, but

with a trace of bitterness. It could've been aimed at herself or her mother, but she shut the door between us before I made the determination.

"And this is why I'm glad I reproduce in the old-fashioned way," Robin said as he balanced the paintings that were too large to tuck under an arm. The Vigil were four men waiting at the end of the hall for us to be finished with our business. They were dressed in uniforms, not brown or gray, but somewhere in between. They could've been movers or exterminators. No one would know or care enough to ask—which is no doubt how they managed to get away with a good deal of what they did. No one noticed; no one cared. Much as I did not care either. I was more curious about Robin's comment than I was about the Vigil's cleanup methods.

"Which would be?" I asked. Not once had I come across in any book a hint as to how pucks multiplied. Since there were no females of the species I was sure it was, if nothing else, noteworthy. And, no doubt, profoundly pornographic. These were pucks after all. Someone had once called Goodfellow a mitotic bastard. It was a clue, but it didn't go far enough for picturing it in your head . . . if you were perverse enough to want to.

"Should I decide to double your pleasure in all things Goodfellow, you'll be the first to know," he retorted with a wicked grin. "Participation isn't strictly necessary, but I always enjoy an appreciative audience. Volunteers are especially"—he caught Promise's eye and shifted smoothly—"but never mind that. I was thinking Thai for lunch. Any takers?"

Promise's gaze moved to meet mine. What I saw there . . . I wasn't sure what it was. A chance? An unwillingness to surrender what we had? Both perhaps, and both still built on secrets. She had compromised with me . . . my half-Auphe brother. Our ongoing battle with those monsters. She had been loyal when it would've been in her far better interest to be otherwise. She had risked her life. Actions are supposed to speak louder than words.

I still wanted the words.

I wanted the truth—whole and unvarnished. I wanted it all. With my mother, I had had nothing. With my brother, I had the words, the action, and the truth . . . no matter how grim it might be. I had no experience with the territory that lay between the two extremes. I didn't know that I could dwell there.

I caught Cal's elbow before it could connect with my ribs. I looked from Promise to him and he tapped his nose meaningfully. "I'm good for another one," he said.

"You're a good brother," I replied dryly. Despite his good, if overly physical, intentions, now wasn't the time to make any decisions. It was time to concentrate on the Auphe—they were certainly concentrating on us.

Cal had said they would come. He'd said it hollowly in the dark of his room where the only light had come firefly-distant through the window and from the sickly gray illumination flowing around his hand. They would come and they would come soon because that's how he thought . . . no, how he *knew* they would think.

I wanted him to be wrong. And it wasn't that the more time without the Auphe, the more time we had to sharpen ourselves, to prepare. It was a good reason, but that wasn't it. I wanted him to be wrong because I didn't want him thinking that his thoughts were the same as Auphe thoughts. They weren't. Cal was not Auphe. In the past, I'd threatened those who'd said that. And I'd hurt those who'd attempted to act on their belief, inflicted a great deal of pain with an even greater lack of regret. I wouldn't have anyone believing Cal was Auphe, not even himself.

But in another way I wanted him to be right. If he were right, then what I suspected from what he had seen in Washington Square Park would be wrong, and I'd never wanted to be wrong so much in my life.

The universe, in its infinite indifference, didn't care either way. The Auphe came that evening.

Filthy, malevolent monsters.

I was oiling the katana when the first whirlpool of tarnished silver light formed before me. I had the dining room table covered in newspaper with the rest of my blades fanned in a semicircle, waiting their turn. I heard a door slam against a wall, the sound of spraying water, and Cal shouting, "Auphe!" If a gate was opened close enough, within a few blocks of him, he'd feel it . . . just as he felt this one.

And the one that followed.

Cal came running down Promise's hall, dressed only in sweatpants, still soaking from his interrupted shower. His face was already set, frozen and blank. He had the knife he kept with him always and the gun he must've taken into the bathroom with him. Prepared. He had believed what I hadn't been able to drive from his head. That Auphe blood was Auphe blood. That Auphe was Auphe.

Two gates . . . one less than he had said. It was a small number, and I was afraid that made me right and him wrong. On the other hand, two Auphe were enough for a suicide run, as Cal had guessed. We would see.

I stood with katana ready. I'd seen my first Auphe when Cal was three and I was seven. I was sure they'd been there since Cal was born, spying, but that was the first time I actually saw one. It had been at our kitchen window while we ate supper. Sophia had been out doing what she did: drinking, conning, or whoring. All three at once, maybe. I'd known from a younger age than seven that that's what her life was. This time she'd gone out instead of bringing her work home with her. It was better that way. Fish sticks and cartoons for Cal. A sandwich and a book for me. Sixteen years later, I thought wryly, things weren't so very different.

I hadn't minded being home alone then. It was safer. There was no yelling or slurred insults or thrown whiskey bottles. There were none of Sophia's "friends," the kind that paid before they walked through the door. There was quiet, Cal's occasional laugh at the tiny TV screen, and *The Lord of the Rings*. The librarian said it was too much book for me, and I'd told her she was wrong. But when I'd lifted eyes to see what shared the winter night against the small dingy window, I wondered if I'd been the one who was wrong.

The glow of red eyes, the triangular white face with tarnished silver teeth so wickedly fine you couldn't begin to count them all. It could've come straight from the pages in front of me. It smiled as I froze. Smiled and then tapped a black nail against the glass. The sound convinced me of what my eyes couldn't. It was real. Monsters were real. Those awful things Sophia said about Cal's father . . . I'd managed to turn my head to see my brother. He was on his last fish stick, face bright and happy as the TV burbled. I jerked my eyes back to the window. Empty. I'd swallowed hard and felt warm wetness at my crotch.

Real. It was *real*.

I'd put Cal to bed, which was my bed too. Sophia wasn't wasting money on two beds when we both fit in one. It was the first time I was glad she was cheap; it let me watch Cal, protect him. And now I knew he really needed it. Sophia was a liar, but the one time I wished she had lied, she did worse. She told the truth. I had cleaned up and washed my pants in the bathroom sink. I didn't sleep a minute that night, and I didn't say a word to Sophia when she came home, but it didn't matter. She saw it the next day—the spidery handprint on the window. Cal was sitting at the

table with the bowl of oatmeal I'd fixed him when she
bent down to be face-to-face with him. "Daddy came,
didn't he?" Her smile had less teeth than the monster's, but it was as cold and hard. "Daddy came to
see his special little boy. His little half-breed freak."
I still remembered the crumpled look of confusion on
Cal's small face—his eyes wide and wary with dread
behind long black bangs.

Every time I saw an Auphe, I saw my first monster.
I felt that echo of that first knowledge that there were
things foul and hideous in the world. But now? Now
I was ready for the monsters . . . the murderers . . .
the dealers of death. And when the Auphe came
through the light, I was ready for it as well. I couldn't
think of it as female, no more than I would've thought
of a shark as male or female—just as death. I sliced
at it, but the narrow head and pale flesh slithered
under the blow so quickly that it was inside my guard
almost before my eyes registered the move. The predator unparalleled.

Almost.

As it lunged at me, it impaled itself on the dagger
I held in my other hand, close to my hip. I didn't say
anything. There was nothing in an Auphe worth wasting words on, but I did smile. It was a Sophia smile,
cold, hard, and satisfied. Then I ripped the blade upward, from abdomen to bony sternum. Where Cal's
blood had been warm on my hand a year ago, this
blood was cool and slippery.

"You are quick." It moved an inch closer, giving
me a smile of its own as bone scraped and caught on
steel. "For a sheep."

I was. I was quicker than Cal and Promise, and
close to a sober Goodfellow. I excelled at what I did.
I was a scholar, a friend, and a brother, but beneath
it all I was a killer, pure and simple. Better at taking
lives than anyone or anything you'd meet walking the

street. I'd made sure of it. And this evil was the reason why.

I ripped the blade free and slashed it across its
throat. But its throat wasn't there. I was quick.

Auphe was quicker.

I felt the claws ripping across my chest and I dove
for the floor. Ignoring the puddle of Auphe blood
pooled on the wood, I swung both blades outward in
an open scissors motion and caught its legs. Barely.
Trailing more blood, it leapt on top of the table and
then back onto me, taking me down. For all the damage I'd done, to an Auphe it was superficial. It could
live with it. I didn't plan on letting it. This time my
blade punctured its chest, but not its heart. They
didn't carry their hearts in the same place as humans,
and suicide run or not, this Auphe had no plans on
going anywhere without me.

The Auphe laughed from above, tasting its own
blood as if it were wine. "A worthy piece of prey.
Struggle all you wish. We shall take you, we shall take
them all, and only then shall we take him." This time
teeth found my throat just as my other blade, strapped
to my thigh, found its heart between its ribs from behind. I felt a jolt of satisfaction as strong as the pain
that flared under my jaw. Getting a knee between us,
I heaved it off.

With my blood flowing down my neck, I was halfway up when it came back with my knife embedded
in its heart. Still fighting. Essentially dead, but still
fighting. I pulled my blade out of it and sliced it across
its abdomen, spilling its guts to the floor. It kept coming, taking one step, another, until it fell. Finally, it
fell. It was the first time I'd ever seen shock in the
eyes of an Auphe. A human had killed it, a sheep
with mere blades.

Then came the second one.

There was silencer gunfire. . . . Cal . . . But the

Auphe was as quick as the first. It came across the hall—touched with some blood, but not much, and moving so fast that I only managed to get the knife in my hand up bare inches before it was on me.

But Cal was on me first.

He wasn't as quick as the Auphe, but he knew where this one was going. Cal had a head start and he made use of it. He hit me hard, his back slamming against my chest, and almost simultaneously the Auphe hit him. We impacted the dining room wall and hung there, pinned. Cal gave a guttural, "No. Me first. You take me first." A human shield between the Auphe and me, protecting me where his gun had failed to. I tried to push him off, but in this he was as strong as I was, if not stronger. Cal would die for me. I knew it, but I didn't have to accept it. I shoved again. Neither he nor the Auphe moved.

Despite the strained bulge of Cal's bicep, one brutal clawed hand held Cal's wrist down and the gun along with it. The other hand closed around Cal's neck. That narrow jaw dropped to reveal its ripping capability in all its savage efficiency. Cal faced it head-on. "Me first," he snarled again. "Take me, you bitch. Go on. *Do* it."

There was a hesitation, then the jaws closed and it laughed. "You do not know. Cousin. Brother. Auphe." It laughed again, and this time when it spoke I thought my eardrums would bleed. The Auphe language was as sharp as my blades, as brutal as a bullet-shattering glass. With every unnatural sound Cal tensed against me tighter and tighter. Then the gate appeared behind it and it sprang backward, disappearing just as Robin's sword blow from the right and Promise's from the left would've taken its head. Instead the gray light took half their blades before the gate vanished.

Cal fell off me. He tried to push away, but couldn't coordinate the movement. He did manage to hit the wall solidly enough to lean against it beside me. His eyes were infinitely aged beyond that long-ago three-year-old boy, but the dread was the same. "You're bleeding," he said, the words syrup slow, before sliding down the wall and sheathing fingers in his still shower dripping hair as he drew up his knees. "I can't do this." He looked up at me with more desperation than he'd ever given an Auphe the satisfaction of. "You have to let me go, Nik. You have to."

And selfish son of a bitch that I was, I kneeled down beside him and gave him my answer.

"No."

Blind. I was so damn blind. I didn't see what he was asking for. Not until his eyes fixed distantly on the gun that had dropped from his hand to skitter across the floor when the Auphe had disappeared. Cal wasn't talking about running this time.

Auphe were quick, Cal was quick, but I'd never been so quick in my life. I grabbed his shoulders and held him firmly against the wall. "You promised me a long time ago. You promised you wouldn't do that to me. You may as well pull the trigger on me first," I said quietly, "do you understand?"

He swallowed thickly and bent his head to butt it against my chest like he hadn't since he was five or six years old. "What did it say?" I asked, moving one hand to cup the back of his head. He'd understood it, one of the flashes that came from those missing two years, picking up the Auphe language. I wished he hadn't, because I'd known without asking what it had said—I didn't need to speak Auphe to understand what I'd wanted so badly to be wrong about.

The Auphe Cal had killed last year in Florida had been male. The last male we'd seen. Turn it around and you could say Cal had killed the last male Auphe.

When Cal had said all the Auphe in the park were females, I'd been uneasy. And when he'd confirmed the last Auphe before them, the dead one, had been male, I'd gone from uneasy to a balance of sharp worry and denial. Then I saw the shock in the eyes of the Auphe I'd just killed. It hadn't expected to die. This hadn't been a suicide run. They thought the four of us couldn't take the two of them. They'd wanted to kill me in front of Cal and to make sure he knew, truly understood their new plan for him. No death. No escape. Nothing half so easy.

"They said . . ." He failed and tried again, but choked on the words.

"Never mind. It won't happen. We won't let it," I denied, shaking my head. "You don't have to say it."

He did anyway. "The last male Auphe." He shuddered with every word, but it didn't stop him from repeating it in dull horror.

"I'm the last male Auphe."

7

Cal

Guts stink.

Human, monster . . . it didn't matter. They were rank, nasty, and had long ago lost the ability to bother me. They say nurses can wipe a patient's ass with one hand and eat a sandwich with the other. It's all in what you get used to, right? I lived a life where I was used to guts on the floor. Lucky me. Yeah, lucky, lucky me.

A pair of rubber gloves, a garbage bag, and I was good to go. I wasn't wasting a Samuel favor on a mess this small, and as I was the only one not wounded, it fell to me. I doubted Promise's cleaning service would've really understood. We don't do windows and we don't do body parts. Sorry.

"She'll have to move. Between the cadejos and this, the stench will never come out." Robin sat carefully at one of the dining room chairs. The flesh over his ribs was clawed and clawed deep, but other than that he and Promise had held off the second Auphe long enough that it hadn't had time to turn its attention to Niko until the first one fell. Promise was worse off than Goodfellow, bitten on her shoulder and hip, and clawed from the nape of her neck to the small of her back, but she would heal a whole lot faster than he would, and feel it less.

Nik had a good swipe across his chest and a shallow bite on his neck. As it was right over his jugular, it would have to be shallow, wouldn't it? A little deeper and he would've bled out before we could've done a damn thing to stop it. He would've died on the floor next to the Auphe and that . . .

Hell, that would've been that.

There's another fact besides the guts-stink one. Sometimes you get pushed so far. . . . So much shit happens that you end up with three choices: You can eat your gun, you go catatonic and wear a diaper the rest of your life, or you can suck it up and go on.

For Nik, I picked the last option. I couldn't have done anything else no matter how tempting another choice might have seemed for a second. Only the Auphe could make torture and death seem like a trip to Coney Island. Only they could make you wish that was the prize you won, being slowly ripped to pieces. That was the winning number and I could rip that lotto ticket up, because I'd lost big. But, hey, here's the consolation prize. I got to be the last male Auphe in the whole damn world. Hybrid or not, pathetic half-sheep mutt that I was, I was all the Auphe had to rebuild their race. Which went to prove I didn't know them quite as well as I thought I did. No suicide for them. The Auphe were mad, sure . . . join the crowd. But they were relentless too. They'd thought of a way to destroy the world before. Give them time and they might come up with another.

I was the time. Robin said Auphe lived nearly as long as he did, if not longer, but even twenty—no, eighteen now—Auphe might have trouble with world domination. But they could bide their time and breed. Build the race back up. And each successive breeding would slowly wipe out the human taint of the hybrid sire.

And Goodfellow thought he was a stud.

I bit back the jagged dark laughter. If I started that, then I *would* be in diapers when the Auphe came to drag me to Tumulus, and I didn't want that. Because if they did manage that, then Niko would be gone and any promises I made would be gone with him. I wasn't going to hell again, not to visit and not to live. The fact that I'd be insane the minute clawed hands threw me on ground glass sand under a dirty, piss yellow sky didn't make a difference. I wasn't adding to the Auphe population. I wasn't making another monster, not a single one. Worse yet, I wasn't making another one like me. Through Auphe arrogance I'd been left with Sophia for my childhood. Niko had raised me. What if the Auphe had instead? What would that baby have grown up to be?

The urge to laugh hysterically changed to the burn of bile against my throat, and I stopped thinking about it. Any of it. I had to focus on the here and now or I wasn't going to make the next five minutes, much less long enough to come up with a way to save all our asses. See me suck it up. See me save my friends and brother. See me completely ignore reality so I didn't lose my fucking mind.

I skirted my eyes around Niko's blood on the floor as I kept scooping Auphe insides and tossing them in the plastic bag. Of all the blood I'd seen in my life, that was the blood I could never get used to—my brother's. "If you think it smells, bring your deodorizer cat over here. That'll fix it up," I said grimly to Robin. "Maybe she could eat this . . . thing for us." I didn't even want to say the name. I definitely didn't want to be touching it, but as I was the most mobile, I wasn't going to let anyone else do it. And Niko had tried. He'd tried to push me into another room. Out of sight, out of mind. If he actually could've pulled the memory of the fight and the Auphe words out of my head, I think he would have. Hell, I know he would have. He'd suspected what those bitches wanted. Not that he'd told me. Never given me a single clue.

He was one goddamn good brother.

Niko wanted the truth in life. More often than not, I was happy with the lie.

"She's dead," Robin said with a snort at my ignorance. "Dead cats don't eat. She only purrs, claws my furniture, and kills man-sized dogs." He frowned at the last bit, then sighed. "What can you do? We are all true to our nature. It's how Zeus made us."

"Then Zeus can go screw himself if he's responsible for this." I knelt beside the body of the Auphe Niko had killed. She . . . *it* didn't look any less against God-and-nature dead than it had alive. Empty red eyes and metal teeth slowly losing their mirror sheen, it gave death's gaping grin. Against God . . . yeah, right.

"If I ever needed proof there's no God"—and I didn't—"here it is. No Zeus. No Allah. If there were, they wouldn't let this kind of evil walk the earth."

I heard the chair creak as Robin stood and walked away. Moments later he returned with a mop and bucket and slowly took care of the puddle of blood I couldn't force myself to look at. When that was done, his hand braced itself on my shoulder as he squatted beside me, wincing as he did. "I don't know. I did meet Buddha once, the skinny version, in India. He gave me half his rice, laughed at my clothes, and told me if I could stay celibate for an entire week I'd reach enlightenment."

"In other words, he was screwing with you."

"In other words," he agreed, green eyes nostalgic. "But he made me laugh. I didn't laugh much in those days, not and mean it. Maybe laughing is better than a god." His hand squeezed, then let go. "Now, let's do something about dumping this pasty bastard . . . ah . . . bitch in the river. I have a feeling Niko wants to pick up a LoJack while we're out and strap it to your wanderlust ass."

Robin had heard what I'd said about Nik letting me go, but he'd taken it at face value. He thought I wanted to leave in hopes the Auphe would follow me—the same idea I'd had earlier when fighting the eel. Probably for the best that he thought that. I didn't need a twenty-four-hour suicide watch with someone holding my hand while I took a piss. Niko knew I wouldn't break my promise. Goodfellow might not be so trusting. I didn't clue him in, instead settling for a noncommittal shrug. And, truthfully, it still wasn't the worst idea—except for the fact Niko would track me down faster than the Auphe, and we'd be right back where we started.

"Leaving might work," he continued. "They may follow you and forget about us. And then again, they may locate you in a few weeks or months and dump our dead bodies at your feet. The Auphe have far more patience than you give them credit for. They don't have to choose either/or. They can have their cake and mutilate it too."

That was an option I hadn't considered on the beach. Seems I wasn't the only one who could think like an Auphe. But I was the only one who could breed like one. Good old science experiment Cal. A male Auphe could impregnate a female human, but apparently a male human couldn't impregnate a female Auphe . . . or at least not as quickly as I could. Sure, I was better, being half Auphe, but it'd be easier grabbing a random guy with no gun, fighting skills, or lethal brother. Although good luck on him getting it up for a nightmare of pale skin, bone-cracking teeth, and eyes of blood. As for me . . . the Auphe and Tumulus would send sanity bye-bye on me. Madness, torture, the memories of probably the same from the past; the Auphe would get what they wanted from me. One way or the other. I just didn't know if being insane would make it better or worse.

"Are you all right? You look like you might . . ." Robin made an obvious gesture with one hand, while patting my shoulder with the other and leaning away from me all at the same time. The guy had talent.

"Fine. I'm fine." Frigging dandy. "I won't run. Nik would find me and make me wish I was dead before the Auphe actually had the chance to do it." It wasn't a lie, just a rehashing of what Nik and I had talked about on the beach . . . before I knew what I knew now. We hadn't told Robin and Promise that I'd understood what the Auphe had said, and when I'd told Niko I was the last male Auphe, it had barely been a whisper, and a garbled one at that. Robin and Promise didn't know that while the Auphe still wanted them dead, they had different plans for me. And I didn't want them to know. That kind of pity I couldn't take. If I saw that on their faces every time I turned around, it would only make all of this more real. And right, now reality was the last thing I needed.

I stripped off the gloves, tossed them on the newspaper-covered table, and reached back to wipe a sweaty hand across the top of my back. My bloody back. Half dried, the sticky residue of Niko's blood was rough against my palm. Before it had itched; now it burned. "Shit," I said. I'd been unable to look at it, but here I was feeling it. The Auphe wanted me, but not yet. First I got to see the big show. Death and despair, and you want popcorn with that?

They wanted Nik first. They wanted me to watch. Wanted me to see. Wanted me wearing his blood.

And I was.

I moved for the bathroom and the shower without another word. I stood under steaming hot water, letting it wash the blood away. I was there a good five minutes before I thought to take my sweatpants off, and it was nearly half an hour before I stepped out nude from behind the curtain. Niko was waiting to toss me a towel.

He leaned against the double vanity as I silently dried off and wrapped the cloth around my hips. He hadn't made a sound when he came in. I hadn't heard him or the door over the thundering water, and I fully expected a swat for it. I didn't get it. "Are you speaking to me yet?" he asked, folding his arms.

" 'Goddamn you, you son of a bitch' was speaking," I told him wearily.

And that's what I'd said to him after revealing I was the Last Damn Mohican, my head burrowing into his chest like when I was a kid, and Sophia had told me another bedtime story about how the monster wasn't under my bed—it was in it. That's what I'd said to him for not letting me go out the quick and easy way.

That was me, shouldering my part and stepping up to the plate as I'd promised myself I would. Way to be a man. Really showing I'd meant it when I'd said things would be all right. Thinking like an Auphe, I'd said I could do it and I hadn't, not by a long shot. Only I could manage to pull off being a monster, but not monster enough. I put the toilet lid down and sat, the back of my head thunking back carelessly against the wall.

"Pity party for yourself?" Niko asked dryly, but behind the sarcasm I could see the shadow of worry.

"Like you wouldn't believe," I exhaled. "BYOA. Bring your own angst. It's festive as hell." The bandage was white against the olive of his skin, but he was alive, and I felt the mental knot unravel a little at that thought.

"Perhaps I'll join you. My brother . . ." He stopped, took a long calming breath—probably to keep from banging my head repeatedly against the wall—and then started again, voice steady as a rock, worry to anger in a heartbeat: "My brother threw himself between me and the jaws of a shark. And if that wasn't enough, he asked the shark to eat him first. Can you imagine how I would've felt if the shark had taken him up on it?"

"I'm guessing grateful's not it." Water—not Niko's blood, just water—dripped from my hair and down my back. Cool and clean.

"No," he replied grimly.

"Going to punch him in the nose? I hear he punched you." The bruising under his eyes was more noticeable in the bright light of the bathroom. It'd been a good punch—short and precise with the exact amount of power I'd meant to go into it. Just as I'd been taught.

"No. That would be far too easy on him." He loomed. Niko could loom like nobody's business. "On you."

"Nik, it wasn't that big a risk. Hell, no risk at all." The dripping water pooled in the small of my back, still cool, but not as cool as Niko's expression. The cooler it got, the more pissed he would be. "We know better now. They won't kill me." No matter how much I demanded. "That's not in their playbook anymore."

"And as the Auphe are completely sane and utterly logical, we'll depend on that? No, I don't think so. It only takes one Auphe to get the taste of your blood and lose sight of its goal." His lips tightened. "Just one. A shark can be docile, but throw one in an ocean of blood and all it would know is slaughter. The Auphe are the same. You can't depend on madness. Or worse yet, they might not be as mad as we think. In that case, they might lose patience with vengeance and just take you. Leave the rest of us for later and take you to where I can't get you back."

It was true, although I had my doubts the Auphe would ever lose their lust for vengeance. If anyone could be mad *and* patient, it would be them.

"You'd have done the same thing," I pointed out,

going around an argument I didn't want to have and crap I didn't want to think about. Not yet. I wanted a few hours of denial. Just a few. Was that so bad?

"Logic? You? Now I know you're desperate." He tossed me another towel from the counter. "And it's my responsibility to keep you safe. The right of the firstborn. Part and parcel of being the big brother." His jaw set. "It could've taken you, Cal, do you understand? It could've taken you or killed you."

I took the towel and scrubbed at my damp hair before countering, "It could've killed you too." I swiped at my wet neck with the cloth. And it had come close. So goddamn close.

He exhaled, "This is getting us nowhere. And waiting to be picked off one by one isn't the best strategic plan spawned in history. We need to find them. Go after them for a change. Surprise them."

Go after them? Okay, that wasn't just crazy talk. That was Hannibal Lecter eating his own foot with Dijon mustard wacko. "They live in *Tumulus*, Nik. Hell's ghetto." It wasn't really hell, but it was a place—far from this world—that would make any mythological hell look like an amusement park. Two years of my life had been swallowed up by a nightmare dimension where time ran in all different directions, which explained how I'd come back to Nik only two days after my kidnapping but two years older. That was the one thing I did know about Tumulus. The rest was so thoroughly blocked out, I had only the faintest of impressions left. Rock and sand as red as blood, a sky the color of pus, and the cold of a long-closed tomb. But I didn't have to remember to know that sticking your dick in a bucket of acid was a better idea than going there.

"I don't know anything about it." I twisted the towel in my hands. "I don't know how big it is. I could open a gate right in the middle of the Auphe, for all I know. We could drop right in their laps, and that's not like Santa's lap, okay? We won't be getting any candy canes out of the deal." Tumulus. Christ. I felt the towel rip under my grip. "Not to mention the me-going-crazy thing. But, hey, why *don't* I mention that?" Only the amnesia, the defense of an adolescent mind, had saved me the other time I'd gone to Tumulus and come back. I knew it wouldn't save me again.

"Not we, Cal. Me," Niko said, absolute. He reached over and took the towel from me. "If you can get me through, I could do a little reconnaissance, that's all. I doubt odds are high that I would walk into the center of the Auphe."

Him, not me. I should've known that and would have if the mere thought of that place didn't have every nerve in me firing in dread and sheer fight-or-flight panic. Nik would never consider sending me over there. It could've been my idea and our last hope and he still wouldn't have allowed it.

"No." I was as absolute as Niko. "That's their territory. You don't take on someone like the Auphe on their territory. You should know that. You taught it to me. They could find you. Time is weird there. You could be gone a minute or a year. There could be pockets of no air." The air had been thin there, hadn't it? High-altitude thin? Hadn't I struggled to breathe when they had dragged me there from home? Hadn't I thought I'd suffocate? I felt my lungs suddenly ache for oxygen before a black curtain dropped down, wrapped around the flicker of memory, and took it away. Banished, like always.

"No." This time I snapped it. "Make that hell no. Fuck no. Any goddamn no you want. I'm not doing it."

"The time component. I hadn't considered that." Which gave away a frustration he didn't allow to show. Niko didn't forget to consider all aspects of a situation. Ever. But he'd been on target. We were basically sitting around, plastic ducks lined up at the carnival waiting for a BB gun to take us out. How do you fight an enemy you can't follow? Can't locate? They wouldn't keep playing with us forever. They'd get serious sooner or later, mad or not, tire of the games, and then. . . . yeah, then.

"What if you kept the gate open? Linking our world to theirs? That might keep time running consistently in both places."

I couldn't believe it. He was still talking about it. Fine. He could have that conversation all by himself. "We need to dump the body," I said, as if the subject of Tumulus had never come up, never existed. In fact, Tumulus was where the Easter Bunny painted his eggs—one big damn fairy tale. "Robin said the river."

Niko frowned, but it was for himself, not me. He'd brought up something he knew I had problems with—profound, mind-melting problems—and for nothing. But it wasn't for nothing. He was trying, and right now that's all we had. Grasping at the thinnest and craziest of straws. I reached over and slapped his stomach with the back of my hand. "Hey, I'm the one not speaking to you, remember?"

The frown faded. "No river. Goodfellow's since had a better idea while you were showering. Promise needs more time to heal before riding to the river is an option."

"How is she?" I asked. More importantly, how was Nik when it came to Promise?

"Resting. She'll be more mobile tomorrow."

"And will you be staying with her tonight or shacking up in a guest room?" I stood, grabbed my sweatpants from the shower, and wrung them out. "Did you decide if you can live with good enough?"

"I don't know," he answered quietly. "Not yet."

Sophia . . . that bitch hadn't done too damn well by either one of us. She'd made me a monster and made Niko the brother, father, and caretaker of that bouncing baby monster. She'd screwed us both up so badly, I didn't think we'd ever get over it. She'd burned on earth and I hoped she was doing the same in hell.

I moved past Nik into the hall and back to my room to dress. He followed. "So what is the plan, then?" I asked, pulling on jeans and a rumpled sweatshirt I fished out of my duffel bag. "Use Samuel again?"

"No." Niko picked up the damp towels from the floor, wadded them into a tight ball, and hit me precisely in the center of the chest with them. You wouldn't think cotton could sting. You'd be wrong. "I'm quite sure the Vigil would like nothing more than an up-close look at an Auphe, a nice and tidy autopsy to find out their vulnerabilities. All of which is one step away from dissecting *you*. They want the Auphe gone, and while Samuel may be willing to give you the benefit of the doubt there, who knows what the rest of the Vigil may have in mind. The less opportunity they have to focus on you, the better." And while I was human on the outside, the inside wasn't quite the same. They'd have something to look it. Good times on the autopsy slab.

"No dissections; got it." Sitting on the edge of the bed, I put on socks. "So what're we doing with it?"

"Robin called in a favor of his own."

That favor was at the door as we spoke. Ishiah's voice carried when he was annoyed, and he was almost always annoyed. This was no exception. As we entered the living room, he was nose to nose with Robin. "Your laziness and sloth know no bounds, do they?" he demanded. "I have a bar to run, my own life to lead. I do not exist solely to be at your beck and call. And I most definitely do not wake up every morning with nothing but the happy expectation of running errands for you. Difficult to believe, I know."

Robin yawned in his face. "You're so very good at that. The temper, the scowl. Absolutely terrifying. You must drink shots of testosterone in your morning coffee." He nudged the oversized garbage bag at his feet. "Here's the package. Dump it wherever you like. Stuff it and mount it as a souvenir in your bar for all I care. Your choice entirely."

"It's not." The wings flared, appearing from no-where, and a few feathers flew free. I picked up one as it drifted to the floor by my feet. Between translu-cent and white with a dusting of gold, it was twice the length of my hand. Robin had Ishiah so frazzled that he was actually molting. The puck was one gifted son of a bitch, I had to give him that. "You are not hand-ing me a bag of Auphe. I know you are not."

"Think of it as a conversation piece." Robin grinned lazily. "And I expect you to take it off my bar tab in trade."

Refusing to believe it, Ish took a step back, bent, and untied the bag. Immediately, the blue-gray eyes darkened in disgust. "Unholy creature." He retied the bag, then wiped the palms of his hands on his jeans. "One. You actually managed to kill one. You've more survival skills than I gave you credit for." He looked past Robin as he said it . . . to Niko and me.

"I've killed Auphe," Robin said in protest. "In fact, I've killed many whilst I saved the entire world last year. Didn't you get the memo?"

"I've always known about your survival skills." Ish-iah picked up the bag with little effort, despite the weight of it. "That's why history writes of the Last Stand of the Three Hundred, not the Three Hundred and One."

"Someone had to live to tell the tale. There'd be no heroes if there wasn't anyone left to talk them up, now, would there?" Goodfellow gave an arrogant tilt of his lips before muttering, "All I wanted was the company of a few hundred half-naked, oiled-up men, and out of nowhere I'm facing the entire Persian army. Where is the luck?"

"I'm certainly getting none my way." Ishiah headed

toward the door. "The next call I expect will request an anecdote for your eulogy. Anything else, and don't bother." He put his all in the growl, but as he'd been the one to save Robin's life days ago, I had a hard time buying it.

Closing the door behind him, I asked Goodfellow, "Did you ever thank him for saving your ass?"

"Gods, no," he denied, appalled. "That's not our dynamic."

"And what would that be?" Niko said. "Rabid annoyance alternating with intense loathing?"

"Exactly." He yawned again. "One shouldn't mess with a proven formula. Wake me for my watch." Yeah, good luck to Nik there, because I had no desire for a dreaming Robin to mistake me for a Spartan, naked *or* clothed.

Hours later, I was pulling my sentry duty, moving through the apartment quietly. Niko could remain still for hours at a time if he wanted and stay completely alert. Not me. I was a pacer. If I was off watch, I could snooze on the couch with the TV blaring, no problem. But waiting—that wasn't my strong suit. And staying still after this last Auphe attack? That wasn't going to happen. So I walked with skin itching and stomach on edge, waiting to feel the tidal pull of a gate opening. I ignored the faint feeling of being watched. After a battle, paranoia and adrenaline went hand in hand. It just came with the territory.

As for trying to anticipate their next move, I couldn't do it. To give me some credit, I'd been half right about the last one—too bad half wasn't nearly good enough. But right now, even with the knowledge of a partially new motive on their part, I still couldn't begin to try. Not yet. Just . . . not yet.

Coward.

As I moved from the kitchen to the living room and down the hall, I saw them. The door was cracked open enough to let me see Niko sitting on the edge of

Promise's bed. I couldn't make out many details in the dark, but I could see his hand resting on her hair as she slept. Couldn't live with, couldn't live without . . . Nik deserved better. A whole helluva lot better. But I couldn't help him make this decision, just like he hadn't been able to help me with George. Everybody had that line . . . the one you couldn't cross. I'd reached mine, which had led to a loss I didn't know I'd ever get over. Of course, it also led to Delilah, a wolf with benefits. Life—what could you do?

I didn't know where Nik's line would take him, but two days down the road, cabin fever was taking us all someplace. "Why the car lot?" I groaned as Promise's driver pulled up into the lot Robin owned. "It's not my idea of a good time." Although at this point I wasn't sure anything would be a good time. I would be happy if something just took my mind off the Auphe for a while. I'd given myself a night of denial before forcing myself far from the shores of humanity to where only monsters dwelled, thought, and planned.

But what were those plans? The thoughts came easier. Much too easy. If I could think those same blood-soaked thoughts, maybe I was treading water out where I belonged. I did know if I stayed too long, I wouldn't make it back to shore again. The more I tried to think like an Auphe, the more I was an Auphe, and I couldn't deny it. Niko could, but I knew better.

"Yes, yes. I'm sure your idea of a good time is us dropping you off at that werewolf's place and waiting in the car while you bump furries," Robin scowled. "But if I'm not getting any, no one is getting any. And for your information, as much as I dislike work, I have a business to run. One that keeps me in fine suits, a magnificent apartment, and wine that would make one weep."

"Work," Niko said. "Don't you mean robbing innocent consumers blind?"

"Caveat emptor. If you're brainless enough to be ripped off, then you deserve it. Pure economics. Survival of the fittest. Besides, I'm a trickster. It's my calling." It was twilight, and the lot was closed for the day. Robin used his key to let us in. We'd come at this time of day for Promise. She was already almost completely healed, but a wounded vampire was extra sensitive to light. Her hooded cloak wouldn't be protection enough for another day or so.

We followed him into the building and I got a look at a few cars way beyond our reach, although with the pearls we had . . . nah. Niko had a freakish attachment to his beat-up old car. So obsessively neat in every other way, he always drove a piece of shit. When I asked him why he was so fond of something that didn't work half the time, he'd answered, "I'm fond of you, aren't I?" And he called me a smart-ass.

"Look at the toys." Robin waved his hand. "I'll be in my office. And Cal, do try not to drive through the display window again. As a matter of fact, try not to touch anything. My insurance agent is only so understanding."

"Ass," I muttered as he walked away. He was never going to let me live that down. Possession didn't cut it as an excuse for driving through the plate glass in one of his cars. Just for his comment, I ran a hand along the sleek red hood of a classic Mustang. "If you're going for old, why can't you buy something like this?" I asked Niko.

"Because eating and paying rent is preferable," he answered.

Yeah, the money from those pearls was going into the bank, no doubt about it. No new toys for us. Unless it was a weapon, but those could be fun too. I opened the car door and slid in. Nice. Very nice. "You know, we could really mow down some monsters in this. It'd take them out better than my Glock."

"Stop dreaming, little brother, and get out of the

car. We live in New York now. One car is more than plenty."

Parking, she was a bitch. We were lucky Robin let us keep Niko's antique at his lot for free, because New York was definitely far more city than we'd been to when Sophia had dragged us around. She preferred the smaller towns. The cops weren't as sharp there when it came to con artists. Although there'd been nights, sometimes weeks, we'd spent alone when she was in jail. Niko and I had gotten good at telling any nosy neighbors that Mom was at the store or the post office, or at the homeless shelter serving up goddamn soup.

I ran a hand over the steering wheel, sighed, and got out of the car. Maybe a motorcycle. The great monster fighter cruising around on his hog . . . that wasn't a cliché, no. Fine. I'd be a monster fighter who rode the bus. It didn't get any more bad-ass than that. Yet I didn't have a problem picturing Delilah on a motorcycle, and it didn't seem a cliché at all.

"You can always drive my car," Niko reminded.

"I can drive the crapmobile. Jeez, how'd I get so lucky?" Of course, I could take some of the money and buy one if I really wanted it, and Nik wouldn't say a word after the fact. It was our money after all, but it *would* be a toy. While we might be flush with money now, who knew when our next paying job would be? But Niko being right didn't mean I couldn't give him a hard time. "I could feel the wind in my hair as I pushed that stalled piece of shit down the road. Can't get a thrill bigger than that."

"My limo is always at your disposal," Promise said, still paler than normal. Niko offered her the receptionist's chair, but it was done more with courtesy than the affection he'd shown her two nights ago while she slept. I wondered if she even knew about that. I still didn't know which way Nik was going to go, and I wasn't exactly sure which way would be best. He had been happy with Promise, and I liked that. But she'd broken his trust and that I didn't like . . . at all. Not my decision, not my relationship on the line, but it didn't stop me from trusting her less. I'd thought she'd always do what was best for Nik. I wasn't so sure now. Then again, considering Cherish's personality defects . . . the selfishness of a vampire teen, and the late, great ex-mate Seamus's homicidal ways, maybe she was—in her own way. It just wasn't the right way in Nik's eyes.

"No, thanks," I told her. "I'd feel like the oldest guy at the prom."

"Junior prom," Niko corrected. "At best."

"Yeah, yeah. We hear from the anal-retentive chaperone." I wandered off, moving between the cars. I took a look into the empty offices, more out of boredom than curiosity. Framed pictures of happy families, happy kids living their happy, happy lives.

Good for them. Life wasn't looking that rosy for us right now.

I shook my head and put the picture I'd been holding back down. I needed to try harder to see through Auphe eyes. Seeing . . . *knowing*, it came from a place I couldn't go to, not here. I needed to be alone. I needed quiet. Swimming with the monsters in my subconscious wasn't enough. I needed talons clawing their way through my mind, gray light, and a twist of black shadow pulling it all together. And even then I might not know any more than I knew now. Only one way to find out.

Later.

"Cal."

Niko's voice was low and serious. Instantly, I moved back into the showroom. "What?" I said, putting a hand inside my jacket and pulling the Desert Eagle from my holster. This time I'd brought the big gun, but not explosive rounds. After the eel, the cadejo, and the Auphe, I was ready for some sheer destructive power—but it was hard to justify blowing a hole through a wall and taking out Mom, Dad, and baby in a stroller on the other side. Hard to justify to Nik anyway. I, myself, was on the fence about it.

"Ten o'clock." He didn't look in the direction of the glass wall he was indicating, and I made sure to grab only the quickest of glances from the corner of my eye. White eyes were studying us . . . white with elliptical black pupils.

"Robin, get your ass out here," I said. Casual. Oblivious. "Now." Whatever it was, it was big. The eyes were the size of lemons. And whatever it was, it wasn't buying my act. It came through in an explosion of glass as Cherish and the cadejos had. I heard Robin swear as he came out of his office, "*Skata*. Caliban, you bastard. Not again." But then he saw it wasn't me in one of his cars. It was a cat, the kind that was way too fucking big for any litter box. The size of a panther, one damn huge panther, it was black except for thin silver stripes at its shoulders. The tail whipped as white eyes fixed on us, the pupils dilating . . . a giant tabby focusing on dinner. Us.

"All right," Robin said, freezing in place, "I don't enjoy at all that kind of puss—"

"If you value your life, do not finish that sentence," Promise warned, rising carefully from the chair. I had the Eagle at my side and I pointed it very slowly at the cat's chest. Quick moves weren't good with your regular pissed-off cat. I didn't think it'd be any different with this one. The tail continued to thrash as it took a step forward, its head lowering and its jaw dropping. My finger tightened on the trigger before Niko ordered, "Cal, no."

"No? You gotta be shitting me," I said incredulously. "Fluffy is coming for our asses."

"No, he's sampling our scent." True, it was chuffing air in and out and not snarling, but it didn't make me feel any better or any less like a zebra about to get its neck snapped.

It took another step and another, this time toward Promise. Niko drew his sword as slowly and carefully as I'd raised my gun. The black lip wrinkled up to show teeth that weren't pantherlike at all . . . unless a panther was crossed with a school of piranha. No way it came from the local pet store.

My finger tightened again, but as before, the cat only drew in air. Then it snapped its jaw shut and growled. Apparently, it was a signal, because someone who had to be Oshossi appeared.

About six inches taller than me, maybe more, and two or three taller than Nik. Dark skin, black hair. Kind of weird there, though. Slick like a cat's fur. Gold eyes, bright gold. Leopard's eyes. He also had the pointed teeth of a cannibal. They showed in a coldly satisfied smile. "I see we've tracked down the mother. Now where is the thief?" The cat could pick out a relative of Cherish's from smell alone? In this city? That was one talented bad-ass kitty. Cherish was lucky Oshossi and his pet had picked Brooklyn to search first, or she'd probably be cat chow right about now.

Glass crunched under black boots as Oshossi stepped forward. He wore a long black coat, black pants and shirt, and a choker-style necklace of small off-white beads. No. Teeth. They were teeth. And you could bet your ass they were human teeth, because, hell, that's just the way things worked in our life.

"Give me the thief." His voice was smooth as glass. It was the voice of a boa constrictor. "Come, walk right into my open mouth. Don't mind the fangs. Just decoration, that's all." Then one swallow and you were gone—your dumb ass gobbled up while you thought, Gee, what a nice guy.

This nice guy was carrying two machetes. Big, shiny, and as capable of chopping through our limbs as if they were trees. I had to make a decision: Keep the gun on the cat or on Mr. Slice-and-Dice. I kept it on the cat. No matter how fast Oshossi was, I was betting the cat was faster.

"The thief." The gold eyes flared and the pupils dilated just like the cat's.

"You cannot have her," Promise said.

"No?" The pointed teeth were shown in another smile, this one feral and savage. "I think I can. I think I can skin her alive if I choose. Rip her organs free and feed them to my pets before she dies. Tear away her eyelids so she has no choice but to watch. I think I can do all those things and you can't stop me." The smile widened, upper and lower teeth separating widely—I'd never seen a mouth open so wide on a human-looking face. I heard the jaws pop like firecrackers. Through that mouth they came. His voice was as hypnotic as a snake's, and that's what boiled free. A small river of serpents.

Six feet long and as big around as a rattlesnake. They were as black as the cat, and the venom-dripping fangs were the same color. They hit the floor and slithered in our direction. "All right," Robin said as he backed up, "that is more than a little disturbing."

"No shit. You think?" I pulled the trigger on the cat. We had more than enough to worry about. We didn't need Fluffy too. The first three shots hit it in the chest, blowing ragged holes the size of silver dollars in it. It didn't faze it one damn bit. My next shot missed as it leapt literally over our heads and ended up behind us. The snakes were in front of us, the cat behind, and Oshossi . . . Oshossi turned and walked off into the night. As if we weren't worth his time. He'd left us a few presents, and so long, suckers. The son of a bitch. It wasn't enough to leave his pets to kill us, but he insulted us too? Saying that's all we were worth? Like siccing a Chihuahua on the mailman. A definite lack of respect.

Then again, giant cat, a carpet of snakes . . . that did beat a Chihuahua—in deadliness, if not crankiness.

I turned, knowing Nik would protect my back, and fired at the cat again. I only clipped it as it leapt again at the same time I fired. It landed close enough to take a swipe at me, the kind of swipe that would open you like a giant can opener and spill your yummy gravy 'n' nuggets on the floor. I dove, hit the carpet, and rolled. Not under it. I'd seen what cats do to prey that end up under them. Those hind feet would rip me from breastbone to lower abdomen. Once again . . . guts on the floor.

There are lots of ways to go. That wasn't one I'd pick. I fired again into its side as triple rows of teeth were bared in a snarl that sounded like a hundred lions. I was suddenly sorry Niko had made me watch the Discovery Channel, because I could all too easily picture those teeth buried in my stomach. Hot breath on torn flesh, what should be inside of you would be outside instead . . . in efficient jaws. The gazelle bites the dust. I didn't want to be the gazelle.

The bullets hit a rib bone. I heard one break and shatter the two around it. Lucky me? Not so much. I was aiming for something a lot more vital. It jumped again, and this time I dove over the receptionist's desk, which promptly shattered under the muscular black bulk.

Shit.

I turned at the enraged hiss by my face. One of the snakes was about a foot away. The venom falling from its fangs was sizzling and burning holes in the carpet beneath it.

Shit.

There was a quicksilver slice and the snake's head spun free of its body and landed on the floor. Its body continued to thrash, but I didn't have time to enjoy the show. I jerked my eyes back to the cat. Promise was on its back with a dagger in her hand. The point was aimed at the thick neck as she slammed it home.

The cat hissed and twisted, throwing Promise off, and then it was gone after its master. Did I mention I was in the way? I shot it again as it hit me. It sent me flying from the shoulder that connected with me, and I was on the floor again. The bullets I fired went through its throat. It narrowed eyes back at me and sneezed a mist of blood into the air, bared its teeth again, and then was gone. The night swallowed it up.

I wasn't sorry to see it go. I was all for finishing a job, but when a Desert Eagle barely makes a dent, that is one tough pussycat. Next time I'd try for about ten rounds in its brain and see what happened.

I sat up, this time on the other side of yet another desk, with three more headless snakes' bodies finally stilling, then disintegrating. Like the venom, it burned the carpet when it went, leaving an S-shaped scorch mark. Niko appeared and held down a hand and pulled me up. All over the room I could see similar brands. The smell of acid-singed carpet was in the air as Promise and Robin moved over to us. I assumed no one was bitten as no one was down and writhing in agony. Humiliation maybe, but not agony.

Robin wiped his sword on the carpet and slipped it back under his coat. "Cherish," he said, looking around at the broken glass, destroyed desk, and smoking carpet with irritation. Extreme irritation, if the audible grinding of his teeth meant anything. "Promise, I fully expect your daughter to reimburse me for damages incurred, along with punitive damages for my emotional trauma and suffering. Intense trauma and suffering." He shook his head as he focused on the desk. "I just bought that. Five hundred dollars for what is supposed to be the sturdiest one on the market, and that ccoa takes it out like a catnip mouse. *Skata*."

"A ccoa?" I lowered the gun to my side, sucked in a breath still soaked in adrenaline, and cocked my head toward Niko. "You're really lying down on Name That Monster. And by the way, you are never making me watch Discovery Channel again."

"Educational channels are good for you. It kept you ungutted, didn't it? And I'm aware it was a ccoa," he said in annoyance. "Usually found in Peru. It appears that Oshossi has shipped an entire zoo from South America."

"And where is he keeping it?" It was a stupid question. Central Park was the only place big enough, although the mama boggle there was notoriously territorial. "Boggle won't be happy."

"You might be surprised, little brother. This Oshossi seems to have a way with predators, and she is nothing if not a predator," Niko disagreed. He didn't resheath his sword, just as I didn't put away my gun. Oshossi and the ccoa appeared to have left, but appearances were nothing if not deceiving.

Boggle, murderous and unsanitary as hell, wouldn't be at all pleased if we tried to question her. As a matter of fact, she and her brood might try to eat us, and they might succeed. There were enough of them and they had every reason not to like us. "We could ask her," I said, lip curling in doubt and disgust as I remembered the stench of her mud pit.

"Ask her?" Robin echoed with a disbelieving snort. "You and Niko are responsible for her being half skinned alive. She's practically summer sausage. Talking is iffy, and spooning is completely out of the question."

Which was true. We'd hired her to help us with our Sawney problem two weeks ago and things hadn't gone quite the way we'd planned. Boggle was the shit, Central Park's Queen of the Jungle, but Sawney . . . he'd been nearly indestructible. And almost as insane as an Auphe.

"Robin's right. Flippant and annoying, but right." Niko turned the katana until the flat of the blade caught the light, studied the flash. "You do know where the ccoa is going next, don't you?" He looked up at Promise, his gaze like a winter river—reflecting nothing. Any emotion he might be feeling was caught deep in the undertow.

"Yes, I know," she answered, a shadow of worry passing over her face. "Will you come?" It was said without desperation, said proudly. Even injured, Promise was more than a fighter in her own right. Together she and Cherish could probably take the ccoa. Maybe.

If there was only one.

This Oshossi who had sent in a whole pack of cadejos . . . I doubted he'd send only one ccoa to do the deed next time. We'd sent this one running for its life—that was my story and I was sticking to it. Oshossi would know better in the future. He was smart. As for helping Cherish . . . Niko had said before he would help, but that was days ago when Promise's lie was fresh.

Funny thing about lies: They don't get better with time. They fester and turn and chew a raw hole in you; they make you wonder if it was only one lie or were there others. It didn't help we'd spent three years living a lie ourselves. Niko wouldn't have told those lies if it weren't for me, but he couldn't help but remember how easy it was. People see what they want to see and believe what they want to believe. Hell, they all but lie to themselves. There was hardly any work involved at all. We practically never needed our fake IDs.

And, really, did anyone ever just tell *one* lie? Then again, weren't Niko and I lying now? Or at the very least not giving all the information we had on the Auphe—on me. It wouldn't make a difference in Promise and Robin's fate that they didn't know mine. But it was a damn slippery slope. Niko and Promise had already seen that.

I spoke up before Niko could. Made the choice so he didn't have to. "Yeah, we said we would. Let's go kick Garfield's ass. Maybe catch one and take it home to breed with Robin's cat."

Robin, eyes slanting in Niko's direction, caught my line of thought, tucked that ball under his arm, and ran with it. "Oh yes, another wonderful idea from the man whose refrigerator spawned the cheddapet, the cheddar-based life form with a thick and luxurious coat of mold. Magnifique." He was walking, gesturing to us with an impatient hand to follow, and already on his cell phone with his lieutenant sales pitbull. "Yes, yes, Jackson. You're mother is in a coma. I'm aware," he said crossly. "So she won't even notice you're gone then, will she? Now come down here to the lot and get the glass fixed before someone makes off with the inventory, your job, and what little ass you'll have left after I'm through kicking it." He snapped the phone shut.

"Pure evil," I said. "Not that I'm surprised."

"That's the fifteenth time in two months that his mother's been in a coma. That may work with the teary-eyed customers, but not with me." He gave his patented sales-shark sly grin. "Besides, I was the one who taught him that line. Great salesman, rotten short-term memory." He opened the door to the limo and looked back at me. "There's still a position available, you know."

Talk about Get thee behind me, Satan. I used a little of my Rom half to fork the evil eye at him. "How many souls a week to I have to rack up? Is there a quota? Do I have to sign anything in blood?"

"That Faust, he never could keep a secret." He gave a slick smile and got in the car.

We beat the giant hairball hacker to Seamus's loft. I could still smell the faint trace of death when we arrived. Old blood. Scrub as hard as you want, the scent still lingers. As for Cherish's scent, my nose wasn't good enough to detect relatives. I had no idea if she smelled like Promise at the genetic level or not. I could only detect a mix of pears and brandy. She smelled exactly like a dessert Robin had ordered once when he'd dragged us . . . well, me . . . to some expensive restaurant. Niko and Promise had enjoyed it, but I'd had to break out my good shoes: the black sneakers. What a pain in the ass. I'd take pizza any day. You can eat that in jeans. Hell, you can eat it buck naked on the couch if you want. As long as no red-hot cheese dripped on the important parts, you're good to go.

"Madre." She stood at the door, dressed all in white this time. There was a long white silk skirt that skimmed below her navel to reveal an amethyst on a silver hoop. She also wore a high-necked top that was a backdrop to a web of more silver and amethysts. Unlike the fake vampires that hung around the Goth bars, there wasn't a whip, leather bra, or thigh-high boot in sight.

She kept us waiting for a second and then shook off the surprise to step back. "I'm sorry. Come in. I'm glad you're here."

Once we were inside, I smelled new blood thick over the scent of the old. I also smelled goat. The chupa, Xolo, was sitting on Seamus's couch, watching a television, which looked new. I hadn't noticed one in the loft the last time we were there. Seamus probably hadn't spent a lot of time watching TV, what with all the painting and murdering. That kind of thing's time consuming.

The chupa's mild brown eyes were dazed and content as he drank the goat blood from a large glass. Apparently, that beat the tequila that they normally drank hands-down. The things were smart enough to carry around money, dress themselves, go to a bar, and point to a drink—I'd never heard one speak—but that seemed to be the sum total of their brain power.

"You sure he doesn't need a sippy cup?" I asked. The whole thing was weird. Did Cherish want it as a pet, or the next best thing to a kid? Was her biological clock ticking, but she didn't want the commitment of the real thing? Did she have a rhinestone collar for it, or a college fund? Did I actually care either way?

Nope.

She ignored me. Closing the door behind us, she fingered one of the teardrop amethysts on her necklace as she faced us. "I wanted to . . ." She trailed off and smiled, mostly at herself. "How awkward to find fault with yourself. I wanted to apologize to you, *Madre*. I'm a selfish creature, I know. But even I go beyond the pale to put my mother in danger when she's already there to begin with. I am selfish, but not so selfish I want to see anything happen to you." She dropped the amethyst and reached for Promise's hand. "You are my only family. Thirty years may pass between my visits, but you are my *corazón*. You gave me life. I don't want to have a part in taking yours."

Promise curled her fingers around her daughter's hand as I drawled, "What about the rest of us?"

That dimpled smile reappeared. "Oh, the rest of you are as disposable as last month's fashion."

"Excepting the whole millstone around our necks dragging us to certain death, you're quite entertaining." Robin gave her what looked like a leer to me but probably had a more sophisticated name. I didn't waste time trying to guess what it was. With Robin all roads led to Rome, and Rome was apparently in his pants.

Cherish's own smile slid to something with more heat in it. "You aren't wrong, *cielito*."

"Little heaven?" He raised his eyebrows. "Not so little, *anasa mou*. And you owe me several thousand dollars. Perhaps we could arrange a trade?"

"We did come here for a reason," Niko said, with little patience for the flirting. "Although I'm sure Oshossi and his ccoa would happily wait to let you consume each other before they consume you."

"Oshossi? A ccoa?" Her eyes suddenly black, Cherish dropped her mother's hand and went to the slit in her skirt. A knife appeared in her hand. "What did Oshossi say?"

"Threats," Niko answered. "Very inventive threats. I doubt you'd want to hear them."

"No, probably not." The eyes stayed black. "I can handle a ccoa. You should go."

"You could." Promise lifted her hand to touch a smooth strand of Cherish's hair, but dropped it before she did. Her expression clouded. "You were always brilliant at whatever you've done. Fighting, dancing, riding. . . ."

"Lying, stealing." Which Promise had remembered, if not said. The dimple disappeared and the smile turned rueful. Her eyes cleared. "Go, *Madre*. I'll send you its fur when I'm done. It'll make a nice coat."

"No." Promise shook her head. "You could handle a ccoa, but a ccoa and Oshossi, I'm not so sure."

It damn sure hadn't been a walk in the park for us.

"He's impressive and he seems clever," Niko remarked, as neutral with the daughter as he was the mother. "Is he?"

"He is. He is very, very clever. The stupid rarely have anything worth stealing, but if I'd known how clever he is and how determined. How proud . . . No one who steals from him shall go unpunished. And I was a fool not to have determined all this beforehand." She shook her head. "But it is done now. Until he kills me or I kill him, these attacks will never stop."

That pretty much said it all.

Niko said, "Tell us more about Oshossi. How did you meet him? What weapons does he favor besides machetes, or does he prefer to let his animals do his killing for him?"

"It was at a party. An embassy affair—not your sort

of party at all," she aimed at Goodfellow. "The nudity was partial at best."

"It's not the quantity, it's the quality," he said loftily, "but go on. Tell us how you circled in on your mark."

She went on to describe meeting Oshossi—an embassy party, he must've invested in some seriously inventive dentures to cover those pointed teeth. Both immediately recognized the nonhumanness of the other. They enjoyed each other's company, each rolling in the dough. Jewelry for her, fancy suits for him. Cherish's stolen, Oshossi's his own. "He's handsome," she said, toying with her necklace again. "Yet . . . not. He's hard planes and angles, much like an Aztec statue. But I'm sure you saw that for yourself. I never saw him carry a weapon." She frowned. "I should've known by his eyes."

"What about his eyes?" I asked. Those cold leopard eyes. Predator through and through.

"They were my eyes. Not the color, but the weighing and measuring. The assumption that everything is yours for the taking. That the world is for you to pick and choose." She yanked the necklace from her throat in one fierce motion and let it fall carelessly to the floor. "I took my measure in mirrors of gold and found myself wanting. Too bad I only realize that now."

"Yeah, too damn bad," I commented with a lack of sympathy that had Promise giving me a glance of exasperation. I understood she wanted to protect Cherish, especially as Cherish seemed to be trying to change her ways. So I could see her wanting to protect her, just like I wanted to protect Nik, but the difference was Cherish had brought this upon herself. She could have a change of heart, but she couldn't change that.

Too goddamn little, too goddamn late, and, worse yet, at the wrong goddamn time.

Niko folded his arms in consideration for a second, then told Robin, "Try looking among your kind for Oshossi."

Goodfellow frowned, "The pucks?"

"No, the rich assholes with money to burn," I said. "He's probably staying at some fancy hotel if he's not in the park. Nobody knows the room service in the city like you do."

He smiled in fond memory. "The Once and Future King, that is I. If the food is worthy of eating and the bed of breaking, then I have ruled there. I'll make some inquiries."

Cherish looked surprised we were still considering helping her. She had finally managed to put herself in Promise's place and seen the picture wasn't one you wanted hanging on your refrigerator. Not the slightest bit bright, pretty, or optimistic. No rainbows or kittens—not one damn puffy cloud or shining yellow sun in sight.

But while it was nice she didn't want to get her mother killed, it didn't much matter. Promise *was* her mother. I'd heard that makes a difference. Maternal instinct. I'd read about it in a book once. Could've been a fairy tale for all that it related to me and Nik, but with normal people—and vampires—I guess it did exist. Promise was sucked into Cherish's problems. She'd stood firm earlier, knowing that the Auphe were worse than anything Cherish faced. And they were, but you didn't have to face the Auphe to die. Lesser things can kill you. The cadejos were one thing. Now there were ccoas and Oshossi, who, like the Auphe, wasn't ever going to give up. Cherish was up to her neck in it, no doubt about it.

And so were we . . . times two.

But there was Promise, reclaiming Cherish's hand with a mixture of determination and resignation, and Niko, who was looking at me with a bemused quirk of his lips. Promise wasn't ready to give up on Cherish, and Niko wasn't ready to give up on Promise. That could only mean one thing. I sighed, went over to the couch, swiped the remote from the chupa, and started surfing for porn.

It was going to be a long night.

I woke up to the low mumble of the TV and a light touch on my skin. I reacted instantly. Promise's hand caught the heel of mine before it hit her nose and rammed shards of bone into her brain. "I'm sorry to disturb you, Caliban." With one hand she put aside the remote she had retrieved from my sleep-loosened fingers, and with the other she squeezed my hand. "It's your watch."

I pulled free from her grip, yawned, and ran a hand through tousled hair. "Yeah? Okay." I yawned one last time. "Sorry about trying to kill you. I'm not a morning person."

It was the plus side of not knowing any normal people. They could handle it. Although I didn't usually come out of sleep in a homicidal flurry. But when the Auphe were around or I had a nightmare or I was running on fumes, instincts were difficult to hold back. Hard to explain to your average-Joe roommate why you crushed his larynx when he snuck in your room to borrow your jacket.

"So I've heard." She watched as I sat up and pulled my hair back into a ponytail with a holder I took from my jean pocket. "It's almost morning. I don't believe Oshossi will be coming. Not yet. Maybe when the night comes again."

"Can't wait," I grunted. "I hate to say it, Promise, but your daughter is almost as much trouble as the Auphe." Actually, I didn't hate to say it. It was true. No, I didn't mind saying it one damn bit, not when that trouble was one more burden Nik didn't need right now. I cared about Nik, I cared about Robin, I even cared about Promise, although I trusted her a whole lot less now. But Cherish? Her I didn't have room for.

"I know. She's nearly as much trouble to me as you are to Niko." The smile was gentle, but it cut with the best of any of my knives. "But we both love you all the same."

Damn it. Promise was so smart too.

"If you start saying things like that, being a liar will be the least of your problems," I said matter-of-factly.

I wasn't pissed that she'd said it. It was true. I hadn't asked to be born, much less born a freak, and I hadn't asked for the Auphe to first use me, then to try to kill me and everyone around me, and now want me as a sire to renew their goddamn race. No, I hadn't asked for any of that on my Christmas list, but I'd gotten it anyway. And because I had, so had Nik. I was the very worst kind of trouble to him—I knew it. But I couldn't tell him that, because he wouldn't listen. No one else could tell him either, especially Promise—because he *would* listen then. And he'd be extremely unhappy with what he heard.

Niko was the most practical, grounded person in the goddamn world. Self-delusion wasn't something he gave in to, but he did have one huge-ass blind spot. Me. He knew me, faults and all, better than I knew myself, but he didn't know—refused to believe—he'd be better off without me. And pity the person who suggested it, even if the person was Promise.

He wouldn't let me go, but he might turn Promise loose. If she pushed it. She had pushed me once before and had sworn never to again. She had one lie on board now, a big one. Add betrayal to that and it would sink her—permanently; it didn't matter if she was telling the truth. If Nik had the faintest suspicion she might betray me for his own good, they would be over and done with just that fast.

She flushed, then the color faded along with the anger as she backed down. "I know she brought it on herself," she said solemnly, "but she is my daughter. I don't want to hear the truth about her any more than Niko wants to hear it about you. Even if it is a different truth."

She was right. I'd been an ass, just as I always was an ass. This was her family and you didn't get to talk shit about family unless it was your own. "Yeah, I get that. Sorry." I held out a hand. Surprised, she took it, and I pulled her a few steps closer to me as the gray light behind her shimmered then blinked out of existence. Like a popped soap bubble, the gate was gone. The gate that had led to a very bad place. Tumulus. Auphe home. Auphe hell.

One push . . .

I hadn't been pissed, not really. She'd only said the truth, and what was the point at being pissed at that, right? I didn't care if that truth reminded me I was a freak. I knew I was a freak, a thing, a monster—one even acceptable to the Auphe now. Sometimes I'd forget, let Niko convince me differently, but deep down, that knowledge was always there. And in that deep is where gates are made.

It had been there a split second before I saw it. I'd *made* it, and I hadn't even tried. I hadn't even known . . .

One push.

Holy fuck.

8

Niko

I woke up to the sound of Cal vomiting. I pulled on my shirt and was in the hall in seconds. Robin, Cherish, and that Xolo creature were sleeping in the upper part of the two-story loft. I'd taken Seamus's room, while Cal had the couch and Promise first watch. Now Promise stood outside the closed bathroom door, looking bewildered and not a little worried.

"I woke him for his watch. He was fine. We talked . . ." She didn't finish the sentence, setting a hand against the wall beside the door. "And then he said he was sick." Truly confused, she shook her head. "Humans. You get sick. Does he need a doctor?"

Humans got sick, but Cal had only once—when he was small. At the time, I'd thought it was stomach flu, but as time passed more and more I was beginning to think he'd drunk something toxic while I wasn't watching him closely enough. A lethal dose of Sophia's whiskey, perhaps—something that would've killed a completely human child, because he'd never been sick before or again. An advanced immune system; the only good thing to ever come out of an Auphe genetic inheritance.

And she, our doting mother, had so many bottles lying about that it was impossible to dispose of them all. Not that I hadn't tried . . . for Cal's sake. But Sophia had been a lost cause long before I was born.

"No," I said immediately. "No doctor." No doctor to spot what shouldn't exist in the mundane world.

"Yes, I forgot." She stepped back as I turned the knob and opened the door.

"Wake Robin for watch," I suggested as I stepped through.

"No. I'll wait. I couldn't sleep anyway." The worry deepened. "We were but talking," she murmured, with a touch of guilt in her voice. It was a guilt I'd have to worry about later.

I closed the door behind me. "Cal?"

Done for the moment, he had his forehead resting on the toilet seat. He turned to look at me, sweat-drenched strands of black hair plastered to his jaw and forehead. "She never saw it," he said hoarsely. "It was right behind her and she never saw it. Oh, Jesus." He threw up again, more dry heaving than anything else, and when he was done, I was there with a wet washcloth and a white tube.

"You know it's a crappy day when you're using a dead vampire's toothpaste. Ultrafright—it figures." He gave me a sickly grin to go with the bad joke as he washed his face, avoiding his reflection as always, then put an inch of paste on his finger and started scrubbing his teeth with a grimace.

I waited until he was done spitting and rinsing before asking, "What didn't she see?" The glance he slid me was so lost and glassy, I hated to ask again, but I did. "What didn't Promise see? You were talking to her, you became sick. What didn't she see?"

"No wonder they want me. No wonder they're so goddamn sure I'm the answer to everything. I am." He threw the tube of toothpaste in the sink and slammed both fists against the bathroom mirror, the lost quality turning to fury. The mirror cracked, but stayed in one piece. That wasn't true of the glass surrounding the shower when Cal ripped the toilet lid free and slung it. The glass flew inward, some down to the tile floor, some bouncing off the tile wall. If he'd had his combat boots on, the other wall would've been kicked in in several spots. As it was, he had to settle for a few deep breaths to regain control.

"Done?" I asked. I didn't dwell on how quickly he had done all that damage—how he'd been much faster than he normally was. As fast as I was, which he never had been, and nearly as fast as the Auphe.

A hank of hair had broken free of the tie to hang down several inches past his jaw as he turned his head to stare at me. "We have to go. Just for an hour or two, but we have to go." He moved past me, flung the door open, and was yelling Robin's name.

It happened in a remarkably short period of time. Robin, as well as the others, was told that Cal and I were leaving. When Robin protested about what had happened to the staying together to save our lives scenario, Cal had replied, "Call my cell. One ring and I'll make a gate. We'll travel back. Nik and I both will. We'll be here in seconds." He knew how I felt about that and shot me a darkly desperate look, and I'd given a nod of agreement. Something was wrong, obviously. The sooner I found out what it was, the better. Ignorance is never bliss, it's only ignorance— often with a less-than-tasty coating of your oblivious blood.

It's always better to know.

And I still thought that when we sat on the outskirts of Seward Park and Cal told me what had happened. He huddled under his jacket against the cold. "I wasn't mad." He'd hooked his fingers through the metal of the park bench on either side of his legs and clenched them there until the skin blanched white. "I wasn't even that pissed. Hell, I'd started it, trash talking her kid. I wasn't mad," he repeated, dropping his head with that still-loose piece of hair swinging low.

"You weren't angry," I said, though I knew better. Weren't angry? He was *still* angry.

I reached over and pulled the tie from his hair, letting the rest of the mess fall free, and put the holder in my coat pocket. "Not at Promise, who brought up feelings about your past and about who you are. Who was saying you're a burden to me." Which I did not expect to hear repeated—would not tolerate being repeated. Not about my brother. "But more importantly, not at Promise, who has hurt me." I rested a hand on the back of his neck and squeezed. "There are so many layers within us, Cal. Stairs, really. Standing at the top, you were fine. Truth is truth, uncomfortable or not. But go down those stairs and on every one something is waiting. Me, Promise, you yourself—with two monsters as parents. Go down far enough and anyone who's lived your life will find anger. You said something unkind; Promise said the same back. And then, to make matters worse . . ." I moved the hand from his neck to briskly swat his head. "You want to protect me. Ass. Rest assured, whatever happens with Promise, I can protect myself fine."

He rubbed the back of his head, but not with much spirit. "The human half of me might know that, but the Auphe part didn't get the e-mail. I don't remember doing it. Swear to God, Nik. I don't remember."

"Of course you don't. You didn't do it purposefully." I sat for a moment, trying for just the right analogy . . . one that could make him understand. "Do you see that squirrel?"

He looked up and saw it scampering in long dead leaves across the way. "Yeah. Fluffy. Cute. Whatever."

"Watch." I took his ponytail holder and tossed it at the rodent. It ran immediately, scuttled up the tree, and cursed me fiercely. Dye it black, and it would be a good imitation of Cal and his morning bitching. "It ran. Did you see?" Before he could respond, I asked,

"What do you think a cat would've done? Would it have run?"

He shrugged, the wind whipping his hair. "Nah, he would pounce on it. It's a cat thing."

"It's an instinct thing," I corrected. "Humans and Auphe have instincts too. Humans get angry and they snap, turn red, maybe yell, maybe even hit . . . maybe on a very rare occasion, kill. An Auphe gets angry . . ." I inclined my head toward him.

"It always kills," he finished slowly. "It gets angry and it always kills."

"You can't erase evolution." I went after the tie and brought it back to him. "You have some Auphe instincts; there is no way to avoid that. You're like the cat, only you didn't pounce. You started to, a half-grown instinct drove you to, but you didn't. And you won't."

"You don't know that." He took the tie and shoved it in his own pocket.

"I do know that," I countered without a shred of doubt. "You could've kept silent and she would've stepped backward through the gate, but you took her hand. You closed the gate and you kept her safe. You were sleepy, annoyed, about two hours away from real consciousness, and you still ignored instinct and kept her safe. You have an unbreakable will, Cal."

It was true. The Auphe had once broken his mind, but they had never broken his will.

He shook his head, not completely convinced. "You always think the best of me. When it comes to the Auphe part anyway. One day you're going to be wrong, Cyrano."

"I'm never wrong." Completely untrue, but he needed to hear it anyway. Because he was right. I'd been wrong in the past, I'd be wrong in the future. But I would *not* be wrong about this. "And trust me, the last time I thought the best of you was before you spoke your first word."

He gave a half grin. "I come by that naturally. Good old Sophia probably knew words I still don't."

"At least 'mother' was part of it. Couldn't leave the other half off, could you?"

Not true, of course. His first word had been much shorter. He still said it every day. Like this moment.

"Nik, do we . . ." The words trailed off as he settled back against the bench, the anger visibly reduced. Still there, but faded. He exhaled, "Stupid. There's no 'do we,' is there? We have to tell everybody. Hate for someone to have to die for taking the last piece of pizza." It was a joke, yet it wasn't, and it deserved only one thing.

"Idiot." I swatted again. "(A) You are not going to kill anyone over artery-clogging food. (B) We tell them only if you want to." I said it and I meant it. Without reservation.

"After what Promise did, keeping an entire family secret? You think that's okay now? Not telling them something that important?" he asked with a skeptical curiosity. "Me being the last . . . you know." He grimaced, but went on, "That won't make a difference to their survival, one way or the other, but this might. And you don't think we should tell them?"

There it was, wasn't it?

"Just because I'm your teacher doesn't mean I still don't have a thing or two to learn," I answered ruefully. "I haven't lied to Promise about you since the entire mess first came out with Darkling, but . . . I would." How odd I hadn't known that about myself. I'd assumed a situation wouldn't come along where I, the so highly principled Niko, would stoop from my pedestal of unyielding truth and honor to actually lie to someone I cared for.

I would.

Cal was my brother, but I had also raised him. My brother, my family, the one I'd protected from the moment he took his very first breath. I would tell any lie to anyone to keep him safe. Make any omission. Promise had told her lies for a different reason . . . to keep herself safe from the heartache of her failure and the blood-soaked memories of her past family. But all the lies originated in the same place. To protect. I wasn't in a position to be her judge.

"So good enough can be good enough?" he asked.

"That makes absolutely no sense, and, yes, maybe it can." For Promise and me—if she understood what Cal was to me and it wasn't a burden, maybe it could be enough. I spotted a hot dog vendor setting up down the block. "Hungry yet? You can eat all the mystery meat you want, and this once I won't say a word."

"Really? Mustard, chili, onions, the whole nine yards? And no bitching?" He stood and dug for a few dollars in his jeans. The crumpled paper appeared and he folded the bills back and forth as he hesitated. "Nik? You're not afraid, then? Of me?"

"Afraid of you?" I leaned back to drape an arm along the back of the bench and cross booted ankles. "I'm still waiting for your testicles to drop so we can buy you a cup for sparring. Now go eat your hot dog," I commanded.

The glower, snarky grin, and annoyed mask he wore as armor against the world—I'd seen the making of those over the years, and I'd seen through them just as long. This time I didn't have to. There was nothing to hide the emotion: relief, pure and strong. It was in the loosened set of his jaw, the curve of his mouth, the lightening of his eyes. Then he shifted his gaze away for a second before looking back again with the armor once more firmly in place. "Just for that, you bastard, extra onions," he promised vengefully. "Until it comes out my pores."

"And that would be different from a normal day how?" I snorted. "Bring me back some bottled juice.

And remember, just because it's orange does not necessarily make it juice. Look at the label. Try a little of that reading thing you hear so much about."

He was thinking of flipping me off, I knew it. But I also knew he was thinking of what had happened the last time he had. Ah, the interesting process of making a brace for a sprained finger using a Popsicle stick. Education at its finest. Grumbling under his breath, he turned and crossed the grass to the sidewalk. I put on my sunglasses against the just-risen sun and watched him go. Jeans, old cracked and worn combat boots, and a beat-up black leather jacket. Wind-tangled mop of hair and a scowl only a native New Yorker could've equaled. Despite what he thought, he was so human, in all the very best and worst ways there were to be human. Grit, loyalty, determination. Anger, vulnerability, fear.

Afraid of him? No. Afraid for him? Every day. Every single day.

He came back with a bottle of something purple that consisted, per label, of nearly two percent genuine fruit juice. It was effort on his part and so, against my better judgment, I drank it. The chili cheese dog was half eaten and the rest tossed to the squirrels brave enough to face the onion fumes. There weren't many.

"You only get one bitch-free one," I reminded him as he tossed a piece of bread with mustard toward a squirrel sitting on a brightly colored swing set. "You shouldn't waste it."

"I know. Just not all that hungry." He threw the last bit and wiped his hands on his jeans. After a minute of quiet, he said, "When I opened the gate, I had a flash . . . a feeling. It was what I was thinking before, but this . . ." He shrugged. "It might confirm it. I don't think the Auphe are done playing with us, with you guys yet. I think they still want their fun. The end game is coming. . . ." When they would kill us and take him to an existence a thousand times worse than any death. "But right now?" he continued. Rubbing a thumb along the arm of the bench, he studied the faint rust smear as if it held the secrets of the universe, before looking up at me and saying flatly, "I think they still want to play. Pick you off one at a time and let the rest of us wallow in it. But . . ."

"But?" I prodded.

"I don't know for sure. Hey, I'm only the diluted product." He gave a humorless grin. "Watered-down whiskey. The half-and-half of the evil empire. But still good enough for stud service. Lucky me." He gave a minute twitch that I saw him refuse to let grow into a shudder.

I ignored it. He would've wanted me to. Sometimes support is all that keeps us standing, and sometimes it's what lets us give up and fall to our knees. So instead, I snorted. "Only you could make a dairy reference melodramatic." If that were his best guess, that's what we'd have to rely on, because the Auphe followed no logic of battle I'd read of. They had the driving purpose of a dying race. They had obsession and sadistic madness; it was a mixture that was difficult to predict.

"Also, I've been thinking. . . ."

"Thinking? That's astounding, little brother," I interrupted, tilting my head down to peer over the top of the dark glasses. "Would you like a gold star for that? I'd hate for excellence to go unrewarded."

"I've been *thinking*," he repeated between gritted teeth, "maybe we should ask Delilah about Oshossi. He could be holed up in Central Park or staying someplace else and just keeping his pets there. She might know."

Or he could simply want to put off returning to where he'd lost control and opened up a gate to hell without even realizing it. Either way, I could see the benefit. He needed time, and we could use the information. Cherish wasn't going to go away, no matter how tempting it was to wish that she would. At least she'd made the offer to stand on her own. That had meant something to Promise.

I checked my watch. We had another hour before we'd said we'd be back, and a quick trip to Delilah's work shouldn't get her noticed by the Auphe. "If anyone would know his movements, it would be the Kin," I commented. "Is she at work this early?" An extra hour wasn't going to have Cal forgetting about what had happened, but as for distracting . . . I thought Delilah was up to the task.

"Yeah," he tried for a grin, but as with the chili dog, he only made it halfway through. "I think they have a breakfast buffet."

He was right. The strip club did have a breakfast buffet. I avoided it like the plague it was. We sat at a table while Delilah, not as picky in her nutritional needs, methodically made her way through an entire pound of bacon. As bouncer, she apparently ate for free. At least it was cooked. She looked at me and shook her head as she delicately snapped another piece in half and chewed. "You fight like wolf and smell like sheep. Strange." I wasn't a complete vegetarian, but I was close, and I suppose to a wolf I did smell less than predatory. Cal, on the other hand, must have smelled like the great stalker of pepperoni and cheeseburgers that he was. A meat and nitrate eater through and through.

When she finally finished the pile of pork, she pushed the plate away and leaned elbows on the table. "You two come here. What happened to not safe? What happened to Auphe? What happened to no sex? No sex." Blond eyebrows lifted mockingly in Cal's direction. "You think you are so special? You think your dick is so . . ."

I gripped Cal's shoulder sympathetically and decided that being elsewhere for this discussion was a good idea. I rose and crossed the room, dodging tables and early clientele. The bathroom was cleaner than I would've given it credit for. It was barely offensive at all . . . except for the incubus. He was one of the dancers, unless the leather chaps and G-string were simply personal-preference morning wear. With an incubus, you never knew. Like his sister succubi, he had blue and silver hair. It was tied back in a long tail that rested across skin that glittered like mother-of-pearl. Makeup and dye to those who didn't know better. Liquid black eyes took me in as he finished his business. The lascivious smile he flashed me didn't show his snake tongue, but I knew it was there.

One might think it odd for an incubus to work in a male strip club that catered to gay men, as opposed to one for women. It wasn't. Incubi and succubi had one priority, and that was to suck a human dry of energy. The sex of their victim didn't particularly matter. Did it matter to the average diner if his steak came from a cow or a bull? Incubi and succubi were no different. Male or female victims, they'd weaken or kill them and move on. I wondered how many customers had dropped dead of "heart attacks" since this one had started work here.

The Vigil had their philosophy: Humans were all fair game as long as you didn't get noticed while eating them. Cal and I had once had a philosophy as well. You don't bother us, and we won't kill you. When you were on the run, you didn't have time for other people's problems or playing hunter to lions gone man-eater. You looked after your own and kept moving. But now we'd settled. This was our home. If the occasion arose that I could make it a slightly safer place . . .

And practice was practice.

I turned and opened the bathroom door. "Delilah," I called in a low voice, knowing her wolf ears would pick it up easily over the thumping music. "Incubus. Yours or mine?"

She waved a hand and said loudly enough for my human hearing, "He started yesterday. My day off. Idiot human boss. Bad for business. Yours."

I turned back and closed the door behind me. The incubus's salacious smile turned to a baring of impressively long snake fangs. He had more than the teeth; he had the quicksilver agility of a snake as well. That helped him for nearly ten seconds—which was impressive for an incubus. They didn't often have to fight. Their prey was usually more than willing. This one, though, he was more challenge than most. The bathroom was too cramped for the katana, and I pulled my shorter wakizashi sword in one hand and my tanto knife in the other. He reared back, then jerked toward me in an attempted strike. It got him gutted for his trouble. It didn't stop him. He slithered backward, bones suddenly liquidly malleable. He streaked up one wall and across another before hurtling through the air at me. I swung my blade. A neck parted. Practice was over. Quickly.

Disappointing.

His body continued to writhe, serpentlike, for several moments, the nearly invisible scales whispering against the tile floor. When it stopped, I cleaned the cobalt blood from my blades with paper towels, and sheathed them. As I stepped out of the bathroom, Delilah was there to lock the door and slap an out-of-order sign on it. "Full now," she said. "Will eat for lunch."

I had no idea if she was serious or not, and I didn't ask. I had a thirst for knowledge, but there were some things I didn't need or want to know. This was one of them. There was something else, however, that I was curious about. The table where we'd been sitting was now empty. "Cal?"

"Manager's office." Her smile wasn't as lascivious as that of the incubus, but it was close. "Watch front door. Ten minutes."

"This, Delilah, is my *brother* you're talking so glibly about," I said sharply, catching her ponytail in a firm grip as she started away. When she lifted her upper lip in a challenging snarl, I added levelly, "Twenty minutes. He's had a difficult morning."

The snarl faded as she said, amused, "You are good brother. Twenty, if he survives."

He did, and looked a little more relaxed for it. Outside the bar, I inquired, "You did take the time to ask about Oshossi, I'm assuming. Much in the same way I'm assuming I won't have to take you to the dojo and beat a measure of sense into you."

"I asked," he responded defensively, although there was a brief sliver of panic on his face as endorphin-soaked brain cells struggled for the memory. "The Kin doesn't know anything about Oshossi. They did notice the extra wildlife in Central Park, though. So we're one for two. But she said she'd look into it."

"How much?" I asked.

"You saying the mind-blowing sex isn't payment enough?" He grinned smugly.

"No, of course not. You're a stallion," I said blandly. "How much?"

"Two K." Disgruntled, he put his jacket back on. "Bastard."

"You'll think 'bastard' when we start meditation exercises today," I said, entertained by the look of distaste that crossed his face.

"Oh, Christ, just sitting there, not doing anything. Not napping or watching TV. It's not natural." He flagged down a taxi and gave Seamus's address. "And it looks boring as hell. Why the hell would I want to do it?" he finished.

"It's about control, Grasshopper," I said, trying to keep it light. We had enough of the dark at the moment without adding to it. "Control is useful in the restraint of emotion."

"Control," he echoed. "Control is good." He went

silent for the duration of the drive. I was fairly sure he believed me when I said he wouldn't hurt anyone. Opening a gate was a far cry from picking up his gun and blowing away whomever was annoying him— which he had done in the past. But they had deserved it. Still, there were easier ways to kill than a gate to Tumulus, and he knew that. Instinct . . . reflex, whatever you wanted to call it, you might not be able to erase it, but you could blunt it, redirect it, control it. Unfortunately, Cal had a lot of anger—most of it justifiable, but that it was didn't make things any easier.

Control was the answer, at least the best one I had. No, Cal wouldn't use his Glock or his combat knife over a loss of temper with anyone he actually cared about, but opening a gate instead wasn't desirable either. Sooner or later something was bound to come out of one of them. Cal had told me once that the gates were two-way. You could go in or something— the Auphe—could come out. But with enough will you could hold it, you could make it one-way. He had done it once, but with this—opening them unconsciously—an Auphe might very well slip through before Cal could close it or lock it to one direction.

Cal stared out the window, hand tightly fisted in the pocket of his jacket. I could see the round outline of it. Cal knew all about control. He had it in spades, although it might not appear like it to anyone else. To anyone who caught him napping on the couch, snarling at the Ninth Circle's patrons, or slamming a revenant's head repeatedly against a wall until brain matter came out its ears, it might not seem that way, but every minute of every day Cal was exercising a control he wasn't even cognizant of. His mind used it subconsciously to keep two years of his life lost, to keep it from driving him insane—literally. He himself used it on a more aware level to not kick daily multiple asses of every creature out there that mocked, scorned, or outright hated him for his Auphe half. He used it to stay in one place when running, from the police seeking Sophia and then from the Auphe, was all he had ever known. He used so much of it, in fact, that I wondered . . .

Was there any left?

When we finally stood outside Seamus's building, Cal took several seconds to carefully scrape back every strand of hair and tie it off. Stalling. Thinking. "I think it might be best," I offered before he could speak, "if we waited until later to worry about telling them about the gate. With Cherish and that chupacabra there—they have no need to know, even if we knew they could be trusted."

He nodded immediately with relief. "When all this Oshossi and Auphe shit is over. Yeah, then."

I slipped off one of my Tibetan prayer bead bracelets. I wore a double row of them on each wrist. Made of steel, they were as good at deflecting a blade as they were for meditation. I handed it to him and he stretched the mala curiously, then put it on. "Robin will think we're going out," he snorted.

"I'm quite sure I don't want to know what Goodfellow thinks about anything dating related. There's only so much depravity I can face on a daily basis." I tapped the beads around his wrist. "It's for meditation. Say one mantra per bead. Do the entire bracelet every hour."

"Mantra, huh?" he said. "And what's my mantra?"

"Whatever you want it to be." The temperature had dropped drastically, and the sun was gone. Several scattered flakes of snow blew past, a few hitting my jaw. "It'll work best if it's tailored for you. A word or two or three that makes you feel calm. Safe."

" 'Thermonuclear warhead' is a mouthful." He fingered the bracelet, then pulled the jacket sleeve down over it. "So is 'wholesale Auphe genocide.' "

"Why do I think you're not trying?" I asked dryly

as the wind picked up along with the snow, and we stepped into the building. Cal, calm and safe. Unfortunately, I had to ask myself if there'd ever been a time when he'd felt that way. I paused by the stairs as it hit me. It was the memory I'd had just days ago. The Auphe at the window. It wasn't the best of ones for me, but for Cal maybe that wasn't true. It had been our routine. When Sophia left us alone, it was our time and it was a welcome time. A safe time. "Fish sticks and cartoons."

He looked at me warily as he pushed open the door to the stairwell. "All that granola and carrot juice has melted your brain. What are you talking about?"

I didn't blame him. It sounded ludicrous aloud, yet . . .

Fish sticks and cartoons; he'd been three when Sophia had taunted him about his father, but he'd been five before he really understood, before he actually saw an Auphe himself. Five years old before he'd started searching every window he passed for the nightmare that usually lives only in a child's darkest imaginary closet. Up until then, Sophia's words had just been words, ugly and frightening, but just words. When she was gone, he and I were alone with our ritual. After he was five, he never thought we were alone again. And for the two years prior to that, I hadn't ever let him think that I knew we weren't. Of all the things I'd done in my life, I thought I was proudest of that than of anything else.

"It was a long time ago." He'd been so damn young, we both had, but some memory had to linger. And if not a memory, then a feeling. "Just say it, or my new mantra will involve your head, the nearest wall, and twenty-four prayer beads an hour."

He didn't bother to say "You wouldn't," because he knew I most certainly would. Instead, he grumbled, then muttered low under his breath. I couldn't hear it, but he had said it. I could tell by the spark of surprise in his eyes. "I feel . . ." He climbed up a step and another before stopping. "Hell, I remember. I watched cartoons and you made me fish sticks." For a moment he was only a twenty-year-old caught in a pleasant memory. No monster father, no malicious mother. No impending Armageddon. Carefree. Unburdened. What he should've been, and what he never could be.

"Yogurt isn't tartar sauce, Nik," he sniped, but there was a smile behind it.

"You thought it was." And our neighbor at the time, ninety with ten cats, had given me free containers of it if I dragged her garbage can to the curb for her. Her granddaughter bought the yogurt for her, and the old woman hated it with a passion. It might be my health-conscious nutrition had begun with a mother who rarely bought groceries and a cranky cat lady who'd survived nearly a century of dipping everything in lard and didn't see a reason to change her ways.

"I was dipping fish sticks in goddamn cherry yogurt." He started back up the stairs. "I should so kick your ass."

"You should," I agreed amiably, as he moved fingers under his sleeve to bead number two and repeated his mantra silently.

"You tell anyone about it and I'll kill you." Bead number three. "Dead."

"And you'd have every right," I said as mildly as before, and far more self-satisfied than could be good for my karma.

"Damn straight I would." Bead number four. Calm and controlled, he was working his way there. Slowly, perhaps, months away—a long, long path, but he would get there. If he continued to work at it. And if I had to throw him to the floor and sit on him every hour on the hour to accomplish that, so be it.

But there is only so much meditation can do. What we found upstairs was enough to destroy an entire five hours of meditation, much less five minutes' worth.

I opened the door to see Cherish and Robin sitting at a table with cards in hand. The former had a pile of clothes at her feet, and the latter was nude except for one sock. Unfortunately, that sock wasn't in a place that would've provided the rest of us with any comfort. I said a mantra of my own. It didn't help. There was only one answer to this. I started walking. Fast.

Goodfellow had once told us he had invented the game of poker. I doubted that was true, but I didn't doubt he excelled at it. The only excuse for his catastrophic loss, catastrophic from my point of view at least, was the desire to show off his puckly attributes to Cherish. As Cal had once told me after accidentally interrupting one of Robin's more dissolute fests, there was a good deal to show off.

Green eyes turned brightly sly at the sight of us. "Niko." He knocked on the chair to his left. "We have room for one more."

"I think you already have three at the table," I said. And if I walked even faster, I wasn't the slightest bit ashamed. I, usually the hunter, in Robin's case knew very well what it was like to be prey. And as prey, you do what you have to to survive.

Run like the wind.

Cal was somewhat less restrained in his comments than I had been. "Jesus Christ, I cleaned my guns at that table last night, you perv. Where the hell am I supposed to clean them now?"

"Perhaps the same place you got laid today?" Robin said smoothly.

"How'd you know that?" Cal demanded.

"It's a sixth sense," came the complacent answer.

"Being a nosy, sex-sniffing bastard is a sixth sense? Since when?"

By that time, I was in the bedroom and with relief closed the door behind me. Promise looked over from where she was firing her crossbow at a large painting on the wall. It was an especially fine rendition of Pan of the Green Wood. He was playing his pipes for a virginal maiden clad in a sheer Greek stola. Every bolt was buried in two areas: the curly head and those puckly attributes I'd seen in passing.

"Did you know art galleries will deliver within an hour if you pay them enough," she informed me as she turned back and casually fired another bolt into Goodfellow's pride and joy.

"I think Cherish can hold her own with Robin," I said.

"I know she can. That does not mean I want the sight inflicted on me," she replied with exasperated annoyance. It was also said with a maternal protection I didn't think she knew was present. With one last shot, she pierced the chest where the heart would be before tossing the crossbow onto the bed. The room was painted a deep chocolate brown, the same color as the wide streaks in the pale blond hair that was twisted into an intricate braid. She wore different clothes than she had yesterday. The painting wasn't the only thing she'd had delivered. "I had clothes sent from my apartment, including what you have there," she offered as she noticed my gaze. "I thought Cal could borrow some of yours. Robin, of course, had all new delivered. Not many, though," she said. "I expected the entire upper loft to be devoted to them."

"To be fair, no one can go in his apartment now," I reminded. "His cat might very well kill them and use the body as a plaything." And that he'd only had a few clothes was a bad sign that Robin had had all the togetherness he could tolerate.

"Yes, his pet. How very unlike Robin to take on something that requires attention—attention that I'm sure he thinks would be better spent on him."

Pucks weren't well liked by other supernatural creatures. Their trickster personalities—in other words, the lying and stealing—didn't make them very popular. Pucks also tended not to associate with other pucks—ever—which was understandable. All those massive egos gathered together, each vying to be the center of attention—as Cal had said, "All those drama kings in one place . . . no way that would be a pretty picture."

"He gets lonely." More precisely, he anticipated being lonely. Despite having us now, not to mention the continuous faceless stream of sexual partners, one day Cal and I would be gone. When you live thousands of years, it's the price you pay for befriending humans. A mummy cat would be around much longer. Although there was Cal's Auphe blood. It was possible he could live longer than your average human. Could, but wouldn't.

I'd been the only constant for his entire life. I'd been the one who raised him. I'd been the one to help him back to sanity after he'd escaped the Auphe following two unimaginably horrific years as their prisoner. He was rational now, but even so, he lived his life balanced on the thinnest of tightropes. I'd seen the suicide run he'd once made to save me. I wouldn't be around to see the one he'd make to join me, but I knew it would come. I also knew that as much as I tried I couldn't change that.

"True, Robin and I don't always see eye to eye, but when the time comes I'll do what I can." She laid her hand on my cheek. "I hope he can do the same for me if . . ."

I knew what she left unspoken. If we made it past this. If we were still together. If I could forgive her.

Now I knew there was nothing to forgive. I tilted my head down and kissed her. A warmth of lips, a fleeting touch of silken tongue, and a taste so familiar it seemed I'd known it all my life. "I was a bastard,"

I said quietly, taking her hand and intertwining fingers with hers. "I expected perfection when I'm far from it myself. I'm sorry for that. We all have secrets. Or will."

An emotion flickered behind twilight eyes. Regret. Her hand tightened on mine. "Now I know how it feels to be on the receiving end. It's not a pleasant sensation. I'm sorry for that, no matter what my reason."

I nodded and said quietly, "Cal." Now worry joined the regret in her eyes. "You have to know and you have to remember, if there had been no Cal, there would be no me. I don't know who or what I would've been, but it wouldn't be the person I am now. I do know this though: It wouldn't be a change for the better."

"Niko . . ."

I didn't let her finish. "Just remember."

Her eyes cleared. "I will. I promise."

Time would tell.

The bedspread on Seamus's bed was brown and gold. The sheets were ivory, the same as Promise's skin. The light brown of my skin was a stark contrast to hers, yet it fit. Just as we fit—as we always fit. The touch of my hands on her breasts, stomach, hips; the feel of her beneath me, wrapped around me . . . how could that not always be?

Rosewood blinds hid the now afternoon sun as I finally lay relaxed in a way I didn't often allow myself the luxury of. There was a kiss in the dip of flesh where my neck met my shoulder. Only a kiss. Promise didn't bite, not even gently. The lightest of nips, more of a caress, really, was as close as she came. Teeth were for food to her. They had been for spilling blood and ripping flesh for the majority of her life. When that was true, biting wasn't erotic. It was the equivalent of using a steak knife during foreplay.

I imagined Seamus had felt differently. But a sociopath's preferences, whether vampire or human, weren't worth wasting thought on. I twined a mixed strand of dark brown and pale blond hair around my fingers and tugged lightly as she raised her face to smile down at me. "Are things better now?" I didn't need my brother's name added to the question to know that she wasn't talking about her and me. The warmth of her draped over me was more than answer enough to that. As for Cal . . .

I told my first lie to Promise and kept my first secret.

"Cal is fine."

I met her eyes as I said it. I could've hidden that it was a lie, covered it up with my mother's skill. Or I could've looked away to soften it. I didn't. In my mind I had no choice.

If there had to be dishonesty between us, then I would be honest about it.

9

Cal

That evening Niko and I had driven to one particular junkyard we'd been to more than once in the past. We'd passed through the unlocked gate when I let Niko know what I thought of the new arrangement between him and Promise. Honest dishonesty?

"As philosophies go," I observed, "I gotta say: That's fucked up."

"No one asked you to say. It's between Promise and me." Niko eyed my wrist and narrowed his eyes.

"Jesus, yes, I've done my meditation. Give it a rest, Buddha." I had done it, and I tried to do it every hour. So far it had worked. Either that or no one had really pissed me off. I had to say it was probably the second one, but I was still in there, meditating my ass off. Shoving the monster down. Niko said it would help, and if he said so, then that was gospel in my book. I'd do it until it became habit, and who knew? It might have me slamming less heads against the bar at work. "I'll pay my tab next week," my ass.

Habits. Meditation might make it there, but there was another old habit between Nik and me that I never needed reminding of. Without warning, I twisted sideways and jammed a foot in his abdomen. "See?" I said. "Meditation. My foot is one with your stomach."

"Forgive me. I shouldn't have doubted you. You

seem so much more at peace." Instead of the hands on the ankle and the wrench I expected, his leg twisted around mine and took me to the ground. The knuckles of his fist pressed just hard enough against my larynx to make the memory stick. "By the way, sometimes the fish sticks were fried zucchini," he added, "and cartoon Great Danes don't actually solve mysteries."

"So you were born a diet Nazi." I waited until he moved to sit up. I didn't try anything else. There was no countermove to having your larynx crushed. Choking and dying tended to take up the rest of your attention. "And now you're talking trash about Scooby. You are one evil bastard."

"So I've been told." He held a hand down to me. "By you. Repeatedly."

I took his hand, got to my feet, and dusted off the jeans I'd borrowed from him. Black, of course. "It's hard to be a ninja-slash-samurai-slash-Buddha-loving bad-ass in regular blue, huh?" I muttered. "God forbid." I picked up the bag from the ground and started deeper into the piles of metal and trash that surrounded us, following the zigzag path. I didn't limp as I went, but I wanted to. "I thought Buddha was about harming no living creature," I grumbled on.

"Buddha was a wise man." He walked beside me, apparently unaffected by my blow to his stomach. "I am not." He didn't seem particularly affected by that either.

"Maybe you should work on that." I went ahead and limped as the muscle in my leg spasmed. What the hell. It wasn't as if he didn't know.

"It'll pass," he assured me, not especially sympathetically, as I limped on. "In approximately sixty seconds. And next time you'll remember."

A few seconds of discomfort were worth a few extra years of staying alive—because staying alive or sane was looking like an easy option now—but the smell out here? Nothing was worth that. Saturday in a

Bronx junkyard—what's not to love? I pulled the
sleeve of my shirt over the heel of my hand and covered my mouth and nose. In reality, it wasn't the junkyard so much as the waste station just up the river. But
smell or not, this was where Mickey lived, and Mickey
was who we needed to talk to. Which was why we were
once again separated from the others in the loft. With
Oshossi and the Auphe, it had come to the point
where it was impossible to stay together all the time,
not if we wanted to eventually get our asses out of
the gigantic frigging sling they were in. I didn't have
to tell Niko that sooner or later the Auphe were going
to seize the chance and attack the others while we
were gone. Or us. More likely us. You didn't need
Auphe genes or a crystal ball to see that coming. Just
a brain cell, and you were set there. But our choices
were pretty much nonexistent, and sucking it up was
the only thing left to do.

We'd run into Mickey two or so years ago when
looking for parts for Nik's decrepit car. You wanted
parts for a decrepit thing, you came to a decrepit
place. Mickey wasn't decrepit, though. He could find
pretty much anything you wanted. Nothing too new,
of course, but anything used showed up in a junkyard
sooner or later. Mickey had seen us walk in back then,
smelled the difference on me, and offered up his
services . . . for a price.

Luckily, Mickey's price wasn't as steep as Boggle's
tended to be. Where Boggle loved jewels and gold,
Mickey was all about the food. He wasn't your typical
junkyard rat, content with rotting leftovers. He wanted
the real thing, he wanted it fresh, and he wanted a
wide variety. Chinese, Greek, Italian, Mexican, whatever; he liked it all. That didn't mean he didn't catch
his own meal on occasion if times were hard. In that
he *was* like your typical junkyard rat.

He ate his own.

"Smells good."

The voice was oil spreading across concrete, smooth and slick. Very slick indeed, which was Mickey all over. I slowed and looked up at a pile of cars to see liquid black eyes reflecting the setting sun. Cool and cunning, I couldn't be sure if they thought it was the Mexican food that smelled good or me. So far, the preference had been for takeout, but it didn't pay to take anything for granted. "Hey, Mick. Brought you tacos this time." And about a dozen burritos. Mickey had an appetite. A tamale to go wasn't going to get it for him.

"Been long time. Yes, long, long time." Black fur and skin slithered over shattered safety glass and rusted metal to hit the ground next to us. He was the same inky color as a cadejo, but where they had been doglike, Mickey was what I'd labeled him: a rat . . . if a rat crouched four feet high, had dark-skinned human hands, and talked. Niko said that there were old Rom legends about a shobolon, a giant rat with human characteristics. There were also legends of wererats. Whatever Mickey was, he wasn't saying. Although considering the thick accent, I was betting he had something in common with Nik and me. And we weren't part wererat.

Besides the accent, Mickey had a sense of humor. Okay, maybe not so much, but he didn't have a bad temper, which wasn't always the case with our informants. He was fairly mellow, considering what I called him. I doubted it was even close to the name he'd been given at birth.

A thick-skinned hand dropped the gnawed dead rodent it was holding and took the bag from me. Within seconds, red sauce was dripping from wickedly large yellow incisors. A naked gray tail wrapped around his feet as he ate. After the first seven tacos, he slowed down and licked his hands clean. "So, so, valued customers, picture of part. Picture of car." Mickey wasn't a mechanic by any means, but with a picture he could

track down what you wanted in a matter of thirty
minutes. Sometimes less. In a yard this size, that was
something.

"It's not about a car part," Niko said. "Not this
time. It's something a little more . . . interesting."

"Interesting." The round eyes took us in with sudden calculation. "That is new word from you, this
interesting."

"Yeah, interesting." I leaned against the cold metal
hood of a totaled car. "Because you know what,
Mickey? You sound bored. You probably are bored."
I thought about adding that he could get a nice big
wheel to run around in, but didn't figure that would
help our cause. Maturity; it was no damn fun. "We're
here to help you with that. Wouldn't you like to get
out? See some trees. Frolic in nature. Good times."

"Frolic." Another dead rat tumbled from above
where Mickey had been perched. It was the size of a
beagle, and it landed on my foot. Mickey clicked yel-
lowed teeth in a rat smile. "But, as see, frolic fine
here."

I eased my foot from under the heavy weight. The
fur was spiky and stiff with dried blood, the mouth
frozen in its last snarl. There was one poor damn bastard that wasn't going to be working at any theme
park. "Yeah, I'll bet you do." I wondered what would
happen if Mickey were to meet Robin's new cat. You
wanted interesting—that would be interesting.

Niko picked up the strand of persuasion since I
didn't seem to be accomplishing much. "This would
be an entirely new endeavor for you. Spying versus
procuring. It would pay well. Lunch every day for
three months." And while I had my suspicions that
I'd be the one making that daily delivery, Niko went
ahead and filled Mickey in on the details. Oshossi, the
basics of what we wanted to know, the zoo . . . cadejos,
ccoas, and who knew what else.

Mickey had finished the tacos and started on the

burritos, as Niko finished. "South America?" Whiskers slick with either blood or hot sauce bristled dismissively. "Tourists." With his accent, that wasn't quite fair—I doubted he had his green card. But either way, he didn't seem impressed. It was a good sign. If we could get Mickey on the inside for a day or two, long enough to find out where Oshossi was—Central Park with his animals or elsewhere—we'd be ahead of the game. For once.

Delilah had tried, but hadn't been able to find Oshossi, and his creatures wouldn't talk to her people— if they even could talk. Still, if Oshossi didn't control it, he didn't trust it, and his crew seemed to follow right along with that. And no wolf was going to bow his neck for a nonwolf. That put going undercover out for them. So what we needed was a spy, one who didn't give a damn about pride and usually gave dollar for dollar value. You hired him; he'd come through. Mickey was as close as we had to that.

If we went into the trees of Central Park ourselves looking for Oshossi, chances were we'd never come back out. There could be a hundred ccoas in there, for all we knew. They knew we were standing with Cherish, lucky us, but Mickey would be a new element—a local yokel to clue them in on the city. He'd been here at least the two years we'd known him; that put him up on them. They should see him as an asset. He might be able to find Oshossi. At the very least, he could get a head count.

If they didn't eat him first.

The thought had occurred to him too. "Three months. Your humor, such wit." He gave a chittering wheeze that was what passed for a rat laugh. "A year. Two meals a day. Every day."

And the negotiations began. It was too bad Goodfellow wasn't here. The Rom lived to haggle, but somehow that gene had skipped us. Niko had cold silence and his sword. I had my temper and my fists.

If those didn't work, we were screwed. Wheedling and schmoozing didn't come naturally to us.

But Nik did his best and we ended up with six months, two meals a day.

No way I was coming out here twice a day for half a year. Hell, there had to be delivery services that would do it. Leave the food at the gate. I didn't know who ran the yard, but Mickey didn't seem to worry that much about being spotted.

Speaking of spotting, I saw something worse than the dead rat as the two of them hammered out the deal. In one of the cars one stack over, a hand was hanging out of the window. The fingernails were dirty, the skin gray as only a corpse can be. Mickey didn't kill people—that we knew of—but the occasional bum did die in the yard of natural causes. Exposure, heart attack—it didn't matter. Mickey liked his takeout, but when it wasn't available, he made do with what was. And that wasn't always rats.

I turned away to ask, "You need a ride there? You gonna drive yourself? Or did you have a bad hair day when they took your driver's license photo?" The bared teeth let me know Mickey's lack of temper might not be all I thought it was.

He rode with us in the back of Niko's car . . . after retrieving a jar full of darkly sloshing fluid. The black eyes reflected in the rearview mirror when he lifted his head for the occasional look around. When he did, I could feel hot breath against my neck. Not a good day for wearing my hair in a ponytail. I also smelled things on his breath—tacos, rat . . . human. Digested human flesh; it was a smell you couldn't forget. If I didn't smell it again for the rest of my life, it wouldn't matter. It was something that was with me for good. It smelled like raw pork, but just different enough to make your flesh crawl. It said "You are meat." Whatever you wanted to think in your happily ignorant world, it all came down to that: You are meat.

It was dark by the time we stopped by the park to let him off. He opened the jar and begin to rub the contents across his fur in sweeping strokes. "Is blood and oil," he explained. "Smell scent of you on me." He snapped his teeth together in demonstration. "Kill me, yes. In seconds. Meet here again. Two days." Leaving the jar and large smears of the mixture on the vinyl seat, he slipped out the door and shadowed his way into the trees.

I looked in the backseat one more time after he was gone. "I am not cleaning that up. I'm not even helping you clean that up. That is nasty."

"It wouldn't matter if it were essence of pizza and hoagies. You're a lazy son of a bitch and all the meditation in the world won't change that," Nik retorted.

"Now, would Buddha have said that?" I asked with mock disappointment. "I don't think so."

"Buddha never found your underwear in the kitchen sink."

I had an answer to that ready and waiting as Niko started the car, but my cell phone rang—the cell phone that now was only for emergencies. Gate-creating emergencies. I flipped it open, saw Seamus's number, grabbed Nik by the arm, and took us. I could build a gate and walk through it, but I could also build one *around* me if there was no room for the alternative. It was more difficult, but I could do it. That's what I did in this case. Niko and I were outlined in gray light, and in a fraction of a second we were gone. Then we were at Seamus's loft, right in the path of a charging ccoa.

It was so close I could smell its breath. It wasn't as bad as Mickey's, but it wasn't exactly potpourri either. I could also see the dilated prey-seeking pupils and the piranha teeth. I could probably have seen its damn tonsils if I didn't get my ass in gear and move. I dove one way while Nik went the other. In my quick drop and roll, I could see he was a muddy gray under his olive skin, but he wasn't puking as Robin had when I'd once taken him through a gate, which was good. He also kept on his feet, which was even better. It looked like we needed all the help we could get.

There was no Oshossi, but there were three ccoas. They were quick and had been predators since they weaned from their mama's teat. They were dangerous as hell, and from the dripping saliva, also hungry. I saw the two at first; the third came from above. If they could climb a tree in the jungle, they could climb a fire escape here. And if they could leap from a rocky ledge onto their prey, they could do the same from the upper loft. It came down like an avalanche, as deadly and a whole lot faster. I'd switched back to the Glock .40 from the Desert Eagle, which hadn't done as much good as I'd hoped it would. As he struck the floor, I put ten in the head just like I'd thought with the last one, and swear to God, I almost hated to do it even though the last one had nearly turned me into lunch. It seemed more like an animal than a monster, a smart and beautiful animal. I didn't like killing it, but I did. There was a scream of pain that sounded oddly human, and a tumbling of black and silver fur over a sleek line of muscle. Then there was nothing but a big, dead cat. I shook it off. If it had landed on me, I'd be one dead son of a bitch, my throat ripped out before I could've pulled the trigger. It might just be an animal, but it had been one damn deadly one.

Robin was holding off another with his sword while Promise and Cherish did the same with the third. Promise's crossbow bolts only enraged the one attacking them. The cat was quick enough that Cherish had only struck three blows that I could tell. They were deep blows, but not deep enough to stop it. Nik was with them in seconds. He took the cat from behind. It whirled before he managed to slice it, but that didn't last long. From the corner of my eye, I saw him strike one paw aside, then evade the other, dodge the enormous snap of mouth, and impale it in the heart with his katana.

That was impossibly quick.

I knew Nik could fight. I knew he was better than I was, that he was better than nearly anything or anyone you could name. But sometimes when you saw him in action, you almost couldn't believe it—that a human could be that fast and that lethal. He'd worked at being that way since he was twelve, but I honestly thought he was born that way as well. A genetically superior athlete who could've gone to the Olympics. Instead, for me he became a killer. Too bad for him that they didn't hand out the gold, silver, or bronze for that.

I turned toward Robin to see him just finishing off his as well. And there we were. . . . Three dead ccoas. It sucked. Monsters were one thing, but this was something else. Oshossi didn't give a damn about his pets, and I'd sure as hell rather be killing him than them.

So why wasn't he here with them? He was smart, but that didn't seem smart. If he wanted Cherish so badly and his ccoas had tracked her down, why hadn't he come with them?

Cherish's teeth were bared as the ccoas' had been, and her sword dripped blood onto the floor. She realized it and covered the fangs with lips painted as red as the silk top she wore. "You came." It was said with a gratitude I wouldn't have guessed she had in her. She was coming around. She might have more Promise in her than any of us thought. "*Madre* said that you would, and you did." She gave a formal dip of her dark head. "My thanks." Raising her eyes to Niko, she said with a trace of amazement, a fellow predator's respect, "You are every bit the swordsman *Madre* said you were. I've seen nothing like it. Not in my life. Not ever." The dimple appeared. "Perhaps you could give me lessons."

"If you've seen nothing like it, then obviously you weren't watching me." Robin frowned at the blood spatter across his pants. "And *I* do it with unparalleled panache and style, but of course that wouldn't be noticed while you're so occupied ogling your mother's property."

So Robin wasn't getting anywhere with Cherish. That had to sting. I didn't think he'd not gotten anywhere with anyone he wanted except for Niko. Robin was lethal too, in a whole lot more ways than one. In the bedroom, out of the bedroom— he bragged about both. For a guy who practically excreted Rohypnol out of his pores, this had to be pissing him off like crazy. I gave him a grin to let him know I knew, and he gave me a silent snarl back. Moving over to Niko, I asked, "You okay? I know traveling isn't such a hot feeling when you're not an Auphe." Which, I thought, was why it didn't bother me.

I might not have said it aloud, but he heard it anyway. "You are *not* an Auphe," he said between clenched teeth, clenched probably to keep his lunch down, although the muddy color of his skin was fading and returning to normal. "And I'll recuperate. Give me a few minutes."

"Yeah, okay." It wasn't a lot to ask considering he'd gotten a good feel of what was inside an Auphe, and, like it or not, what was inside me. It was an unnatural thing, ripping a hole in the fabric of reality. You knew that as soon as you saw it, but to pass through that rip, you felt the unnatural twist of it to your bones. It wasn't right. It was unwholesome and awful and it wasn't *right*.

I'd used to feel that. . . . Like Robin had. Like Niko. The wrongness of it.

I didn't anymore.

Whatever that meant, whatever it said, it wasn't good.

But you play with your Auphe half and you can't expect it to stay buried. It *wanted* to play, a lot more than you did.

Robin laid his sword on the dining room table, folded his arms, and sighed. "What now? Samuel and his happy-go-lucky band of game wardens? Or are we pushing our luck there, making them our personal janitorial team?"

"I'll take them." We really didn't want to push the Vigil into thinking we were their version of overt. That was all we needed on top of everything else. And if the Auphe could get rid of an eel the size of a truck, I could get rid of three panthers. "I'll open a gate to the river. If it's good enough for the Sopranos, it's good enough for us."

I didn't wait for Niko to object, and he would have. Risking sharpening the Vigil's attention on us versus me playing with Auphe fire, he'd take the first any day. But that wasn't the right thing to do. Everyone was already in danger from the Auphe because of me. I wasn't going to add the Vigil to that. Who knew how long they'd listen to Samuel that we were okay, that we weren't going to get noticed. I squatted down to study the nearest ccoa. Because, let's face it, we did shit that had a damn good chance of getting noticed.

And we did it a lot.

"What do you think? Two hundred and fifty pounds? Three?" I opened the gate absently.

That was a mistake, thinking it was as simple as the small amount of effort involved. Thinking that I didn't need to pay attention. Forgetting how much my Auphe side did want to play.

But it had gotten so easy. Once it had brought pounding headaches and unconsciousness. Two weeks ago it had brought blood gushing from my nose or ears. Now it was like turning a key in a lock. Normal. No pain. No exhaustion. Just the feeling of doing what I was meant to do.

Maybe what I was meant to be.

The last male Auphe.

It was back . . . the cold touch, the slither of blood-thirsty satisfaction. I laid a hand on wet black fur, still warm, and lifted it back up to stare at my red palm and fingers. I had killed, I would kill again. And, hey, was that such a bad thing? Was that so wrong? To do what you were born to do . . . to follow the fire and ice that burned and seared your blood. To touch blood, to wear it, to spill it, to taste it . . .

No.

No. Absolutely fucking not.

This was not going to happen. That's not who . . . *what* I was going to be. I took all the control I had, made the massive effort, and shoved those alien thoughts out of my mind. They had to be alien . . . otherwise they were mine. All mine. And that couldn't be. It *couldn't*, damn it. Luckily, I pushed them out or down before Niko clocked me one. He'd been across the room; now he was kneeling beside me, looking grim. "Control," he said.

"I've got it. It's gone." I wiped the blood from my hand onto the black jeans.

"Pay attention." That was said with an edge, an edge that had every right to be there.

"I know. Sorry." Sorry didn't quite get it for not treating opening a gate with the cautious respect it deserved. It was wild and feral. I wasn't going to tame it, and if I weren't careful, it would eat me alive. The best I could hope to do was control it and keep it on a short leash. And watch it—always watch it. Keep a wall up. I wasn't what those bitches said I was. I was human, at least enough to stop the part of me that wasn't.

The gate was still open, the cold light spilling through the ragged gash. I sucked in a deep breath. I had it now; it didn't have me. "Let's get them through."

To the side I saw Cherish watching me with the clouded black eyes of a vampire ready for battle. "You *are* Auphe. I thought you were lying."

"Why the hell would I lie about something like that?" I bit off as Niko and Robin helped me heave the first dead weight through the light. "How'd you know?" I went on quietly for Nik's ears only. But as usual, Robin couldn't let anything be for someone else only, not if that someone wasn't him.

"You were speaking Auphe." The fox face pulled into an expression of distaste.

Those two years they'd had me—I must've learned the language then. I'd seen that when I understood the Auphe before—telling me I was the last male. But understanding it and speaking it, those were two different things. . . . And they were just two more things tying me to them.

"What'd I say?" I didn't remember, and I wasn't sure I wanted to know. If it had been anything like what was going through my mind . . . Jesus.

"I have no idea. I don't understand Auphe, and I don't want to. Imagine ground glass shoved into your ear canal. That's what it sounds like, and it's about that pleasurable to hear," he grunted as we tossed the next cat through. "But your brother knew before you started with that. He was already moving."

"Nik?" The last ccoa slid into the gray. I closed the rip and ignored the disappointment of letting it go. Control. I had it. I did.

"You opened that thing and you weren't you. Before you touched the blood. Before you spoke that hell-spawn language. I knew the second you opened the gate and weren't paying *attention*."

It was something Niko didn't allow himself often—anger—and it was completely justifiable. I hadn't paid attention and I'd nearly gotten lost. I'd gone from swearing not to open any more gates, to doing it to try to outthink the Auphe, to emergencies in case of attacks, and finally to just cleaning up around the house.

Which is how the road to hell is paved with a little maid service.

"It won't happen again," I said grimly.

"See that it doesn't. I won't enjoy knocking you out, but I will." I took it for what it was: reassurance. Niko was my lifeline. If I started to fall, he'd drag me back.

"No one I'd rather have beat my ass into unconsciousness," I said wryly.

"Not that this macho brotherly love fest isn't bringing a tear to the eye," Robin drawled, "but I think we need to talk about moving. Oshossi knows where we are now. If we don't go, every night is going to be Sundown Social at the Zoo. Pet the predator. Kiss the carnivore. All things I could do without."

It was a good point. Niko, Robin, and Promise discussed it; Cherish watched my every move with wary eyes; and I, ignoring her as I ignored most of the others who gave me that look, ended up playing Go Fish with Xolo. Which, in a strange way, was what I needed. I didn't want to think about Oshossi and his overgrown kitties. I didn't want to think about the Auphe. I didn't want to think about me.

The chupa had crept out of the back bedroom while the others talked, silently watched them with those large eyes for a while, and then moved over to me. I was on the couch, arms folded and doing my damnedest to keep my mind a blank. No matter what Niko would've said with dry sarcasm, it wasn't that easy. Xolo sat on the floor opposite me and placed a pack of cards on the artistic metal curve of table between us. The shaved dog face regarded me gravely. I scowled back. It was habit. I didn't have anything against Cherish's pet. He tended to stay out of the way, gave up the remote when I wanted it, and didn't eat my leftover pizza in the fridge. As roommates

went, he wasn't so bad. Weird, but not as bad as
Robin, who'd gotten so desperate it wouldn't have
surprised me to see him humping a table leg.

"What?" I asked. "What do you want?"

Just as gravely, he dealt the cards. Seven to me,
seven to him. Hell, why not? I played Go Fish with
him. He held up his fingers when he asked for my
cards. Any threes? Up would go three fingers. It didn't
work so great for jacks, queens, and kings, so we discarded them. Those eyes would blink, moonlike, the
fingers would flash, and the cards would go down. The
bastard couldn't talk, couldn't fight, could barely dress
himself, and he beat me seven games to three.

I turned the cards around to look at the backs. "Are
these marked? Are you cheating?" Or was I less
bright than a mentally challenged chimp?

"I hate to interrupt your vastly important task"—
Niko's hand pulled the cards from mine and slapped
them on the table—"but we've narrowed our
options."

"Yeah? Rafferty's place?" Rafferty was a healer
we'd used before. He'd disappeared months ago, but
as it was most likely a voluntary disappearance, there
wasn't much we could do about it. He wouldn't want
us sticking our noses in his business, and he had a lot
of business to take care of. His cousin was sick, a kind
of sick Rafferty couldn't heal. We'd checked his house
after a month of not being able to contact him. . . .
We had business too, and it frequently called for a
healer afterward. From the looks of the overgrown
yard, the house had been locked up and temporarily
abandoned. Both Rafferty and his cousin were gone.
Rafferty wasn't one to give up. If he couldn't cure his
cousin, he'd find someone who could.

"Figured," I added.

"Or Ishiah's," Nik said. "From what you've said, he
can handle himself well."

"Ishiah's?" I leaned back against the couch.

"You're shitting me, right? One day, and he'd kill us before Oshossi or the Auphe could."

Robin immediately backed me up—so immediately, in fact, that I wondered who he was actually trying to keep safe—us or Ishiah. "All of us shoehorned into that overgrown canary's place? That's an exercise in natural selection waiting to happen. Survival of the fittest. And that walking feather duster is fit." His left eye twitched. "Very fit." This had to be the longest Robin hadn't gotten laid in, damn, at least in the span of human existence—at least once we'd stopped braiding each other's back hair and thinking of lice as a tasty treat. "Desperate" didn't begin to cover the shape he was in.

I was so locking my door tonight.

Rafferty's place. On the one hand, Rafferty did have the nature preserve behind his house, a good location for supernatural wildlife that wanted to eat you. On the other, it might take Oshossi a while to find us there. I said so, and Niko agreed. As for the Auphe, of course they had to be watching us, but following us on the open road in daylight? Doubtful. We'd lost them time and time again when we'd lived on the run. They always eventually found us, but that we lost them to begin with proved they weren't infallible.

"Once we get the report from Mickey, we will definitely have to be more proactive about tracking down Oshossi. Robin and Mickey are doing what they can, but we need to get this resolved more quickly," Niko said. Now that we'd committed ourselves, which I still didn't think was the best idea, he was right. But helping Cherish fight off a few cadejos and snakes was different than actively going after the one who sicced them on her. He was probably going to be a little harder to take care of than the wildlife.

"Tracking him down and killing him in a truly inspired fashion," Promise added. Cherish flashed her a smile that was laced with surprise at the fiercely maternal note. If nothing else, this whole thing appeared to have her seeing the error of her criminally wild and wicked ways and bringing her and Promise closer. Good for them. Not too good for the rest of us trying to avoid maiming, mutilation, and, worse yet, pet-dander allergies, but good for them.

"What is up with Oshossi and that goddamn temper of his? And what did you steal from him," I asked Cherish, "that pissed the living hell out of him?" If I were going to get killed, it'd be nice to know it wasn't over a lamp or a first-edition Mark frigging Twain.

Cherish frowned, but turned a dining room chair around to face the rest of us and stretched languidly on it. Yep, Robin in a female body. I still couldn't figure why they hadn't gotten together at least for a night. She might be the vampire version of eighteen, but apparently had her hormones more in control than Goodfellow did.

"Oshossi," she considered. "Oshossi is powerful. Every forest in South America belongs to him and he engages in constant guerilla warfare to prevent their destruction." She tapped fingers on the knee of one long black-clad leg. "But don't think that makes him some sort of hero. He will kill anyone—*anyone* who threatens his agenda, crosses his path in the forests, or simply annoys him. He is not a creature of patience or forgiveness."

"And you, not doing your research, took him for an easy mark." Robin shook his head. "Even the lowliest of my junior salesmen would know better than that."

She glared at him. "*Regardless*, I robbed him, and that lack of forgiveness is firmly aimed in my direction. Our direction," she amended, glancing at Promise.

"What did you steal?" Niko asked as he simultaneously gestured to me, tapping his meditation beads. As much as I wanted to, I didn't blow it off. I'd seen where a lack of control had gotten me. I fingered the beads around my own wrist and got to work. I still kept part of my focus on the conversation, which had to not help the meditation. But hearing Cherish's story was important. I had at least two brain cells. I could split them up.

"Is that so important?" she countered, tilting her head, the black hair falling behind her shoulders, and her violet eyes challenging.

"Yes," he replied, unyielding. "I think it is."

"Fine," she replied, lashes half covering her eyes with what looked like regret or even shame. "It was a necklace. Gold, diamonds, and chunks of turquoise as big as a baby's fist. I endangered all our lives for one piece of jewelry that was in no way worth the price we're paying now."

"Did it do anything?" I interrupted, remembering the power-draining crown another puck had black-mailed us into getting for him.

"Do anything?" she said with confusion. "It sparkled and it looked quite amazing on me. What else would it possibly do?"

"So you hocked it?" Robin asked. "Once it wasn't quite so amazing?"

"As I said, I bore of pretty things quickly and move on to the next. I'm thinking of changing my ways. It seems a good survival move." She sighed and touched the ruby choker at her throat. I wondered if it were stolen too.

"Yes, then you can marry men with a foot and four toes in the grave. That's certainly more respectable," Robin offered with a smirk.

Promise tapped her crossbow against her leg and said in a voice as sweet as honeysuckle, "I believe, Goodfellow, that I have a painting you should see."

I saw where this was going, and it was going to be long, drawn-out, and something I'd heard a hundred times before. I went back to concentrating solely on the meditation, bead by bead. Boring but calming, as much as I hated to admit it. When I finished, those moon eyes were still on me. "Jesus," I groaned to the chupa. "Okay. Deal another hand."

I played Go Fish for another two hours. I lost again. Lately, it was a familiar feeling.

10

Niko

Rafferty's house was over the Verrazano Bridge on Staten Island. It looked the same as it had the last time we'd visited. A tired and deserted ranch house with a fence in the back large enough to hold the biggest of dogs . . . or wolves. Behind that was the nature preserve, thousands of bare trees. Robin, as always, proved adept at gaining illegal entry. I doubt he even broke stride on the simple lock. There was a click of metal against metal, a turn of his wrist, and we were inside. There the utilities were still turned on, a sign that Rafferty thought his trip would be short, or he didn't have any idea how long he'd be gone. If he'd thought the first, he was wrong. We hadn't been able to contact him in months. Normally I wouldn't have invaded his privacy, but desperate times . . . desperate measures. His place suited our needs perfectly.

There was only one problem. It wasn't on par with the Auphe, Oshossi, or, say, a two-headed werewolf, but it was a problem nonetheless, and one my brother was more than capable of handling. I handed him the toilet plunger as he walked out of the kitchen.

"There's nothing left in . . ." He stopped to stare glumly at the plunger. "Jesus."

"I doubt that. If you were he, you could simply wave a hand, unstop it, and simultaneously turn the water to wine. Sadly, we'll have to settle for your plumbing skills."

"Why me?" he demanded.

"Why not you? Or do you plan on holding it until we find Oshossi and destroy the Auphe? If so, best to avoid colas."

"This is revenge, isn't it?" He took the wooden handle with resignation.

"In a word," I replied without hesitation, "yes. Plus Buddha-loving bad-asses like me have better things to do."

He looked with trepidation down the hall toward the bathroom door. "Revenge for that. Revenge for last night with the gate. Do I even want to go in there?"

I curved my lips. It wasn't reassuring. It wasn't meant to be. He groaned, turned, and trudged down the hall. For the moment, I was alone. Everyone else was outside unpacking the two cars, and I took the opportunity to move to Rafferty's surgery. It was simply a large bedroom with three neatly made beds, shelves of medical supplies, and the kind of cheap tile that makes it easy to mop up blood. God knew it had seen its share of it. This was the place where Cal had nearly died, then did die, and was brought back. There were no ghosts in our world, I knew that, but if there had been, they would've been here.

There was the sound of a footstep. I turned with my sword drawn before my mind had time to catch up with my body. Robin appeared in the doorway, eyes immediately going to the katana. I sheathed it, but didn't apologize. There was no reason to. He'd lived through the nightmare that had happened in this room the same as I had. He knew.

"I suggest we give this room to Cherish and her pet," Goodfellow advised as he walked in and circled to take it in with pensive eyes. "Promise and you can have one bedroom, and I the other."

"And Cal?" Who hadn't gone near the room since we'd walked through the front door. Among the three of us, he'd had the better sense.

Robin raised his voice to carry. "The couch. He is the youngest, and his ass is so frequently glued there anyway." His lips quirked as an outraged "I heard that, you bastard" came echoing down the hall.

He gave a light squeeze to my shoulder. "Let us go from here. This isn't a good place for any of the three of us." Once in the hall, he promptly closed the door to the room. Out of sight, out of mind. Hopefully. "I've called all of my normal homes away from home, the hotels to the fabulous. No one who matches Oshossi has checked in. From the look of him, I doubt he's staying at a flea trap. I'll try the private residences for rent next. I know several real estate agents, most as amoral as I am. Almost." He grinned. "I'll give them a call. Now"—he clapped hands together—"where do we obtain food in this desolate wasteland? I couldn't see a single five-star restaurant from the porch."

"We might want to consider a store," I pointed out.

"Store? Food doesn't come from a store. It comes from restaurants or a personal cook, and I doubt any of you are up to my chef standards. The last time we were here, we ate microwave food. *Microwave.* You may as well circle that monstrous machine with the River Styx and call it the life-sucking Hades that it is."

"And what did you do before there were restaurants?" I asked, torn between patience and drawing my sword again.

"I had nubile maidens to feed me grapes, and muscular men with honey-covered . . ."

I went to see if Cal needed any help in the bathroom.

That evening, we sat in Rafferty's comfortable but definitely suburban living room, finishing off Chinese takeout. Robin, horrified and bemused by the bright orange sauce with the consistency of Jell-O that dripped from his chicken, was shocked into an uncustomary silence. Cal sat on the floor with his egg rolls, letting the rest of us have the couch and chairs. Xolo . . . Xolo had a talent for disappearing into the background. I sharpened my attention and caught a glimpse of his sweatshirt and hairless head through the doorway in the kitchen. He was looking raptly out of the window.

"Cherish, does he see anything?" I asked.

She turned her head, then shook it. "No, he's a simple *perrito*; pat his head, play with him, and he is easily entertained. He just likes to look."

"You did bring goat's blood, right? He's not going to start gnawing on our legs or anything, is he?" Cal said.

I saw the effort she made not to give him the look that so many others did, as if he were a bomb seconds away from exploding into metal, violence, and death. Unfortunately, Cal saw the effort it took as well. He didn't say a word, only stared back at her without expression. "No," she said. "No more than you would. And I brought what he requires."

"No more than I would, huh? You have a lot of faith there suddenly." He pushed the white carton aside and lay on his back, hands behind his head, to stare at a spackled ceiling instead of stars.

"I behaved badly before. I apologize." She exhaled, "So many apologies. I'm turning respectable, *Madre*." She smiled at Promise. "Who would ever have thought?" Then she added, "But I was startled. I had never seen an Auphe before."

"You haven't seen an Auphe yet," I said flatly.

Eyes identical to her mother's started to darken, but Promise stopped her with an upraised palm. "Don't. Niko is telling you something important. You have not seen an Auphe, and if you assume they will in any way look like or act like Caliban, then when you do see one, you will freeze and you will die."

"Chances are you'll die anyway," Robin offered morosely as he let the possibly radioactive chicken fall back into its container. "We all will. Death by Auphe or MSG; both are too hideous to contemplate." He waved an arm at the brown faux-leather couch and the carpet, worn to the nap. "Much like this furniture. This house. This Cordon Bleu–free land of minivans, tricycles, and polyester. This isn't Hades. It's worse than Hades. No. No more." Abruptly, he pushed up to his feet. "I am going home. Now. Where are my keys?"

I'd seen this coming since we'd crossed the midway point on the Verrazano. I pulled the glittering silver metal from my pocket and twirled the key ring once around my finger. "Sit."

"As if I need those to start a car," he sneered.

"True. And I could slice the tires with my katana, or remove the steering wheel, but then you could call a cab. I'm aware." I tossed the keys to him. "This is only for the night. Tomorrow Cal and I have to meet Mickey and see what he's learned. Come and go as you please then. I know we can't stay together as one, not and accomplish anything, not anymore. But let's have one last night where we all have a chance at a good sleep. Watch split five ways is better than two or three, or you up all night at your orgy of choice."

"Then this is our safe house." He made the keys disappear, reappear in the other hand, then vanish altogether. "Not my prison."

"Yes. This is a good place for Cherish to hide temporarily, but it's not a permanent answer. Everyone has Cal's cell number. As with the ccoa attack, we'll come if you call." "We" because he would not be opening any gates unless I was there. He would not be going anywhere unless I was with him. The Auphe weren't taking him from me, not again, and not for a reason so horrifying I could barely think it. I looked down at him. "Can you do that? Open another gate?"

He propped up on his elbows and shrugged. "Hey, it's only sanity." Behind the dark humor I saw his recognition of my trust in his control—that he ruled the Auphe blood, it did not rule him.

"It's not so bad, kid." Robin told him, suddenly cheerful at the thought of freedom. "Think about it. Without the gates and travelling you'd just be another cranky asshole with a gun."

"Don't go home until this is over, if you can help it. Stay elsewhere, but avoid your usual haunts. And try to never be alone even during the day," I went on dryly to Goodfellow. "But I don't think that will be a problem for you."

"And the Auphe?" Cal sat all the way up, the humor gone.

"They have forever, little brother. We don't. As long as we have our phones, you can gather us in a matter of seconds." With the Auphe, seconds was often all they needed, that was true, but the "forever" was true as well. "We can't only react to them anyway, to only expect them, not if we hope to win. Just as with Oshossi, we need to be more proactive. We need to take this war to them." Although how, I didn't know, with Tumulus out of the running. We couldn't go to them. We could only wait for them to come to us.

But Cal seemed more confident. And of all of us, he did have the best chance of thinking of a way. Not because he was Auphe, but because he'd been held prisoner by them for two years. He knew them, subconsciously at least, in a way the rest of us couldn't begin to. "Okay, you're right. It's done," he said simply. He didn't elaborate, lying back down on the carpet with arms folded across his chest and eyes closed.

"Considering they're the most murderous creatures

on the planet," Robin drawled dubiously, "how do you plan on that?"

"I'll tell you when I know," he responded.

"But if you're going to spout such outrageous claims, I think that . . ."

Eyes still shut, Cal held up his forefinger and thumb as if his hand were a gun and pointed it up at Robin, his aim unerring right between the eyes. "I'm a cranky asshole with a gun and superpowers, remember? Try giving me a day to work on it, at least, before you start bitching." Although I imagined he'd been working on it all along, just as I had. I hoped he had more success than I was having.

Robin settled back into his chair. "A day is asking much even for one with the patience of Job. Speaking of Job, the real Job, did you know he single-handedly destroyed the concept of property and health insurance in its infancy? If not for him, you would've had HMOs two and a half thousand years earlier. But he broke the First Uzite Health and Home Insurance Company in its first year."

"You are so massively full of shit." Cal folded his arms again.

"Why do you think all insurance companies now exclude acts of God?" he countered smugly.

He had a point.

The next morning Cal and I stood on the cracked concrete of Rafferty's driveway as I said to Robin, "You're not coming back here tonight, are you?"

He bounced the keys again and evaded, "As you said, we can't live this way forever."

"You think I'm having the time of my life out here getting my ass kicked in cards by something that looks like he's one step away from drinking out of the toilet?" Cal said sharply. "Suck it up."

"Trust me. I plan on it." Cal got the smirk he deserved on that one, but it was followed by an almost apologetic shake of his head, "I cannot do it. No more." Pucks weren't the types to be tied down against their will, whether something as deadly as the Auphe were the incentive or not. I was surprised he'd made it as long as he had. That he'd done it for us didn't escape me. He gave Cal a reassuringly breezy grin. "But the second I crave your sour and sullen company, I'll be back in a flash."

"Maybe I'm only sour and sullen when you're around. Maybe when you're not there driving me nuts, I'm a regular ray of fucking sunshine. Ever think of that?"

I'm not worried about you; you're not worried about me—with their invulnerability to the less testosterone-driven emotions asserted to each other, we were finally ready to leave the playground. "You might want to check on your cat briefly. Very briefly," I suggested to Robin as he opened the driver's door to his car. As I'd said before, his home wasn't safe. "If she killed the neighbor's dog, what might she do to the neighbor herself?"

He winced. "Damn. You would have to plant that thought in my mind. Other than that, I will try to avoid my condo, but I may have to put in a small amount of time petting the hairless zombie for a bit— only to keep my furniture intact and my neighbors alive, of course." He inserted the keys into the ignition. "It's not as if I miss the smell of ginger in the morning or the jingle of her collar."

"You bought that thing a collar?" Cal said in disbelief, missing the real point that indeed Robin missed his cat.

"Where else would I put her identification tag?" Robin started the car and was out of sight in seconds.

"Holy crap." Cal shook his head. "What do you think it says? The tag?"

"Just the basics, I'm sure." I headed for our own car, parked on the street. "Dead cat. If found, please call."

Promise had wanted to stay with Cherish in case there was an unusual daytime attack. We left them behind windows shuttered against the sun and drove off as Robin had, although with less abstinence-induced speed. We were headed for another talk with Ishiah. Face-to-face was always better than the phone. They can't see your knife through the receiver.

Cal bounced from station to station on the radio for several minutes before giving up. "Cherish was telling me stories this morning while you were out back doing your katas." He slapped hands lightly against his knees. "Well, after she flipped out anyway."

"She . . . ah . . . flipped out?" I asked.

He rolled his eyes. "That card sharp shaved dog of hers was standing by the fridge, looking hungry, so I poured him a glass of goat's blood." He pulled a re-pulsed face. "Personally, I'll stick with coffee. But Cherish came into the kitchen, freaked the hell out, and slapped the glass out of his hand. She told me I was 'under no circumstances' "—he gave his best haughty imitation—"to feed her beloved Xolo. I was just doing a favor for the mangy mutt." He shrugged. "But the princess cleaned up the mess herself, actually apologized, and made *me* coffee. Said Xolo was all she had. She knew she was overprotective. Blah, blah, went into some Dr. Phil crap, and I almost dozed off."

He rolled down the window a crack to let in a stream of icy air. I didn't blame him. Whatever Mickey had used to cover his scent still lingered in the back of the car. "I guess she noticed, because then she started to tell me about all the jobs she's pulled. She gives Robin a run for his money. Knows everyone. Ripped off ninety-nine percent of them. Should've been a puck instead of a vampire. She was also asking where we'd learned to fight, who I thought was the best of all three of us. Could we give her lessons."

"I'm surprised the two of you got along well enough to talk," I said as I watched pearl-white clouds hang heavier and heavier. Snow; you could smell it in the air. "And who of the three did you claim to be best?" I asked, amused.

"By the two of you, yeah, I know you mean me," he snorted. "I gave her twenty minutes and tuned her out. That's the best I could do. As for the best, I'm not that stupid, Nik. I said it was a toss-up between you and Robin, but I definitely came in dead last."

With swords that was true. However, with his gates and guns and Auphe genes that were more active all the time, I wondered. If he did lose control for good, Robin and I together might not be enough. I tightened my hands on the steering wheel. But that wasn't going to happen. Cal wouldn't give in to it, and I wouldn't let him.

Unpleasant and unnecessary thoughts, and I distracted myself with others. He had tried with Cherish, because of what Promise meant to me. Naturally, Cal's trying fell under the category of not walking out of the room the second she walked in, but it was effort, and I gave it the appreciation it deserved. "McDonald's drive-thru?" Positive reinforcement; it was a good way to train dogs and brothers.

After a grease-laden bag was dumped in his lap, he took a bite of something that squirted syrup, dripped bits of egg and biscuit, and lost an entire sausage patty to the floor. "I'm surprised it didn't come blended in a cup of coffee. It would've made things much simpler," I said with distaste, sticking with the only palatable thing I'd found on the menu: orange juice. And I was careful to check for chunks of waffle floating within. "Did Cherish have anything to offer other than tales of misbehavior?"

"Nope, not that they weren't fun. She's not that bad once she gets over herself. She told me one story about some sheik, a huge diamond, and how long it takes something that big to go through a camel's digestive system. Gotta say, she worked for the money on that one." He wiped his mouth with the back of my hand. I felt the internal twitch and quelled it. Not every battle is worth fighting. Focus on the war. "Like I said, she was curious about our amazing ass-kicking abilities too, although more you, really. You're apparently a vampire-nookie magnet. Guess that makes my monster half yesterday's news." He finished off the McAngioplasty and stuffed the wadded paper back into the bag. "She also wanted to know where we grew up. How'd you get to be so great a swordsman. Were you always your brother's keeper."

All that in twenty minutes. Cal had been more social than he wanted to admit. "And you said?" It wouldn't be unusual for her to be curious about the man occupying her mother's bed. It would be unusual if she weren't.

"I said it was none of her goddamn business, and went to take a shower." He frowned. "At least I'm pretty sure I did. The coffee hadn't kicked in yet."

"Thankfully you were polite," I said sardonically. Now that was more like the brother I knew.

"I do what I can." He leaned the seat back and rolled over onto his side. "She can get in good with the stepdad on her own time. See you in twenty."

Cal had pulled the last watch. He needed the nap. I didn't mind the silence during the drive. I never minded silence. The lingering smell of greasy pork death I could've done without, but in life there are always challenges.

He slept hard, twitching occasionally, until I parked about two blocks down from the Ninth Circle. I didn't need to guess at his nightmares. They were the same as my own. Insanity, slavery, and far worse. But it wouldn't happen. I wouldn't let it. Cal wanted to carry the burden this time, but no one could carry that one alone. The moment I turned off the engine, he woke up. He blinked once, took in his surroundings, and said, "You know the only thing Ish will be interested in giving us is his foot up our asses?"

"You could be right." Unfortunately for Ishiah, whom I thought so far to be honorable in his fashion, I was more concerned about my brother than I was about his ass-kicking threats. The sooner we solved Cherish's problem, the sooner we could completely concentrate on our bigger one. And by now some information on Oshossi could've surfaced among the bar patrons. "But our options are limited."

"You ever think of just hauling Cherish's ass off to Central Park and dumping her there?" he asked, gray eyes calm and, yes, ruthless. "Let God, Zeus, and Allah sort it out?"

"No." She was Promise's daughter, and although a careless thief, she wasn't entirely without merit. Although even if she had been, I would do what I could for her for Promise's sake. And she did seem to be changing for the better . . . or at least trying to. Putting people if not before her, then at least equal to her. It counted for something, especially in one that young. And she did care for Promise now, and that counted for much more than just something. "Do you?"

He didn't answer, rubbing his knuckles thoughtfully along his jaw. "I think I'll plead the Fifth on that one." Getting out, he slammed the door shut. "Not too fair to Promise to make her think my shit smells like roses if I'm actually thinking something . . ."

"Survival oriented?" I offered.

"That sounds better than 'homicidal.' Yeah, thinking something survival oriented about her daughter. Let's go with that." He started to grin, but it twisted to a frown as his eyes slid from one side of the street to another.

"Cal?" I looked as well, but saw nothing. That didn't mean there was nothing to see.

He looked back at me. "Eh, it's nothing. Just feeling

paranoid. What with the Auphe in heat and a South American ass-kicker after us. Go figure."

We walked the two blocks as the snow began to fall. It wasn't the puffy flakes of Christmas cards and winter wonderlands. It was small pellets of hard white ice that bit at your face and collected under the collar of your coat. Breath billowing in the air, Cal pulled at the handle of the bar's front door. It didn't budge. "Huh. It's past noon. It should be open." He dug in his pocket for the keys, turned one in the lock, and opened the door. He didn't go in; he didn't take even a step. I saw him inhale sharply. His grip on the door handle tightened.

The lights were out, the windows covered, but I could see Ishiah in the interior gloom of the empty bar. He sat at a table alone with a bottle of whiskey and a glass. "Go away." His voice was one of the perfectly sober. I thought he wished he weren't.

"Who?" Cal asked, his own hoarse.

"Cambriel." He lifted the full glass and drained it. "Go away."

Cal closed the door with a jerky motion and rested his forehead against it. He had smelled them as soon as he had opened the door. I hadn't needed to. Seeing Ishiah was enough to know what had happened. Cambriel was a bartender I'd seen before. Cal had talked about him a few times. Had said he didn't quite have the peri temper that Ishiah had, but damn close. When push came to shove and the bar erupted, he could fight like a winged lion. Hold his own against the wolves, the vampires, the revenants.

But not against the Auphe.

Cal had worked at the bar for a while now. Months. Day after day. It was an association the Auphe couldn't have missed, and one we hadn't even considered. "It's just a job, Nik," he said, closing his eyes. "Just a stupid goddamn job. I didn't know Cam. I mean, he poured a mean shot and never turned me in if I took a long lunch, but I didn't know him. Him or Ishiah. They're just guys I work with."

If that were true, and I wasn't sure that it was, for the Auphe it seemed to be enough. "Call Delilah and let her know." He didn't move. I took a handful of his jacket and shook him lightly. "Cal, call. Now."

"Okay." He straightened and stepped away from the door as if it were red-hot. "Call Delilah. All right. I got it."

Keeping my eyes on him, I stepped far enough away that he couldn't hear my conversation with Georgina. She answered on the first ring. "Niko. Hello."

"Will you be there?" I asked.

"I already am." There was the usual gentle impishness in the words.

Georgina had held court at a tiny ice cream shop since she was eight. People came, they bought ice cream, and they asked what they needed to ask. She alone had kept the shop and its Methuselah-aged owner up and running. She didn't take money for what she did. Georgina was like that.

I called Robin next. Friend, enemy, wary ally, whatever Ishiah was to him, he should know what had happened. I caught him in the middle of what I fully expected to and managed to end both his good mood and aerodynamic lift instantly. I disconnected in the middle of his cursing. What he did with the information was his decision, but I had a feeling letting Ishiah drink alone in an empty bar that had been a former Auphe Ground Zero wasn't going to be the one he made.

"Cal."

His eyes, fixed and bleak, were back on the bar door. At my call, he looked away and shoved his cell phone in his jacket pocket. "Delilah's okay. Hasn't seen anything."

"Good. Let's go." I put my own phone away and felt the brush of steel in my pocket. One of the smaller throwing knives I carried—barely five inches long. I had ten on me now, along with my katana, wakizashi, and tanto blades. It was adequate for an average day. It didn't feel adequate today.

"Go where?"

"Do your meditation," I advised, turning and heading toward the nearest subway entrance. We had the car, but seeing Georgina meant a very roundabout approach. I didn't see any Auphe on the rooftops, and Cal obviously didn't smell any now or sense a gate. They probably weren't here anymore, but probably wasn't good enough. We absolutely could not be followed. That meant several evasion tactics, train switches, and fall backs.

"Why would I need medi . . . shit, we are not going to see George. We can't risk that." He came after me, hand on my shoulder stopping me as he moved in front of me. "Nik, no. Okay? Just no."

"It's all we have," I explained. "We'll take care. We won't be followed."

"Can you guarantee that?" he demanded.

I gave him patient silence as the snow beat harder.

"Yeah, yeah. You can." His hand fell away. "I still don't want to take the chance, and I don't want to go. She won't tell us anything anyway. And I really don't want to see her."

Understandable. Hurt; no one wants to embrace that. Cal had done all he could to be rid of Georgina, to save her from precisely the sort of thing that was happening now. The right thing and the easy thing; they could never be one and the same. "She may not, but I want to ask. I have to explore all our avenues, no matter how dim the chance. And you can wait outside." Because separating was not an option.

"Shit," he said again. "Ten blocks down. That's the best I can give you, Cyrano. I'm not taking any chances on them remembering her. You're the best, but I just can't."

I didn't want to take chances with Georgina either, but I was more concerned with his being that far away. But he was stubborn, and if I pushed it, he might take it up to fifteen blocks.

It took us well over an hour to get to the ice cream shop, but the time was well spent. I knew we hadn't been followed and I canvassed a four-block radius around the building. I'd left Cal those ten blocks away, huddled in a corner where a liquor store butted up against the larger building next door. "Hurry up," he said, pulling up the collar on his jacket and sticking his bare hands in his armpits. "My balls are finally getting me some action. Turning them into ice cubes isn't much of a thanks."

"Go inside, then," I said impatiently. "Buy something—a brain cell, perhaps."

"No, thanks. If somebody accidentally dropped a bottle behind me . . . yeah, I think you get the picture. Enclosed places with one way out aren't exactly my friends right now. Now hurry the hell up. Go get jack shit off George so we can go."

It was Cal and his stubborn bravado . . . not at their best, but there. And that counted. I pulled off my gloves, black silk hunting ones. They kept the warmth in and allowed the finer touch for pulling triggers and tossing knives. I handed them to him. I didn't bother to ask where his were. I knew he had no idea. "And don't put them down your pants. Your balls will have to survive as best they can." I left him as he was pulling the gloves on and looking up at a white sky that kept falling. . . . He was doing his best not to imagine a portrait of Georgina through a frosted plate glass window.

It was overly warm inside the shop when I arrived. It was also empty except for its proprietor, reading the paper with hugely magnified lenses, two bodyguard wolves in human form in a booth by the window, and Georgina.

Younger than Cal by two years, she was the oldest soul I'd come to meet. Wrapped in the package of an eighteen-year-old girl wearing a dark red velvet coat that was a bit worn around the hem. Consignment wear, but as with most things regarding Georgina, it was right for her. As this place was right for her. She took what came and always seemed content in it. Her nose was pierced since I'd last seen her. A tiny garnet. She was beautiful, if your eyes were open to what beauty truly was. It was in the softness of chocolate eyes, the pixie cap of dark red waves, skin of deep brown-gold, and freckles that sprinkled a perfectly ordinary nose. She had Samuel's, her uncle's, smile . . . slow and thoughtful.

"Niko." There came that smile.

I sat in the booth opposite her. "Georgina." I bowed my head to her as I had done to all my instructors at the many dojos over the years. In many ways, she was as much a teacher as they had been.

The smile faded. "I'm sorry. I tried. I did."

"Tried? What did you try?" My hopes that she would help us were faint, straw-grasping, but if she were at least making an attempt, maybe they weren't all in vain.

Her eyes were sad as she reached across the table to take one of my hands in hers. "I can't change things, but I'd hoped I could look and see where the path ends. Where you and Cal will be when this is all over. I wanted to be able to tell you that you would pass through this. Be safe." Her hands tightened on mine . . . with fear, I thought. "But I can't. I can't look because I'm afraid of what I'll see. I can't help you, and I can't comfort you either," she said with resignation.

"Georgina, you may be all we have." We might find Oshossi, between Robin and Mickey, but no one could track the Auphe. They were here, there, nowhere . . . a poison-tainted wind.

"I'm sorry." She squared her shoulders to deny, "There's nothing I can do."

Nothing. Nothing she could do. Nothing she *would* do. Her hands were warm on mine. She couldn't be moved any more than a marble saint, yet she felt warm. It seemed wrong. The oldest soul I'd met and the oldest I hoped I ever did come to see. She was wise and compassionate beyond her years, beyond a simple human span of years, in fact. I respected her for it, but lately I'd come to see that the compassion of someone who sees the entire world as opposed to the single struggling ant isn't necessarily a human compassion.

"There's a reason and a purpose to even the darkest of the dark. Hold on to that, Niko," she said softly. "Please."

Purpose. Knowing that your purpose in life will inevitably be fulfilled isn't a comfort when your purpose is to die ripped to shreds before your brother's eyes to drive him insane. And that would be a kind and giving act compared to what would be done to him then. Insane or not, catatonic or screaming day and night, they would use him. Violate him until the day he died. Wishing he were dead before they had that opportunity was the best I could hope for.

Hold on to that? Forgive me if meditation only took me so far.

In many ways Georgina, who was fully human, was less human than Cal. In the two years we'd known her, she'd always refused to meddle with the larger affairs of the universe. She'd find a lost dog, tell if a baby would be a girl or a boy, offer hope that, yes, love was coming, and that your sick relative would pull through. She gave warmth and comfort, but she wouldn't save your life. She wouldn't save her own, if it came to that. In this situation she wouldn't even look to see the outcome. Wouldn't tempt her own philosophy. She had a wisdom only seen in the holiest of people.

But speaking from the ant's perspective, I wished she had less wisdom and a more human perspective, because now people she could've saved were dying. I'd thought that might make a difference. It seemed I thought wrong.

"The Auphe killed one of Cal's co-workers at the bar," I said. "Did you know that?"

"I knew when you called. I am so sorry for Cambriel." She plucked his name from the air like a bit of drifting dandelion fluff. "I wish it were different, Niko. Please know I do, but we all have to walk the road before us. I can't change that." She sounded genuinely sorrowful.

"I had my sympathy for your position, Georgina." But it was gone. "But do you know what they plan to do to Cal? Do you know it's a thousand times worse than any torture, any death? If they take my brother when a few words from you could've stopped it, I'll have nothing at all for you then. Not one damn thing." My hand tensed to stone under hers. "For once break a rule. If not for me, then for Cal."

She withdrew her hands. "I can't," she said with a sudden and sharp flash of anger. I might wonder at her humanity, but she reacted the same as anyone when pushed into a corner. "Do you think I haven't tried? When I was a child, before I knew better? You think I didn't try to save my best friend or my grandmother? Or the nice neighbor who made me cookies and didn't deserve to burn alive in her apartment? I did try, and it was for nothing." She slapped a small hand on the table. "*Nothing*. You can change the twists and turns, you even can make the way smoother, easier, but you can never change what lies at the end."

"You haven't looked, then, to see how all this will end?" I persisted. "You can't at least give us that? You can't at least look?"

"No. I told you I can't. I tried, but I can't. Call me a coward if you want." She lifted her chin. "I know

I've heard it before, but I just can't look for endings anymore. Do you think I'd want to live whatever happens twice?" The anger disappeared as suddenly as it had come, melting to sorrow and regret. "I might have to accept the end of the path, but that doesn't mean I don't cry for it." She wrapped her coat tightly around her, as if it were cold. It wasn't. She looked away. "I miss Cal. Don't tell him. It would only hurt him. But I do miss him." And he missed her, but there was little to be done about that now. Both had stubbornly tied a knot in their relationship there was no getting around.

"Georgina, please." It wasn't a word I said often. I said it now with an angry desperation you didn't need psychic powers to sense.

She pulled the coat tighter around her neck. "Goodbye, Niko, and take care."

A singularly useless thing for her to say, I thought more savagely than I was proud of. Tumble into your razor-lined pit of destiny, but take care as you do so. My friend, my lover, and my *brother* gathered under Damocles' sword . . . a hair from brutal and bloody death, all of them, and that was what she offered me.

"Just look," I said sharply.

She slid out of the booth and began to walk away. I thought I saw tears. I didn't care.

"Look."

She disappeared into the back of the store. I gripped the edge of the table hard for a moment, then surged to my feet, flipping it over with a crash that sent the owner scrambling for the phone. The wolves watched me warily. They knew who I was through Delilah, and they knew I wasn't Auphe. But they also knew I was dangerous. They slunk past me and followed Georgina out of sight, leaving me with the wreckage of my futility.

Outside the store I walked the ten blocks to Cal,

who looked at my face and said warily, "What? What happened?"

I took his arm and pushed him into motion, saying brusquely, "I lost my temper. I imagine the police are on their way. Let's go."

It was dusk as we pulled up to the Seventy-second Street pedestrian entrance to Central Park to wait for Mickey. When we'd dropped him off on his mission, we'd set this as the time and pickup place for his retrieval. Not that it was easy to know it from what lay outside the car. A full-on blizzard had us surrounded by blowing white snow. You could barely see five feet, and it didn't look to be letting up anytime soon. It could be dusk or midnight for all one could tell. The winter wonderland I'd been so skeptical of earlier in the day had shown up with a vengeance.

We'd killed several hours checking to see if our landlord had replaced our door yet, getting more clothes from our apartment, eating lunch, and buying more ammunition for Cal. Not once did he bring up the subject of the scene at the ice cream shop after I'd filled him in, which, to be fair, I'd been tempted not to. Now I wasn't sure if I was grateful, or worried that he'd had some form of mild stroke that had robbed him of the information. He hadn't even said anything about my throwing of the table, true harassment fodder I'd never thought he'd let pass.

"Are you drooling?" I asked abruptly, tapping one of my small throwing knives against the steering wheel. "Numbness in one side? Any incontinence I should be aware of?"

Eyelids half-mast and lazy lifted all the way. "No more so than usual, Nik, but you're a helluva brother just for asking."

"Mmm." I flipped the blade, slid it under my sleeve, back out, and then flipped it again.

He straightened in the seat. "Not that you were exactly the poster boy for meditation yourself there, but do you really want me to give you hell over something I've wanted to do a few times myself?" He planted a knee against the dashboard and exhaled. "I kept thinking she and I, maybe . . ." He shook his head. "If she'd have just *looked*, but hell, no. That *que*-frigging-*sera-sera* thing. What's the point of seeing if you can't change the big things, the things that matter? I used to think it was me that kept us apart, but it's not. It's her. It's always been her." This time his fist hit the dashboard with considerably more force than his resting knee had.

"Infinite insight," I said thoughtfully, "brings only infinite annoyance."

"So it sucks?"

"Yes, indeed it does." I put away the knife before I was tempted to follow my brother down the primrose path to automotive destruction. Just as I did, there was a scrabbling at the door to the backseat, and Mickey scrambled in. There was a splatter of wetness as he shook off melting snow, saying immediately, "Give to me. Now."

Cal passed back a Styrofoam container of the best Thai in the city. "Ah. Is good. Yes, is good." The pointed muzzle was buried in coconut curry chicken. "You starve me with this work. The park, it is picked clean. Oshossi's clan, they devour all. No squirrel, no rabbit. Boggles take the one or two revenants left." Black eyes focused on us both. *"Hungry."* The hunger sounded as black and ravenous as the eyes appeared.

"Okay, Jesus. Hold on. I've got more." Cal gave him two more containers, and I think counted his fingers when he drew his hands back. It wasn't long before Mickey finished and began grooming his hands and whiskers.

"Well?" I tried for patience, but considering the day so far, I don't think I achieved it. "What of Oshossi?"

"I did not see him. He is not in park that I know, and his creatures? They are not quick to speak to others. Not quick to trust. Even for the handsome and suave such as me." The five-inch incisors snapped in a rat grin. "But I talk of the city. Of how to get around. The tunnels. The abandoned places. They listen. But they are not like me. They are not so smart; they are only few steps above animals. They are clever in ways of hunt. Very, very clever. But they know few words. Simple." He yawned, and beside me Cal stifled a gag at the stench of it, rolling down his window a few inches for fresh air. "Finally, *finally*, they say, Oshossi only comes to park to send them on hunt. Where he is other time, they will not say or do not know." He looked sleepy now, the gloss of his eyes dulling.

"How many creatures does he have?" I asked.

"Ccoa five, cadejo fifteen, and Gualichu one." The teeth showed again, not in a grin this time but in fear. "One is enough."

"Gualichu," I mused. "That's a spiritual being per folklore. He has no body. I assumed, then, that he might be a myth."

"He has body. Very large, like spider with a thousand legs." The dull eyes sharpened and looked out the window with unease. "We go now. Home."

"May as well," Cal grunted. "Looking in the dark for a giant cobra centipede that I can't even pronounce might not be the brightest of moves."

"We fight many creatures whose names you can't pronounce, but point taken." I started the car. Cal, more lazy than safety conscious, hadn't bothered to take his seat belt off as we'd sat parked. I began to fasten mine when something landed on the roof of the car, hitting so hard the roof caved inches under the pressure. I let go of the belt and threw myself sideways at Cal as I heard a familiar sound—the sound of metal under tension, a sharp twang. An arrow of black metal as big around as a quarter punched through the roof and impaled the driver's seat I'd just vacated. Oshossi had gone from machetes to a weapon typical of a hunter. A bow and arrow—the kind that could actually kill cars.

Impressive.

One of the backseat doors was flung open and I saw Mickey slither out and disappear into the whiteout with a speed that let me know this wasn't a setup. He had every fear that one of those arrows could very well be reserved for him. Cal drew his gun as I moved off of him and slid into the backseat to draw my tanto knife.

"Forget Shaft." Cal aimed up and pulled the trigger of his Glock. Six silencer-muffled shots punctured holes in the ceiling. "I think Oshossi's got the title of mean motherfucker nailed."

Too many old movies; too much bad TV—the thought was just forming in my mind as I started out of the car. I didn't make it. The world was suddenly revolving in an explosion of glass and the scream of metal against asphalt. I hit the ceiling, the backseat, the floor, and when the car came to rest from the rollover, I was halfway between the front and the back.

It wasn't over. There was a massive force heaving us up and the car flipped end over end. How many times I don't know. I hit upholstery, a door, and then the back window. I didn't feel it so much as recognize the crunch of safety glass spiderwebbing.

And I was free. There was no metal or glass, only the fast whirl of a carnival ride. It spun you in circle after circle until there was nothing left but free fall. But falling is never free. It always has its price. If not now then later.

Now . . .

I didn't know much about now.

There was the smell of snow with a coppery taint. The ground hard and cold under my cheek. The rest of me . . . Was there a rest of me? Hard to say. I could still see. Strange things. A huge metal shape crumpled and compressed against a tree, wheels spinning lazily up at the sky. There was a figure all in black . . . long black coat, black hair, black titanium bow, half a head taller than . . . taller than . . . the other one. The familiar one. Leather jacket, black hair in a ponytail, a gun—a gun that was fired. Soft muffled explosions. Barely audible as the snow crept down thicker and thicker. "You son of a bitch"—savage and hoarse. "You goddamn son of a *bitch*."

He staggered under the shots, the first one—who, Shossi? No. Not right. That wasn't right.

He stumbled but didn't fall. Instead he turned and vaulted over the car, because it was a car. Mangled, barely recognizable, but a car. There was dark skin, harsh angles and planes like stone, gleaming gold eyes, black hair short and sleek as an animal pelt, and then there was only white as he melted away. Into the storm . . . into the park. Gone.

And the snow kept coming. It was peaceful. Calm. Quiet.

Then there was a cry, distant. A child . . . Cal?

No. Cal was fourteen. Not a child. And Cal was gone. The Auphe had taken him and he was gone, pulled through a hole in the world. But I would wait, because he would come back. He had to come back. They took him right out from under me, and he had to come back. I couldn't have failed that badly. I was his brother. I was supposed to keep him safe. I . . .

Was that a siren?

But that wasn't right. The Auphe had burned the trailer to the ground, and the fire department didn't come. Too far in the woods. No one saw the smoke or flames at night. No one saw Sophia burn like a torch, or her blackened corpse. No one saw because no one cared. It was only Cal and me. Always. Only the two of us all our lives, and he couldn't be gone.

"Oh, God, Nik. Shit. Oh *shit*."

There was a hand under my shoulders and one under my neck turning me carefully from my side to my back. A face swam into my vision. Black hair nearly white with snow, a straight slash of dark brows, gray eyes, pale skin, sharp chin. He looked like . . . someone. A cold hand wiped at my face and came away dripping red. Snow? When had the snow turned red?

"Jesus." The pale skin went even paler. "Hold still, Cyrano, okay? Don't move. Let me get them." There were hands brushing over me, at my ankles, my waist, tugging at cloth. A knife appeared and slid between my chest and a snug band. Something long and stiff was eased from under my back. Suddenly against the white there was gray, a hideously hungry gray.

A hole in the world.

That had just meant something minutes ago, but now the meaning was lost.

The hole was swallowing things now. Guns, knives, leather and metal. And when they were gone the hole swallowed itself. I wished I could've swallowed myself too. Out of nowhere, the pain came. My head, it throbbed until I could barely see. But pain was only pain. It could be conquered. It could . . .

Where was Cal?

The sirens were wailing louder. I heard the murmur of distant voices. "It's a car wreck." "They'll never see it." "Wave them down." "Where's the driver?"

"Nik, it's done, okay? The weapons are gone." This voice was closer. The black and gray smearing into the white like a melting candle. Cloth wiped my face and then pressed against my temple. It was soft and warm and smelled oddly good . . . like coconut and chicken.

"Thai," I murmured.

"Yeah, sorry." A laugh, shaky and determined all at once. "At least it's clean. I borrowed it from you this morning." The voice raised, along with others. "Over here!" Then softer. "The ambulance is here now. We're going to the hospital, okay? The hospital. We were in a wreck, all right? If they ask, we had an accident."

To the hospital. No. Cal.

"No." I closed my eyes and the darkness was as peaceful as the snow. "Can't. Waiting for my brother. They took him." And I wasn't leaving until he came back. I wouldn't leave, I wouldn't move, I wouldn't sleep . . . although I was tired.

So tired.

There was a pause, and I felt a grip on my wrist squeezing hard. "Don't worry. He's here. He's back. I promise. You'll see him at the hospital. I swear. You'll wake up and he'll be right there."

I wanted to believe him. He looked so much like Cal, only older than fourteen, and I wanted to believe. Then I forgot what I wanted to believe. I was waiting for someone, but I forgot who.

Sleep, I just wanted to sleep.

Other voices came. Loud and then fading until I could hear only one. The same one. "I'm right here, Nik. These guys are on our side. Do me a favor and don't punch any of them out, all right?" Joke, but not a joke. Very much not a joke. Don't hurt. Don't kill.

Then the voice disappeared. The hand on my wrist went with it . . . as did the world.

And I disappeared with them.

11

Cal

Alcohol, stale piss, and bad cafeteria food.

Infection, sickness, and blood. Everywhere the sulfur sweetness of dying organs, the rot of gangrene, the stench of death. In all my life I'd never smelled so much death. It was on every surface in every room in this god-awful place of the living dead.

I sat in the hard plastic chair beside Nik's bed, my elbows on my knees and fingers locked over the back of my neck. I wanted to rock. Swear to God, I did. But that's all I needed. To have some angel of mercy think I'd lost it and drag me upstairs to the crazy ward.

Speaking of . . . there she was now. Nurse Panties in a Wad. She frowned at me from the door to Niko's room. Gray hair in tight waves, coolly efficient blue eyes, and starched scrubs. The same type of scrub top I'd bummed from one of the ER nurses. I'd used my shirt as a bandage for Niko's head wound. Soaked with blood, it had gone from light gray to dark red. Every inch of it. He'd bled and bled and bled.

I focused on the nurse. She was the lesser of two evils. "What?" I demanded.

"I told you, young man, visiting hours are over. You need to leave."

I don't know why they wear the stethoscopes looped

around their necks. It just made for one convenient strangling temptation. "I'm staying. I'm family."

"He looks like a big boy. Perfectly capable of spending the night on his own. He should come around soon. I'll tell him you'll be back in the morning," she said, folding her arms.

I picked up the remote from the bedside table as if I hadn't heard a word she'd said and switched on the TV.

"Sir . . ."

Young man to sir. Wow. A promotion.

"I'm staying," I repeated through my clenched teeth. "I'm *family*."

With that she gave up. When she was gone, I kept flicking through channels, not seeing a damn one of them. There was a rustle of sheets and I dropped the remote in my lap as I swiveled in the chair. Hazy eyes blinked and Nik said hoarsely, "Making friends . . . wherever you go."

I smiled, one so sharp and relieved that it actually hurt, and wrapped my hand around his arm. "Hey, Cyrano, you really awake this time?"

His hand moved to touch a row of twenty-five stitches along a hairline stained orange with Betadine. "I wasn't before?"

I let go of him to press the button on the rail that lifted the head of the bed up. "You kept telling me to put down my gun and finish my homework. You forgot I graduated Niko's home-school academy with honors two years ago." There was still dried blood in his hair although they'd gotten all the glass out down in the ER. The tie he used to pull the top of it back was long gone, and the stained blond strands fell inches past his jaw, messy in a way I don't think I'd ever seen it. Not even as kids.

"Honors?" His hand dropped back to the sheet and blanket covering him to midchest. "You spilled pizza sauce on the final."

"Yeah, you're awake this time." My smile faltered. It had been hours of silence, then two more of him drifting in and out. I'd cooled my heels in the ER waiting room forever. Security made it clear the only thing I'd get by trying to push my way back there was arrested. Finally, after tests and scans and stitching, I'd been able to go back to see him. He was still out cold. Concussion, they said. Moderate. He'll wake up soon. Here. Fill out these forms. There was enough Rom in me that I promptly lied on every line of them and handed over one of Niko's fake IDs. We'd stopped our running days, but some things would never change.

I'd waited until the registration lady bustled off to make copies before I threw up in the garbage can beside Nik's gurney. Rom, Sophia had said, didn't go to doctors or hospitals, although with good old Mom I thought it was more cheapness than a cultural thing. This was the first hospital I'd been in, and the smell of it was unbearable. I'd thrown up twice more after Niko had been moved to his own room. Fortunately, he had a bathroom there. Made for more convenient puking. Lucky me. Since then, I was dealing with it and this strange, cold, painfully bright place. Seeing Nik awake and finally with it should've made it easier.

It didn't. A bright red string, scarlet as his blood, had run through me, stitching me up, keeping me together . . . so I could watch out for him. Guard him. Wait for him. Now the waiting was over and the string was unraveling and I was unraveling with it. "Want some water?" I didn't wait for an answer, pouring lukewarm water into a plastic cup from a plastic pitcher with a hand that felt just as plastic, and handed it over.

He took it and slowly sipped. "What happened?"

I took the cup back when he finished. "You don't remember?"

"I remember . . ." His brow furrowed, wincing with

the movement. "I remember Mickey getting in the car and . . . nothing. That's all."

"The pizza sauce, you remember. A bad-ass tossing our car around like a Frisbee, that you forget." I slid down in the chair a few inches and rubbed tired eyes. "Oshossi. He picked up the car and flipped it. You were thrown out through the back window. I still had my seat belt on. He shot at us with a bow that could've taken down a rhino, and I shot him with my BB gun." It may as well have been for all the good it did. "Hit him at least five times, and he strolled off into the storm like nothing had happened."

"Then?"

The word prompted me into realizing I'd gone silent. "Then? Oh. You were . . . hurt." I rubbed my eyes harder. "You were thrown through the back window. Someone heard the crash and called the cops and an ambulance. I barely had time to get rid of our weapons. I don't know what the hell the cops made of the giant goddamn arrow shish-kebabbing the car."

Bracing himself on the rails, he sat up a little farther. I could see him taking stock. "Just my head, then."

"Trust me, it was enough." Enough blood, enough worry, enough of the whole damn ball of wax. I looked away at the window. More snow. The city was down for the count . . . buried. "But you're okay now," I said. It sounded kind of belligerent, maybe, but there you go. I resolutely kept my eyes off him and on the window. "And I'm not holding your hand in some sort of made-for-TV brotherly death-scene crap, all right? So stay okay. Don't die."

The sheets rustled again. "I won't," came the grave assurance, as if it were a perfectly reasonable request, and, hell, it was.

This time I looked at him. "Promise, you bastard?"

"I promise."

"Good." I picked up the remote and started clicking

through the channels again. "Glad that's settled. Can I have your Jell-O?"

There was no Jell-O. Only clear liquids and painkillers for the concussion victim. Nik passed on the meds, although by the lines bracketing his mouth, he could've used them. I'd given up on TV and had gone back to the tried-and-true elbows on my knees, hands on back of neck. I kept the rocking in my mind and almost dozed off in that position. The adrenaline of the past five hours had sucked me dry, and trying to keep from a total sensory meltdown in this place wasn't helping either.

"Cal."

I blinked. "What?" I ran back his words in my mind that I'd only half heard in my fog. Promise. He'd asked about Promise. "Yeah. I called her. Told her you were okay. She and Cherish can't get here until tomorrow. The city's shut down." Although a vampire could probably walk the miles and miles through the flying wall of snow. I'd managed to convince her not to give it a try. "Maybe you should call her. She's worried." I patted my scrub top for a few seconds before I realized I wasn't wearing my jacket. Reaching down, I picked it up off the floor and pulled my cell phone out of the pocket to hand to him.

He took it. "I will, but I want you to go lie down. I'm safe now. I have this watch."

Concussed, but he had this watch. And truthfully, concussed or not, he probably had a better handle on it now than I did. "You're okay?" I persisted. "Because you . . ." Because he hadn't been. He'd bled like a stuck pig and had been barely responsive. He hadn't known who I was. Was asking for a fourteen-year-old version of me. He hadn't been okay at all. "You're all right?"

"Cal." He pointed at the empty other bed. "One hour and I'll wake you. Go."

I gave in. Nik was Nik again, and he knew what he

was capable of. I got out of the chair, took off my sneakers, and climbed onto the other bed on top of the blanket and sheets. God help me if I messed up Nurse Panties in a Bunch's clean bed. My head hit the pillow, and the sharp smell of industrial-strength bleach sent a spike of pain like an ice pick through my brain. I didn't mind. The pain faded, and all I could still smell was bleach. No death or rot or creeping decay. It was such an utter relief that I slept instantly and slept hard, dreaming of sheets hung out to dry in the sun, of a thousand hungry rats tearing them down, of a living statue with blazing gold eyes, and of red snow.

It was everywhere. Bloody flakes falling from the sky. Piling so high you could drown in it.

And I dreamed of being watched. Of someone standing beside the bed, looking down at me. Someone who didn't belong.

I might sleep hard and it might take me a while to get up to full speed in the morning, but if the situation calls for it, I can wake up instantly and razor sharp. In this case all it took was the shuffle of a rubber sole. I was awake, across the room, and in the chair just as the Nurse Bitch on Wheels walked in the room. She did have a real name printed nice and neat on her name tag. I'd read it and forgotten it instantly. It hadn't said Satan's Bedpan Pusher of Despair, so it was wrong anyway. No point in committing it to memory.

She eyed the slightly wrinkled empty bed, narrowed that gaze at me, but checked Niko's vitals without comment and told him he might be discharged tomorrow. Maybe. If he stayed alert, there were no setbacks, the follow-up CT scan was good, the neuro doc agreed, and the planets all fell into alignment . . . it could happen.

When she left, Niko looked at me. "Exactly how shut-down are the roads?"

I checked the window again and shook my head. "Unless we can rent skis in the gift shop, it's not happening."

He studied me, weighing the pros and cons. I had to look like shit; I knew that. There's only so much overload you can handle before you shut down, but I wasn't leaving Nik alone either. No way, no how. "All right," he said. "Take us back to Rafferty's." He didn't want to ask, I knew. Hated it, in fact, to have me do what he'd rather I never did again. Didn't want to put me in that situation, but he also knew the situation I was in now wasn't much better.

I could've stood and went to the small closet to get the clear plastic bag that held his clothes, shoes, phone, and wallet. Could've scooped up my jacket from the floor, cradling it and the bag under one arm and placing a hand on Niko's shoulder. I could've taken us out of here in a heartbeat.

I didn't.

I sat, unmoving, in the chair. The hell with my situation. He was in one of his own. "Yeah, right. Traveling when you're perfectly healthy has Robin puking and you five shades of green. It used to have blood coming out of me like a faucet. We're not risking it with you having practically cracked your skull open. We wait for the doctor and the scan. By then the roads will be clear and your brain won't be oozing out your ears from me dragging you through a gate. Hell, that's probably on your discharge instructions. No traveling through rips in space for at least a week. The hospital cannot be held responsible for unnatural horrors of the supernatural world." I saw the pain pills in a small paper cup on the table beside him. "So take your pills, and in the morning we'll be out of here."

In the end, after a lot of squabbling—that would be bitching on my side and calm, forceful logic on his—we compromised. He took one of the pills and I took the pillowcase from the next bed, wadded it into a ball and took a deep whiff whenever the other smells, smells straight out of a slaughterhouse, got to be too much. Niko finally slept after making sure I was hanging in there, and I think I ended up slightly buzzed from the bleach.

It definitely kept me awake and alert, which was good because when Niko woke up at about seven a.m., he wanted every detail I could dredge up about Oshossi and the battle. Other than almost killing my brother, I hadn't been concentrating on those little personal details that make monsters so gosh-darn interesting. Like acid spitting, leeches for intestines, liquefying your internal organs and drinking them like Lipton's Cup-a-Soup—fun stuff like that. When it came to Oshossi, I'd been preoccupied with my brother sprawled and bleeding in the snow, so I didn't pick up much new from what I'd noticed at the car lot.

"I hit him several times with the Glock, I know that," I said as I swiped his blueberry muffin from his breakfast tray. He'd been upgraded to food for people with teeth by the day-shift nurse. Nurse Tiger-Stripe Thong/See-through White Pants Combo. I called her Tigger for short. For that and for her bouncy nature. You know the wonderful thing about Tiggers? Nothing. Not a damn thing. They're annoying as hell with all that bouncing and good cheer.

"He flinched but he didn't go down," I added before chewing and swallowing. "As a matter of fact, he grinned." I picked out a blueberry—it smelled a whole lot better than bleach—and fiddled with it. "Good teeth. Just as sharp as before. His dentist would be proud. Bet he flosses like crazy." Yeah, flossed pieces of punks like me out of those back molars like nobody's business. "Cyrano," I said seriously. "He is bad fucking news."

"Because he rolled, then flipped our car?" He regarded the fake scrambled eggs and hockey-puck sausage with the same distaste he showed flesh-eating revenants. "It would take serious strength and physical framework to do something like that."

"Yeah, but"—absently I gave him the last half of the muffin—"more that, hell, Nik, he wasn't even trying that hard. It was like at the car lot. Like he was fishing, caught us, and thought, Nah, too small. Not worth my time. And tossed us back. You were down. My gun wasn't putting him away. He didn't even draw his bow on me. He just took the bullets, smiled with those freaky teeth, and disappeared. We might've killed his cadejos and ccoas, but he doesn't think we're much of a threat. I think he's telling us to mind our own business."

"From what you say, it wasn't our best showing, and he is a hunter. Has been one for thousands of years. He might consider us unworthy prey." He considered the muffin, sighed, and ate it. "I think I'm embarrassed for us."

"I think I'm glad I'm not a head mounted on his wall somewhere." I focused on the smell of the blueberry muffin and nothing else and managed to keep it down. "You want to get cleaned up? There's a shower in the bathroom. If Promise sees you like that . . ." Bloodstained hair, Betadine, a bruise spreading across his forehead to match the fading black eyes I'd given him.

"No good?" he asked. "I'll definitely enjoy being clean, but I hardly think it would matter to Promise. I never claimed to be as vain as Robin."

He missed it. Niko, who hardly ever missed anything. "You look human, Nik," I said bluntly. "You look way too human right now." Blood, bruises, faint lines of pain. Human. Vulnerable. Promise had seen it before, but not to this degree and not in a hospital. It was a reminder that couldn't do anything but hurt her. I knew I wasn't enjoying it.

He could've died. Could've bled to death in the snow. My family, my only damn family.

Which led to something I was far better at than meditation. Denial. Very big, very bad denial. I took the tray and started in on the leathery eggs. One bite was enough. Jesus. That was physician-assisted suicide right there. "There's shampoo and crap in there. Try not to flash me on the way."

Fifteen minutes later he was back with clean damp hair, the Betadine scrubbed away from the stitches, and wearing scrubs instead of the hospital gown. He was still bruised, but he was steady on his feet, which was a good thing, because Promise was there, having walked past a scolding Nurse Tigger like she didn't exist. They really were fascist with their visiting hours there.

She walked past me the same way she had Tig, so I took the tray out to the hall to give them quality vamp-human time. Cherish was waiting out there in black-on-black with a collar of gold, pearls, and onyx. She liked the shiny stuff, no way around it. She and Robin, they would always be thieves, but there were worse things to be. As long as the thieves were on my side when the chips were down, their private lives were none of my business. Hair swept up into a smooth coil pinned with more pearls, she held the hand of Xolo. He was in a parka, new from the sheen of it, with a hood that kept anyone from seeing anything but large shadowed eyes.

"You saw him again, then? Oshossi?" Her leather-gloved hand tightened on Xolo's.

"You could say that." I dumped the tray on a metal cart loaded with other dirty ones. "You could also say you owe us a car." I folded my arms and leaned against the wall beside her. "I'm hoping you've never seen this guy fight, because I'd like to think you'd have mentioned he invented ass kicking and has a black belt in taking names."

"No, I never saw him fight." Her mouth, painted the color of poppies today, tried for a smile but didn't pull it off. "I saw other sides to him. I do know he has never lost prey once he's started the hunt. He's very proud of that. Too proud, I thought. Arrogant, perhaps even foolishly so. But I was the fool. This is it, then?" she said more to herself than to me. "You and the others have faced him and barely escaped with your lives. I am a fighter." The blackness fogged her eyes, and I saw her fangs, if only for a second. "An excellent fighter, but I've seen you and your brother . . . with the cadejos and the ccoas. You're hunters, just as Oshossi is. If you can't take him, neither can I."

"Hey." I wasn't sure if I was insulted or felt bad for her. I rolled a meditation bead against my wrist and had a flash of that insight everyone's always talking about. Know thyself.

Yeah . . . I was insulted.

Okay, okay, I felt a little bad for her too. "It's not just you, remember? It's all of us. Robin's been around longer than Oshossi, you can bet that. When he has to, he can fight like hell. He might not like it, but he can do it. And if it hadn't been for the car thing, I think Niko would've given Oshossi something to think about."

I touched another bead. "Niko's human, but . . ." I stopped and thought about it. "He's a Caesar, an Alexander, a Genghis, a Minamoto no Yorimasa." And he'd always said I never paid attention to the history books he'd used to teach me. "Some people are born warriors. He's one of them. What it takes some creatures hundreds of years to learn, Nik was born knowing. Every once in a while the world comes up with a natural-born predator. We're lucky nature screwed up and gave Cyrano a conscience along with it, or it'd be Alexander all over again."

Huh. I'd gone through the entire mala, bead by bead, and hadn't noticed. And I'd talked more than I usually did about personal things, and what the hell was up with that? So what if Cherish was Promise's daughter, and Promise was with Niko. So what if that sort of made her family. So what if . . . damn, I was getting soft in my old age. Twenty—who knew you went to instant pudding then.

I grabbed my cynical nature and pulled it back into place. She was *not* family. She might have come around to care for someone other than herself, but that didn't mean I trusted her.

My phone rang, and I walked down the hall from her. I'd brought my cell out of the room with me to call Robin. I'd called him last night, and I was hoping he'd learned something between then and now. He'd beaten me to the punch. "How's Niko?" he asked.

"Good," I said. "Once he gets his CT scan we're out of here. You find out anything about Oshossi yet?"

"I did indeed," he responded smugly. "He's renting a brownstone in Harlem, the entire thing. He apparently likes his privacy."

"It only makes things easier for us." I pressed against the wall as a gurney went flying by, nurses doing CPR as they ran. It was pointless. I could smell the death on the guy.

"Easier?" Robin said incredulously. "You did say he flipped over your car last night, didn't you? I can't see there will be anything easy about this."

"Hell, he might just spank us and send us on our way," I said wearily. That hour of sleep hadn't done me much good.

"I'm going," Cherish said over my shoulder, having moved up behind me. "That will keep him there. After all, it's me he wants. Anything, anyone else is incidental."

She had a point, although he'd known her location when he'd sent the ccoas after her and his cadejos had followed her. He hadn't been there then either. The only time he'd shown up was to warn the rest of us to back off, and that's what it had to be because he could've made things much more nasty for us if he'd wanted. Maybe he wanted his animals to do his work for him to show the contempt he had for a common thief.

Whatever it was, it didn't matter. With Promise involved, we were up to our necks in it. I looked back toward Niko's room. Not that I liked it, not one damn bit.

"You coming back to the house?" I asked Goodfellow.

"No. But I'm on the move and, no offense, I'm better off on my own. I've honed my escape abilities over the years." That was probably true. The fact that he'd stuck with us for so long, confined unnaturally for any puck, yet had been ready to help when the fight came, that said something about Robin. Something better than you could say about me.

"But I am staying in those hotels worthy of my presence," he continued. "If you need help, you'll know where to come for me." That was the thing about traveling. I had to know where I was going. I couldn't open a gate blindly to a place I'd never been or seen at a distance. And Robin had filled me in on what hotels were good enough to suit him. . . . There weren't many. I knew all their locations, passed by their doors in my years in New York. "And call me when you're ready to take on Oshossi. Just make sure there are no cars readily available when you do." With that he disconnected.

I shoved a hand through my hair. I needed a shower too. I'd cleaned all of Nik's blood off me in the sink last night, scrubbing until my skin was red and stinging, but there were moments where I could still feel it. It was something that was happening way too much lately. It was easier to be irritable than thinking about that, and I turned my attention to Cherish and Xolo. "Seriously," I asked with annoyance, "what is up with that thing? Why don't you just get a dog? Alpo's easier to come by than goat's blood."

"Some of us aren't as fortunate as the four of you," she said with an edge of bitterness, and turned to walk back to the room. "Sometimes pets have to do."

Not many pets played Go Fish, but she was right. I was lucky, and I intended to stay that way. No matter what I'd thought on the beach when the Auphe had taken the eel. No matter that I thought we were going to die. No matter that I'd found out it was even worse than that. Whatever happened to me happened, but I was keeping Nik safe and alive. The real shitfest had yet to come. So let it. I wasn't going to lose what I had, even if I lost myself.

Denial: Sometimes it was all that kept you going.

I took my shower while Promise and Cherish watched over Nik, who would've been offended that I thought he couldn't take care of himself even with a concussion. They came to take him to CT while I was in the shower. Promise went with him. By the time they came back I'd gotten our weapons back from Rafferty's, where I'd tossed them before the ambulance had come. The hospital had metal detectors at the ER entrance, but Cherish had said the front doors were clear. Good news, because walking out of this place unarmed wasn't my idea of smart. Promise and Cherish had brought extra blades for us, but I felt more comfortable with my own and I definitely felt better with my gun—not that it had done me any good with Oshossi.

I'd shoved them in the closet. With Cherish standing outside the room door guarding it, I passed over Niko's katana and various other blades. As he dressed, he slid them into place and put his coat on to conceal them all. His clothes were clean except for a blood-stain on the shoulder of his coat and the shirt beneath. I was still in the scrub top. My jeans were all right, though, as was my jacket. The nurse came back to say the CT had come back normal, and Nik would be discharged soon. When soon dragged into the second hour, we left. What the hell? The ID they had was false, and no one noticed as we walked out.

No one but the Auphe.

We were on the stairs when the gates opened. I didn't have to warn anyone. They opened on the landing a floor below us. A straight shot and that's what I took, firing several shots at the first of the seven, but it had already slid to the side as my finger pulled the trigger. Then I felt two more gates open behind us. Nine of them, four of us. That wasn't even odds, nowhere near. One of the ones who'd appeared behind us was carrying something. At first I didn't recognize what it was. I didn't recognize it because I didn't want to.

Cambriel's head.

It was held by a handful of copper hair, the normally neat braid a tangled mess, the light brown eyes filmed. "I brought you a present, treasonous cousin. Traitorous brother. To put you in the breeding disposition. We hope it pleases you." Scarlet eyes were bright with homicidal glee. "We made sure that he knew he died because of you." The metal teeth flashed. "He had a long time to think of that before we finished. So very long."

I didn't think about that. I couldn't. If I did, I'd make a mistake, and we couldn't afford one now. *"Mi Dios,"* Cherish murmured in dread. She had called me Auphe, but now she saw the real thing. Walking, talking carnage. Even vampires feared the Auphe, were their victims like anyone else.

We hadn't been able to handle two before between four of us with Niko in top shape and Robin with his thousands of years of experience there. I didn't think we could take nine. I *knew* we couldn't take nine.

I didn't know if I could build a gate around all of us, four and Xolo too. That would be a big one, bigger than I'd attempted before. And a half-ass gate? I didn't know what that would do. Take half of our bodies out of here, leave the other half? It was risk that might be as dangerous as the Auphe. So I opened one behind us, between the two Auphe and us. I concentrated. I stayed in control . . . God knew how. They were there. Right fucking there, and if we didn't get out of there someone was going to die.

My gate was open, tarnished and greedy and big enough for two people to pass through at the same time. "Go!" I rapped. Promise didn't hesitate. Cherish did for the briefest of moments, but then followed, dragging Xolo behind her. The Auphe watched them go, unmoving—their silver teeth showing in wider, contorted grins. Then Niko and I lunged for the gray light of the gate.

The Auphe closed it in our faces.

I felt them jerk it out of existence, collapse it into nothingness.

I hadn't known they could do that. I hadn't . . . oh, Jesus. It was Niko they wanted first. Last time, this time. The one person I could least afford to lose. The one I *couldn't* lose.

The two who had appeared behind us on the upper stairs moved apart, leaving the way clear between them. "Run," the one with Cambriel's head said. "Give us our chase. Give us our thrill. Run, meat. Run, whore. Run."

We did. We ran up eight flights. For anyone else with a concussion it probably wouldn't have been possible. For Niko it was not only doable, but he had to slow down so that I could keep up. Ultraconditioned athlete or machine, take your pick.

At the fourth-floor landing a man in scrubs and a lab coat was scanning a clipboard. With one quick motion Niko gave him a hard shove back through the door and slammed it in his face. We went up four more before the scream came. He hadn't stayed behind the door like he should have. I didn't have time to feel guilt over his death. I didn't have time for anything but the running, lungs burning and legs propelling with all the strength they had. We were still ahead of them, but only because they let us be. They were taking their time, drawing it out. Having their fun.

The last door was locked. I shot out the lock and we were on the roof. We could've gone out onto one of the occupied floors, but I didn't think that would stop the Auphe. Not this time. They were in the heat of the chase, insane with it. A cold insanity and ready. They were so damn ready. Niko and I ran to the edge. At least sixteen floors up, there was nothing below us but the street. Nothing to hold on to, no way to climb down.

The door slammed open across the roof and they were there. Blood on their teeth and claws, dripping down pointed chins. Running. So quick I barely had time to point the Glock, but not time to pull the trigger—they were so fast they were almost on us when Niko tackled me and we went over the edge. I felt the concrete ledge hard against my knees, the breath-sucking tumble. Then there was free fall, lights flashing past us, and the hard thud of the ground beneath us. Not the street, but the bristle of winter grass.

I'd tried one last time. Tried one last time on the way down to be Auphe, and the Auphe had let me.

Niko rolled off of me to lie at my side, and I stared at the morning sky above Rafferty's backyard. I waited slow seconds as the air finally began to wheeze back into my lungs. I'd created the gate one floor down as we fell from the hospital roof, the gate open one moment and closed the next. The Auphe had allowed it. Why? Because even in the madness of the hunt they knew what they wanted.

Me. And Niko had played on that when he'd pushed us over the edge. Him they wanted dead, but me they needed alive. They'd still been at their homicidal vengeful play, trying to take him, then the others.

I had a feeling, though, playtime was about to be over. They might live almost forever, but they didn't know that I would. They'd tire of the chase and soon. Torture was good fun and all, but they had their plans too. Then they would all come, and it wouldn't be long. Not two, not nine, but every last one of them—which would accomplish both their goals. A massacre, and me pulled back to hell to remake the Auphe race.

I coughed and said hoarsely, "I never thought my dick would save our asses."

"You had to say it, didn't you?" Niko studied the sky with me. Blue and clear—a good day to still be alive. "But in this case you're an idiot whose penis *did* save our lives. And I hope I never have to say or think that again." It had been our only chance, Nik's plan, the only way I wouldn't have seen my brother die before my eyes while they held me back.

And if for some reason it hadn't worked, hell, hitting the pavement would've been one goddamned better way to go.

12

Niko

I hadn't known that the Auphe would let us escape the relatively painless death of a sixteen-floor fall. I'd strongly suspected, but I hadn't known. I had known the only other option was not preferable. I turned my head, the grass rustling in my ear, and watched as Cal continued to stare at the sky, memorizing it, as if it were the last one he'd ever see. The faith he'd once had at the beach, the determination since, had drained away, leaving his face blank and empty. I watched it go as the stomach-wrenching nausea from the gate slowly began to subside. Cambriel, and the stranger who'd gotten in the Auphe's way at the hospital—it was all hitting him now.

He'd kept his word, anticipating the Auphe twice . . . as much as anyone could. You could anticipate a tornado, a tsunami, yet there were times when there was no place to go to escape them. This, I thought, was one of those times.

"Did you flip them off on the way down?" I asked.

"Hell, yes, I did." He gave a small smirk, but it faded away almost instantly, and the emptiness was back again.

I sat up, reached over him to take his right hand that still held his gun, and placed it on his chest. "If the time comes and we can't win," I said steadily, "you go first." I'd done all I could to protect him his entire life. I would protect him at the end of it as well.

His knuckles tightened on the Desert Eagle. "That won't stop them from killing the rest of you."

"No, but it will infuriate them, madden them. If I take the one chance their race has at survival, they'll take the rest of us quickly. They'll be too infuriated to do otherwise." And if they didn't . . . we'd fight until our choices were gone. If it came to the torture the Auphe had promised, we would have an escape. A clean death. I'd rather die by my hand than the hand of an Auphe. Either way, Cal wouldn't have to see it. I might not be able to save his life, but I could save him that, and I could save him from much worse. I would never let the Auphe take him again.

He looked at me with eyes unutterably exhausted and far older than they had any right to be. "Together."

"Together," I promised. I held up a hand and he let go of the gun to clasp it, hard and desperate, then he pulled himself up to a sitting position.

He let go and rubbed his face. "I think we have codependency issues."

"There's no one I would rather have them with, little brother." I stood and nudged his hip with my foot. "Up. You need to sleep. One hour in a day and a half doesn't quite qualify."

"Cyrano," he responded. The shadows under his eyes had advanced to circles so dark they were almost black. "I don't think I'll ever sleep again."

I thought he would've proven that true had I not palmed two sleeping pills at the hospital. Slipped into his coffee, he'd collapsed on the living room couch, dead to the world. Promise, who stood beside me, leaned down to brush the hair from his face. She didn't bring up the breeding remark the Auphe had made on the hospital stairwell. Either she didn't truly want to know or knew Cal wouldn't want me to talk about it. "We're not going to survive this, are we?" she said softly.

I said nothing. It was answer enough.

"Perhaps you, Cherish, and Robin would if you ran," I said eventually. "If you hid. Once Cal and I are gone, they'd have little reason to follow you. You can't torment those who are already dead. Wasting their time on you would be pointless."

"But the Auphe are mad. What is pointless to us may not be so to them." Her hand wrapped around mine. "All my life I've only survived. With you, I've actually lived. That is worth dying for."

To say I had mixed emotions on that was an understatement. Pride and automatic refusal. But I could refuse all that I wanted. Promise would do what she wished.

Cherish would run. Oshossi would suddenly seem not quite so bad. He could kill her, but the Auphe *would* kill her. As for Goodfellow . . . a knock on the door, a scant moment of metal scraping the lock, and he was there. "So," he said impatiently, "are we going after Oshossi or not? I had to perform with someone far, *far* below my standards to get this information. I would hate for it to go to waste." His annoyance faded as he took us in. My stony face, Promise's determined one, and Cal limply unconscious and worn to his last reserves.

"*Arhidia*, what's happened now?" The apprehension was easily read in his tense frame.

I filled him in. Halfway through, he was on one of the chairs with his head in his hands. When I reached the part about us plummeting over the edge, he was muttering over and over under his breath, "*Gamiseme. Gamiseme. Gamiseme.*"

I spoke enough Greek to agree with him. I repeated the same thing to him that I had to Promise. "You should go. When the three of us are gone, they'll have no reason to come after you. And as long as you've lived, no one could be better at hiding than you, assuming they could even pick you out from the other pucks. None of us expect you to die with us."

His shoulders braced and he straightened to lean back against the chair. "And miss all the fun?" The careless smile disappeared. "I've run from battles all my life, counted my own life as far more important than anyone else's. You, on the other hand, have faced death with me. For me. No one in all my years has ever done that. I stand with you now." He turned a little green with the words, but he was resolute all the same.

It wasn't what Cal would've wanted. It wasn't what I wanted, but bravery and loyalty could be unshakable. In this case, I knew it was. We would, if nothing else, give the Auphe something to think about.

"Tell us what you learned of Oshossi," I said, changing the subject. There was nothing more to say about it. Nothing more to do but to go down fighting.

Cal had mentioned the brownstone Robin had told him about on the phone. And as far as the puck could tell, Oshossi had no backup locations. "It's that or the park with his zoo. If he kicks our asses, well, that was that. But if we come out ahead on this one and he makes a run for it, then we'll only have eight-hundred-some acres to search for him. What could be easier?"

"Soon. Coming soon." We turned as Cal mumbled in his sleep, and it wasn't Oshossi he was dreaming of. That I knew. His hand clasped open and shut. It was the serrated-edged combat knife he always slept with that he was missing. I picked it up from the coffee table and slipped the handle into his hand. His disturbed breathing smoothed out and he dropped into a heavier sleep.

"One last time," I said to Cherish who had appeared at the hallway entrance. "We'll try one last time for you and then, unfortunately, I believe you'll be on your own."

"It's more than I could ask," she said gravely.

It was much more, but Promise was willing to die with us. I owed her daughter at least one more effort. Although I was beginning to wonder—all this over a necklace? Oshossi might have his pride on no prey escaping him, but this seemed excessive over a handful of rocks and metal that held no other purpose. There is pride and then there is obsession. And to walk away when he might have easily killed us, it gave one pause. But I'd given Promise my word and I would live up to it this one last time.

Cal slept nine hours, knuckles white from his grip on the knife's handle every minute of those hours. I ignored the ache in my head and watched him. There had been a time when he had slept that way every night, except he had done it under a bed curled in a ball. The first time the Auphe had taken him, when he'd come back he'd spent months that way.

During that time I'd slept little as I watched for the Auphe. Cal hadn't talked much then; some days not at all. We'd been hiding in Charleston, South Carolina, at that time. I'd studied martial arts since I was twelve. Whatever city Sophia had dragged us to, I'd find a dojo. I'd collect cans or, when I could fool someone about my age, work any job I could find to pay for those lessons. I'd never forgotten that face at our kitchen window when I was seven. Or the others I'd seen since. And at eighteen, almost nineteen with a barely responsive brother, I went every day for as many hours as I could, taking him with me. I hadn't known the Auphe for what they were then. I thought I would have a chance.

I became a warrior, a killer, but all I had managed was to put off the inevitable.

Eighteen Auphe. It may as well have been a hundred.

I detected the change in Cal's breathing and looked

up from the blade lying across my lap. "We've had a helluva run," he said. "At least those bitches will remember that."

We had. The steel that suddenly ran through me was as solid and real as the one that rested on my legs. "We have and we will. We are not giving up." I couldn't. I'd spent my life refusing to give up. I wasn't going to start now. "The Auphe closed your gate. Do you think you could do that to one of theirs?"

He sat up and thought about it. He had a crease across his face from the couch cushion, and what I suspected was a slight hangover from the drugs. "Yeah, I think I could. I felt how they took it. How they tore it apart. I'm pretty sure I could do it. But what good would that do? The last thing we want is to keep them hanging around. If they want to take off, I think letting them leave the party is our best bet."

"I don't know if we can use it in our favor or not, but it never hurts to have information." It was a piece of an impossible puzzle, but there were times amazing things could be done with one piece. "We're going after Oshossi tonight," I said, moving on. "Are you up to it?"

He looked at his watch to check how many hours he'd slept and scowled. "You mean after you drugged me?"

"Yes, that's exactly what I mean," I said without remorse.

"Bastard," he said affectionately, before yawning. He then shook his head, getting rid of the last of the drowsiness. "Yeah, I'm up for it. Hell, compared to this morning it'll be like a vacation." He tapped the black blade of his knife against the mala bracelet around his wrist. Putting down the knife, he pulled the beads off and handed them to me. "Thanks, Nik, but I think being Auphe now might be the best thing when the time comes. If Midol deosn't work, I'll give them a little taste of their own medicine." He gave a darkly feral flash of teeth. "Next time they call me family, they'll have reason to."

I fingered the beads, then slipped them back on. It was his decision, whether I agreed with it or not. And I wholly did not. His grin faded and twisted. "Sorry I didn't get us out of this like I said I would. I thought being like them would be enough." It wasn't, because he wasn't. But he couldn't see that.

"It's not over yet," I said.

Neither of us would let it be.

As Cal had not been in the mood for the revenant outside the Ninth Circle days ago, I was not in the mood for Oshossi. I was also not in the mood for Cherish having brought Xolo along. At best he'd be a distraction for her; at worst he'd be killed. It was not my problem or my responsibility, but it was an annoyance.

"You will not be at top form if you're watching out for him," I told her. And watch out for him she would. He seemed to have the defensive capabilities of a sloth.

"Do not worry," she assured. "He hides well, and I'm not leaving him alone. If the Auphe discover the house, he'd have no chance at all."

Cal was studying the brownstone, along with the rest of us, from across the street. It was midnight, with snow still piled in heaps off the sidewalk. "Nik's right. He has the kick-ass moves of soggy breakfast cereal. You could've put him in a kennel. He could've had some nummy-nums and a nice scratch behind the ear."

"You're not going to get over the fact he beat you in cards, are you?" Robin drawled.

"Shut up. It was a fluke, okay?" Cal was only going through the motions. He'd seen Oshossi nearly kill me, without even making much of an attempt. He was, let us say, pissed. Or homicidal. Both words worked.

"Of course. Bowser couldn't possibly be smarter than you," Goodfellow said smoothly. "Perhaps you can get matching flea collars."

If Xolo understood any of the conversation, he didn't give an indication of it, his eyes staring dreamily as they always did. He didn't have to understand it. I did and was tiring of it. "Enough," I said. "Let's go. Promise, Cherish, you take the third floor. We'll take the first. If he's not on either one, we'll trap him between us."

On the other side of the street, Robin picked the lock of the door and Promise and Cherish swiftly climbed—almost floating—their way up the stone facade, Xolo clinging to Cherish's back. We were inside in ten seconds, and I heard the breaking of glass above us. "The second floor is mine," I said, spotting the stairs. "You two search down here." Cal hesitated— obviously Oshossi's scent was everywhere in the house; unable to pin it down, he followed the command.

The runner on the stairs was as richly expensive as the first floor of the house. Oshossi apparently liked to live well. I was curious to see if he would die as well.

I had my chance to find out almost immediately. He was waiting just past the top of the stairs, his machetes in hand. "Stubborn human. I spared your life last time, ineffectual prey that you are." The pointed teeth bared. "I make no exception this time." Long black claws sprouted from his fingertips, curving as the machetes did.

I simply appreciated the lack of snakes. Unholy waterfalls of serpents, I could do without.

I caught the first blow of his machete on my katana; the second as well. He swung each blade with equal skill and he was quick, quicker than Seamus had been, but not as quick as he thought he was. He couldn't use his enormous strength. The metal of his weapons would shatter as easily as mine. I continued to fend off his whirlwind of blows one-handed while I drew a throwing knife. He lunged to one side, and I missed his throat, but I didn't miss his shoulder. He narrowed his yellow eyes. "Not so ineffectual after all." The predator teeth flashed in satisfaction. "I will enjoy this."

Ordinarily, I wouldn't have. Killing was a fact of life, not something to take pleasure in. But this time, having lost so many times in the past days, I was going to enjoy this as well. I shouldn't, but I was.

I already had another knife in my hand and threw it as well. He knocked it aside with one of the machetes and lunged at me with the other, swinging it in a quicksilver blur. I came under it, then dived to one side before it could change trajectory and bury itself in my back. It tore through my coat as I rolled and sliced my katana to hamstring him, but he was already across the room. I didn't give him any breathing space, and was on him again in an instant. He was fast, a challenge, but he was no Auphe. And he might not realize it yet, but he wasn't me either. Not blade to blade. Hand to hand would be a different story, but for now . . . he was mine. It wasn't overconfidence. It was fact.

I couldn't knock either machete from his grip; he was too strong for that. But I could go around them, under them, over them. I sliced his thigh and a path across his ribs as he did across mine, then I got behind him and slammed a foot in the small of his back. He hissed in disbelief, but he didn't give up, whirling to face me before I could bury a blade in his back. I doubted he could remember the last time he had been defeated. What was good for the ego could be disastrous in battle. Humility could go a long way toward keeping one alive.

Cal had said bullets had barely staggered him. It was time to see what a blade through his heart would do. He dropped the machetes and reached for me with hands that had flipped over a car. At the same time,

I'd pulled my tanto knife and was jabbing it directly toward his heart. Or rather, where I was making an educated guess his heart might be.

And that's when they came down the stairs: Promise, Cherish, and her shadow, Xolo. Oshossi's gold eyes widened, his hands dropped away, and he ran, throwing himself through the second-story window before my knife could hit home. There was the crash of glass, the thud of running feet, and as I moved to the window, I saw him disappear, weaving through the traffic.

A fighter so fierce, so unyielding, that he couldn't recognize he was seconds away from death, yet the sight of two vampires sent him running. With an ego so large, I imagined he would've thought he could take them as well. Yet he had fled.

"He's gone," Cherish said bitterly. *"Maldígalo al infierno."*

Xolo's eyes were brighter than I'd ever seen them as he eased down the stairs behind her, but they dulled just as quickly when he saw Oshossi was gone.

"We have to go," Cal called from below. "Cops are coming."

All the shattering of glass was bound to have drawn attention. As for staying downstairs, he knew I'd call him if I needed him in the fight. Otherwise I needed him to stay out of the way. I needed the room. If only Promise and Cherish had known that.

I put away my katana, fetched my fallen blade, and moved down the stairs to the first floor. "For the best hunter in South America, he spends quite a bit of time either escaping us or letting us go," I mused. I gazed over my shoulder at Cherish and wondered if she was telling the truth—the entire truth. Xolo's hazy eyes drifted over me. Then again, Cherish was guarding what seemed the most helpless of chupas, and she was Promise's daughter. Something completely worthless couldn't have come from Promise. Could it?

No. No, Cherish deserved a chance.

"Nik, you okay?" Cal's hand urged me toward the door. I'd stopped, unaware. "Your head hurt?"

Slightly foggy, I shook off my Cherish thoughts for another time and then we were on the sidewalk, moving fast. "No. I'm fine."

"I'm surprised Oshossi didn't pick you up and catapult you through the floor," Robin said. "Much like a Three Stooges movie."

"We fought with blades. He's good." I slid the knife back in its place. "I'm better."

"Unless he starts throwing cars around again, that makes you hot shit." Cal was looking over his shoulder with distant eyes. He'd been doing that quite a bit lately. With the Auphe searching for us and finding us more often than not, I wasn't surprised.

"Cal?"

He jerked his attention back to us. "Yeah, the cars. Stay away from the cars." He said it to Cherish. "Or start running again, because we're done. Probably in more ways than one."

Back at Rafferty's, Cal watched the snow from the kitchen window. It was falling again, although in scattered swirls rather than the blizzard of before. "Are you hungry?" I asked, about to fix what few groceries we'd stopped and obtained on the way home. I'd already patched up the shallow slash on my side.

He shook his head and kept watching.

"What is it?" Cal wasn't much for introspection. Unlike Xolo, if he was looking, there was something to see. I moved to his side and saw nothing but snow and hundreds of bare trees.

He narrowed his eyes and kept them on the window. "One of them is watching us."

The Auphe.

"Right now," he added grimly.

13

Cal

"I can't see it," I said, calm. Maybe a little too calm. The bogeyman was right outside, but look at me. Look how calm, cool, and collected I was. Like ice. You could frost a beer mug on my ass. "But it's out there." The Auphe bitch. I breathed on the glass and wrote in the condensation I SEE YOU. I didn't really see it, but I felt it—as much as if it had been standing outside the window, inches away, facing me, all grins and murderous cheer. "It must have opened its gate pretty far away, because I didn't feel it."

"But you feel it now?" Niko stood by my side and kept his eyes focused on the night beyond the glass. "This is new, isn't it?"

"Yeah, new." New, fun, and exciting. Feel a monster's eyes on you. Hurry and call in now for a sample. Comes with a free prize. "All the traveling I've being doing lately. Maybe it's another instinct thing that finally popped up. Pack animals sensing their own kind."

That sense of being watched for days—it'd started out small, like a small dose of paranoia, and it had grown and swelled, to the point that I was looking over my shoulder every hour or so, until I'd looked out of the window today, this very minute, and *known*. "They've always known where I was, Nik. Always.

Since the day I was goddamn born. It was part of their plan." And remaking the entire world in their image, that had been one helluva plan.

"We guessed they were watching us since we stopped running, but this makes even more sense," he said. "They wouldn't have to watch us all the time to know where we were. And it would explain how they followed us all those years. How we wondered why we never lost them for long. How they always managed to track us down again and again."

"They could sense me, no matter where we went." A biologically built-in tracking system. GPS built into the genes. The results were slower but as sure. Sticking together these past few days had been the worst thing we could've done, all of us, because *I* led them to us. The Auphe could sense themselves in me. Sense their blood just like I was one of them. It was one more repulsive goddamn tie to them and a hideous thought, but that thought, as horrible as it was . . .

It gave me another one.

I grinned darkly and saw the reflection of my teeth in the glass.

A really nasty idea.

One every last piece of shit of them deserved.

Timing. It was all about timing. The same way setting off a bomb is about timing, because the Auphe were a living bomb. Too late and you might miss your target. Right on time, way to go. Too soon? Too soon usually meant you weren't going to be around to appreciate the other options. . . . You were going to be tomato-colored paste on a wall somewhere. And when the explosive had a mind and an agenda of its own, yeah, you were probably screwed. It didn't bother me that my whole life hung on a "probably." Hell, it always had.

The next day, Delilah, who had refused to talk on

the phone, refused to fear any Auphe, now shivered with an all-over body twitch of disgust when I sat in the cubicle beside her in the main branch of the New York Public Library, the mythology section. It seemed appropriate. "You stink." She cupped her hand over her nose. "Of *suburbia*." It was as close to horrified as I'd ever seen her.

I wasn't sure what suburbia smelled like. Pink flamingos, Virgin Marys, waving flags, and Big Wheels, maybe. "If you weren't so damn stubborn, you wouldn't have to smell me," I retorted.

Every time I'd tried to talk to her on the phone she'd disconnected, until I'd finally agreed to meet her. Since I was an Auphe homing beacon, I made sure she was there a half hour before I arrived and she'd promised to stay a half hour after I left. Then again, promises and Delilah—I wasn't sure she was patient enough to always keep them. Smart enough, yes. Patient . . . different story.

"Better clean death than your stench." She left her cubicle to sit on the desk of mine, very obviously not there for the book learning.

"The Auphe won't give you that."

"Yes, yes." She rolled copper eyes. "To wait thirty minutes. Sneak like weasel. Cower like sheep. I understand." Her silver ponytail hung over her breast. "Where is your keeper?"

"Safe." Nik was a lot safer alone and on the move than he was with me. Not that it hadn't taken some convincing . . . on both sides. We'd had to convince each other and ourselves that it was the right thing to do. If I was wrong about the Auphe being imprinted on me like Satanic baby ducklings, if they were simply following with more skill than any creature should have, I could lose Nik. If I was right and the Auphe got pissed off that I was the only one they could find . . . then Nik could lose me.

Of the games they'd played with us the past week this time, I was finally dealt in. And my hand was good—aces high, because I didn't think I was wrong.

Not this time.

And that promise I'd made to Nik, how I'd outthink them, how I'd get us out of this—I might just be able to keep it.

They were all gone now—Promise, Cherish, and Robin. They'd scattered before the sun had come up. The Auphe watching that night had been joined by another one and had stayed put as the others left. Both had melted out of existence when Niko and I had driven off that morning in his car before going our separate ways in the city. I hadn't felt one since. Not yet. Definitely not when Niko and I had split up.

It had to be one of the hardest things I'd ever done. I knew the Auphe wanted him, almost more than they wanted me—because of me. Walking away from him based on a feeling, an ability I barely knew existed—"tough as shit" didn't begin to describe it.

And for him to let me go? He almost couldn't do it. Literally. He'd spent his life making sure I kept mine, and to not be there to watch my back now? I didn't think he could take that first step away. He didn't think so either. This wasn't a fight with a mummy or a battle with a werewolf. This was the big time—the real monsters. *Our* monsters.

Walk away? Now?

I saw it in his eyes. Impossible conflict. My big brother, who'd guarded me since my first breath, and he couldn't do it. Not even if it meant saving us all. He believed in me—he did—but when belief runs up against a lifetime of habit, belief can be kissing the canvas in a heartbeat. Just that one step . . .

I took it because I knew he couldn't.

"Tell the son of a bitch Samuel hey for me." I grinned before turning and merging into the crowd on the sidewalk. If it was the last look he ever had of me, I wanted it to be of the same cocky, cynical, stubborn bastard I'd always been. That thanks to him, I'd lived long enough to be. When I finally gave in and glanced back, he was gone.

It was the right thing to do, but I'd never felt more alone in my life. Your brother watched your back and you watched his.

Always.

God.

But he was safe. I believed it. I believed it because I had to.

"Safe." In the library Delilah leaned down to whisper by my ear. "Safe is overrated. Safe is not fun."

I let my thoughts shift from Nik to the image of a very nude, very limber werewolf, then gave myself a metaphorical smack back to reality. Not that doing it in the stacks with Delilah wouldn't have been entertaining, not to mention some stress relief, but I didn't have the time. And not really the concentration. Knowing the Auphe could appear on the top of a shelf any second and snatch me away while I was going at it was enough to take the lust out of anybody's thrust.

"Safe is all I've got right now, if I want to stay above ground and kicking." I ignored the warm press of her upper leg against my arm. And I didn't sweat. No court in the land could make me swear otherwise. "I need a favor."

She sighed, bored. She didn't pout. Wolves don't pout. They may get indigestion from eating you if you annoy them, but they don't pout. "Favor? What favor?" she demanded with a careless yawn.

It was an easy enough one for her, just information, though for what she charged you'd think it was much harder. Before I left she did kiss me with a punishing nip of teeth and the soothing silk of tongue. It had me wanting to rethink safe, but I couldn't. I'd been heading for this moment my whole life. Whether I lived or died, it ended now.

I left the library, hoping Delilah was smart *and* patient enough to stay behind as long as she'd said, because I had one of them on me now . . . watching. It had just moved into range. Of course, I wasn't sure what that range was, so it wasn't too helpful to me. I assumed within eyesight. I didn't look around. We had one small advantage in this, and I didn't want to give it away. My phone rang while I was clambering down the bottom of the stairs. I answered to hear Niko say brusquely, "You alive?"

"It's cute how you worry." I grinned, equally relieved to know he was in the same shape himself. "How'd it go with Samuel? Did they go for it?"

"They did. More importantly, they have the equipment upstate, although they also said officially it didn't exist." For some reason that seemed to amuse him, but he didn't say why. "They flew it down from Fort Drum. I met them and was instructed on it. What's the address Delilah gave you? I'll call it to Samuel."

I gave it to him. Flew it down from the army base. Damn, the Vigil did have some unbelievably serious influence. "You haven't seen any of them following you, have you?"

"No, I'm clean as far as I can tell. You were right. They are homed in on you. Do you have any?"

"One."

"One." Nik didn't say it like it was good news. To him it wasn't. One could as easily call in the other seventeen, and he wouldn't be there. That was the bottom line. He wouldn't be there.

"Just one. Broad daylight. Thousands of people." All separately might not have stopped them, but the combination could pull it off.

He exhaled, sounding calm and matter-of-fact, and absolutely not fooling me one damn bit about any of it. "Samuel said they can be ready starting tonight."

"Be nice if one time was all it took." The sky was as pure blue as yesterday when we'd come tumbling out of it. "Everyone else crawled in a hole and pulled it in after them?"

"Yes, although Promise and Robin aren't too happy about it." Promise and Cherish had gone to New Jersey. If Oshossi's animals could sniff them out in that smell, more power to them. Robin had gone wherever Robin went. Someplace where condoms were stored by the crate and clothing was not only optional but highly frowned upon.

It made facing the Auphe a shade less terrifying.

"It was you and me in the beginning, Nik," I said. "You and me in the end." It was the way it was supposed to be. Meant to be. Fate coming full circle.

"If this time in the beginning you could come already potty trained, it would be a big plus," he said dryly before disconnecting.

I snorted and slid the phone into my jacket pocket as the second watcher joined the first. Five minutes later, there was a third. They had to be curious. Annoyed. Ticked the hell off. Where were the rest of us?

"Yeah, you keep watching," I muttered. I'd been right when I'd talked to Nik on the beach days and days ago. If I'd ran while the others hid—even if they'd had to do it all their lives—they would've been safe. Although Niko was like the Auphe. They might have genetic GPS, but in a way, so did he. There was no guarantee who would've found me first.

I ducked my head against the cold wind and started walking. It was going to be a long day of dragging these bitches from place to meaningless place. And the night? I didn't want to think about the night. That's when it could go wrong in all the worst ways.

I had hours to kill before that, though, and there was one thing I'd always meant to do. If I was going to go out, good hand or not, and chances were much better than ever that I was, I wasn't going out with that on my body. *That* was a black and red tattoo I had on my bicep. I'd been possessed once—yeah,

yeah, old news—and my pilot during the whole ordeal thought it would be an absolute blast to get MOM surrounded by a heart on my arm. To say I'd considered peeling the skin off with my combat knife didn't really give the flavor of how much I hated it. Had hated her.

I wasn't going to die with that on me. I found the nearest tattoo parlor, waited my turn before sitting, taking off my jacket, rolling up my sleeve, and saying, "Cover it up."

The guy—big, fat, and with a curly beard—blinked, bored. "With what?" Whether I didn't love my mommy or not anymore wasn't his concern.

"With damn Big Bird for all I care. Just cover it up."

It wasn't that easy. It's *never* that easy. A whole slew of them came over to discuss the situation. A tattoo was a reflection of your inner self, your true blah, blah, blah. You couldn't just slap anything on there. Well, obviously I had, as no one had fought me about the whole mom issue. Apparently moms got more respect than Big Bird. One guy had actually suggested that it would be easy to blend the tattoo I had now into a dragon, as if that wouldn't get me laughed out of the bar. Assuming Ishiah ever let me back in after Cambriel's death.

A dragon. Christ. While piles of flaming lizard crap from the sky were deadly enough if you weren't careful, it certainly wasn't worth bragging about to have survived. I could never wear a short-sleeved shirt again.

Finally I pointed at a red and black band on the wall. Funky lettering. I felt the invisible Niko *thwap* me over my ear and corrected myself quickly. Latin. It was Latin. "What about that? What's that?"

"Armband. A lot of our guys retiring from the military are getting that. It says 'Brothers in Arms,' " Curly said.

Huh. How about that? The right colors and, this time, the right sentiment.

Last time it hadn't hurt or the thing inside me had enjoyed the pain. Hard to say. This time it did. I didn't mind.

The things that matter are worth it.

You could still see the heart with the MOM, but just barely, and only if you knew where to look. The ghost of gone. Just like Sophia herself. She was gone, but if you knew where to look in me, you'd still see her. It was the best that I could hope for, though, and I was happy with it. I let them tape it up with gauze, paid, and headed outside. Hours had passed and the light was bleeding from the sky.

Timing. Now was when I found out if I was on the right side of it—or tomato paste on the wall.

Radioactive tomato paste, as it turned out.

Because that note in Nik's voice on the phone? Can I just get a "Holy shit" from the choir, please?

"A nuke? A goddamn nuke? A fucking nuke? A . . ." My mouth was still moving, but nothing was coming out. I'd run out of curse words to say. Me. That hadn't ever happened in my life. "What's wrong with a nice normal bomb? You know, in case things go wrong, we only take out a few buildings, not the whole damn city."

Robin had found Niko and me a place to stay temporarily. It was a furnished studio apartment, the best he said he could do on short notice, but it was on the first floor. That's all we needed. The first floor. I met Nik there and I would've wrinkled my nose at the smell of old cat piss dried into the floor if I didn't have other things on my mind—radioactive things.

"First off, there is no such thing as a nice normal bomb. There are bombs dropped from planes. There are missiles. Trucks filled with fertilizer and diesel fuel. And there are multiple charges placed around a building to detonate it. None of which fill our need. Besides, I thought the mere idea of a nuclear weapon would make you happier than the porn you hide under your bed. It certainly puts your Desert Eagle in the shade," he replied, a wickedly amused glitter in his eye while his face remained passive.

Despite my love for my Eagle and various other weapons of semiexplosive destruction, I wasn't, believe it or not, turned on by the thought of a nuke. "There has to be something. We brought down the last warehouse without a stick of dynamite."

"That's because then you were the bomb."

Not much you could say to that.

"Well, what the hell were you asking for when you called Samuel?" I asked, sitting on the fold-out couch that sagged a good half foot in the middle cushion. I didn't think Robin had tried as hard as he said he had. I doubted he appreciated those days and days of celibacy.

"I thought since the Vigil has contacts within the police and city government, they would most likely have agents within the military as well. Thousands of years of conspiracy does give one maneuvering room for job placement. And the military has weapons, including explosive devices, that the public know nothing about."

"Seems complex." I grunted. "There are bombs out there that should wipe out anything the size of a couple of football fields that you don't need a truck to haul around. I've seen them."

"There are?" Niko asked as he leaned against the cracked wall. It held his weight, surprisingly. It looked like a forty-pound five-year-old could take it down. "Where did you see them?"

"You know, TV, movies. *Mission: Impossible* wouldn't lie."

He closed his eyes. "I tried, Almighty Universe. I

did my best." Straightening, he went on, "Since the Auphe move so quickly, we need a large area of destruction, and since you cannot build a gate big enough to drive a truck through, the Vigil suggested a suitcase nuke as being the most appropriate for the task."

"The Vigil trust us with a nuke? Even a baby nuke?" I asked skeptically. A nuke? The Vigil *had* a nuke? They did have a finger in every pie, pretty scary pies.

"Probably not, but Samuel does. He's seen what we would do to keep the Auphe from taking the world back. I didn't say what their plan was this time." He wouldn't. Niko wouldn't tell anyone that. "But that they had one and they had to be dealt with. Now. He convinced his superiors that whether our plan worked or not, we would make sure that the city would be safe. We'd die to keep that promise."

"Dying's the easy part," I muttered. As plans went, it was like most of mine—semisuicidal—but even I hadn't come up with the damn nuke. And the Vigil knew the Auphe. They knew that even eighteen could one day, no matter how many hundreds or thousands of years it took them, take back what they thought was theirs. They still must have trusted the hell out of Samuel . . . and Niko. If they knew anything about the supernatural community, if they had investigated Nik, they knew he would keep his word. NYC would be safe.

When they'd investigated me, and I'm sure they had, they must've thought it was a good thing they had Nik to fall back on. I was one of those guys who didn't look too good on paper, or while being possessed, or creating mass chaos going undercover in the Kin.

Or being the last male Auphe. Good thing they didn't know about that. Even if a human male would do, just not as well, I was sure the Vigil would think long and hard about popping one in the back of my skull to be on the safe side and try to deal with the Auphe another way.

But there was no other way.

I didn't want to think about this anymore, the pressure of not taking out NYC with me if I bit the dust. Thinking about if we did pull it off, I still might not be coming back—the rational part of me anyway. Really, *really* didn't want to think about it. I rested my head and stared at the ceiling. A nuke. Goddamn spy movies. And why did our government have suitcase nukes? Weren't only terrorists supposed to have them?

"How many followed you?" Great, a subject worse than nukes.

"Three." I looked back down at Niko, my ass already complaining from the couch. I didn't think it'd be any more comfortable when we folded it out, but it didn't much matter. Sleep was going to be hard to come by until this was over anyway.

"Three," he repeated grimly before adding, "fifteen more to go."

I got up to check out the bathroom, because the thought of eighteen Auphe in one place—that'll make your bladder sit up and take notice. "Shit!" I called out. "Is there such a thing as a giant supernatural cockroach straight from the depths of hell?"

"No. Be a man and deal with it."

I could've shot it. It was that big. I kicked it in the toilet and flushed. Three times. Then I returned to Cat Urine Central. "Okay. The world is safe for pissing again. Enjoy."

"And to think I worried about you today, being alone." Niko drew his katana and looked it over. "Almost."

I snorted. "I think I feel a tear coming on."

He turned the katana over and laid it on the back of his hand. It balanced perfectly. "You are sentimental, I will give you that." He sheathed the sword.

"Your plan or not, you're coming back, Cal. All of you. I won't have it any other way." I'd made it clear I wasn't too damn sure about that, and it showed. I could hide a lot of things, but not that.

But what the hell? Sanity was overrated. What had it ever done for me anyway?

"I'm sentimental. You're optimistic." I dropped back on the couch. "Watch out, Snow White. There's two new dwarves in town."

He wasn't distracted. "Are you ready for this?"

"I've been ready a long, long time."

And I had been.

Before I was born. When I was nothing but a pile of gold in a whore's hand, I'd been ready.

Waiting, like timing, can be a bitch.

I'd hoped it would be the first night. I wanted it over with, and I wanted it over with now. Of course it wasn't. The next night, I felt five outside. My stomach tensed, I carried my gun with me the entire night, and didn't sleep one minute of it. Five could be enough. Five might do the trick for Niko and me. But they'd tried four times before. Two times playing, two times in sincerity . . . although it was a mocking sincerity. I didn't think there would be any mocking this time. I thought they were coming for Nik, coming for me, and game time was over.

The third time is the charm. Isn't that what they say? It didn't feel like a charm, but it felt like a chance, and that was the best we could hope for.

I'd been dozing on the couch off and on that night. Staying awake three nights in a row turned out not to be doable, but the feeling brought me out of the drowse instantly. Eighteen. Eighteen of the bitches were out there, and they weren't going to stay out there long. All they needed was the time to catch a glimpse through the window, to see where they were going, and they'd be there. That's why we kept the small window covered with a blanket, and it was the only thing that gave us the time we needed.

"Nik, *now*." I bolted off the couch fully dressed, shoes on. It was the way we'd catnapped for the past days now.

I hit the door running, Niko right behind me. We were on the street in seconds and in a cab in minutes. We moved fairly briskly through the nighttime traffic and were at the warehouse district in less than a half hour. Delilah had given us the address—long abandoned by humans or Kin, and abandoned was what we needed. It was a hulk of a building with windows.

Huge, unobstructed if grimy windows. The Auphe had good night vision. They could see where they wanted to go—see the way in. And they were there, every last one of them, following us from rooftop to rooftop, maybe. From the top of a bus or truck. I didn't care. They were there, and that's what mattered.

Niko and I pushed through the front doors, then slammed them behind us. They were unlocked. Wasn't that lucky? Yeah, right. Planning is better than luck any day.

It was a trap. The Auphe knew it was a trap. A paste-eating, booger-picking kindergartner would've known it was a trap. That was the Auphe weakness. They were strong, incredibly fast, fanatical, hard as fucking hell to kill, but they were arrogant.

Promise, Cherish, Robin, Niko, and me. What could the five of us possibly accomplish against their eighteen? Take one or two with us? Maybe. But other than that, not a damn thing.

But there were no Promise, Cherish, or Robin. There were others, though, those who wanted the Auphe gone almost as much as we did.

Niko and I made our way to the center of the warehouse. He didn't draw his sword, one of the strangest things I'd seen in a battle—Niko without some blade drawn. "Samuel!" he rapped. From twenty feet away, Samuel tossed him a large metal briefcase that just happened to contain a nuclear device. *Tossed*. Okay, Nik had explained a suitcase nuke was much smaller in destructive power than the kind dropped from a plane that can take out whole cities. But it would take out a chunk, and they were tossing it like a basketball—even though Samuel had told Niko it weighed only about fifty pounds.

"Don't worry, Cal. It's not volatile. It has to be triggered, not dropped," Samuel said.

Right. That guy should watch more TV.

I didn't pull my gun from my holster, another first for an expected battle. I looked at my brother and wanted to repeat what we'd said after we'd fallen out of the sky. I wanted to ask if he was sure. He still had a chance to make a run for it. He still had a chance to live.

He anticipated me. "Together," he repeated.

I barely had time to nod when the eighteen gates opened behind us, and Niko and I dropped to our knees instantaneously. That's when the Uzis of thirty of the Vigil who had been waiting in the warehouse moved between the Auphe and us and fired. Just as Niko had planned it with Samuel and his companions four days before, they formed a shield for us, to give us time to do what was needed. They were a line of the best-equipped human assassins in, if at least not the entire city, definitely a fifteen-block radius.

They might as well have been carrying Super Soakers.

The Auphe had smelled them, smelled more than the five they'd counted on, smelled a far bigger trap than they'd been expecting, and they didn't care. Nope, a shit they simply did not give. And if it had only been the Vigil, they wouldn't have a reason to. They couldn't have smelled anything in the air but a cloud of fear sweat. The Vigil had been around, and

Uzis were fun and all, but this was the Auphe. The Vigil might be the only humans alive besides Nik who knew what the Auphe were and what they could do. They had every reason to be afraid, and the Auphe proved it. A blur of motion, they leapt from their gates, some up to the walls and some across the floor straight toward the men and into the near wall of bullets.

I was occupied wrapping a cloth over my nose and mouth and tying it behind my neck. It smelled strongly of the oil Niko used on his swords. I was going to use my gun oil, but something that smelled of Niko . . . it had a better chance. Gave *me* a better chance.

"How many seconds?" Niko asked as he opened the case.

We'd discussed this at least twenty times in the past few days, but it came down to me. How fast I could open a gate and how fast I could shut eighteen down. Then there was moving through and . . . shit. Shit. I didn't know. I could only guess.

"Cal."

Niko had his hand hovering above a computerized trigger. The Vigil were being torn to pieces around us. Bullets, bullets everywhere, but these were the Auphe. If they couldn't dodge it, and most they could, it didn't matter unless it took their head off, and I didn't see a single headless Auphe torso. Which I happily would've wanted an eight-by-ten glossy of if I had. I did see human guts, heard screaming, limbs ripped from bodies, and throughout it all the switchblade stab of hyena laughing. I saw it all—the future of the world. If the Auphe had their way.

Fuck 'em. They weren't getting it.

I wrapped the second cloth over my eyes. "Five seconds. Go." I heard the click of the timer being switched on, and I opened the gate to hell. Tumulus. It was half of the plan. Forget gating. The Auphe can run too. We needed someplace we could blow up the size of a few football fields. Even the Auphe couldn't run that fast. Especially with what Niko was packing.

When I said "Go," I tore a hole in reality. I couldn't see it, but I could feel it—inside me, howling in glee, all but screaming my name. And I discovered there was something better than meditation for pushing down my inner monster; the thought of a nuke three feet from me.

Niko's hand grabbed my arm and yanked me through. I felt the ripple of pure power and then we were there. I couldn't smell it, only the oil-soaked cloth over my mouth. I couldn't see it, thanks to the blindfold. But it touched me. The biting cold on my face, the grit of glass sand under my hands and through the knees of my jeans. I was back.

Four seconds.

Niko had said no when I told him back at Rafferty's what we needed to do. He'd seen me the first time I'd returned from Tumulus. He'd heard and seen what I'd done when hypnotized to recover the lost memories of this place and what had happened to me here. We both thought the same. If I went back, that'd be it. No lost memories to save me. No juvenile traumatic amnesia this time. More likely the two years I'd lost to begin with would all come flooding back and do to my brain what the Auphe had done to the Vigil.

But it could be that wasn't true, I'd argued. Maybe every time I thought of going back to Tumulus and losing my sanity, I was thinking of being dragged there by the Auphe. Maybe it wasn't just the place but the monsters that went with it and what they would do to me if they ever took me there again.

Three seconds.

I felt the eighteen gates open around us.

I'd argued with Niko for hours over it. Saying it was worth the risk. He wouldn't agree—it wasn't going to happen—until I said the Auphe were following me. They wanted Niko dead. They wanted me alive. Either way, if Niko went through to Tumulus without me, there was no guarantee all the Auphe would follow him and his bomb. Some would stay for me, and Nik knew it. It was the only reason he'd given in. It was him, naturally, that came up with blocking my sense of sight and smell. Blocking as much of Tumulus as we could. And it seemed to be working.

And the time element . . . if I kept the gate open, like Niko had suggested when he'd wanted to go through alone earlier in the week for reconnaissance, if I kept it anchored to our world, it might keep the time flow there and here the same. Although, hell, at this point, the time difference was the least of our concerns.

They came through their gates. I heard the whisper of sand under their feet and claws. I felt their eyes on me the same as I'd felt them watching me the past days.

Two seconds.

I didn't think they knew what the bomb was, but they did recognize a trap that would actually work. Smelled the confidence on Niko, the vicious triumph on me—not the fear they'd scented on the Vigil. Mad, feral, but smart as the most cunning of predators. A predator like that would retreat, think things over, see what would happen.

Too bad I slammed their gates in their faces. At Niko's harsh "Now" and hard squeeze of my shoulder, I closed them all.

I knew how they did it. I knew it *in* me—when they had done it to mine, they'd taught me to do it to theirs—but knowing and closing one was one thing. Closing eighteen. Could I do that? Guess what. I'd learned last year, if you're willing to die, physically you can do almost anything before you go. To kill the Auphe, I was willing to die. . . . But I didn't. I closed their gates and my brain didn't explode. Did it hurt? Jesus, yes, it hurt, but I was still conscious, and that's what mattered. Niko hit me midchest and knocked me back through the only gate left—mine. I felt the concrete floor of the warehouse under my back, his weight on top of me and I closed the door to Tumulus instantly. It was gone.

One.

The world shook. I pulled off the rags from my face as the pounding in my brain continued. There was no light brilliant enough to burn away the flesh from your bones. No force strong enough to take out city blocks. There was nothing, but the world still shook. The glass didn't quiver in the windows; the dust motes floating in the dim lights set in the ceiling didn't drift a millimeter. I didn't care. I still felt it. A part of a world—not this one—but a part of some other world had just died.

I started to ask Nik if he felt it too . . . but I saw it. Quicker than the other seventeen. More of that razor-edge intelligence. It couldn't open its gate, so it used mine. It came through with us, fast and alive when it should've been dead. Metal teeth that had grinned through so many of my childhood windows and adult nightmares. Eyes more radioactive than any mushroom cloud. Claws, transparent skin, jagged joints, death . . .

No.

Red glass granules on my hands cutting them . . . like before.

No.

That thin, cold air that wanted to suck your lungs inside out.

The bitch should've *died* there.

I growled and threw Nik off me, before he saw it behind him. Threw him off like he weighed nothing. The sand, the cold, being naked in caves, being fed meat, and told what kind it was only after I was done. Discovering as bad as eating it was, being forced to eat it again after you'd vomited it on the ground was

worse. Beaten and clawed and fed handfuls of it from
the stone. Fed by what could've been the same goddamn bitch. Because they needed their tool healthy,
to open a gate back in time to when the world was
new and wipe out the humans before they had a
chance to get the smallest grip on life.

My teeth were in its throat, ripping it with one
smooth motion as I took it to the floor. It had moved
to evade. I had moved with the same speed. Used the
same throat tearing I'd seen them use on the weaker
or wounded ones. Or sometimes they killed each other
just for the hell of it—in the caves or under the boiling
sky. A game. And now I got to play too.

Black blood flowed down its chest, but it wouldn't
kill it. It would only slow it down for half a second . . .
a second. More than enough for an Auphe to take
advantage of, and I did.

I'd seen them use their claws in those caves, not
just their teeth. I didn't have claws, not homegrown,
but I had others. My hands went into my jacket and
came out with two dirk daggers, one in each hand.
Narrow blades, the perfect size to fit the eye sockets
that held those pools of lava and blood. I sheathed
them there to the hilts and punctured the malignant
tumor of a brain. Its body bucked under me, its claws
trying for my face, my side, but the spidery hands
went limp first and fell to the ground.

"Unworthy," I hissed. I withdrew the blades and
slammed them home one more time. It bucked again,
and the faint hiss of air bubbled through the blood
that was still pumping from its throat, but more slowly.
And slower still.

Then there was no more gurgling. No more fighting
to escape. Only the last escaping breath ripe with the
smell of Vigil flesh. There was a bead of moisture on
my bottom lip. I'd ripped out its throat with such
speed that only a drop of blood touched my mouth. I
touched it with the tip of my tongue, sampled it. It

tasted like poison and death and the rich earth of a long-forgotten graveyard.

It wasn't half bad.

"Cal. Come back."

I looked up, a boiling acid glare through the strands of black hair that fell over my face. "My kill. Mine." The words hurt my throat. Weren't right. They twisted and knotted the air, they didn't flow through it.

"Cal, I told you I was bringing you back with me. All of you. I meant it. Now come back." I recognized that voice. He was there the first time I'd come back from . . . that place. He'd been there, waited for me. My brother.

Like he was waiting for me now—in the warehouse, not at a burned trailer. No, not waiting. He'd been with me to hell and back. Blown hell to hell and back.

I laughed. It didn't sound quite right either, but better than the words I'd spat.

"Cal, *now*." There were hands on my arms, gripping hard.

I let go of one of the dirks and rubbed my eyes, then the blood from my mouth. "Nik."

The random mixing of colors I'd seen settled into olive skin, with a touch of green from the gate travel, dark blond hair, warning eyes. My brother's face. "The Vigil," he said softly enough only I could hear and steely enough to let me know I was on the edge of Auphe-ing myself into the Vigil's classification of overt as King Kong pregnant with Mothra's baby, and telling Oprah all about his mood swings.

I'd been as fast as an Auphe, killed an Auphe in seconds, spoke Auphe, had been considering . . . no one needed to know what I was considering. I didn't need to know. But I did know. I knew what Auphe did with their prey.

The Auphe's heart stopped under me.

It had stopped breathing a moment before, but sometimes the heart takes some time to catch up. It did, and this time my brain did explode. I fell off the Auphe, over onto my back, and began convulsing. There had been lights in my brain. A dark and grim constellation, always there but I'd never known it. I knew now because they all blinked out. They very last one wavered, faded, and disappeared. The half-genetic, half-telepathic web was gone. I'd only known about the connection for days, but it felt like millions of neurons were dying. It was as if every single star in the universe went out. Every single one.

Now I really was the Last Mohican.

Nik's hand was on my shoulder as he turned me from back to side, in case I vomited. "Get away," I heard him snap, probably to Samuel. Let's face it, all the Zen in the world wasn't getting Nik over Samuel's onetime serving of the Auphe. Seeing me actually taste Auphe blood, though, no big deal. I had the little-brother-get-out-of-jail-free-forever card. Big brothers. "Cal, can you hear me?"

I could hear him, but I couldn't keep my teeth from chattering long enough to answer. And I thought three things—the last was the worst by far and away. The first, seizures were bad. The second, seizures could kill you. Third, seizures could make you piss your pants. Dear God, don't let me piss my pants, I thought desperately as the thrashing turned to shuddering and from there to utter limpness. Niko moved me onto my back again. Someone had already dragged the Auphe away. "Can you hear me?" he repeated tightly.

"Tell me . . ." I swallowed and blinked, vision clearing. "Tell me . . . I didn't . . . piss myself."

He bowed his head for a moment, shoulders relaxing, then looked up to slap my face lightly. "Not so much that you'd notice, little brother."

I glared with hazy eyes. "You suck, you know that?"

Samuel ignored Niko's warning for a moment, either a brave man or a stupid one, and moved closer. "They're watching," he muttered low. "If Niko hadn't pulled you out of it, I don't think they'd just be watching."

Yeah, I'll bet the Vigil was watching—or what was left of them. "He still sucks," I mumbled. I tried to get my hands under me to push up. The dizziness was sharp, my muscles like spaghetti, and I nearly fell, but Nik braced me with one hand behind my back. My legs weren't cooperating yet. "I think I'm going to puke." I closed my eyes. "Or die. Or both." A hand grasped my face and shook it carefully until my eyes opened. Niko looked into them. Apparently, what he saw satisfied him and he exhaled with more emotion than he usually let show. "I think you'll recover, wet pants and all."

I looked down automatically and scowled at perfectly dry jeans. "I repeat, you suck."

"So you keep saying. Do you remember anything?" he asked, pulling my face back up to get my eyes on his. "You acted like you remembered something. From before."

"Before" meant only one thing with us. When the Auphe had me for two years. I frowned and for a second . . . I had known something when I took out the Auphe. Remembered something, hadn't I? To kill it like I had, I would've had to, because that wasn't me. I was good at killing, but not like that. Not that fast, not that *hungry* to see death. I held my breath, scared shitless, that I did remember. That the flood-gates would open and wash me away. But it didn't. My head hurt and felt weirdly empty and dark, but no lost memories lurked there. At least not anymore. "No." I slumped slightly in relief. "Not a damn thing." I looked over to see five remaining Vigil, not counting Samuel, rolling the Auphe up in a tarp to put in one of their vans that was pulled up to the now-open door.

"They took out twenty-five Vigil in, what, two seconds? Twenty-five men with machine guns. How the hell did we pull it off?"

"You said you would outthink them." Nik helped me to my feet. "You kept your word." He sounded as if he hadn't expected anything different. Like I said, big brothers. They had faith in you when you'd forgotten what the word meant.

With an emotion so huge I didn't have a name for it, I watched as the last Auphe in the world was hidden from sight. The hell with the dizziness, the bile burning my throat, my brain turned to red-hot cinders. They were gone. Jesus Christ, they were gone.

Except for one half-blood who for at least a minute had been every bit the Auphe he had killed.

"Think we got them all?" Samuel said, his still-smoking Uzi in one hand, as he steadied me as I swayed with his other hand. Niko allowed it . . . barely.

With Nik on one side, his hand now gripping my upper arm in protective support, and Samuel on the other, they managed to keep me upright as the relief faded a little. "I thought that once. I'm not sure I'll ever think that again." But the darkness in me told me different—they were gone.

"But for now . . ." Nik said.

"Yeah, for now." It wasn't a grin. It was too twisted for that, but it was satisfied, like I'd never been so satisfied in my life.

"Time for you to go," Samuel said. "Even around here someone was bound to notice this." The Vigil were already bagging up their own dead now. "And I think you might want to consider us even now. At least from the Vigil's point of view, if not mine. No more favors."

Then he let go of me, face serious. "Stay strong. Keep your head down." Then he walked toward the doors and passed through.

Keep it down, because the Vigil had seen what I'd

done. I didn't think I could do it again, had no idea how I'd done it at all, but in their eyes, half Auphe might be too much Auphe.

As I steadied myself on my feet, the dizziness and headache were fading fast. Too fast for a human. But probably about right for the last Auphe. The Vigil might be right, saw what Niko didn't want to. That was definitely a thought for another time. I wasn't ruining this. Nothing could ruin this. I said, "I think I want a beer. If Ish will let me in the place. I want one beer, and I want to feel normal."

"No bar. No beer. Convulsions and beer do not mix," Niko retorted. "And you always were normal."

I cocked my head. "Cyrano, seriously, you have delusions only massive drugs could explain."

"Normal to me," he countered firmly. "As far as I'm concerned that's all that counts."

As we walked outside, the dizziness disappeared as did the headache, and I was good as new in record time . . . the sort of time that definitely wasn't normal, no matter what Nik said or thought. I ignored the feeling and felt around for more Auphe out there. None. We were clean. Suddenly, I felt good. Right. This was right.

"You going to Promise and Cherish's new hideout?" I asked as we kept walking. A taxi might take you here, but it sure as hell wasn't going to be cruising here for pickups. We could've called, but walking felt good and right too.

"No. This is our night. Tonight we go home," he said as if there was no other choice. No hot vampire girlfriend waiting. He was right, though. It was our night. The Leandros brothers, who'd turned survival into an art form like nobody else ever had.

"Tomorrow I'll see them. I especially want to discuss the Oshossi situation, which I'm finding more questionable as time goes on." He looked back through the door at the dark stains of blood that were scattered across the floor. "It's over." There was an odd note in his voice, part satisfaction, but mainly puzzlement.

I knew he meant, How can it be over?

It was a good question, and one I could still hardly understand. One with an answer I wasn't sure I could admit to. After all that had happened, after a lifetime of watching for, running, or fighting a nightmare, how could it really be over? It was almost unbelievable.

"You want a hug?" I drawled, just as unsure myself. "Will that bring you closure?" Normally he would've swatted me a good one on the back of the head, but convulsions gave me a free ride there for now. And I was bullshitting anyway, because I felt the same. Relieved, strong, yet . . . how? The Auphe were dead. They were gone. But I was like Nik. How could it be over? After all these years . . .

How could we be free?

But I knew one thing: Their whole race had nearly been destroyed in a warehouse. It was goddamn poetic we could send the last ones out in one just like it.

We went home, a place truthfully I didn't think we'd ever see again. There was a new door and a bill taped to it courtesy of our landlord. Hell, I was relieved it wasn't an eviction notice.

There we were with our battered couch, battered table and lamps . . . battered everything. Right then it was better than a mansion in my eyes. We didn't have to worry about watching, waiting. We didn't have to stay alert every second for death to come tearing out of the air. We could relax. We could sleep, not that half-assed dozing you do when something's breathing down your neck. We could really sleep.

Neither one of us did.

We sat on the couch until the sun lightened the morning sky. Who wanted to waste the first real taste of freedom on sleep? I had my brother. I had my life.

I was going to enjoy every damn second of it. All that was missing were the fish sticks and cartoons.

The sky streaked with tangerine, pink, and violet-blue, and the sun peered through the shadow-black buildings. It looked to be a damn gorgeous day.

One of the best of my life.

Robin called me that afternoon after Niko had already left to see Promise and Cherish. He wanted to meet at the bar and get the story up close and personal. We'd called everyone the night before to clue them in on the survival thing, but Goodfellow liked details. Lots and lots of details. It was the next best thing to being there. And he would've been there if we'd needed him to be, but I thought he was damn glad we hadn't, especially once I mentioned the nuke. He'd taken that about as well as I had.

"So it's over." Reliving it all hadn't been as tough as I'd imagined. Skipping one part of it had certainly made it easier. I'd managed it so thoroughly I kept half forgetting where I'd lost my dirks. Not the eye sockets of an Auphe, nope, and it was the end of the Auphe. How could that be bad? Forget it and go on.

I had a flash of a thought that the real end of them might not come until I was gone, but what we'd done the night before . . . it was good enough. I'd made the decision not to rain on my own parade, and I was sticking with it.

Despite Nik's order from last night, I had a beer. Last night was last night and today was seventeen hours later. That was a long time—in my book anyway. I nursed it, though, as it was the single one I tended to allow myself. Sophia had been the type of alcoholic that would've needed a 112 step program. It didn't pay to tempt fate.

"Thank Zeus, it's about damn time." Robin was working on a bottle of wine, fancy glass and all. "The

Vigil came through, eh? I suppose Samuel is as remorseful as he says he is."

"Sorry is sorry, but I think he probably considers thirty Uzi-armed Vigil and a nuke cleans the slate." I took another swallow of beer.

"Nuclear weapons." He shook his head and swirled the wine in his glass. "I'm not sure humans are too far from the Auphe in some ways."

Being both, I wasn't much in the position to make that call. "How was the orgy?" I asked instead.

"Actually, I picked up Salome and spent quality time with the shriveled feline." He went on defensively, "I didn't want her snacking on the neighbors."

Sure. That was the reason. I grinned into my beer.

Halfway through my beer, Ishiah came up to the table. He hadn't said a word when I'd come through the door. He'd looked at me briefly, then went back to serving a customer. It wasn't an engraved invitation or anything, but I took it to mean I wasn't banned. He didn't mention Cambriel when I went up for my beer. I'm not sure he ever would. I wasn't sure I wanted him to. Cambriel deserved better. To be remembered. But to think of him was to think of his severed head dangling from the hand of an Auphe, and I couldn't. I couldn't go there, knowing if it weren't for me he'd still be alive.

I finished my beer in several swallows, nursing it be damned, but the memory didn't disappear as easily as the alcohol did.

"So," Ishiah said to Robin, "you survived the Auphe."

"I did," Robin said smugly, as if he'd actually been there. But I'd give him credit this time. It might not be lying, bragging, or his enormous ego. He could be referring to the entire crappy experience instead of only last night. "I was beyond brave, an unparalleled fighter, a morale booster with no equal."

"And he didn't get laid once," I added, which seemed the bigger feat to me.

Ishiah raised a disbelieving eyebrow. "You're saying after all these years you're finally listening to me?"

"Listen? To you?" Robin scoffed. "If I listened to you and your thousands of years of bitching, I'd be a monk. A poorly dressed, destitute, horrifically celibate monk."

"I simply wanted you to behave like a halfway rational creature," Ishiah retorted.

Oh, this was going to be good. I leaned back out of the way.

"*Behave*? Oh no, what you wanted is for me to cut back on the drinking, the lying, the stealing, the conning, and the whoring about. The very things that make me the magnificent specimen I am today," Robin said indignantly.

"Maybe if you had, you wouldn't have ended up on the verge of being killed by descendants of former worshippers," Ishiah pointed out, brutal but true.

Robin sputtered, "Please. As if you weren't chased over sand dunes by a band of Israelites desperate for a holy souvenir. They plucked you like a chicken. You looked like a mangy pigeon when I found you."

Looking less like Niko by the second, because where Niko's anger was cold, Ishiah's was red-hot, Ishiah said dangerously, "I did *not*."

Robin countered spitefully, "They could've barbecued those things and served them up in a sports bar."

Oh yeah. This was good, all right. And I didn't even have to pay for a ticket.

They were leaning over the table, almost nose to nose, eyes narrowed to slits, faces flushed with rage. Robin huffed out a breath and said between gritted teeth, "Are you coming back to my place or not?"

Ishiah growled, "No, we're going to mine. It's closer." He tossed me the apron. "Close up the bar tonight. I won't be back."

I caught it, surprised. That wasn't the way I'd thought it would go at all. Then again . . .

Niko and Ishiah resembled each other. It'd taken me a while to notice, but it was true. Dark blond to light. Dark skin to pale. Gray eyes to blue-gray, but still, they could've been brothers. They looked a lot more like each other than Nik and I did.

I'd always thought Robin had a thing for Niko, but now it seemed more likely that Niko had reminded him of someone else. Although he hadn't been a substitute—from Robin's hounding, it had definitely been a true attraction, but now . . . the truth came out. Niko would be one relieved son of a bitch.

And as soon as I closed up the bar, Robin and Ishiah wouldn't be the only ones getting some.

I hoped.

14

Niko

The New Jersey location Promise and Cherish had chosen was a house much more elaborate than Rafferty's had been. Promise was like Robin, although she would hate to admit it—she liked the luxuries in life. I scanned the arched ceilings and doorways and gave an appreciative murmur, although truthfully between spartan and opulent, I would choose spartan. But one tried stalling techniques when he could. Unfortunately, it didn't work.

Promise had been relieved we'd survived the Auphe and furious we had not let her participate in the plan. But as it had once started with my brother and me, it had ended with my brother and me. It was the way it should have been. The way it was.

"You could have died," she snapped.

We could've worse than died, and what had happened to Cal . . . one more thing I hadn't shared with her. The slippery slope, but it was what we had, and as I'd told Cal, I'd have to see if good enough was good enough. What had happened to my brother I wasn't sharing with anyone. It had been one moment brought to life by a trip he shouldn't have had to ever make again, and an Auphe who refused to die with the others. He had come back, though—his mind somewhat slower than his body, but he had come back. No one else would've had the will—the absolute stubborn hardheaded will. No wonder I could never get him to pick up his dirty clothes.

"Died," she repeated.

We could've died anytime in the past week, but I thought it wiser not to bring up that point. Promise, normally cool and collected, rarely showed her temper, but when she did it was best to ride it out. Perhaps do a mantra or two during the experience. Focus on the lotus . . . an expression of beauty from the dull mud that spawned it. Trace the soft colors of its petals. Regard the glitter of its inner jewel. Or, as a change of pace, imagine the precise sweep of the blade required to disembowel a revenant. The silver shimmer . . .

I realized several seconds of silence had reigned, and I refocused to see fangs bared and her eyes, black as night, on me. "Are you listening, Niko, because I would hate to think that you are ignoring me."

Buddha had no teachings I knew of on domestic disputes with vampire partners, so I went with silence and a raised eyebrow. Cherish reclined nearby on a black silk couch, and laughed. "Where is the celebrated strategist now?"

"Discretion has always been the better part of valor."

Promise's eyes didn't turn any less black at my words. "Tell me again. Every detail. I want it all."

I repeated it all, minus the first exception and Cal's urination phobia. I didn't think the last was a revelation he would appreciate my sharing. Promise paced, murmuring words under her breath that were no doubt unladylike. With her long life, she probably could've taught my brother a few obscenities. "There were so many ways that it could've gone wrong. So very many."

"But it didn't. It worked as planned," I pointed out,

finally sitting. This was looking as if it might take some time, and I still had Cherish to interrogate.

"Because Cal did something he shouldn't have been able to do. Shut eighteen gates. One day he won't be so fortunate," she said, facing me.

He hadn't looked particularly fortunate seizing on the floor, but I knew what she meant. "Now that the Auphe are gone, truly gone, he shouldn't have to go to such extremes." I wouldn't let him push himself that way again. There could be no reason desperate enough and no call to close any gates ever again. Gates in general . . . we would have a very long talk about those and their use. More importantly, their disuse.

"He won't have to do what he did again," I countered. "There will be no other gates to close."

"Only his own," she said. Implacable and true, and as I'd said to myself, I would take care of it.

"Cherish." I looked away from Promise. There was no further place for the conversation to go. Cal was my responsibility. I would help him take care of the monsters in his life, even if only their shadows remained. "I want to talk to you about Oshossi."

She curled her legs under her, much as I'd seen her mother do many times. The smile was different, however. Cooperative but wicked, with a quick flash of pointed canines. "What do you wish to know?" Xolo had climbed on the couch and leaned into her side. Beauty and the beast. Granted, a very small beast—a very small beast with very large eyes. Amazingly deep and large.

"I find it difficult to believe even the proudest of creatures would chase you across country after country, transporting all his creatures, to take vengeance over one piece of useless jewelry." I finished flatly, "Very difficult."

"Not so difficult, if you know the kind of creature

he is. How his sense of pride is his greatest treasure. How none can defeat him. His ego simply won't allow it." Her fingers stroked the pale cheek of the chupa, its eyes brighter than usual. "You can see how that might be."

Promise, who'd once called her daughter a liar and a thief, a shame to her, agreed immediately. "There are those like that. Niko, you've told me yourself. Wasn't Abbagor the same?"

Actually, Abbagor had not been the same. The troll's tastes had run to slavery, and to his final battle looked forward to the majority of his life, but vengeance over a necklace? It was beneath him, and I would've thought beneath Oshossi.

"No," I responded. "I would think only madness would lead to extremes, and Oshossi seems anything but insane."

"Pride can be a kind of insanity," Cherish said lightly. "Can't it? Can't you see that, Niko?" Xolo leaned his head against her shoulder, his eyes still on me—dreamy and drifting.

Perhaps . . .

Perhaps she was correct there. Madness could take many forms. We'd seen that over the years. Although Oshossi didn't seem that way, it was possible I could be wrong. And even if it weren't a necklace that had inspired Oshossi to such radical methods, maybe it had been something else. Something . . .

But was that really important? I shook off a sudden spell of light-headedness. Lingering effects of the concussion, no doubt. But that wasn't important either. Wasn't dealing with the problem now more important than anything else? Anything at all? The dizziness began to dissipate.

Yes, it was much more clear now. With the Auphe gone we would be able to concentrate more on helping Cherish. Because whatever she'd done, she shouldn't be hunted like an animal. She was Promise's daughter.

Helping her was simply the right thing to do. Hadn't I thought nearly the same thing at the Harlem brownstone? There was no need to doubt now.

We spent the rest of the day into the evening discussing Oshossi, plans to track him in Central Park— nearly impossible—and any other information Cherish had about him, what I'd gathered from mythology books, and what little more Robin had provided through acquaintances. Once or twice more the vertigo returned, but my train of thought would shift and the feeling would eventually vanish. The time passed quickly and it was nearly two a.m. before I was home. I'd taken the PATH train into the city and ran the rest of the way for the exercise. It was cold, but unlike Cal, I didn't mind the cold. It scoured your lungs, made you feel alive, aware, calm, and free.

And we were free.

The pound of the pavement under my shoes, the chill air against my face, it was a return to normality. As close to normal as Cal and I would come, and it was good. Up to then we'd had to search for the good . . . the light, but it was here and now. No matter how long it lasted, it was here and now.

I ran up the stairs in our building, the cold streaming away. Our hall was empty, and the walls were painted a battleship gray. The same as it always was. Normal.

Until I saw our door, partially open.

It was never unlocked and it was never open unless we were walking through it.

I silently drew my sword and slid into the apartment, only to see Cal lying on the floor. For a second I was annoyed. He'd ignored our safety protocols, leaving the door open. He'd ignored some of the most important rules of our lives. Defeating the Auphe was no reason to ignore the rules. Besides, we had work to do, finding Oshossi, and my brother was taking a nap. He was always napping. Lazy as a cat, had been his whole life. This time he hadn't even bothered to get on the couch. He just lay there in a pool of dark red, staring at the ceiling as if he hadn't heard me come in.

My breath burned my throat.

As if I wouldn't notice the mess.

I felt the katana fall from my hand.

As if I wouldn't give him hell.

As if I wouldn't . . .

Wouldn't . . .

"Cal?"

The floor was hard beneath my knees. There was blood on my hands, soaking my shirt as the heavy weight of his head rested against my shoulder, black hair covering his face . . . except the eyes. They were half open, the gray dull. Not the cocky and sly eyes that looked at me across sparring swords. Not the ones I'd seen as I walked him to the first day of first grade—clear and solemn. Or the roll of them with his first glimpse of NYC, combined with the sarcastic drawl: "One helluva roach motel."

Not the terrified madness of them as I yanked the steering wheel under my hand to drive us away from the burned-out shell of our trailer—a teenage Cal curled in a fetal ball in the passenger's seat, twitching whenever I spoke and pulling out of reach desperately if I unexpectedly tried to touch him. Months later I'd seen his first smile fleeting in the gray after being taken by the Auphe; a year later I saw his first laugh catch there. I saw his determined stare at his first gun, his grip uncertain. His first kill, a grip like iron and eyes just the same. I saw the ferocity in them the first time he'd saved my life; I saw defiance there the first time he had died.

The first time he had died.

This time, the very last time . . . I saw nothing.

Nothing.

The gray of gone.

My brother was gone.

Then I was in the hall, the katana I didn't remember picking up back in my hand, my mala beads discarded. The blood seeped through my shirt, sticking it to my skin. My hands were covered with it. There had been ccoa around him . . . five dead. I knew who had sent them.

I was the gray of gone as well, but I heard a familiar whisper. Cal telling me the same thing I would've told him.

Wake up.

Telling me that, because brothers know you can fight like this but you shouldn't. But waking up wasn't an option. Waking up to his surviving the Auphe but not a South American immortal. No. If I woke up, I wouldn't be able to do what I had to do.

Wake up and I'd know.

I couldn't know. Not now. Not yet.

Not until every last one of them was a cooling corpse.

I didn't listen to any more whispers, and I didn't know anything after that. I made sure of it. I didn't know how I made it to Central Park, but I was there. I didn't know how long I searched for them. I didn't know if I found them or they found me. I didn't know if it was cold. I didn't know if there was snow or grass beneath me. I didn't know anything. There was only a whiteness in my head, an emptiness with only one thought. One concept. One word.

Death.

There were cadejo, slippery black canine shapes. They lunged and retreated. Came and went. I sliced them to pieces. They couldn't touch the white void in me. Nothing could.

The ccoa were quicker, some on the ground, some leaping from the trees. They didn't die as quickly, but they died. My hands, still covered with blood . . . now dried a red-brown, swung the katana and they died.

Some with slit throats, some with open bellies. It didn't matter . . . as long as they died.

The Gualichu came—the spider with a thousand legs. A thousand to avoid. A thousand to cut.

It was timeless in the void . . . the cadejo, the ccoa, the Gualichu. They were swallowed and gone in the whiteness. To note how long it took was to care. I didn't care about anything anymore. Beyond death there was nothing.

Only the white.

Only the void.

My blade cut through the spider's bulbous body. Thick fluid poured free. I moved through it to chop the creature in half. It may have screamed. It may have not. Everything was muffled, wrapped in layers of cotton—sound was distant, the moon an amorphous haze, the lifeless bodies around me meaningless shadows.

Only one thing was clear, one figure sharper than anything seen in my life.

Oshossi.

"All this for a thief." He stood on the swell of a hill. "All this fury and rage over a common thief."

Words. Meaningless words.

I walked toward him, unable to even feel the ground beneath me. Unable to feel the air in my lungs. I didn't need air. I only needed this. Death. Vengeance.

I'd said I'd keep him safe. I'd told him that before he even knew what the word meant, and then I'd turned my back and this piece of dead flesh standing before me had made a liar of me.

A liar to my brother.

A *failure* to him.

A crack appeared in the void and the white filled with blood. My lips peeled back from my teeth. I had no words for Oshossi, because there were no words for what I would do to him. No way to express the agony in which he would die. There would be blood in my head, on my hands, and filling the air like a warm rain. After that, I thought that red-drenched void might then swallow me as it had swallowed everything else, and it would be a long, long time before I came out. If I ever came out.

I'd lied to him, I'd failed him, and I'd lost him.

I took another step, a double-handed grip on my katana. I met gold eyes and moved to extinguish them.

"Nik?"

It was the only thing as clear as Oshossi. The voice. His voice.

I turned my head, so slowly—the air as thick as glue, and saw him. Impossibly solid, impossibly there, impossibly real.

Caliban Leandros of the Vayash Clan.

Cal.

My brother.

Whole. Not bloody. Not torn. Not dead.

How could that be? It couldn't. It was impossible. A trick. Just another shard of broken glass that sliced my brain.

"Nik, what the hell are you doing here alone?" He had his gun in one hand and his cell phone in the other. The GPS tracker connected to mine. Beside him a white wolf whose back came as high as Cal's waist snarled silently.

A trick . . .

I looked down. My hands were bloody but not with the dried blood of before, not Cal's blood. This was fresh animal gore. My coat was streaked with it, too, but my shirt that had been stiffened and caked with the blood of his body held against mine, head cradled on my shoulder, it was clean cloth again.

But which was the trick?

"I came home. The door was wide open. Your mala beads were on the floor." I had dropped them, hadn't I? They'd held nothing for me anymore. He looked past me and growled, "What did this piece of shit do to get you here alone?"

Only a *goddamn* trick.

I fell to my knees, let the katana tumble from my hands, and pressed my eyes with the heels of my hands. Cal's hands were instantly on my shoulders. I recognized the hard grip of them, recognized the urgency. "Come on, Cyrano. You're starting to scare the shit out of me." I looked up, seized his jacket, and pulled him against me in a rough hug, one hard enough I know his ribs groaned under the pressure. His eyes—worried, determined, fierce—and alive. Not the dead, dull gray. They were alive.

"Nik?"

I rested my forehead on the top of his shoulder and struggled to find my way out of my own Tumulus, my own private hell. He smelled like beer, wolf, and my herbal soap, since he could never be bothered to buy his own. He smelled like my brother. He smelled like one last chance at sanity. A hand cupped the back of my head. "Nik, what the hell did he *do*?"

I pulled air into my lungs, breathed for what seemed like the first time since I'd seen him dead on the apartment floor. Straightening, I let him go but refused to release my one-handed grip on his jacket. If this was the trick, I didn't care. I would take it and not look back. I turned my head to see Oshossi still standing on the hill, unmoving. "You said thief." My voice was guttural and thick. It had been one of the few words to penetrate the void. "You said a common thief."

"You know nothing, do you? You truly do not know," he said, gold eyes narrow with disdain. "You only spring to the defense of family, *vampire* family, take her word, no doubt, until she could have Xolo force you to take it, whether you wanted to or not."

"Xolo? What's this have to do with that goat sucker?" Cal demanded, gun between Oshossi and us. Behind us the white wolf, Delilah, stood stiffly with head lowered and ears back.

Oshossi whirled his machetes casually. "Nothing.

You literally know nothing. It's amazing. Criminally so." He jammed one machete into the ground at least eight inches and kept the other one in movement. "Xolo is mine. He is special among his kind. Most chupacabras have mild telepathy, only enough to immobilize their simpleminded goat prey." The pointed teeth smiled. "They are nearly as simpleminded as the goats themselves, but, ah, our equally simpleminded Xolo has much, much more mind control than his average brothers and sisters. He is a potent weapon, an idiot savant with a rare talent. Once he has time to study his new prey, to feel out the workings of their mind, he can push their thoughts here and there. And he can make anyone see anything. Put a picture, a memory in their head that is as real as any genuine one. All he needs is someone to pull on his leash and tell him to do it. You can see how valuable that would make him to me."

A picture . . . a portrait of my brother and blood and death. How easily I'd been persuaded to Cherish's way of thinking today and earlier at the Harlem brownstone. As soon as a doubt would surface, so would the dizziness, and then they would both just as quickly disappear. The more I questioned, the further I'd been pushed into ignorance and compliance. Xolo. All Xolo. He hadn't known us long enough to map out our minds until now, and as we'd previously agreed to help Cherish, she hadn't needed to order him to manipulate us that much. Not until I started questioning. And then Cherish had him make a kamikaze of me.

"Christ, I get it now," Cal cursed. "That's how she pumped my brain about Nik at Rafferty's and the hospital—what a fighter you are. Were you the best of us? Were you my keeper? No wonder I'd talked so damn much. I never talk that much. Not about us. Not about family. And I never would've thought she was part of the family without that damn chupa. She was looking for the perfect weapon. And, shit, Niko, you *are* the perfect weapon."

That was it, then. My questioning earlier in the day might have hurried her plan a little, but it had been her plan all along. It was why she'd watched us spar so closely, watched us all fight. Robin, Cal, and I; she chose among us the one she thought best able to defeat Oshossi.

She had also made the most fatal mistake of her life.

"You can see how valuable that makes Xolo to me, the things he can do. You can also see why I could not allow him close to me with his new mistress. Why I depended on my creatures to dispose of her and bring him back. He is completely docile to whoever has him and feeds him." Which was why Cherish had become so alarmed to see Cal trying to give blood to him in Rafferty's kitchen. "And he knows well the workings of my mind. He could have me drown myself in the river, if so ordered, while thinking I'm but walking through the forest." Which was why he could walk into the car lot but fled the brownstone where Xolo had been.

He stopped the motion of the last machete and let it point down toward the ground. "I use him to save what forests I can. To save what belongs to *me*. I want him back. I need him back. He can move the minds of men . . . the will of governments."

"Then take him. If you have more creatures, find her, kill her, and take him," I said, my voice empty and savage all at once. "We won't stand in your way." When I didn't come back from Xolo's illusion, she'd know either Oshossi had killed me or we'd killed each other. Either way, she wouldn't stick around. In fact, I was positive she was gone already.

"And if she were here now?" he said, dark face curious.

"I'd kill her myself," I responded flatly.

Oshossi looked around at the death that surrounded

us. "My pets." His stony face set dangerously, then relaxed slightly. "Victims, all of us. Go. But stand in my way again and you'll be *my* victims next time."

We went. I couldn't feel my legs, but they still worked. Cal had come up from his crouch with my katana and wrapped my hand around its hilt. My other was still firmly fisted in his jacket. "Do you want to tell me what the son of a bitch Xolo made you see?" He had a good guess, I knew, but a guess wasn't the same as details. Details I could not do.

"No." There was snow beneath us—I could see it now—white and pristine as the void had been . . . the void that had shattered into a thousand pieces of sharp-edged, blood-streaked milky glass inside my head.

"You have interesting lives. Even Kin life not quite so interesting." Delilah walked beside us in human form now, the change so quick it was a blur. Her bare feet walked through the snow without hesitation. "Pretty boy, give jacket now."

"I lose more jackets this way," Cal grumbled, but his worried gaze was still on me. "And stop calling me pretty boy. Upgrade me to smoking-hot man-meat, at least." Delilah laughed until she nearly howled . . . a genuine wolf howl. Cal waited with uncustomary patience as I managed to unlock my fingers from his coat. He passed it over to a still-laughing Delilah while I immediately grabbed a handful of the back of his shirt.

"Where were you?" I demanded, and shook him. Shook him hard. And he allowed it without complaint. "Where *were* you?"

He didn't bring up that I'd been gone only a half hour less than he had. He let it be. "I closed up the bar and met Delilah back at our place about two thirty. Like I said, the door was open, your malas were thrown down. I knew something was wrong." His jaw tightened. "Really wrong. I used the GPS in our phones and tracked you to the park. I made a gate, Delilah came along for the ride, and we pinpointed your location." He looked over his shoulder at what lay behind us. The Vigil would be busy tonight, if there was anything left that Boggle and her brood didn't eat. "You killed everything, Nik. Everything." He didn't say it with awe—he said it for what it was. Fact. Cherish might have needed proof, but Cal had always known what I was capable of.

"I'm not done yet. She almost got her way. That evil bitch almost got her way," I said with an emotion so dark and jagged it cut more easily than all the blades I owned.

"You want me to call Promise and tell her?" he asked. "Fuck it. That's a stupid question. I'll call her."

He did. I didn't listen. I, who listened to everything, paid notice of the smallest detail, didn't listen. I hadn't listened to much since two a.m. I knew she would be hurt, even after Xolo's effects had worn off and she remembered how she'd trusted her thief and liar of a daughter with such an unnatural ease, considering their history. I knew she would be shamed and guilty that Cherish had risked all our lives over a lie and a lust for power to equal the Auphe's. I imagined she ached for me, although Cal couldn't tell her exactly what Xolo had made me see. She would guess like Cal had guessed, and all the guesses in the world couldn't equal what I'd seen. I'd seen Cal die twice in my life. Two failures to protect him; one real, one illusion, both as carved into my memory with the same sharp edges.

Could a four-year-old be held to a promise?

Yes.

Could he do it justice?

Not always.

We were headed for the subway when Delilah began to peel off in another direction, the jacket making her barely legal. Her copper eyes looked through

me, one roughened pad of her finger touched my forehead, then my chest. "Sick. Run it out. Hunt it out.
Fight it out." She shook her head. "Or go to the
woods and never come out."

Because that's what a sick wolf would do—go to
the woods, whether the woods were trees or a jumble
of empty buildings, and wait to die.

As far as I could tell, it was better than that hospital
bed I'd spent that night in. The wolves weren't wrong.
Cal had been listening to Delilah, because he had us
off the subway ten blocks from home and had us running it. Ten blocks was nothing compared to my normal regimen, but after the battle I barely remembered,
it tired me.

But not too much. The moment we entered the
apartment, I pulled my tanto knife out and savagely
slashed the rug in front of the coffee table to shreds
before tossing it into the hall. It was where I'd seen
Cal, seen the circle of blood. I still saw it, not with
my eyes, but I still saw it. I couldn't have that thing
in here. Not with me.

Cal closed the door behind the flying cloth and gave
a light shrug. "Never liked it anyway. Too Pier 1."

I stood in the center of the floor, with no idea where
I should go or what I should do. "You keep dying,"
I finally said. I didn't mean for it to sound accusatory,
but I thought that it did. So much for my lifelong
vaunted self-control. "You keep dying, and I keep
breaking my promise."

"I'm still here, so you haven't broken it yet." He
moved in and peeled off my coat. Stained in blood and
fluids, it probably wasn't salvageable, but he tossed it
in the sink anyway. "But, yeah, I can see how it'd
seem that way." He took my arm and moved me
toward the bathroom. "You were supposed to let me
carry the weight this time, Nik, remember?" He
turned on the shower. "And I did. At the last second,
I figure out how to get rid of the Auphe. And guess

what? You still get screwed." Once possessed by a creature that had lived in mirrors, he'd had a fierce phobia of the reflective surfaces for nearly a year. Fighting the fading but still-lingering effects of it now, he looked at himself in the simple square of glass bolted to the wall. "I don't look like so much to be such a huge damn Achilles heel, do I?"

I wondered how long it had been since he'd actually seen himself full-on, not just in quick snatches. His hair had grown since the phobia had started, but he kept it cut at shoulder length, so no change there. His face had become more lean, his brows darker and thicker, but his eyes . . . Once you're no longer a small child, the color of your eyes doesn't change, but what's behind that color does. Whatever lurked there had gone darker in Cal. And then I looked at myself to see the same thing. After this week . . . after this night, I'd gone darker as well.

"I think I need a haircut." His faint grin faded as he went on. "I'm probably going to die before you, Nik." His eyes locked with mine in the reflection. "I'm not as good as you are. I'm not as smart. And it won't be your fault. It'll just be life and death and all the fuckups in between. You made a promise to yourself eighteen years ago when you should've been playing with Legos. Well, you did it. You kept me alive. Despite Sophia and the Auphe, you managed to keep my ass alive. Now let it go. It's my responsibility from now on." He bumped his shoulder against mine. "Keep watching my back, yeah, and I'll keep watching yours, but bottom line . . . you've put your time in. If I go, it's not because you failed. It's because whoever I was taking on was better or luckier than me or, shit, I was just having a bad day. And, hell yeah, still kill the son of a bitch who took me out, make it hurt too, but . . ." The smile was dark, worried. "Just try to do it with a little less suicidal fury. Homicidal fury is good. Suicidal, bad. Got it?"

"And you'll do the same if it goes the other way?" I already knew the answer to that. I'd seen him dive headfirst into death twice in the past year to save me. He'd do the same to follow me.

"Yeah." He hung his head for at least a minute, then shook it ruefully. "We're screwed, aren't we? Okay." He exhaled, straightened, and accepted it. I couldn't do any less for him than he would do for me. "So we go out together, then. Just like with the Auphe. Sounds like a plan." He pushed me toward the streaming water. "You're a bloody mess. I doubt you want any souvenirs of tonight, much less spider intestinal goop on your leg."

He left and I showered. When I was done, we sat side by side on my bed, his shoulder resting against mine to remind me what was true. I couldn't even go in the living room without seeing the lie in vivid detail—an afterimage on the floor that was as bright and real to me as any camera's flash. Like the night before, we watched the sky lighten. This time it wasn't celebrating our freedom. This time it was me not being able to close my eyes for more than a minute without seeing Xolo's handiwork, and it was Cal not letting me spend that time alone.

The sun came up on a new day.

I hoped it was Cherish's last.

15

Cal

We ran our asses off in the next week. Literally. My jeans were getting a little looser. But if that's what it took. I followed Delilah's recipe—run, hunt, fight. Because she was right—Niko was sick. If I'd come home to find his dead body on the floor I'd have been sick too. Way past sick. Homicidal/suicidal—just opposite sides of the same coin.

And although Nik hadn't said, my body had to have been on the floor, apparently with a lot of blood soaked into the rug around it. As the rug had been eight-by-six and he'd slashed it all to pieces, that illusionary pool of blood must've been pretty damn large. Pretty damn horrific.

When I'd seen him in the park, he'd been gone. What was left was a Niko-shaped weapon, a human killing machine. No emotion, no thought, no soul. Whatever he had seen on that floor couldn't be erased by destroying a rug, but if it made him feel better, I was happy I'd held the door open for him to throw it through.

He didn't talk much in the days after, not that Nik was ever one for running off at the mouth. So I did the talking for both of us. Considering my conversation skills—pretty damn lacking—he probably wished

I'd died after all, but it kept him occupied. Occupied, annoyed—they were close, right? At the end of the week, finally . . . *finally* I got a swat to the back of my head when I asked whether werewolf sex or vampire sex deserved the most porno points.

We also hunted that week—revenants, mostly. They were easy to find, only moderately difficult to kill, and so disgustingly fond of eating human flesh that chopping the head off one didn't bother me at all.

We fought too. We sparred in Washington Square Park, me cursing the cold. We sparred in dojos. We sparred anywhere you could swing a wooden sword or throw a human body, but not at the apartment. We didn't spend much time there at all. I was already checking Craigslist for a new place. Nik would never be able to walk into that apartment again without seeing me dead at his feet.

Toward the middle of the week I scooped up the mala beads that were lying carelessly on the coffee table and handed them to him. His lips had tightened. "I'm not sure those are for me anymore."

"They better be, because you have to teach me more about this meditation crap." I held back one bracelet for myself. "Now that the Auphe are gone, I need to deal with this gate shit. I need to be at peace and one with the whatever. You know, less of the creepy blood-licking homicidal monster thing." I half grinned, half grimaced. "It seems to put people off."

"You didn't lick the ccoa blood off your hand," he pointed out.

No, but I'd damned sure thought about it when I'd opened the gate to the river. "I did worse in the warehouse," I responded honestly. And I had. The Auphe weren't gone, no matter what I said or what the Vigil thought. As long as I was around, the race lived on. There was a different race going on inside me, and right now the human half wasn't too damn far in the lead. By a nose, maybe, and I was hoping for better than a photo finish. I might not want to rain on my own parade, but denial takes you only so far.

So we meditated. He might not have been moved to do it for himself, but he did it for me. I only fell asleep fifty percent of the time, which put me in the A-for-effort column. We also did the meditating in the park. Talk about being at one with the world. Sit on the frozen ground long enough and you'll be one all right—practically need a crowbar to separate your icy butt from the packed snow.

Niko talked to Promise daily on the phone, but she didn't come to our place and he didn't go to hers. I didn't know if it was just understood or they'd talked about it. As Nik had thought, Cherish had disappeared nearly thirty minutes after he'd left the New Jersey house. Gave her confused mother a malicious smile and spat at her feet, saying, "Seamus was a better parent and a better vampire than you. And I was a far better lover to him than you ever were." Death, vengeance, and betrayal weren't enough—she had to toss in a gothic soap opera too. Then with gloating laughter, she had taken Xolo into the night. Gone. And with Xolo holding her back, Promise hadn't been able to do a thing to stop her. Although Cherish had manipulated us so well that she'd barely needed the chupa up until the end. Robin was humiliated he hadn't spotted it, and jealous that he might not have been able to pull it off half as well.

I only heard snatches of those phone conversations, but I could tell Promise was ashamed. . . . No, that wasn't the right word. It was worse than that. She felt disgraced by her daughter. Ashamed, dishonored, guilty—as guilty, I thought, as if she'd been the one to shred Nik's mind herself. It wasn't her fault, though—as much as I'd wanted to think it was.

Because her I could reach. Cherish was gone.

But Promise had warned us in the beginning about

her bitch of a daughter. It hadn't mattered. We'd been pulled in by our ties to Promise, and the fact Cherish had apparently changed. Our loyalty to her mother had led us into the trap, and Xolo had closed the door on it. Not intentional on Promise's part, no, but it had happened all the same. Sucks, but there you go.

Then at the end of the week I'd come back from the deli, counting myself lucky Nik let me out after dark by myself, and stopped at the top of our stairwell to see them standing in our doorway. Niko had taken her hand. I slid back out of sight to give them privacy.

"I think," I heard him say after a brief hesitation, "that I can't be with you for a while." There was nothing but solemn silence from Promise. "When I see you," he continued, "I see her. And when I see her, I see Cal. I see him dead." The calm in his voice sheered sideways—an earthquake sliding the side of a mountain into fragments far below. "More than that," he managed roughly, "I see him butchered like a piece of meat. I feel his head on my shoulder as I pull him up, trying to hold him together. I could barely hold him together, Promise. He was all but in pieces."

I leaned against the wall of the landing and didn't slam my fist into the concrete block wall. I didn't, but God, I wanted to. I wanted to. Over and over again.

The mountain firmed. The ground settled as he went on. I don't know how he went on, but he did. "When the memory fades some. When I don't see it every time I close my eyes to sleep or when I open our apartment door." Fuck finding a no-fee apartment. Robin's pricey real estate friends could get us a new place. Next week. *Tomorrow*.

"I don't expect you to wait," he added somberly. "It could be weeks or months."

Or never.

"I will." I heard the sad smile in the next words. "Who knew after the lies there could come something so much worse? I told you she was a liar and a thief with a care for no one—and so charming she made us forget that, I think, even without Xolo's help."

"You had to help her. From what you knew at the time, you had to help your daughter."

"No," she answered Niko. "I could've remembered a hundred times in the past. I could've remembered that those who forget history are condemned to repeat it. But I didn't. I trusted her and I trusted Seamus. I was such a fool. Niko . . ." Tears don't have to be tangible to be real. They could be something you hear rather than salt and water you can touch. I went back downstairs and came back fifteen minutes later. Goodbyes, permanent or temporary, shouldn't be said in front of others, especially those sneaking in the stairwell.

That weekend we moved. Unheard of in New York, right? Found a place in a day. Where there's a will . . . or where there's a will, a handful of pearls, and one of Robin's more unscrupulous pals, and we had a new place. It reminded me a little of the one we'd had the year before, only fit for human beings this time—half-human ones too. A SoHo loft with a wall full of windows, a polished wood floor, and a bathroom you could actually turn around in. Amazing what a difference having money makes in your life. The one job that had actually made us successful, and the Auphe had done it for us. I shook my head.

"What?" Niko asked as he dropped a box on the floor and took a look around at walls painted an oddly, some might say hideously, butterscotch yelloworange. Very trendy, though, I'd bet.

"Nothing," I replied. "Some place, huh?

Still eyeing the orange, he gave a nod. "It will do."

"Do? We never had it so good. That one place we lived in when we first moved here didn't even have a stove."

"Cooking food robs them of most of their nutrients anyway," he said, unperturbed.

I opened the refrigerator door. It was bright, shiny, and new. Unbelievable. "And the fridge didn't work, not to mention the homeless guy that was living in there."

"We paid him fifty bucks to leave, I made you fix the refrigerator, and all was well." He looked at me, mildly smug. "It took you only one DIY book and three months. It was a learning experience and a trade to fall back on when you forget to practice."

Yep, this was home. From crappy to better than we'd ever had, the snark moved with us.

We painted the walls a cool, restful green—Zen green, knowing Nik. I eventually stopped looking for giant mutated roaches in the toilet and learned ice came from refrigerators. Water, too. Who knew?

I'd also been staggering to the bathroom early Saturday morning when I passed Nik's bedroom. I heard him suck in a harsh breath and lurch up to a sitting position. That's when it hit me: every morning he woke up thinking I was dead—with that vision the first thing in his mind. I didn't know how many seconds it took for his memory to reset to reality, but however long was way too long.

Cherish had done this. Of the three of us, she'd picked him. I was obviously a little unstable, what with the uncontrollable gates and spouting Auphe while finger painting with blood—no way to know which way I'd crack. And she couldn't get a grip on what would drive Robin to a suicidal rage, homicidal maybe, but facing Oshossi required both. Nik was the perfect fighter and the perfect choice. I was the switch and she'd flipped it. Now he lived with that every day, and every morning I was dead—at least to him.

That night after he'd gone to bed, I went in to his room and taped a picture to his low, spare headboard. "What could you possibly be doing?" he asked in the darkness. I knew better than to think he wouldn't wake up when I crossed the threshold.

"I'm making like the Tooth Fairy." I snorted before ordering, "Wait til morning. You're always giving me chore lists. Here's yours."

Niko tended to sleep on his stomach, hand on the hilt of the sword under his mattress or on the knife under his pillow, and I knew when he woke up Sunday morning, the first thing he saw was the picture. It was the cheap instant kind they took when you were posing with Santa. And I *was* posing with Santa, hopping up and down on his balls for never bringing Niko and me any presents for Christmas. And five-year-old feet can make a real dent in a department store Santa's balls, from the pained expression on the chubby face. I'd scribbled across the bottom of the picture: *Cal's alive. Now get off your ass and fix him breakfast.* I didn't know if the alive part helped or not, if it beat or canceled out the false memory, but he did make me waffles, so it couldn't have hurt.

As I ate them, he studied me before looking back toward his room, back in the direction of the picture. "How did you know the presents were from me and not Santa Claus?"

"Because you didn't get any. And if any kid deserved to be on the Good Little Boy list, it was you." I leaned back and patted my stomach. Real, non-soy food was so amazing.

"And if anyone deserved to be on the Bad Little Boy list?" he asked, eyes lightening just a little.

I grinned. "Ask that department store Santa. Bet he couldn't walk for a week."

That Monday, Nik went back to teaching at NYU. I met him on his lunch break. As he moved through the crowd, I left the corner vendor with my hot dog and a lemonade for him. I handed it to him, and as he opened it, I said, "I was just talking to this guy on the corner. See him over there?" I pointed. "I know I'm a moody, whiny, sometimes possessed, killer genetic monster freak with mommy issues, but do you think Scientology could honestly be the answer to all that?"

Glass bottle held in front of his lips, Nik froze, then laughed. Yep, the Buddha-loving bad-ass actually cracked a smile and laughed.

I smiled to myself and took a bite of my hot dog. Things were going to be okay. They really were. It might be months before Niko was completely his old self again, or as close as this life would let him be, but we'd get there. I doubted a lot of things in this world, but I didn't doubt that.

That night I went back to work too. It was the first time I'd been back since Robin and Ishiah had exited in a storm of feathers and angry, sexually charged words. Ishiah wasn't there, which was a good thing. I would've had to say something, then he would've had to kill me, which would make finding another job a bitch.

Robin did show up, though, and I sat down with him on my break and had a beer. Before he could open his mouth, I held up a hand. "No details. I don't want even a hint of a detail, okay? I have to work with this guy. If he looks over and sees me picturing you, him, and a feather duster, he'll ram a beer tap into my neck and serve me up until I run dry."

Goodfellow smiled slyly. "Coward." But he drank his Scotch and didn't even mention how far down a peri's feathers went. Relieved, I told him how the move had gone, that Cherish was still missing in action, and that Nik was mostly Nik again. He'd already heard what Cherish had done, what Xolo was, why Oshossi was really chasing the vampire.

"I still can't believe she fooled me. *Me*." He stared broodingly into his glass. "I'm losing my touch." Sighing, he finished the Scotch and said, "There's one thing I still wonder about. Not about Cherish, but about Seamus. Who killed him?"

Well, damn, that was out of nowhere.

"Seamus?" I took a pull of the beer, bored. "Old news. Who cares?"

He persisted. "I've come to the conclusion that Samuel and his colleagues didn't do it. They wouldn't have called us before the cleanup in that case. They were suspicious of him becoming blatant with his killings, but they hadn't made their move yet. I wonder who did. Was it someone who caught wind of Seamus's off-the-wagon ways even before the Vigil confirmed it? And the Vigil *were* watching Seamus. How'd the killer get in without being seen by them?"

Robin and his curiosity. He couldn't let anything go. No one else had even thought about Seamus in the midst of all this mess.

Almost no one.

I said nothing, just rang the glass of the beer bottle with my finger.

"You?" he hissed quietly. "It was *you*? Does Niko know?"

"He knows." I rolled the bottle between my hands. "I didn't tell him, but by now he knows."

"How?"

The same way I knew he was across the street, watching the bar, watching me. Keeping me safe.

Nik was mostly Nik again, but at the finish line wasn't across it. He needed time. If he needed to spend that time watching me, that was fine. No, I didn't have to see Niko to know he was there. I knew. Just as he knew about Seamus.

I gave Robin a shrug and steadfast gaze. "He's my brother."

I'd killed Seamus before I knew about the dead girl in his bathtub. Killed him before I knew he'd gone rogue. I'd smelled the blood, but I didn't know she was dead. Didn't know it wasn't some voluntarily given juice. I did know he was trying to kill Niko, and that wasn't going to happen. My brother had integrity. He wanted to face him head-on, wanted to face that ambushing son of a bitch fair and square. As if Seamus gave a rat's ass about face-to-face and honor, but Niko did.

Niko had the honor that he always denied existed in battle. It was true in a way, that denial. . . . He was the only man or monster alive that had that kind of honor. The rest of us were just doing whatever it took. Nik was better, and I wasn't going to let him die for it. Wasn't going to let some vampire bastard have the chance to kill him for it. I hadn't been willing to wait until the Auphe were gone. Seamus had the time that we didn't. My brother—a good man, the best man—could take the high road all he wanted. Seamus was different. He was about the low.

How'd you do it?" he asked with disbelief. "He was one hell of a fighter and you didn't have a mark on you those following days."

Simple. It had been so simple. I'd opened up a gate in Promise's guest room late the night Cherish had shown up—that night I'd thought those god-awful things trying to anticipate the Auphe. God-awful thoughts they were, yeah, but clarifying. The clarity had carried past Cherish's arrival. Seamus and the Auphe were one thing. Add Cherish and her trouble to the mix . . .

Too much. It was too much to handle at once. Too many ways for things to go from sugar to shit. But there was an easy solution to that.

While Niko slept and Robin kept watch, I'd traveled to Seamus's loft. I came out right behind him. Luck, you can't buy that kind. He hadn't known I was there. Never saw it coming. Too bad for him. I took his head with one brutally fast and forceful swing of the sword. Guns were practically useless against vampires unless you nailed the brain or the heart. I like guns, but sometimes a sword is better. As I'd watched his head bounce as it hit the floor, I'd thought, Yep, sometimes a sword worked just fine.

Then I was back in my room, gate closed. I cleaned my sword, went to bed, and slept like a baby.

"How?" Robin demanded again.

"I'm sneaky." I gave a grin, dark, secretive . . . and maybe just a little Auphe.

Yeah, Seamus had been all about the low road. And if that's what it took to save my brother . . .

Then so was I.

Robin had leaned back slightly at the sharp curve of my lips, so I touched the beads at my wrist to remember who I was—who I *really* was—and let the grin slide into something less lethal. "Okay, give me at least one story to hold over Ish's head. Just nothing that'll make my ears bleed or swear off sex for the rest of my life. Can you do that?"

Seamus and the Auphe in me instantly forgotten, Goodfellow gave a grin equally as scary as anything I'd shown, I was sure, and drawled, "Let's start off with a hypothetical question: If someone endowed with flammable feathers cooks in the nude, is that a lifestyle choice or a death wish?"

I dropped my head into my hands and groaned.

I hoped Niko was having a better night of it than I was.

16

Niko

The bar didn't have any uncovered windows to speak of. The Ninth Circle's patrons liked their privacy, but it did have a few tiny stained-glass panes here and there that gave little away . . . unless you were very observant. I was. Through one triangle of grape-colored glass I saw Robin's arm gesticulate wildly. In annoyed surprise or shock, I guessed. He'd been caught up on the entire ordeal in the past week. Now, what could possibly surprise him to that extent?

Ah.

Seamus, I thought with a little annoyance of my own. Resigned amusement as well. Cal. He did for me what I did for him. Hard to take him to task for that. I would at some point certainly, for going without my knowledge and for using a gate when it was still quite dangerous. Although, considering the efficiency he'd shown, it was hard not to want to reward him with one of his favorite cardiovascular-damaging foods. Positive reinforcement—it truly was the best way to train children and animals, and I'd say Cal fell about halfway between those two.

Yes, he'd handled Seamus well. I'd rather he'd have let me handle it, but spilled milk is just that. I leaned back against the cold surface of the building directly across the street from the bar and folded my arms. I was surprised, however, that it had taken Goodfellow this long to figure it out, although we most definitely had been occupied. I supposed he could be forgiven the lapse of his usual inquisitiveness.

Cal wanted to handle someone else besides Seamus. He wanted Cherish, and he wanted her badly. "For what she did to you, Nik," he'd said adamantly. "I'm not letting her walk away from that. I don't give a damn about Xolo or Oshossi or all the other shit she put us through, but for what she did to you, I'm not letting that slide. I will blow her fucking head off, swear to God. And if she's lucky, that's the least of what I'll do to her."

I'd given him the one reply, the only reply that would change his mind. "She's mine." That wasn't enough. "I need it, little brother." That was.

I didn't ask for things often. I didn't need them often, but if I did . . . Cal would move heaven and hell to get them for me. This time he had only to step back and, for me, he did.

I kept my eyes on the bar. Only two weeks, and I stood here across the street. Cal had done well by me; otherwise I would've been standing in the bar inches behind his chair, breathing down his neck. He had done everything he could, done everything right, and here I was . . . in one piece, physically and mentally. More than slightly cracked, but held together with the best glue Cal could produce.

He had run, which he hated. Meditated, which he also hated—when he managed to stay conscious. Fought, which he actually enjoyed, except for its direct conflict with his inherent laziness. Delilah had been smart, Cal driven, and the result was I could actually go almost an hour at a time without picturing what Cherish had Xolo shove into my brain. It was an improvement—a vast improvement.

A man walking down the mostly empty sidewalk caught my eye. The Ninth Circle wasn't in the best part of town. You were unlikely to see crowds drifting along, and there was the feel of something different and strange that kept most humans away. But once in a while, the stupid or the unlucky didn't pay attention to what their subconscious was trying to tell them. Predators ahead. I focused and saw the faint glitter of a blade held against his leg as his jittering eyes hit me. A junkie and his knife. In other words, a rank amateur. Breaking the well-known rule of "Don't let a man see your knife until it's in him," I raised an eyebrow and held the side of my duster open to show a glittering array of nine blades strapped within. He twitched, hesitated, then ran across the street and went into the Circle.

Stupid and unlucky. It would be the last anyone saw of him.

My cell phone rang and I answered it. Samuel spoke without preamble. "Your buddy Oshossi took a walk off a very tall building in Atlantic City. We were cleaning him up with sponges." We'd asked him before for Oshossi's location when we'd believed Cherish, when we'd been desperate, but he and the Vigil had been silent on that subject. But now they knew. I'd been very clear in letting them know what Xolo could do, and several guesses what Cherish would do with him. She could rule at least a country or two if she and Xolo had access to the right people. It seemed that was potentially overt enough for the Vigil to provide some assistance. "Our psychics say your other friend is in room seventeen-eighty at the Borgata Hotel. Now, seriously, Niko, don't call me anymore. This was an exception because of what that chupa can do. We are even. You know that. You're an honorable guy. The Vigil won't stand. . . ."

It was the same thing he'd said in the warehouse. No more favors. I gave it the same weight now as I had then. "I couldn't care less about the Vigil," I interrupted him to say levelly. "For what you did to

Cal, we will never be even. Keep taking my calls or we'll talk in person. Trust me, Samuel, you don't want to talk to me in person." I disconnected before he could reply.

Honor. People were so quick to talk about my honor. Promise, Robin, even Cal, who should've known better. I did my best to have honor, my best to maintain that core in almost every aspect of my life, but where my brother began, honor ended and instinct took over. Instinct knew very little about honor, and cared even less.

With this call, I knew what had to happen. What was going to happen. I could only hope Promise felt the same way, because for me it was the only way.

I dialed her number and waited as it rang. So Cherish hadn't gone far. I had thought she wouldn't. Oshossi was at a disadvantage in a city, and no matter how it had ended when she had Xolo send me after him, she knew if he were alive he'd be either wounded or without his creatures. A city wouldn't be his friend, but it would be hers.

And it had been. Oshossi was dead. He'd gotten too close to her and Xolo after all. Instead of being swallowed by a river, he'd fallen to his death, all the while no doubt thinking he was but walking in the forests of his home.

"Hello?"

I didn't hesitate. "She's in Atlantic City. Oshossi's dead. She still has Xolo." With whom she could do whatever she pleased. Control anyone. Rule anyone. Kill anyone. Surround herself with mind-warped puppets. None of it was good, and none of it began to approach my problem with her.

I heard Promise exhale, lost and certain all at once. "This can't go on. She has to be stopped."

I waited.

There was a hesitation; then her voice was weary. "She's not my daughter. She's a monster." There was silence as I knew she was thinking of taking the matter into her own hands, that Cherish was her daughter and her responsibility. But in the end, she couldn't. "I wash my hands of her," she said tonelessly, which said while she couldn't do what had to be done, others were welcome to. Specific others. There was the buzz of a dial tone in my ear, and I slowly flipped the phone shut.

Four hours later, I was in an Atlantic City hotel. Mickey had managed to make it back to his junkyard after Oshossi had flipped our car by the park. He hadn't been too enthusiastic about getting involved until I told him Oshossi and all his creatures were dead. Then—for a price, naturally—he came along. I'd borrowed one of the cars from Robin's lot. Aside from the clumps of rat fur in the passenger's seat, I didn't think he'd mind.

In the past year, I'd had Robin teach me some of the more rudimentary points of lock picking. When it came to a casino hotel door complete with keycard, I accessed the lock via the heel of my boot. I did it as quietly as possible, and at four in the morning the hall was empty, if you didn't count the woman passed out by the elevators.

Mickey, huddled in a hooded trench coat, streaked past me into the darkened room, and by the time the lights flashed on scant seconds later, he said, "Is done."

I could see it was done. Mickey was nothing if not quick. He had swaddled Xolo up in the bed comforter. Covered from head to toe, there was no chance of those large hypnotic eyes catching mine. As Xolo had never met Mickey, he hadn't mapped his brain yet. He couldn't control the rat before he was contained, not like he could have me.

I closed the door quietly behind me. Cherish stood beside the other bed, where she'd been sleeping. She was dressed in a white silk nightgown and held a sword in her hand. She could've tried lying or playing innocent, but with one look at me she knew. Lying, charming, thieving—none of that could help her now.

Once when Cal was seven, he'd been chased by a dog. Hammer. A vicious giant of a canine, it had broken its chain and leapt on Cal. It had ripped his backpack off with one tear of its massive jaws, and I knew my brother's neck was next. Hammer was the first thing I'd ever killed. I'd run, snatching a rusty pickax off the rickety porch of one of the trailers, and with one swing buried the sharp end between the dog's amber eyes, deep in his brain. That was the first time. I'd killed for Cal many times since.

This time I did it for myself.

She could rule masses of people with Xolo. It was true. I could say there was the threat she could come back for us. With what Cal could do, with the way I could fight, if she could have the chupa control us, there wasn't much in this world she couldn't have. That was true as well. Saving the world like a genuine hero. It was a good reason for what had to be done.

But it wasn't mine.

"I can make you see him die every minute of every day for the rest of your life," she hissed, the normally beautiful face twisted and ugly as murder itself. "He'll scream for you, and you'll fail him. Every time he dies. Every single time."

Once had been enough, and that was my reason.

It wasn't long before I was looking down at her fallen body. Her sleep-tousled black hair was spread around her now still face, Promise's violet eyes wide and empty, the smallest amount of blood staining the white silk over her heart. Her sword at her side. I'd given her a chance, warrior to warrior, and she'd wielded the weapon admirably. She'd been almost as skilled as she was beautiful. She'd also been intelligent, charming, charismatic, clever, and with the potential for so much more.

I'd felt worse about killing Hammer.

He couldn't help what he was. She could have. A monster, her own mother had labeled her. She could've gotten Promise or any of us killed with her lies. She nearly had. She'd been a kidnapper and a thief, made me an assassin, killed Oshossi, and counting all that, I doubt she had even warmed up. But worst of all, she'd cost me my brother. Temporarily or not, she'd taken him away from me.

Now when I closed my eyes, maybe I'd see her body instead of his.

I turned to Xolo, wrapped passively in a blanket as Mickey watched it all with ink-spot eyes. I suppose the chupa belonged to me now. Oshossi was gone, Cherish as well. All that was left was a living weapon that could rend your mind in half. A living, breathing nuclear bomb. We didn't need any more of those.

I took his head swiftly and painlessly. With the muffling blanket he never saw it coming. Like Hammer, it wasn't his fault he was what he was, but he was too dangerous to let live. I suppose there were those who thought the same about me.

It's all perspective, and you did what you had to do.

Cherish's eyes were beginning to film over. Her mother's eyes fading from purple to an ordinary dark blue behind the fog. I wondered whose choice it would be now. Would I ever be able to look at Promise again without feeling my world fracture? Would she be able to look at me without seeing a little girl with dark hair holding her hand and smiling the sweetest of smiles? She'd known what had to be done, she'd given her consent, but consenting and facing the one who'd carried out that consent? Vastly different things.

Would either of us be able to look at one another again without seeing our families die?

Five months later I found out.

It took two months before I stopped waking up

knowing Cal was dead and gone—*seeing* it. Although once in a while his note hit me before the memory did. Pain-in-the-ass little brothers—occasionally they knew what they were doing. It didn't mean I fixed him waffles every morning. Rewarding good intentions; encouraging laziness. It was a fine line.

It took another three months before every monster—every revenant, every sylph, every djinn—that I killed no longer had Cherish's face. Three months before I could kill and not *enjoy* the killing. When that happened, I chose an afternoon and went to her door. I knocked, and when she opened it, I saw her. Not Cherish. Not Cal, bloody and limp. I saw her. Promise. Pale skin, unpainted mouth, wise eyes, the coffee-and-cream tumble of her hair. I saw all the things between us, the good and the bad, and the more I hoped to come.

What did she see?

Past her I saw her piano. The picture, the old-fashioned photo of her and the little girl, was gone. In its place was a single calla lily I'd once given her. Both it and the vase that held it were crystal. The brilliant glassy shine of the petals was the same color as her eyes. A long-lived flower for a long-lived love, I'd thought when I'd given it to her. I hadn't said it aloud. That wasn't my way. She knew all the same, though, because she'd seen me. She had seen me then.

And she saw me now.

She smiled and held out a hand.

I took it.

Read on for a taster of the next instalment in the
Cal Leandros series:

Doubletake

Coming in August 2012

1

Black Sheep

Family . . . it is a fucking bitch.

Just like he was a bitch. I had seen him—wallowing amongst the game, but never tasting of the herd. More perverse, he lived with prey, had been raised by prey, had been taught the ways of the world by prey, when I'd had to teach myself. Clawing myself along, I had chewed my way through knowledge as grimly as I'd once chewed discarded putrid meat and bone. Everything I'd earned, I'd earned with blood, mine or someone else's. I had done what no one else could do.

The castoff failure, but look at me now. Damn right, look at me. Look hard and look good—right before I gut you.

Then there was him, the golden boy, yet look at what he had done.

Naughty and bad, bad and naughty. But much worse: disobedient. Not what they'd expected of their one true success at all.

I laughed at the irony of it.

I laughed, but I hated him, hated him, hated him, hated him, hated him.

Not for what he'd done, but that he'd been the one instead of me to do it.

That was all right, though. That was fine and fucking dandy, as someone I used to know once said. Fine and fucking dandy, because I hated everyone anyway. The only difference was, I was related to this one . . . and that made the hate sweeter. Hate was all I'd known. All I had ever been given and all I had ever had. I was created from it, molded by it, lived by it. Hate was like air, necessary to life. I wore my hate as a second skin and let it warm me when nothing else did.

I saw him through binoculars from where I lay atop a roof far enough away that he wouldn't know I was there. It was night, but I saw him clearly. Light was for the fearful herd; the night was for me. Not that it was ever truly dark in this immense mound of misbegotten roadkill waiting to happen.

Yes, I saw him. He had black hair, pale skin, light-colored eyes. Nothing like I was at all. That I didn't hate. That I liked—I was better, purer, closer to the truth.

It was all about the truth.

The new truth.

My truth.

And he was part of that, whether he wanted to be or not.

Family was a hateful bitch; it was. I had the hot poker scars of that burned into my flesh to prove it, but, scars or not, sometimes family was all you had worth playing with. Maybe he would see that. Maybe he would want to play too. I played rough. I played to win.

Did he?

I'd bet he did if given the chance, not that this boring

*scuffle I was watching was anything to go by. It wasn't a
fraction of the challenge I'd give him.*

The Unmaker of the World, they had called him.

*Unimpressed, I waggled black-gloved fingers in a mock-
ing wave. We'd see. Sooner or later, we'd see exactly what
family and blood meant to him. He might look like one of
the cattle, but he would never be one.*

*Besides, if he could unmake the world, how much
more fun would it be for me to remake it instead?*

2

Family . . . it is a bitch.

The thought came out of nowhere.

Or maybe not, considering my current situation. There was no denying that it was true. Everyone thought it sooner or later, didn't they? If there's only you, you're good—lonely maybe, but good. You can't fight with yourself. If there're two of you, it can still be good. Your options are limited. You make do and appreciate what you have, unless it's the stereotypical evil-twin scenario. Then you aim for the goatee and blow his ass back to the alternate dimension he popped out of.

A kishi—better known as my paycheck in the form of a supernatural hyena—hit my back with staggering force. I flipped it over my shoulder and put a bullet between its eyes.

Yeah, normally two was a doable number for family. It was when you hit three and higher that things started to go bad. That was when the bitching and moaning started, the pitting of one against another, the slights that no one forgot. No one could tell me that Noah didn't pitch a few of his relatives kicking and screaming off the

Ark long before the floodwaters receded. It was no familial *Love Boat,* and I believed that to my core.

Which brought up the question: Did that wrathful Old Testament God kill the sharks? I don't think he did. You can't drown a shark. I think they were snacking on biblical in-laws right and left. Noah, Noah, Noah . . .

I swung around and kicked the next kishi in the stomach as I slammed another clip home before putting three in its gaping, lethally fanged mouth as it jumped again. It sounded easy, but considering the one I also had attached to my other leg . . . it was a pain in the ass.

Family-wise, I had no pain in the asses. I was lucky. I had one brother and he was a damn good one. Once we were on our own, I'd escaped the curse of screaming Thanksgiving dinners. . . . I had a turkey pizza; Niko had a vegan one. No bitter arguments around a Christmas tree . . . Niko gave me a new gun; I gave him a new sword. Absent was the awkward discovery of first cousins shacking up at the summer vacation get-togethers at the lake. I didn't have to wait for summer. I saw my brother every day when he winged my sopping towel off the bathroom floor at my head or I asked—after the fact—if I could use his priceless seventeenth-century copy of some boring book no one but him and the author had read to prop up a wobbling coffee table.

Summer vacations . . . if you thought about it, what kind of people actually gathered together at a lake with cabins and all that crap anyway? Hadn't they ever watched *Friday the 13th*? Jason? Hockey masks? Machetes? A good time for me, yeah—oh *hell,* yeah—but not as much for the members of your average Prius-driving middle class.

Stupidity is everywhere.

But for me, right now, things were good. My brother

and I kicked supernatural ass for fun and profit. I had a shirt that said that with our phone number. Humans wouldn't take it seriously. Humans didn't know what the world really hosted. But the kind that hired us—nonhuman—they knew a walking billboard when they saw it. Running your own business is a bitch. You have to advertise. Promo. Market. Niko did that. I couldn't be bothered with that crap—unless it resulted in my offensive T-shirt slogan. He and I had been doing this for four years now. Before that we'd done the same, but it had been a hobby, not a career.

Okay, I say hobby, but it was self-defense, pure and simple. When you're half human and half of the worst monster to walk the earth—a creature that ate the supernatural for appetizers without putting hardly any effort into it—you weren't popular with the other monster types. And there were thousands of different kinds. Some immediately attacked me, sensing the half human in me and assuming it would make me weaker—they were wrong. Some ran—they were smart. And some didn't care either way—we hung out and had a beer.

Good family. Interesting and well-paying career. Half monster . . . well, everything couldn't be perfect, but otherwise right now things were good. I was hoping they stayed that way. Except for Niko. I didn't have to hope when it came to family.

The rest of my life might be challenging in some other areas, like at the moment as an adolescent kishi was either trying to eat my leg or hump it to the bare bone, but family? I knew I had that under control. I watched my brother's back; he watched mine. We were a Hallmark card dipped in blood and made of unbreakable steel. I'd never had a doubt about my family and I never would—no matter what the kishi, who had brought the topic to mind to begin with, were doing to annoy me on the general subject.

No, it was all smooth sailing, rather like this current job, until my cell phone rang. "Niko," I said, shooting another adult kishi with jaws stretched wide enough to swallow my entire head. It had leaped downward at me from a fire escape of a condemned tenement apartment building long crumbled in on itself—no demolition crew needed. Gravity worked for free. "Can you get this one off of my leg before I need sexual assault counseling?"

Niko said to not kill the babies, although at one hundred and fifty pounds "baby" was pushing the definition, but I was doing my best, more or less, to be a good boy. Although it would've been much easier to be a bad boy.

So very bad. So very fun.

For my brother, however, I reined in that part of me—that nonhuman half of me, choke-chaining it with a practiced grip. It was the price I paid to keep my brother satisfied. Bearing in mind that if it weren't for him I'd be dead or sanity-challenged ten times over, I owed the man. I was also fond enough of his bossy, anal-retentive ass to die for him.

More important, to kill for him.

And to have chosen the darkest of roads to make that happen.

All that made ignoring a giant baby with an equally giant bite easy enough. As I fished for my cell, Niko was less than awed at my babysitting skills and said so: "If you can't do a minimum of three tasks at once, I have failed you with all my training and instruction. I'd blame myself, but clearly it's entirely your fault, your laziness, your total ineptitude."

Not that we shared the fraternal fondness out loud. How manly would that be?

It wasn't as if I hadn't heard that all before. If adults heard lullabies when they slept, that would be mine. I shook my leg again, shot another kishi bounding down the side of the next building, equally as dilapidated as the first, putting three bullets between its blazing silver eyes. They shone brighter than any streetlights in this part of town ... until their life seeped away and left only the dull gray of death. I felt bad for them—almost—but they had turned a block that had once hosted scavenging homeless, thriving drug dealers, and sullen hookers into a desolate wasteland. In my opinion, I didn't have a preference for one over the other, kishi or human. The mayor wanted the city cleaned up. The kishi clan was doing the job one block at a time ... even if it meant eating quite a few people.

Were those people good people? If I knew anything, I knew that these days, starting four months ago, I wasn't in the position to make the call on whether certain people were worth saving or leaving to the predators. That I left up to Nik. I simply stepped over their bodies and went on with the job.

Regardless of whether they were good or evil, those people belonged, whether they knew it or not, to the Kin. The Kin, the werewolf Mafia of NYC, weren't pleased to be sharing their money or their snacks with Johnny-come-lately supernatural hyenas from the depths of ... um ... I should've paid attention to where those depths were during the premission rundown—maybe Africa, but Niko knew. That was enough. I didn't think it mattered much. They were encroaching on Kin territory, and the Wolves didn't like that.

Unfortunately for the Kin, the kishi, as a race, howled at a decibel level that would have any Kin Wolf's ears bleeding ten blocks away. Curled up in homicidal furry balls, moaning for their mommies, they hadn't had much success in taking down the kishi. Luckily for Niko, me, and our bank account, human ears couldn't hear notes that high.

And although I wasn't entirely human, my hearing was. That made us the go-to guys for this job. It had seemed easy from the hiring and the half our fee slapped into my palm—if it hadn't been for Niko's research, finding out the kishi were highly intelligent preternatural hyenas, if extremely malevolent. That meant the adults were fair game, but the younger kishi we had to pat on the head and find a goddamn supernatural foster and rescue organization for murderous fur babies to raise them right, socialize their asses, put rhinestone collars on them, and take them off our hands.

How many of those do you think were in the phone book? Nada? Good fucking call.

But the bottom line was, it was all about family, which had to be where that thought had originated. The adult kishi taking down prey for their young, which luckily was only one at this point, feeding him or her, setting up a nest, claiming this place for their own. They were doing what evolution had bred in them to do. Evolution worked the same for nonhumans as for humans. Kishi were predators to their bones. They would slaughter anything they thought they had a chance of bringing down, but to give them credit, they looked after their family.

That's where family became a bitch in yet another way. You eat people for your family, you piss off the Kin for your family, you die for your family.

As a random bully had once said to me when I was a kid in the fourth grade as he demanded my sneakers and backpack, life isn't fair. I agreed with him by punching his annoying teeth down his equally annoying throat. If that's the way the world wanted to be, I'd go along. I didn't make the rules. I only played by them.

Since when?

Since never.

This wasn't a schizophrenic voice; at least, I hoped not. This was just my subconscious, my new subconscious. Since I'd let a small piece of me wither and die months ago to save *my* family, the swamp in my mind that made up the subliminal me was considerably more shadowed. It was more prone to the bad thoughts people think, normal people too, that they shouldn't, don't like to admit to, and don't act on. But as I wasn't normal and wasn't exactly the Webster's dictionary definition of a person, my bad thoughts were much badder than most and I wanted to act on them. Sometimes or often or frequently or very frequently, depending on my mood . . . no judgment needed or wanted. If I thought it, I absolutely wanted to do it.

But I didn't.

The voices/thoughts were almost as much a bitch as family could be, the squabbling, but I'd learned to mostly tune them out. Many psychotherapists would be proud of my progress—the ones who hadn't met me and, if they had any sense, wouldn't care to.

I wasn't good or bad. I was only me, and I was neither.

They'd have to invent a new bizarrely long German psychological description for what I was. How did the German say, "To see him is to piss your pants in fear"? Freud would've known.

I shook my leg futilely one more time and exhaled in irritation at the molten mercury eyes, the dark red coat dappled with silver spots, the milk teeth—as large as a German shepherd's adult teeth—that continued to gnaw at my thigh. "Three seconds and he's a rug under the coffee table. Your move, Cyrano."

Did Niko have a proud, hawklike nose? Yes, he did. Did I give him hell over it? What do you think?

I answered my still-ringing cell phone as I shot the last kishi that leaped through a boarded-up window. Wood split, glass shattered, and bone splintered. The combination made for one dead kishi whose stomach was rounded and full with its last meal, which, I was guessing, had been the last occupant of this street. From the hypodermic the para-hyena coughed up in its dying throes, that meal had most likely been a tweaker.

They say drugs kill, but does anyone ever listen?

"Yeah, Leandros," I said into the phone. "Death and destruction by the dollar. The meter's ticking. Go."

I hadn't had a chance to check the incoming number, not with Kishi Junior both seducing and making a meal of my leg. But it didn't surprise me to hear a familiar voice. Five people total had my personal number. Our business number was an untraceable phone with voice mail lying on the floor of an otherwise empty storage locker. Niko and I'd been sorry before—we went with safe now. "Kid, thank Bacchus." I heard the relieved exhalation. "I need you and Niko at my place now."

The three seconds was up, and I had the muzzle of my Desert Eagle planted between toddler kishi's moon eyes as it gnawed harder at my lower thigh. I had a high pain tolerance—you learned to in this business—but to balance it out, my tolerance for nearly everything else remotely irritable in the universe was low. *Damn* low. Contaminating part of your soul will do that . . . if you believed in souls. I hadn't made up my mind, but either way it was too bad for baby. It was night-night time. I might as well stop the pattern now. The same as its parents, it would grow up to be a killer anyway.

Like you did?

As if I didn't know that.

But I was a done deal; the kishi wasn't, not quite yet. "Goodfellow? You in trouble?" I started to put pressure on the trigger and tried to overlook the shadow of guilt. It *was* a kid. A killer kid, but a kid. Couldn't I relate? On every single level? Then again, did I care if I could relate? Was I Dr. Phil? Hell, no. I was, however, Niko's brother. That had me yanking harder at my internal leash while frowning crossly at Niko as I gave him a few extra seconds to move over and slide his katana blade between my leg and the kishi to pry it off with one efficient move.

"You owe me," I grumbled at him.

While it squealed, barked, yowled, and laughed hyena-crazy through a toothy muzzle, Niko threw the last kishi down and hog-tied its preteen fuzzy ass. My brother—he wasn't a bleeding heart. There were more dead monsters and people in whatever version of hell you wanted to believe in who'd testify to that. He did like to give a break when he thought one was due, though—or when he thought their birthright shouldn't automatically condemn them.

He'd learned that raising me and adjusting to my birthright—a lifetime of habits, right or wrong, was hard to break.

Robin's voice was in my ear, catching my attention again. "Am I in trouble? Ah. Hmmm. It's more like everyone else is in trouble with the exception of myself," he hedged. "I'd rather explain it in person and give you the keys to the bar. Ishiah left them for you."

Ishiah was my boss at my day job/night job/afternoon job, whenever I wasn't out doing what pulled in the real rent money—disposing of monster ass. He owned a non-human bar—not that humans knew the supernatural existed—called the Ninth Circle, was a peri, which was a winged humanish-type creature that had spawned angel legends, and was generally neutral on whether he should kill me or crown me employee of the month for making it a week without icing a customer while serving up their liquor of choice.

Why would he want to kill me? We had a lot of unpaid tabs because I hadn't once made that said employee of the month. But hand held to the empty, godless space that filled the sky, if I killed you, you usually had it coming. Or you just weren't that quick. In my world, the two were practically the same.

"The keys? Why did he . . . Ah, hell with it. We'll get the story when we get there." I looked down at Niko crouching on the street, rhythmically rubbing the kishi's stomach. It crooned mournfully, my blood on its teeth, the silver of its eyes surrounded by the white of fear. "Fuck me." I sighed. Before I let Goodfellow off the phone, I added, "By the way, do you know anywhere we could drop off a baby kishi to be raised up all good with God? Religious, righteous, and true? Oh, and non-people-eating?"

"Your imitation of a Southern drawl is pathetic, and yes, drop him off here." He rattled off an address. "They take in strays all the time. But you'd better do it in the next hour or they'll be gone."

"Gone where?" I asked.

"Who knows? It doesn't matter. They'll all be gone. Everyone. Now hurry the hell up. I'm paying your bill this time. I'm a puck, a trickster, and a used-car salesman. Don't think I won't squeeze every penny out of Niko's well-shaped ass if you don't perform this job to perfection." His phone disconnected in my ear.

"Who was that?"

I grinned down at my brother. "Robin is hiring us for a job, and I'm thinking seriously about taking a dive in the fifth, because it's your ass on the line if we screw up."

"Goodfellow will be a good client. He wouldn't cheat us." He'd cheat anyone else—man, woman, or child, but not us. Niko finished the knot on the rope and slitted his eyes at me. "And let us leave my ass out of it. Why I claim you as my blood, I will never know."

It wasn't true. *I* didn't know why he put up with me, but I took it on faith that Niko knew something that made me worth keeping around. Niko inherently knew extraordinary things that most others didn't know and wouldn't ever know. He was like that. Then again, very rarely, Niko screwed the hell up, wasn't the infallible older brother—because no one was infallible. No one. I hadn't kept count before, the times he was wrong, but if I'd known what was headed our way, I might've starting adding them up now.

Number one was a little over sixty minutes away and headed for us like a freight train.

Tick-tock.

Robin Goodfellow, Pan, puck, trickster, car salesman, and more identities than I could memorize in a lifetime, lived off Central Park. That might have had something to do with his being rich and his kind having a history of spending a lot of time in the woods running around nude, which I didn't once picture in my brain—not once, okay? It was a goddamn shame my booty-call werewolf, Delilah, or Puppy Le Screw, as Robin liked to call her, had tried to kill my family and friends, and was considering the same for me if she had the chance, because I really, *really* needed to get laid.

Regardless of my pathetic condition, squatting on the

outskirts of Central Park was Goodfellow's best option in NYC—if he wanted to revert to the old days of forest flashing and if you could call a three-million-plus condo squatting. His condo board hated him ... something to do with his wanting to install condom machines on every floor, and the thinly veiled orgies. Although in the last year, the orgies were a thing of the past. After nearly a hundred thousand years of debauchery and extreme horniness, he'd embraced monogamy. I suspected it was a puck brain tumor. Or it would pass in another few months. A monogamous Goodfellow was as if aliens came to Earth and didn't want to hunt you, eat you, or screw your women.

Extremely unlikely.

We'd dropped off the kishi kit and now I stood pounding on Goodfellow's door. "Porn and pizza. Asses and anchovies delivered in thirty minutes or it's free." The condo board didn't care for that either, which is why I did it. Unless it was advertising our business, Niko had threatened to kill me in my sleep if I wore any more T-shirts with obscene, violence-encouraging, or just plain fun-with-chainsaw slogans on them. I had to get my entertainment somewhere else now. No big deal. I was versatile.

I'd bandaged my leg, tying a thick gauze strip on the outside of my jeans and popping some Tylenol in the car as we drove the kishi to demonic day care. I'd do a real version when we eventually made it home. If I could help it, I kept my pants up around Goodfellow. A year of monogamy versus a hundred thousand years of frenzied pansexuality kept me cautious. I'd seen him talk a convention of ninety-year-old Catholic priests into a nudie bar. All right, thinking about it, maybe not that difficult to accomplish, but I didn't want to be the next test subject. He did like a challenge.

After dumping the baby, we left Niko's junker on the curb in front of Robin's building. The doormen were used to us by now and drove it to the nearest parking garage for seventy bucks, which was the first charge on Robin's bill. On the way over we'd seen Wolves, vamps, revenants, vodyanoi, and more. They were in cabs heading toward LaGuardia or JFK, in their own cars, slamming their horns headed for the Holland and Lincoln tunnels. Many were so desperate they were going toward the George Washington Bridge. Jersey to escape the city? That told you right there something was going on and it was worse than the ten plagues of Egypt and Chernobyl combined. Some Wolves were just running, no vehicle necessary. People on the sidewalks were glaring around for the dog walker who'd screwed up. Robin hadn't been exaggerating. Everything with claws and paws and fangs was getting the hell out of Dodge.

I banged against the door again. "Pony play and pad thai. Get it while it's hot." I didn't have to see Niko's hand to know it was aiming for the back of my head. I ducked with the instinct of a thousand received swats and stumbled into Robin's condo as he opened the door beneath my pounding fist.

"You," Robin said, catching me by the back of my shirt to keep me upright, "are going to spend months, nay, years of sleepless nights wishing you had never said that, not in this particular situation." I expected him to sound amused, as that was the kind of joke he would make, but he looked nothing but deadly serious.

Once steady on my feet again, I walked in. Same expensive rock-crystal coffee table, same buttery leather wraparound sofa—an identical replacement, rather, as I'd been indirectly responsible for destroying the last one—same enormous flat-screen television set hidden in a recess in the wall behind an original Waterhouse—Nik told me—painting. Same rich and expensive everything, although one addition was fairly new and a gift from me to Goodfellow, or rather from me to Goodfellow's roommate, Salome. She was a Grim Reaper on four paws and I liked to stay on her good side. So a few months ago I brought her a boyfriend.

"Spartacus," I called, "how's it hanging?" Probably not too well. Once you're dead, had your organs removed, and are resurrected as an undead mummified cat, your testicles probably looked like old raisins that had rolled under the couch. Raisins didn't tend to . . . hang. But it was the thought that counted. I caught him as he slithered out from under the couch and leaped through the air, a zombie feline missile. He looped around my neck and purred in my ear. And if his purr sounded like skulls being crushed under an iron boot, again, it was the thought that counted. His bandages were long gone, and I stroked the hairless black-and-white-spotted wrinkly skin. "You're living under the couch? Is Salome giving you a hard time?"

Another purr erupted from atop the massive refrigerator. Salome, unlike Spartacus, was gray with a small hoop earring in one pointed ear. They both had eye sockets that housed flickering lantern lights that reminded me of Halloween. Salome had followed Goodfellow home from the Museum of National History—against his will—and had lived here since, when she wasn't out stalking senile, ancient pet Great Danes in the hallway. Salome had killed man and beast and probably hadn't considered either one taxing. That was why I'd brought Spartacus to keep her company. I did not want to get on her bad side.

A mummy, Wahanket, who'd lived in the sublevels of

the museum, had made Salome and Spartacus. Although a sometime informant, he had tried to kill me twice and he did kill cats. I didn't approve of either hobby. I made sure Wahanket didn't get to play his King Tut games on anyone else, which Spartacus seemed to appreciate. Salome didn't much appreciate anything, from what I'd seen. I gave the cat's bony ass one last pat and plopped him on the floor. "Be a man," I told him. "Show her who's boss." He gave me a dubious glance and disappeared under the couch again. Apparently being a man was overrated.

Niko removed his duster, hot for late summer, but necessary for covering up katanas and various other swords. "You're hiring us for a job, Goodfellow? That seems odd. You assist us so often you know we'd be more than willing to do you a favor for free."

Robin shrugged, his normally cat-that-ate-five-canaries green eyes glum, and waved a hand at the kitchen table on which rested a meatball sub with double cheese and a tea that stung my nose enough for me to know it must cost a hundred bucks a gram at least—the type of tea Niko loved above all others. "There are favors and then there is ripping your own heart out to tape to an extrarealistic Valentine's card. This is the latter."

I moved closer to the table to catch the precise smell of the sub. "Gino's? Gino's extra-sauce, extra-cheese, extra-garlic meatball sub?" Gino's, where the grease was so thick in the air that it contaminated the entire block and Robin refused to even drive down the street. That combined with the stink of a tea that was available only from one ninety-eight-year-old mean-as-a-snake woman in Chinatown. You had to walk across a path of nails to prove you were worthy of this damn tea, and I was not joking. He'd gone to serious trouble to tempt us, and Goodfellow didn't go to serious trouble to do anything. He manipulated, deceived, lied, but not this. Honesty, money, and snacks?

This was bad.

"Shit. I don't even want to know what the job is." But I didn't mean it.

It was Goodfellow. Our first friend when we'd been on the run from the other half of me, a race called the Auphe. The first murderers born of this earth. All the other supernatural feared them, bowed before them, died under their teeth and claws. The Auphe were gone now, as was the handful of half-breeds like me, but I didn't forget that Robin had been the first to help Niko and me.

Even now . . . he was one of very few. The Auphe had been at the head of the supernatural food chain and they had large appetites, torture always being the cherry on top—which explained why I wasn't too popular. Everyone had feared them and no one had missed them when we wiped them out. Although many didn't know that they *had* been destroyed, that I was the last left, not that that would've made me any more popular. Quite a few had taken and still did take that unpopularity and hatred of Auphe up with me. They couldn't kill an Auphe, but I was only half Auphe and half human. And humans were weak, nothing more than sheep. They thought that was worth a shot.

They thought wrong.

Robin, though, had always been loyal, always had our backs. We'd be piss-poor friends if we didn't do the same. I sat at the table and grabbed the sub, taking a large mouthful. "So what's the job?" I asked as I chewed—the Miss Manners of the monster-maimer crew.

Niko agreed with me silently by sitting down and drinking the tea that they probably cleaned gutters with in China. Both of us looked expectantly at Goodfellow.

He exhaled, folded his arms, shifted from one foot to another ... nervous tics — all the things the ever-smooth, fast-talking puck didn't do. This was looking worse and worse by the second. After several more twitches, he finally managed to get it out.

"It's my family reunion.

"The whole of the puck race here in New York City.

"Tomorrow."

I choked on the bite of meatball, feeling the suck of it into my airway, and halfway hoping it would do the favor of killing me before I could cough it out. Niko gave me an unconcerned smack on the back, which only had the hunk of meat lodging deeper, while murmuring, "We should have asked for more money."

"You haven't asked for any money yet," Goodfellow pointed out.

"It doesn't change the fact that we should have and will ask for more." Niko slapped a hand between my shoulder blades again, saying, "One more cough and if that doesn't do the trick, Robin gives you the Heimlich. The key concept in Heimlich being 'from behind.'"

I promptly expelled the chunk of Gino's finest onto the table and welcomed the darkness that had begun to slice across my vision. If it was dark, I couldn't see. And I didn't want to see ... pucks, everywhere. All identical, wavy brown hair, sly green eyes, smug smirks, rampaging egos, and an appetite for sex that made Caligula seem like a hundred-year-old virginal nun. One puck had taken a few years to get used to. More than one? Hundreds? Maybe thousands? All exaggerating, lying, stealing, trying to screw anything that couldn't outrun them ...

The end of the world had come, and not with a bang ... okay, yeah, with a bang. It could be lots of them—the largest planet-wide orgy to date. If that was true, I was eating my gun right then and there.

"How many of them?" I said hoarsely, taking the tea Niko passed me to soothe my abraded throat. It tasted like donkey piss. The way the night was going I wasn't surprised.

The puck seesawed a hand back and forth. "It's hard to say. That's the point to the reunion. We count how many of our race are left. If the amount is too low, then we have a lottery and the schmucks with the unlucky numbers have to reproduce to make sure we don't go the way so many other of the *paien*—the supernaturals' word for their kind—races have. Extinction. We meet every thousand years. We all hate it, but it's a necessary evil if we want to keep the magnificence that is Puck alive on earth." He took the same hand and opened a drawer to fish out a checkbook. "My best guess: between seventy-five and a hundred will show. See? Not so bad. When you live pretty much forever you don't need that many to keep a race intact. So? Fifteen thousand dollars? Does that sound good?"

"Thirty," Niko corrected. If Robin was offering fifteen it was worth at least two to four times as much. "And you haven't mentioned precisely what you want us to do."

"Babysit mostly." He handed over the check with a sharkish smile that said Niko should've asked for fifty thousand. "All our well-deserved high self-esteems"—unbearable egos from hell—"in one place tends to lead to disagreements . . . some verbal abuse . . . small fights . . . attempted murders . . . large riots. That sort of thing. You'll be like bouncers, keeping everyone in check, the two of you alone. You're the only two in the city who can do this. We'll meet at the Ninth Circle, get it over with in one night, tomorrow night, and then everything can go back to normal."

"What about everyone else in the bar? The Wolves, lamia, Amadan . . . the usual. We saw them running like bats out of hell on the way over here. I guess we don't have to worry about them." I shoved Niko's poisonous tea back at him.

"Indeed. No worries there. No one else will be at the bar, as no one else will be in the city. No one but humans." Robin's smirk had turned into something darker—beyond old, from the impenetrable forests that swallowed travelers whole, and from under a sky where the stars were the blood-tinged eyes of mad gods. "Every living *paien* creature will flee this place. They feel it."

"They *know*."

"The Panic has come."